THE SUN BOAT

a fairytale

by Roger Maybank

Note for Librarians: A cataloguing record for this book is available from Library
and Archives Canada at www.collectionscanada.ca/amicus/index-e.html
ISBN 1-4120-6452-X

*Printed in Victoria, BC, Canada. Printed on paper with minimum 30% recycled fibre.
Trafford's print shop runs on "green energy" from solar, wind and other
environmentally-friendly power sources.*

PUBLISHING™

Offices in Canada, USA, Ireland and UK
This book was published *on-demand* in cooperation with Trafford Publishing.
On-demand publishing is a unique process and service of making a book
available for retail sale to the public taking advantage of on-demand
manufacturing and Internet marketing. On-demand publishing includes
promotions, retail sales, manufacturing, order fulfilment, accounting and
collecting royalties on behalf of the author.

Book sales for North America and international:
Trafford Publishing, 6E–2333 Government St.,
Victoria, BC v8t 4p4 CANADA
phone 250 383 6864 (toll-free 1 888 232 4444)
fax 250 383 6804; email to orders@trafford.com
Book sales in Europe:
Trafford Publishing (uk) Ltd., Enterprise House,
Wistaston Road Business Centre,
Wistaston Road, Crewe, Cheshire cw2 7rp UNITED KINGDOM
phone 01270 251 396 (local rate 0845 230 9601)
facsimile 01270 254 983; orders.uk@trafford.com
Order online at:
trafford.com/05-1363

10 9 8 7 6 5 4 3 2 1

To Richard Vick

She climbed the hill very slowly. The wind blew straight at her; it tore at her clothes and her long hair, and made her fall again and again to her knees. With one hand she lifted herself up again, while with the other she held her cloak as close to her body as she could. She fell against boulders, and held to them, and sheltered a moment in their lee, and continued climbing upwards through the fading light of the wintry afternoon. There were fine flakes of snow now on the wind, and with every step she took there were more. With one hand she drew herself on from thin sapling to thin sapling, themselves arched like bows in the black and white wind, placing her feet with care so as not to miss-step, so as not to fall; never for a moment releasing her arm which was wrapped round her belly, holding the cloak as well as she could round her body. The snow became so thick that time and again she had to brush it from her face which was sweating from her struggle; and the stony ground was softening with the snow and the footprints of her passing remained in it. All the crevices of her cloak were filled now with the snow, brightening it as the ground was brightened, so that she could still see her way although the light in the sky had dimmed almost to darkness. But she could see only a few feet ahead into the streaming wind.

Darkness fell. The only light came from the snow, which was deep now, so deep that she could make her way forward only very slowly, lifting her feet high to clear the snow, and falling over into it again and again, letting herself fall easily, and resting a moment or two where she had fallen before lifting herself to her feet again, always with one arm only, always with the other wrapped round the cloak round her body. She moved ever more slowly and her breathing was ever heavier, as she stumbled and dragged and drove herself on and up into the night and the icy wind and the fine biting flecks of snow, stopping only when there was a small tree round which she wrapped her free arm and squinted up into the darkness ahead of her. But there were fewer trees now, and fewer boulders, and fewer hollows into which the snow had settled and where she could lie in the white softness somewhat sheltered from the bitter wind until she had the strength to crawl to the edge of the hollow and drag herself to her feet and lean into the wind and continue. There seemed to be no more such hollows now, nor any other shelter for her or for the snow which was shallower now, with every step she took it was shallower, it was being driven off the rocky earth by the wind; so when she stumbled her fall was harder, broken only as best she could by the one arm she allowed herself, not broken well. At last she stumbled on something she couldn't see, for without the snow the earth was as black as the sky, and lost her balance and was thrown back swiftly by the wind, like a leaf; but she fell to the ground like a woman, a heavy woman, and she cried out with the pain, and for some while lay where she had fallen. Then, as she peered into the wind from where she lay, and as the snow began to gather and to shine white where it was caught by her body, she saw something high in the air which held her gaze, and she lifted herself slowly to her feet and wrapped both her arms around her belly and staggered and stumbled forwards over the stony ground, no longer trying to see where her feet were landing, falling to her knees again and again, ever holding her gaze to the same place in the darkness, as high in the darkness as the top of a tall tree.

The hillside levelled out, but the wind against her was as harsh and bitter as before. She walked now as if she didn't feel it. Her hair streamed behind her and her cloak billowed and flapped about her knees, but she held it closely over her belly and continued making her slow and steady way towards what she could see in the darkness ahead of her.

It was a shape darker than the night. It rose from the stony ground high into the air, many times higher than she was, many times broader than she was: an uneven shape, its black edges weaving up through the dark, unmoved by the wind. The nearer she approached it, the fiercer the wind was against her, until each step she took was of only a few inches, and it took all the strength left her to continue at all.

There was more than one dark shape. There was another to the left of the first, and a third to the right of the first. She made her way inch by inch towards the space between the first shape and the third, until she could stretch out a hand to the first shape and touch its rough surface with her fingers; she held to it with her fingers and drew herself by her fingers very very slowly and painfully around the edge of it into the very teeth of the shrieking wind.

And the wind died. She let her hand and her other hand fall to her sides, and stood still where she was in the still air, and looked up in the gentle light at the great stone just behind her rearing high into the grey sky, and then at the stone beyond it and the stone beyond that and beyond and beyond, until the stones circling round to the left met the stones circling round to the right, all rearing up to the pale grey sky; and outside them all the raging wind; and within the circle of them stillness and soft unchanging

7

light. Still gazing about her with slowly blinking eyes, she sank gently down to the grass and fell asleep.

When she woke, the light and the stillness were the same. Her body ached from the struggle of her climb and her arms and legs felt bruised from her falling, She sat up with some difficulty and unwrapped and opened her cloak from around her body, so that the unchanging light fell shadowless on her full womb, and she laid her hands gently upon herself and felt what was not herself moving.

After a while she lifted herself slowly and painfully to her feet; and then walked slowly over the grass and small flowers towards the centre of the circle where she could make out something gleaming. It was a small pool. She stood at its edge and looked down into it, and at her reflection in it, then let her heavy cloak slide from her shoulders to the grass. Slowly she removed all her other clothing, and stepped into the pool and sank down into it until her whole body was in it, and stayed there until all her aches and pains melted away. When she lifted herself up out of the pool and onto the grass her strength ebbed so suddenly from her that she sank again, almost falling, to the ground beside the still quivering pool. And slept again.

She woke to the rhythm of her body giving birth. She surrendered herself to the rhythm, flowing back and forth with the shocks, pushing and being pushed, flowing through the silvery silky water and tumbling and breaking in blood on the rough shore; until the body inside her body pushed its way out of her. She took it in her hands and saw that it was a boy. She bit through the umbilical cord and knotted it, and lowered him into the pool and washed him, gazing as she washed at the patterns of light which danced round his glistening body. Then she lifted him from the water and brought his mouth to her breast, and while he sucked at the nipple greedily she gazed down at the pool

8

where the last ripples of his bathing were slowly
away.

"Your name is Matthew," she said. He was holdi
each of her forefingers with each of his hands, and walking after her over the grass as she very slowly backed
away. Beyond him, in the distance, the great stones reared
up to the pale clear sky, and beyond them she could still
see the bitter wind bending the trees. But by the little lake
the air was as still and soft as on the day he was born, and
the light of the sun high overhead fell gently on their bodies, and glistened like pale gold on the water. She led him
to its very edge, and he sat down by it and bent forward
and made it ripple with his fingers.

"You will sail on it, when it is time," she said, bending
close over him and laying her cheek against his golden hair.
He splashed both his hands in the water and laughed.

She watched him playing by the shore of the lake. his
shadow lying close around him on the sand. He was brown
from the sun and his curling hair was pale gold from the
sun and he was strong.

"Boat," he said, pointing to the tree she had drawn for
him in the sand, so that he should know. The wind-beaten
trees beyond the tall stones were too far away to see. He
pointed at himself and across the lake to where the tops of
the tall stones rose out of the water into the sky.

"Boat. Me."

"Yes, my darling," she said, holding her hands in her
lap to keep them from reaching out towards him, to enfold
him. "Soon. Soon you will go." She pointed to the shape
she had drawn in the sand on the other side of him. "That
is the boat, my darling. This is a tree." He turned his head
to look at it.

"Boat," he said, looking at it steadily. "Boat. Boat."

He sat in his boat on the sand, and pushed at the sand with a stick.

"It's a good boat, isn't it?" he said. She nodded.

"Will it float?"

"I hope so."

"Shall we try it?"

"No, not yet. Not just yet," she said, fear suddenly passing through her like a cloud. but the sun melted it again and she was warm again and smiled at him. "You haven't finished making your paddle."

He climbed out of his boat and picked up a long flat piece of wood from the sand and brought it over to where she was sitting and laid it down beside where she had drawn a picture of a paddle in the sand. She laid her hand on his strong brown back, and caressed him lightly as he bent over his piece of wood and sliced pieces off it with his knife. After a while he measured it against the sand-pattern.

"Is it a good paddle?" he saked, looking up at her.

"Yes, very good," she said. "It will be."

"Will it take me to my father?"

"I don't know. It will help," she said, gazing out over the still and golden lake which stretched away in every direction from their island.

"Has he been waiting for me a very long time?"

"I don't know, my darling. I don't know if he's waiting at all. But I know he'll be very glad to see you whether he's expecting you or not."

He nodded, and bent over his carving again. And then he looked up at her again, and his face was troubled and his deep blue eyes were clouded.

"But what will you do while I'm gone?"

"Oh, don't you worry about me," she said, smiling to reassure him. "I'll be with you."

"My boat's not big enough for two."

"No, my darling, no it's not. I shall drift on the wind above you."

"Will you?" he asked, golden reflections from the lake glistening in his eyes. "Will you really? Will you fly?" Then, as she didn't answer him but only stroked his golden hair, full of love and sorrow, his eyes clouded again a little.

"What's wind?" he asked. "I forget what wind is."

She fanned the air in front of his face with her hand.

"That's wind. That's small wind. When you're in your boat on the lake the wind may be very big. It may blow your boat for miles."

"That will be wonderful," he said excitedly. "And the whole while you'll be flying above me. Like a bird. Like the birds you told me there are. Will you be the biggest bird of all?"

"The very biggest. My wings will stretch from one horizon to the other. I shall be as wide as the sky."

He lifted his eyes from her face to the sky, which was as blue and clear as his eyes, except where the sun, directly overhead, was pouring its light down to the lake. He lowered his eyes to her face again, and looked so troubled suddenly that she wrapped her arms round him before she knew what she was doing.

"What happens when you get tired?" he asked. "Where will you rest?"

"I won't get tired. I'll rest on the back of the wind. I won't be as heavy as I am now, I'll be as light as any feather." She continued holding him in her arms, and tears without her willing flowed out of her eyes and over her face and over his body, and all she could see was shimmering golden water.

"Tell me about my father," he said, facing away from her, standing at the very edge of the lake and gazing far across it to where it met the sky. His young bare body was all sunbrown. Her own was greyishbrown, and her hair falling over her sagging breasts was greyish-white.

"What shall I tell you, my darling?"

"What is he doing? What is he doing now? And now? And now?"

She gazed at the horizon where he was gazing, where a brilliant white light seemed to be parting the lake from the sky, and she smiled.

"Well then," she said, "He has put a few things in a satchel and has flung it over his shoulder and is walking into the forest. You remember what a forest is?"

"I remember. It's many, many, many trees. Are they big trees?"

"Very big trees."

"Is the sun shining? Is the sun shining like here?"

"No, my darling. The sky above the trees is all grey, and there is a fine rain filtering down through the trees. But he doesn't notice it. And anyway he likes the rain."

"Will I like the rain?"

"Will you be like him?"

"Yes!"

"Then you will like the rain. Your father would always go walking in the rain, and come home with his hair hanging in wet ringlets against his cheeks and with the clear light of the rain in his eyes. He is looking up into the trees now, at the big waterdrops which have gathered underneath branches from the fine rain and are falling big and fat and bright from leaf to leaf. He likes to see that, he is smiling. He is lost, I think, but he doesn't mind. He never seemed to mind where he was. He is listening to the birds singing in the shelter of the leaves, and breathing the wet smells of the forest. And yet, he is not so very happy, he is troubled behind his smile. I think he misses the ocean."

12

"Why did he leave it then? Why didn't he go out on it in his boat?"

"Because I took the boat, my darling."

"Oh yes. I forgot. Didn't you have another boat?"

She shook her head, gazing steadily at the knifeedge of bright light at the horizon. He turned round to look at her.

"Why did you go?"

"Because it was time. Because it was nearly time for you to be born."

"Did he know you were going?"

"No. I don't think he knew. He wasn't there."

"Is he looking for you now? Is that why he's in the forest?"

She glanced at him and smiled fleetingly.

"I don't know. I don't know what he's looking for. I never did." Tears suddenly welled in her eyes and melted the bright horizon, and flowed down her cheeks. Matthew ran to her and tried to wrap her in his small arms.

"Don't cry, Mama. Don't cry." He reached up to smooth away her tears with his hand, and they died down of their own accord.

"It's nothing, my dearest, it's nothing. I was only re-membering."

"Is my father a good man, Mama?"

"Oh yes, yes!" She held him tightly and rocked him in her arms. "Your father is a very good man." She wiped her wet cheeks against his golden hair. "It was only that he thought it was time for him to stand...and...to stand there. And it wasn't. That's all. He wanted to stay, he said, to live, between the forest and the ocean. And he built us a very comfortable log house there on the beach, just above the reach of the high tide. And there was food from the ocean and food from the forest, all the food we wanted.

"But from the day the cabin was finished and everything was in order, your father began again to wander, only a little at first. He couldn't stop himself. I would find him some way along the beach, gazing down at something…a branch, or an old piece of iron, half-buried in the sand. Gazing as if asleep. Or enchanted. Sometimes he gazed for an hour at sunlight resting on a rough rock. I saw him, but he never saw me.

"And then he began walking further, along the beach or into the forest. At first for hours, and then for days. The first night he didn't come back I was very anxious….and frightened, because there was nobody else in any direction for many miles, and there were wild animals in the forest. But he came back, smiling and with a far light in his eyes, just as the sun was rising. And we made love in that early light. I was dry, but cold from fear for him, and he was dew-wet, but warm from walking and love of the forest. The air was so clear that the blue of the sky seemed far off, and the fresh sunlight was bright and sharp….and even while I lay in his arms and could feel his heart beating, I knew that he was looking past me at the flowing of the sunlight over the sand. And it was then, just then, that you came into the world through our bodies."

"Did you see me come?"

"No, no, my darling. It was only later that we knew. I knew, and then he knew. But still he couldn't stay by the house. And so, when he was gone for many days, I took what I needed, food and clothing, and laid them in the boat, and pushed it out to sea at high tide; and was carried out with the ebbing, and with rowing. So I was gone by the time he came back."

"Could you see him coming back?"

"No. I couldn't see him then as I can see him now. But he always came back. I was the weight that kept him from drifting too far. I was his anchor. Or his chain. And so now he is free and he is lost. He is lifting his head and

14

trying to smell the salt breath of the ocean. You will go to him, won't you? You will go and find him?"

"Yes, yes, I will go," he said. "When I'm bigger," he added, snuggling down deep in her lap.

"Only you can find him. If you don't go he will wander forever."

"But I don't want to leave *you*," he murmured. "It won't be the same if you're flying somewhere up in the sky."

"Yes it will," she said. "It will be just the same." She slipped her hand under his chin and turned his face upwards to hers. "Look, my darling, look into my eyes. You see the lake there, don't you, and the sky?" He nodded, his own eyes a clear, dark blue. "Well then, what is there to be troubled by? When I am no longer here to hold you and you are in your boat in the middle of the lake, you have only to look into the water to see my eyes. And you will hear my voice in the least moving of the air. I will be with you always. You will be as you are now, in the very midst of me. And yet you will be free, as you are not now, to move and wander as you need. And I will not be, as I am now, between you and the sun; the sun will always be with you. You will remember that, won't you? The sun and the moon and the wind and the water are for you alone. Now you sleep."

His eyes were already closing sleepily, but they opened wide a moment and looked at her questioningly.

"What's the moon?" he asked.

"You will find out, in time."

He nodded, and his heavy eyelids drifted over his eyes and his head sank against her breast and he slept within the shelter of her body.

He knelt on the sand beside her and she smoothed his hair back from his ear and threaded a little gold ring into

15

the lobe of his ear. He turned his head the other way and she threaded another gold ring into the lobe of his other ear. Her old arms felt very heavy, her old arms felt very weary.

"It is nearly time," she said. "You must be ready."

"I'm ready," he said. His little round boat with its paddle inside it was sitting on the sand at the water's edge. The lake stretched away in every direction from their little island, still and golden to the far horizon.

"You must be careful of islands," she said. They may be good and strong, or they may be only mirages. Be careful you don't land on a mirage."

"What are mirages?" he asked, playing with the old flesh of her shoulder and breast, making it roll over her bones in small tired waves.

"They are pictures of islands, that someone has made. It may even be so well made that it will seem solid to your touching, that will be the danger; for if you walk on it, it won't bear you, not for long; you will sink deeper and deeper into it, and not find your way back to the lake. Or out to your father. You will be lost in the island, because it will be a kind of magic island, which someone where your father is has invented. And all you will see there at last will be the big frightened eyes of a wizard peering in at you."

"What will he be frightened of? You said wizards are wise men, so why will he be frightened?"

"He will be frightened of you."

"Why? I won't hurt him."

"I know you won't, my darling," she said, laying her old hand very lightly on his smooth shoulder, and then withdrawing it, feeling that light as it was it was still too heavy. "But others are not so strong as you are. They are much nearer dying, what is called dying. Don't ask," she added, as his eyes filled with questioning. "It is too dif-

16

ficult to explain. But if people turn away from you, even wizards, it is because they have to, because they are not strong. Let them go."

"But my father?"

"You must be careful of him too. If you come upon him on a small island, a very small island, before you reach the Mountain, then you can go to him, then it will be all right, he will be able to see you clearly. But it's not at all likely."

"Doesn't my father want to see me then?"

"He will *want* to, my darling. But it will be difficult for him. He has been away a long time. You *will* be careful of him, won't you?"

He nodded, and both of them gazed across the golden lake to the glittering line of light at the horizon.

"Is that the way to the Mountain?" he asked at last. "Is that the way? Which is the way?" She didn't answer.

"What does it look like?" he asked. "Draw it for me on the sand." She shook her head.

"You will know it when you see it," she said quietly. "It will be there. Look at me now. Look into my eyes."

He turned and looked at her.

"You have only a moment now, a moment or two; so listen to what I have to say. You must land where you will. But be careful. A small island is better than a big island. The smaller the better."

"What is big and small?" he said. "How will I know?"

"It will be small enough," she said, "If you can paddle around it in a hundred strokes and one. Will you remember?"

He nodded, his deep blue eyes gazing steadily at hers.

"If you go ashore there, it will hold you. And you may find your father there. But it is much to expect. It is almost

17

certain that you will have to seek him through the Mountain." She looked at him for awhile in silence, and slowly and with difficulty brought her feelings to stillness.

"And don't lose your earrings," she said at last. "Don't give them away for no reason, or let anyone take them. They are your father's. That is how he will know you. Unless," she added. "And it may be so, someone asks for them with a pure heart. Then you must give them."

"How will I know when that is?"

"You will know. And you will give them without knowing. Now. Close your eyes." He closed them, and knowing she would not see them open again, tears began to well in her own. She took his hand in her hand and they stood up together, and she led him to his little round boat; and he stepped into it and, guided by her hand, lay down in it; and as she smoothed the air over his face with her hand he fell asleep. She gazed down on him a little while, and tears streamed down her old face and body and soaked into the sand. Then she lay on the sand herself, at full length on her back. Her head touched the water of the golden lake at one shore of their island and her feet touched it at the other. She lay a moment unmoving, and then her breath stopped.

Matthew woke. He opened his eyes and looked at the sun right overhead. He sat up, and found himself floating in his boat in the middle of the shimmering golden lake. His mother and the island were nowhere to be seen. He was alone.

He wondered what to do. He picked up his paddle and held it as his mother had shown him to hold it and as he had practised holding it, paddling in the air over the sand of their island, and lowered the blade of it to the gleaming golden surface of the water. As it broke the surface, the gold scattered in dancing lights, and he saw through it into the lake, which was clear green. He leaned over the side of his boat to see better while it turned slowly round on itself. He looked as far as he could into the water of the lake, but all he could see was the green growing darker and darker until it was black. And then, as he stopped moving his paddle, the golden surface flowed back over the green, reflecting the sky and the sun and his own peering face.

Then he saw that his paddle was dripping water, and where the drops landed holes opened in the golden surface and he could see again into the green depths. And the holes grew larger and joined one another, and he thought he saw something then moving in the water, but the golden surface filtered over it again. He dipped his hand into the water. It felt cold and then it didn't feel cold. He pulled his hand out again and held it over the golden surface and drops fell from his fingers and broke the surface and melted back into the lake. And in the holes they made, and as they met and made one big hole, he saw something moving, something glistening in the green.

"A fish," he murmured. His first fish, the shape of it was like the sand-fish his mother had drawn for him. But she didn't draw the small pale-green lights which filtered from it through the water, she couldn't draw it swimming, she said; but if it wasn't swimming too deep he would see it by the light of the sun; and he did.

It was gone. The surface closed over the lake again. He dipped his hand into it again quickly, and let drops fall from his fingers again. But there was nothing now, only the clear green water. The golden surface covered it again. Discouraged, he sat down in the bottom of his boat and gazed over the lake to the horizon. There was nothing that way, nothing except the lake. He dipped his paddle into the water and slowly turned his boat round on itself, looking the whole while over the lake to the horizon. There was nothing in any direction, except at the very horizon where there was a line of bright white light, which his mother said was a mirage.

So it didn't matter which way he went, it was all the same; so he began to paddle straight ahead, as straight as he could, the whole while watching his arms move the paddle and feeling his arms move the paddle, and seeing the surface of the lake roll back in pale golden waves from the green water under them; alert the whole time for a glimpse of another fish. Then he was tired of paddling, and he sat in the bottom of his boat again and looked around at the horizon again. But there was nothing. He was still nowhere.

He began to miss his mother. The air was as still as always, so he couldn't hear her voice the way she promised, and he hadn't seen her eyes in the water, except the green of her eyes, it was the same green as her eyes. He leaned over the side of his boat and looked down at the water, but all he could see was his own face in the middle of the shadow of his own head. He touched the surface with his fingers to open it, and as it opened he saw little glistening lights, were they her shining eyes watching him? They were gone. The surface closed again. He opened it again quickly, and saw the lights again, deeper now in the water, and saw that they were many small fish. He trailed drops onto the water with one hand and then with the other to keep back the golden surface, and the longer he watched the more fish he saw: big fish and little fish, round fish and long fish, striped fish and spotted fish, fish of all colours. Delighted, he followed them with his eyes as they swam from one edge of the open pool of green he made with his dripping hands to the other, until they slid away under the gold. The light from the sun sparkled all over their backs, except when they swam into the shadow of his head on the water; they were as dark then as the shadow was, all the light went out of them. Then they were bright again.

A long black fish swam through the pool, into his head shadow and out of it; when it was gone he saw that all the other fish were gone too. He picked up his paddle and broke the golden surface with it as widely as he could to find them, but he only saw the black fish again. It had a long narrow head which turned this way and that, what was it looking for? Keeping the golden surface back with one dripping hand, he held his paddle between the long fish and the sun; in the darkness of the paddle's shadow it almost disappeared, and then in the light again it seemed brighter, flashing black lights. Then it was gone.

There were other fish again. A round orange fish was swimming just below the surface, swimming one way and then the other, passing again and again through the shadow of the paddle, from bright orange to dark orange; it was swimming deeper it was turning yellow, it was only a little ring of pale green. but other fish were swimming this way and that way, passing in and out of the paddle-shadow and the shadow of his head, their sunlit eyes were brighter than their bodies and then darker than their sunlit bodies. then they were gone. He spread back the gold with his paddle as far as he could, but all the fish were gone. there was only the clear green water. He sat down in the bottom of his boat.

He thought he heard his mother's voice. Where was she? He looked up into the air, hoping to see her big wings, but there was nothing in the air except the sun right over his head. And the air wasn't moving, so how could he hear her? He fanned his hand in front of his face the way she had done, then he laid his paddle on his knees and fanned his face with both his hands, but the little wind he made was too small it seemed because he couldn't hear her. So he began to paddle to make a bigger wind against his face. He paddled and paddled as hard as he could, until he was hot and tired; and always he felt he was just about to hear her voice, but he didn't. So he stopped paddling, and drifted, letting his paddle trail in the water beside him as he drifted, and flipping it back and forth to make little waves of gold with long narrow valleys between them of green. But the green was empty, it wasn't like his mother's eyes, they were always full of dancing lights. Why did she say she would be with him always in the water and the air? Discouraged, he was about to let the gold flow right over the green, when he saw that the green was suddenly full of tiny lights. Was it his mother, had she heard him? He leaned eagerly over the side of his boat until his nose was almost touching the lake, and stroked the gold back with both his hands and peered down into the water, and saw that the lights were many many tiny silver fish. And as he watched them happily he saw other fish among them, larger and rounder and golden, with green bands on their bodies, like the water itself flowing through them. And then in a moment the silver fish quivered and scattered and a big rosy-grey fish appeared out of the depths and seized one of the round gold fish in its mouth, and carried it down again into the darker and darker green, while he watched in delight until both fish were gone, and all the fish were gone; and he remembered the long black fish which had cleared the water before.

He kept the golden surface of the lake back with his hands and wished the rosy-grey fish would come back so he could see it eat another fish, the tail of the gold fish in its mouth danced like the sun on the water. But there were no fish now. There was only the clear green water deepening to black.

Something was happening in the black. It was like it was growing. He peered closer, holding back the gold. Yes, it was growing, it was pushing up into the green. It was a fish. It was an enormous fish, and it was all black, its scales were all shining and black. It was swimming upwards very slowly through the green water, it was filling and filling and filling the green water. It burst out of it, only a little way ahead of him it was breaking through the surface of gold. It was still lifting up and up into the air, its scales were shining black in the sunlight.

It stopped moving. It was lying still just ahead of him, half in the water and half out of it. As the waves it had made died away and the golden surface settled smoothly against its side, he paddled eagerly nearer to it, and when he was right beside it and it rose high above him, he reached out his hand to touch its black scales. But they weren't scales, they were stones. Big black stones, and not bright anymore, slowly turning grey as the sun dried them; it was an island.

He sat back in his boat, with his paddle on his knees, and looked at the stones uncertainly. They were piled four and five and six high, much higher than he was, and they curved away to the left and right as far as he could see. If it was an island they were making, it looked like a big island. Or maybe it wasn't an island at all; maybe it was the Mountain. He wanted to climb onto it, up the big stones, and see what it was like, so much land. but he remembered what his mother said about much land, so he stayed in his boat. Not knowing what to do, he began paddling slowly alongside the smooth stones, counting the strokes he took and watching the little waves from his boat ripple through the golden surface to the rocks and stain them a darker grey. All the stones were the same, all smooth and round, and there was nothing among them for him to mark and remember, to know when he came round to the same point again. He began to look for the stains from the waves of his boat, but there weren't any. The sun might have dried them. And the sun was so high his shadow never changed, though his mother said it would, she said the sun would change, it would move, but it never had it was always right

23

overhead, and his shadow was close about him in his boat. So he couldn't tell where he was or where or how far he was going, so after he had paddled a hundred and fifty strokes and still the smooth stones looked just the same, he stopped.

If he could mark the surface of one of the stones, he thought, he would know when he came round to it again. but they were too hard for his paddle to mark them, and he didn't have anything else. And he didn't have anything to leave, there was only himself and his paddle and his boat. He looked hard to find a small stone he could set on one of the big stones as a marker; or a stick, or anything; but there were only the big smooth stones, there was nothing he could leave as a sign.

And then he thought of his earrings. His mother said not to give them away. But this wasn't giving them, it was just to mark the place on the land so he would know when he came round to it again, and if he didn't come round in a hundred and one strokes he would come back, and take his earring back. Pleased with his plan, he reached up to his right ear and forced the ring apart where his mother had joined it, and slid it out of his ear. Then he reached up to the nearest stone and laid the ring very carefully on it, so it wouldn't slide off into the lake, and pushed his boat back a little way out from the land.

Suddenly he was frightened. His ear without the ring felt cold. What if the land was only a mirage, and it melted? Or if it was a fish after all, and it dived under the water again? He almost paddled back to the stone to take back his ring, but then he remembered that his mother said that his father might be on an island; maybe he was on this island, if it was an island, maybe he was only on the other side of the big stones. So he looked once more uneasily at his earring shining in the sun, and set off paddling as fast as he could along the shore, to be back as soon as he could,

24

counting the strokes as he paddled. The shore looked just the same as the shore he had paddled by already, so he couldn't tell if it was exactly the same shore or a different part of the same shore, there was no sign of any kind that he had been there before. But when he had paddled ninety strokes he thought he saw a glint of gold on one of the stones ahead of him. He was very tired but he kept paddling, and then he could see that it was his earring all right on the stone, so the island must be only a hundred and one strokes around. So he could land. He let his boat drift in towards the stone where his ring was lying.

Suddenly his whole boat was darkened by a shadow. He looked up and saw, just over his head, a big black bird floating in the air and looking at him with one unblinking eye. It couldn't be his mother, she didn't have eyes like that. Now its eye was looking at his earring.

"Go away!" he shouted at it, and waved his paddle. "That's my earring." But the bird only glided to one side, and suddenly swooped down on the ring. It picked it up in its beak and flapped its wings and lifted itself up again into the air.

"Give that back! he shouted. "That's not yours, it's mine. My mother gave it to me." But the bird flew slowly away over the island, so he climbed as fast as he could out of his boat and wedged his paddle between two of the stones, so its other end was inside his boat to keep it from floating away, and scrambled up the stones to their top, and stopped there and looked.

It was a big island. It was a big valley surrounded by stony hills. The stones at his feet were as bare as right by the water, but a little below him on the slope down into the valley there were bushes with bright red berries on them; and he could see them further down the slope as well, there seemed to be hundreds and hundreds of them, only these bushes, no trees anywhere on the slopes, the only trees he saw were right in the middle of the valley, all gathered together, and the big black bird was flying slowly towards them. He watched it until it reached them and disappeared into the midst of them. He would find it there, he thought, and he would get his ring back, he would make it give it back, because there nowhere else it could go. And maybe he would find his father there too, maybe his father lived in that grove of trees, maybe the bird was his father's bird and so his father would know when he saw the earring that he was coming to him. Happy in thinking this, he started down the slope, over the stones which were dry and warm and rough against the soles of his feet. But the bushes pricked and scratched him, so he had to be careful not to touch them; and when he bent to rub his leg where it hurt particularly, he saw a thin red trickle on his skin, that was his blood his mother had told him about blood, it was the same colour as the smooth glossy berries on the bushes. He touched it with his fingers and looked at it on his fingers, and tasted it and licked it off his fingers and licked his lips. It was still trickling down his leg, it trickled over his foot onto the grey stone; it was still bright for a moment like the berries, and then it darkened and then it was only a dark stain on the rock, and then it was gone, the stone was again just as it had been. And the blood on his leg was gone too, and all sign of the little wound. He smiled, and smoothed his hand over his leg, and continued on down the slope.

There was earth between the stones now, reddish-brown earth; and small flowers, he thought he could smell them, there was some sweet smell in the air. He stooped down through the bushes to three or four little blue ones growing together, and smelled them; they smelled beautiful, but it wasn't the smell in the air, it was a smaller smell. He smelled the earth around them it smelled beautiful, and the grass growing out of it, and long old grass

26

growing over it. There was grass once on his island, he remembered his mother showing it to him when he was very small, but he didn't remember if it smelled beautiful like this grass, and then later it wasn't there at all, only sand.

He remembered the big black bird and stood up and continued his way down the slope towards the grove of trees. The slope was levelling out now, he was nearly in the valley bottom, and the bushes were fewer, he could make his way easily among them, and they had flowers on them, pink flowers with five big petals. And the beautiful smell was much stronger now, he thought it must be these flowers and he bent his nose down to one of them and it was the flower that was making the beautiful smell he didn't remember anything smelling so beautiful. Then he sneezed, because the dusty yellow centre tickled his nose, and a very small bird which was sitting on another flower of the same bush opened its wings and fluttered them and flew into the air. It was bright orange and it didn't have any body, only two big wings as fine as leaves, and two long whiskers in front. It wasn't a bird, he remembered now, it was something else, his mother had drawn it for him on the sand. It was a butterfly. It settled on the flower he had just been smelling and closed its wings together over its back. And there were others like it, in all different colours, like the fish; they fluttered round him as he kept on his way towards the grove of trees; they fluttered closer and closer around him, looking as light as the air, and some of them began to land on him; but even when their feet were resting against his skin they continued to flutter their bright wings. And more and more of them, all colours and patterns of them, landed on him, he could see them fluttering all over his body, and even where he couldn't see them he could feel their tiny feet. They were fluttering on his head and on his face, even all around his eyes, so he could hardly see where he was or where he was

27

putting his feet. But there was soft grass under them now and the sharp smell of it in his nose blurred the smell of the pink flowers, and the bushes seemed to be not many now, maybe there weren't any. He was nearly at the grove, the thin white trunks were just in front of him. He stretched out his hands carefully, not wanting to disturb the butterflies, and touched the trunks, they were very smooth. He went in among them and he was shaded from the sun by their leaves, the first shade that had touched him, except the black bird's shadow, since he found himself alone. He walked slowly, not being able to see except right in front of him because of all the fluttering butterflies.

He thought he saw something move in the trees ahead. He turned his head to see it better, but he lost it. then he saw it again out of the corner of his other eye, and again he lost it. He was more in the open now, in the shade of all the pale green leaves of all the trees, and he could look round a little better because the butterflies were fluttering more gently.

What if what he saw moving was his father? He wouldn't know him with the butterflies on him, he wouldn't see his earring. He thought he saw the moving again, but when he turned his head quickly to see it better all the butterflies began fluttering as quickly as before, and he couldn't see anything. But it couldn't be his father anyway, because his father wouldn't hide from him; even if he didn't know him he wouldn't hide, his mother said he was very brave.

He saw the moving again, he was sure now that it was somebody, just in the trees to his left. But it couldn't be his father, whoever it was looked more like his mother; he turned eagerly to go where she had gone through the trees. They were bigger than before and growing close together, so the light in among them was dim. The butterflies were quiet now all over his body, their closed wings like many

28

leaves on their sides, and he had to make his way very carefully through the trees so as not to hurt them.

Then he was through the trees and in a big gloomy space all hidden from the sun by the tangled branches overhead. It was so dark that he could hardly see. But he could see the woman. She was right on the other side of the big gloomy space and there was a pale light around her and she was looking at him, it must be his mother. He started across the clearing towards her, but before he had gone any way she was gone.

She wasn't his mother, she couldn't be his mother, his mother wouldn't leave him like that. He caught a glimpse of pale light shimmering to his right; but when he looked full that way the butterflies began fluttering and the light was gone. Then he saw it to his left. Then it was gone. Why wouldn't she stay for him? She was so beautiful, she was like his mother when she was young.

She didn't want to be looked at, he thought, that was what it must be. So when he saw the light again, just with the corner of his right eye, he kept himself from looking right at it; but he followed just behind it with his eyes as it glided round the gloomy space, round and round, gliding from tree to tree to tree. And inside the light she was dancing, whoever she was, he could just see her turning and smiling and her long hair floating out from her head; but if he looked too near her he could see the light beginning to fade and draw her away, and the butterflies quivered nearly into fluttering. He turned round and round in the middle of the big gloomy space while she danced round its edge, and he thought she was very beautiful and he felt very happy.

A sudden loud noise overhead made him look up, and he saw the big black bird perched in the high tangled branches. Its beak was open, it was deep red inside; and his earring was falling down towards him, glittering in the dark air. As it fell past him he turned his head to see where it landed, and saw it fall with a small splash into a tiny pool he hadn't seen was there; and a brilliant flash of light burst out of the water and lit up the gloomy space and the butterflies all over his body began fluttering wildly and for a moment he couldn't see. He knelt down quickly and reached into the pool for his earring, but he couldn't touch the bottom; and as he reached his arm deeper and deeper into the water, and the butterflies climbed higher and higher up his arm to escape the water, the light from his earring swirled round and round his arm up through and out of the water and round and round the dark glade; but he couldn't reach the earring, the pool was deeper than the whole length of his arm; so after a moment he pulled his arm out of the pool and stood up and looked down into it at his earring still sinking and still leaving behind a trail of light which flowed up into the glade, but every moment more dimly. At last there was only a small point of light in the middle of the pool, and then nothing at all, and the surface of the water became still. And the butterflies were all still. He looked around the glade for the beautiful woman, but there wasn't any sign of her, or of the light she danced in. He looked up, and saw the big black bird perched on the same branch, absently furrowing its beak through its feathers.

"That wasn't your earring," he shouted at it. "That was *my* earring." But the bird only continued furrowing in its feathers. "I'll never get it back now," he said to himself. "I've lost it and she told me never to lose it." He felt cold in the gloomy empty glade, and shivered. "What if I won't ever find my father now?"

He looked around him, wondering which way to go, and saw that there were little patches of sunlight here and there on the ground. He stretched out his hand into a sunbeam near him, and the butterflies on his hand opened

their wings and waved them slowly back and forth, and
then one by one left his hand and fluttered away into the
sunlight which was spreading every moment further. He
moved a little so he was standing full in it himself, and
all the butterflies on his body rose in a rainbow cloud
about him, and he saw then that the trees weren't any
longer high over his head. They hardly even reached as
high as his head. Some of them weren't any bigger than
bushes. And the butterflies were as small now as bright
bees darting in among them, and he could see the sunlit
grey stones. The lake was right beside him again, and his
boat. He loosened his paddle from the stones where it was
wedged and sat down in his boat, and watched the island
shrink to a black drop on the golden surface of the lake,
and disappear.

He was glad to be in his boat again, with his shadow
close around him; but his right ear felt cold to his fingers
when he touched it and he kept seeing his earring falling
from the black bird's red mouth to the deep pool. He held
the ring in his left ear and told his mother he was sorry,
and saw the other ring sinking and sinking and sinking
and the light of it slowly dying.

Then he thought he couldn't just sit there, he had to
find his father. So he started to paddle in the direction he
was facing, and he paddled and paddled, not fast, but not
stopping.

He saw something ahead of him, something black. He
paddled straight at it and when he was nearer he saw that
it was a black rock, rising just above the surface of the
lake. And someone was on the rock, sitting cross-legged
and facing him. It must be a man, he thought when he was
nearly to him, because he had long hair growing from his
chin, as his mother had drawn it once for him on the sand,
it was white hair and the hair on his head was white too,
and hair on his chest and belly, a little bit, right down to

31

where his johntom was, which was bigger than his own and all wrinkled; all his skin was wrinkled, the way his mother's was when he left her. So he was old, so he couldn't be his father. But the rock was only a bit bogger than his boat, so it was safe for him to go right up to it, even to touch it. Though the man was so close and facing straight at him, he couldn't tell if he was seeing him because his eyes were all golden like the lake and weren't blinking.

He stood up in his boat as it touched against the man's knee, so his eyes were level with the man's eyes, and he saw himself in them, in the middle of the shining gold. He reached out and touched the man's shoulder and the man's throat quivered and his dry lips slowly parted and a deep sound came out from between them, as if it had rumbled up from a long way inside him.

"What...do...you...want?"

"I'm looking for the Mountain." Matthew said.

"Why?" The man's face was blank and his unblinking eyes were still golden except where Matthew could see himself in the middle of each of them.

"Because I'm looking for my father, and my mother said that was how I could find him." For a moment the man sat unmoving; then he slowly closed his left eye and his throat began to quiver again and his old mouth to open.

"Come...closer. Look...in...my...eye."

Matthew leaned nearer to him, until his own reflection filled the old man's eye, which slowly turned darker and greener, with shapes moving in it slowly and small bright darting dots.

"You've got fish in your eyes," Matthew said. "I can see them swimming."

"Look...well."

Matthew looked as well as he could, and he saw that

32

the slow-moving shapes were trees, many trees together, big trees; and the little darting shapes were bright birds in the trees.

"Is the wind moving the trees?" he asked. "My mother said I would hear her if I heard the wind. But I haven't yet. I can't hear the wind in your eye."

"She...is...there," the man said. "You will hear...her... when you...are there."

One of the birds Matthew could see was bigger than the others. It was grey and it had flown out of the trees and it seemed to be flying right towards him because it grew bigger and bigger, until it was almost all he could see in the man's eye it was blocking out everything else. In its beak it was carrying something red, something small and round.

"Is it coming out here? Won't it hurt you if it comes out of your eye?" he asked. But already it had wheeled sideways and was beginning to grow smaller again. He could see land just below it now, and houses and fences and some animals, maybe they were cows, like the cows his mother had drawn for him on the sand. Or horses they could be, the bird was flying too high for him to see them well. Its shadow was flowing over the fields and fences like water.

"Where is it going?" he asked. The man didn't answer.

"Did it steal what it's carrying?"

"No."

"A bird stole my earring. It was a black bird. It dropped it in a pool."

"That was the...raven," the man said. "He likes bright things and...steals them. Was it a deep...pool?"

"Very deep. I watched my earring sinking until I couldn't see it anymore. It took a long time."

"That was a...well...then. Someone...will be caring for...it...below."

"Who will? How will I find them?"

"Someone. Watch...the bird." It was flying lower

33

now, over more houses; and where it was flying towards were more houses still, as many houses together as there were trees where it came from, it must be what his mother told him was a town. The bird flew down nearer the roofs of all the houses, they were very close together now, he thought there must be hardly any space to move between them. The bird flew over the roofs to the highest house in the town, right at the far side of the town, and landed on the highest windowsill of the highest house, and strutted back and forth on the windowsill, watching with one eye and then the other what was happening in the room.

"What kind of bird is it?" Matthew asked. "Is it a raven too?"

"No, it is…a dove. It is used…for…carrying things. It is…tame."

At that moment a tall thin man opened the window and reached out one hand and wrapped it around the bird and held his other hand under its beak. It opened its beak and the red berry fell into the man's hand and rolled about for a moment and was still.

"There were berries like that where I was," Matthew said. "Where the raven stole my earring. There were lots and lots of them."

"They are rose…berries," the man said. "Rose… hips."

"What are they good for?"

"They make…roses."

"Did the man ask the dove to bring it?"

"I don't know," the man said. The man in the window closed his hand on the berry and left the dove walking on the windowsill, and sat down at a big table in front of a bright clear ball. He opened his hand with the berry and laid his other hand beside it and rolled the berry from one palm to the other, watching it.

"What's he doing?" Matthew asked.

"You will...see."

"Is he my father? He's not my father. Is he?"

"No. He is...not your father."

As the man continued rolling the berry from palm to palm the clear ball in front of him grew brighter and brighter, as if it had light inside it, and then it seemed to have shapes inside it which were moving. The man leaned closer to the ball and rolled the berry more and more slowly back and forth and the light and the movement melted together and there was a man in the ball, a man who was walking in a forest of trees so big the light around him was all in shades of green.

"Is that my father?" Matthew asked in a whisper.

"Yes," the old man said. His breath drifted up Matthew's nose.

"Where is he?"

"He is...lost."

"Where is he lost?" The old man didn't answer. "My mother said she could see him wandering in a big forest. Is it this big forest?" The old man didn't answer. His father was climbing over a big fallen log now, and jumping down the other side of it, and water splashed up around him and bushes caught at what he was wearing on his legs.

"Those are trousers, aren't they?" Matthew said. "He's wearing clothes. My mother told me about clothes." His father had stopped walking, he was turning round and looking up out of the clear ball, past the man who was bent close over the clear ball, right out of the old man's eye.

"He's looking at me," Matthew said. "Isn't he? He's looking at me."

"He is...looking up at...the sun," the old man said.

"This sun? The sun above us?"

"No. The sun...above the forest...where he is...lost."

"He's beautiful. Isn't he beautiful? Is he beautiful?"

35

"He is…beautiful. Yes."

"And he's young, isn't he? He's younger than my mother."

"He is much, much…younger than…your mother."

"Is he looking for me? Does he think I'm in the forest?" The old man didn't answer. And the clear ball was growing smaller, so it was harder and harder for Matthew to see his father in it. He leaned still closer to the old man's eye, until his nose was almost touching the old man's cheek, but still his father grew smaller and the clear ball he was in grew smaller, and the tall bony man bending over the clear ball, and the room he was in and the house he was in, everything grew smaller, all the houses in the town were like toy houses now, like the sand houses he used to make while his mother sat near him and stroked his hair. He could hardly even see them anymore, there was only something like an island in the middle of the old man's eye and two other islands near it, they were bright and it was dark; was it the Mountain his mother told him about? Then he saw that it was only his own eyes and the end of his nose, and he backed away from the old man's eye; and he saw the man's other eye slowly open, and both of them overspread with the golden reflection of the lake. And he saw too that the old man's body was wet and shining in the sunlight; and the sound of his breathing was heavy.

"Are you all right?" he asked him. "Have I hurt you? My mother said…" The old man slowly shook his head, but his body was still shining and his sweat was trickling now all over his old flesh.

"Can't you please tell me where my father is? Can't you tell me how to find him? Is he very far away?"

The old man didn't answer. But he seemed to be trying to answer. His throat was quivering and his lips were opening. Sounds came out of his mouth, but they didn't sound like words, and his body was shining brighter and brighter.

"Ho...ly..." he said at last. "Holy...Moun...tain."

"That's what my mother told me. But she didn't tell me where it was. Please tell me where it is." But the old man's mouth closed again and the quivering in his throat died away. His whole body was covered in sweat and he was so bright he was hard to look at. The edges of his body blurred and the gold of his eyes melted into the shining of his body, and the gold of the lake beyond him began to show through his body, he was only patches of brightness in the gold, he was gone.

Matthew sat down in his boat and looked at the empty bright horizon and didn't know what to do. He took up his paddle and paddled slowly round in a circle, looking for anything, even the smallest rock; but there wasn't anything. Then he held his paddle over the water and looked down into it where the drops from the paddle pushed the gold back from the green. And he saw fish swimming, big and small fish, and big fish eating small fish, that he had been so happy to see before, and even a fish so big that he could see himself and his boat mirrored in every one of its scales as it swam slowly under him; but all he could think of was his father struggling through the green forest, and he wished the old man would come back and tell him how to find him.

After a while he looked up again, to see if maybe an island had appeared anywhere near him, maybe the big fish had turned into an island, and he saw what looked like the same rock with the same man sitting on it, only a little way off. Eagerly he began to paddle towards it. But it wasn't so near as it seemed to be. He paddled and paddled and paddled, until he was very tired, and all the while he paddled the island grew bigger and bigger; and he realized it had only seemed so small because it was so far off. But there was a man on it, like on the other island, the rock; but he was much bigger than the other man, nearly ten times as big, so he still nearly covered the whole island. He was fatter and redder as well, and he was lying on his side with his hands tucked between his thighs, as if he was asleep.

Reaching him at last, Matthew saw that the sandy edges of his island, where he wasn't lying, were almost covered over with fish of every colour and shape and size; and some, still alive, were wriggling and sliding back into the water over the bodies of others. He stopped his boat in front of the man's big belly and leaned forward and cautiously poked it with his paddle. The man stirred, and opened his eyes to slits, and when he saw Matthew he seemed startled and sat up so quickly, rising up like a high hill, that fish all around him were pushed off the island and sank through the golden surface of the water; but he didn't seem to notice. He looked steadily at Matthew with quickly blinking eyes.

"I'm sorry I woke you up," Matthew said, looking up into his big red face, "But I wanted to know…"

"That's all right, my son," the man said. His voice was as big as he was. He started scratching all the red hair on his chest. "I didn't know I was asleep."

"You were though," Matthew said. The hair around the sides of the man's head was red too, and the skin on top of it, and his big beard. And all the skin of his body was covered with red freckles. "You were when I touched you."

"Was I? It's difficult to know. I thought I was listening and thinking." He glanced down at the fish lying all around him on the shore of his island. "I thought I was listening to the sound of them, of others like them, swimming and brushing past the underside of my island. And the sound of the ocean flowing under it. He brushed sand from the ear which had been lying against the ground.

"It isn't the ocean. It's a lake," Matthew said. "My mother told me. You can drink the water." The man peered down at him and seemed surprised and uneasy; he slowly lowered his hand, with his forefinger outstretched, to the water. He pushed it through the golden surface and pulled it out again, and put it to his tongue and licked it. And his eyes grew wary.

"You're right," he said. "It's fresh water."

"And you can't hear it floating under you," Matthew said. "Not right under. Because that's not a boat, it's an island. It comes up from the bottom and it can't move. That's how islands are. *This* is a boat," he said, looking down at his own. The big man looked down as well from his great height, and didn't speak and looked uneasy. Then one of his feet suddenly jerked, and he reached down eagerly to his big toe.

"A bite," he said. He lifted up the line which was tied to his toe and began to pull it in hand over hand. "He's going to fight," he said. "He's going to be a good fight. This'll be worth watching. Just stay where you are." Then the taut line went slack. "Ah, I've lost him. No, no I haven't, he's still there, he's just given up. Maybe he'll give a lastminute jerk, that's often their way." But it didn't. He pulled it in smoothly through the golden surface, and held it up for a moment in front of Matthew; it was round and flat with violet scales, and big. The man laid it on the sand and removed the hook from its mouth and stroked its bright flank sadly.

"So I'm stranded here," he said. His face looked all fallen and dark. "Just like this poor beautiful fellow. I thought I was floating and you say I'm not. I thought I was floating to the Holy Mountain."

"Do you know where...?" Matthew began excitedly, but the big man just kept gazing down at the violet fish.

39

"Where I'm not," he said mournfully. "Not here. And now I can't go there. Where it is. Because you say I'm not floating." He glanced suddenly and sharply at Matthew's watching eyes. "But I could if I had a shell, a shell like yours." His eyes were darker, and narrowing.

"What shell?" Matthew asked.

"The one you're in."

"It's not a shell. It's my *boat*."

"It's a *shell*. Look, you can see where the nut was once pressing against its walls. It's a walnutshell. Which shows how small you are. I could hold half a dozen walnuts in the palm of my hand. So could anybody."

"It's my boat," Matthew said stubbornly. The man slid his hand under the violet fish and picked it up and held it a little way above Matthew's head.

"Would you like it?" he asked, and suddenly let go of it, and Matthew was just able to fend it off with his paddle, so it fell into the water with a big splash beside his boat and set it rocking crazily for a moment, and the man and his island and the whole lake and sky turned round and round. Then, as the fish sank down in the water and slowly began to move in the water and then slowly swim away, and the golden surface closed again over the water, Matthew looked up at the big man, who was now bigger still, and was trembling for some reason.

"I'm sorry about that," he said. "That was a mistake." Matthew looked both ways along the sandy shore of the island and then began to paddle along beside it, carefully counting his strokes. The big man looked down at him paddling and seemed every moment more uneasy, more afraid. "I get lonely, you see. I'm always alone. And there's nothing to do but fish. It could be a floating island, why couldn't it be? I've heard even the Holy Mountain's floating, that's why you can never find it. Maybe there're logs under the sand and they're floating. Maybe they were cov-

40

ered over by birds sitting on them and shitting on them, so they don't show."

"What birds?" Matthew asked, keeping up his slow paddling and counting. The big man looked up at the empty blue sky.

Is it moving now?" Matthew asked, pushing his paddle into the firm sand just beneath the surface of the water. "My boat's moving."

"How can I tell? the man said. "There's nothing to measure it by. Sometimes I seem to be moving like the wind, but then it's only the clouds overhead, or their shadows passing by me on the water, and over me."

"What clouds?" Matthew asked. The man glanced up again at the empty blue sky with the bright sun in the middle of it.

"Well, there aren't any just at the moment," he said. "But it isn't always like this, you know. There are other times as well. Like sunset."

"My mother told me about sunset," Matthew said, pausing in his paddling and holding the number of strokes in his head.

"That's a good time," the man said. "That's something to see. All the fish melt away then, you know, every last one of them. They begin flowing about me here and for awhile it's like sitting in the middle of a lot of rainbows, and they flow over the edge of the island and back into the water, they sink into it; some of them seem to be heavier than others, blue's heavy, it sinks almost straight down. And then soon enough the sun's sunk down as well and there's just some phosphorescence about for a little while and then that's gone too, and it's dark and here I am, all alone, for the rest of the night."

"It's too big," Matthew said, stopping his counting, and paddling a little way off from the island.

"Don't go away," the big man said. "You can stay here

41

with me, why don't you stay here? There's room for you. And there's plenty of fish for both of us. I can teach you how to catch them."

"I have to find my father."

"Would you take me with you then?" His voice was soft and gentle; but Matthew looked at his huge body, and began paddling backwards as fast as he could.

"You're too big. You're a hundred times too big."

"I'd sit very quietly. And I don't have to be so big, I can be very small. I just want to feel what it's like, float-ing over the water, with the gold floating under you. And we'd find the Holy Mountain, wouldn't we? We'd find it together." He had risen up onto his knees so he was tow-ering right above Matthew who back-paddled his boat as hard as he could. The man lifted his great heavy body to his feet, until his head was nearly between Matthew and the sun. "I can make myself very small. I'll make myself as small as a mouse, or a bird, will that be all right? Or an ant. Ants are no weight at all." Matthew kept paddling away from him. "Oh please don't go away. I'm not really big, I only made myself big to catch more of the sun." He was stretching out both of his arms now towards Mat-thew's boat, and where their shadows fell on the golden surface of the lake they broke it and churned the water under it to waves of black and silver. But they didn't reach as far as the boat, it was a good way off from the island now.

"It's not a small island I'm offering you," the big man called. His arms were still stretched out and the shadows of his great hands were following close behind Matthew and the waves they made were splashing over the golden surface and breaking it everywhere, except right around his boat. Matthew paddled with all his strength to keep the man's hands from coming between him and the sun. "And I can make it bigger, I can make it as big as you like, oh don't leave me. Often I make it big, very big, and I live many days in the shelter of big bright boulders that look now like grains of sand. Wouldn't you like to see that? And in the caves among them I can hear the ocean, wouldn't you like to hear it with me? I crawl in there when the wind blows. Oh please please don't leave me, it's starting to blow now. It's growing cold. It will be colder and colder. I only want to lie and sleep in the warm sun." The air between his outstrtched arms and the water was pitch black, and the waves they were making were higher and higher, they were beating all round his island, they were even rolling right over the island, all the fish were being washed away, and the man was swaying and staggering, it looked like he could hardly keep from falling over into the waves. It was the air around him, Matthew saw, it was blowing. Was that his mother, was she making it blow? The man's voice was still calling, but it wasn't strong anymore, and his body looked like the wind was tearing it and breaking it, was it his mother? It was all broken now, it was like dry leaves blown high into the air. The man was gone. And the island was gone too, under the waves.

The storm died away to nothing and the smooth golden surface spread again over the green water. Matthew stopped paddling and gulped in air in big breaths until his heart was beating quietly again. Then he saw some dry leaves drifting down to him through the bright air; they landed lightly on the water near him and floated there like little boats, sandy and red in colour like the man. He lifted his paddle over one of them and trailed waterdrops onto it from the end of the blade, and watched and smiled as it filled and sank through the gold into the green of the lake and disappeared. Then he tried to make a storm in the midst of the other leaves, splashing the water this way and that with his paddle, and swirling the air above them, hoping to raise a wind, hoping to hear his mother's voice.

43

But he hardly disturbed the golden surface and the leaves sank out of sight through it, and he found himself alone again in the middle of the lake

He sat for some time then in his boat, unmoving, gazing blankly over the golden surface which nothing anywhere was breaking; and in his head he saw his father walking and struggling through the thick forest the old white-haired man had shown him, and whichever way he gazed over the lake all he saw was his father struggling through the forest, and when he closed his eyes all he saw was his father struggling through the forest; and still he was nowhere himself, he was where he was from the beginning, and he didn't see how he was ever going to find the way to his father.

Then, out of nowhere, a bird flew past his boat. It flew low to the water and it was white, and its wings were widespread. He followed it with his eyes and lifted his paddle to follow it with his boat, but in hardly a minute it had vanished into the shimmering line of the horizon. Then another, just like it, flew past on his other side. He lifted his paddle again to follow it, but it too was soon out of sight. But a third bird came past and a fourth and a fifth, where were they coming from? Was his mother sending them?They were all skimming the surface of the water, and weaving back and forth now in front of him. And then one touched the surface, skidding over the gold, scattering silver, and came to rest. Others too came to rest, many others, they were all around him now on the water, all white with long yellow bills curved at the end, and they were glancing at him again and again as if they wanted something. He paddled slowly and carefully among them, and they let his boat pass right beside them; but when he stretched out his hand to touch them they were always just beyond his reach.

And then he saw that he and the birds both were

among grasses just breaking through the golden surface, and when he looked down through where he was breaking it with his paddle, he could see the grasses growing up through the water, and they were thicker with every stroke he took, and he could see a sandy bottom below the water, not very far below, and crabs, he remembered his mother drawing him a crab he wanted her to draw it again and again, little orange ones were scuttling over the sand below him. The grasses around him were ever thicker and taller, they were growing out of the water now as high as he was they were nearly too thick for him to paddle through; but just ahead of him the white birds kept opening a narrow path which wound deeper and deeper among the grasses, until they were thick behind him as well as in front, and so high now he couldn't see over them, and there were big reeds among them with long brown furry heads. The path broadened out and closed in again and wound this way and that, and there weren't so many of the white birds now, they must be gulls he thought, his mother told him he would be sure to see gulls; there were only one or two following after him now. And ahead of him the water was all golden-green, as if the surface was melting; and there was a tall grey bird on thin legs standing right in the water by the reeds and looking down at him as he passed. He didn't seem to have to paddle now, there was a current in the water that was slowly carrying him forward, was he come to the Mountain at last? There were other, smaller wading birds at the edge of the stream, and bright yellow birds sitting and singing on the reeds and rushes, and bees and butterflies were flitting over his head; and flies, glistening black ones, were buzzing all round him. A bird appeared suddenly out of the water in front of him and then sat on it; it was all black and shining and the waterdrops glittered in the sunlight as they rolled off its back. Another tall grey bird lifted its head out of the stream as he drifted past, and gazed blankly at him, and the shape of a fish slid slowly down its long throat. A brilliant blue bird flew past him and caught a bright fly in its bill; and another kind of fly, big and glistening green, with long filmy wings, darted around him, catching one fly then another and another. And then a frog, sitting on a small rotting stump at the edge of the stream, a big frog, bigger than any his mother ever drew for him, shot out a long thin black tongue which touched the big green fly and it was gone. So quickly that Matthew laughed, and all about him the birds and insects disappeared; but when he was quiet again they came back.

Then something else seemed to disturb them, something in the direction in which the slow stream was carrying him, because they were cocking their heads and turning their heads, and hovering on quivering wings. He couldn't see anything himself, the stream kept turning one way and then another and the reeds and grasses on either side of it were two and three times higher than he was; and he couldn't at first hear anything either. And then he thought he heard a voice, a high voice. He thought maybe it was his mother's voice and she was calling him to her, even though there still wasn't any wind; and he stirred the water in the stream, hoping to see her, but the water wasn't clear any longer, the gold and the green had melted together and however he stirred it he couldn't see into it.

He heard the voice again, it sounded like a kind of cry, and the birds nearest him were turning their heads this way and that and seemed more uneasy, and a long snake slid off a log into the water; and a furry black animal standing in the mud on the shore lifted its sharp nose in the air and seemed to have stopped breathing. As the cry went on, and was broken and began again and was broken, the animal too slid quietly into the water and swam away past his boat as smoothly as a fish.

46

The cries were more and more frequent, and the birds were more more restless, and the tops of the rushes and grasses were beginning very softly to rustle. It must be the wind, he thought, the wind his mother told him about, if he could reach it he would hear her. He stood up in his boat and stretched himself up as high as he could, but the rushes were much higher and too thick, and only their very tops were ruffled; down where he was the air was as still as always. And the stream was still flowing quietly, and on its smooth surface now there were some pale green lily pads and gold-and-white lilies open to the bright sun.

The flies were quiet now, they were all clinging to the grasses, not one of them was flying; and the small birds were clinging to the grasses as well, or hiding down at their roots, and the water birds were hardly moving on the water, they were drifting as he was drifting, listening and listening to cry after cry. As he passed another tall grey bird, standing on one thin leg, it suddenly spread its big wings and drew its leg up into the air after it and tucked it up against its body and flew back along the stream the way he had come, its wingtips nearly touching the rushes to either side. One of the water birds, all brown and white, flapped free of the water and circled up into the air until it was as high as the tops of the rushes, where the wind caught it and blew it away sideways. It was a high wind now and full of sudden gusts, little bright birds trapped in them tumbled by high over his head; it couldn't be the wind his mother said he would hear her voice in, the cries were more like the fat red man's when the wind was blowing him; they were louder now and nearer and more. The water birds were all leaving now, they were all flying after the big grey bird along the stream. And there weren't any little birds, he couldn't see one anywhere, or any frog or snake, or even any insect; there were only the tall rushes on either side of the stream, their tops lashing about in the high wind.

There was something in the air just above the stream a little way ahead of him. It was round and full of colours and it was floating on the quiet air just below the wind; he watched it as he drifted towards it and it drifted towards him. Then it began to rise, until it was even with the tops of the rushes, and the moment the bright streaming wind touched it it burst with a flash of light and a loud sharp cry, and the tops of the rushes near it were flung wildly about. Another one like it, and others smaller, were drifting towards him now over the winding stream, and as they came near him they rose like the first one and burst in the wind like the first one; more and more drifted after them, all sizes of them, all of them with rainbow colours sliding all over their bright surfaces. The waterlilies now were thick around him on the water, but they were all slowly closing, they closed one by one as he passed them; and he couldn't any longer see the surface of the water, it was entirely covered with lily pads. But still his boat continued its slow drifting throught them, and still the big bubbles came drifting towards him, they were as thick in the air as the lily pads were on the water, and one after the other they rose into the wind which was as wild above the rushes now as the wind that broke the big fat man in pieces, and burst and burst, so the sky was white with the brilliant flashing light and the still pale air around him was filled with all the loud sharp cries. He wanted to touch the bubbles before they burst, to see what they felt like and if his touching would burst them, but every one he reached out to rose too high as soon as it was near him. So he sat down in his boat and watched and listened.

And then, just below where all the bubbles were drifting and just above the lily-pad-covered water at the furthest stretch of the stream that he could see, he saw the legs of people. He crouched down in his boat and he could see more of them then below the bubbles, he could see halfway up their bodies; and he could see from their bodies that some of them were men and some were women, and they were all standing on thin stumps right over the water. As he drifted nearer and nearer them he could see more and more of their bodies, because the bubbles that seemed to be drifting out of them rose up higher. But they weren't drifting out of them, they were drifting out of the grasses behind them, they were drifting just over their heads and the heads of more and more people he could see now, standing in a long narrow opening, it must be a path, stretching back through the grasses. The people standing over the stream were leaning forward now and stretching out their arms to him and their faces were smiling and bright with silver trails over their cheeks that changed colour all the time as the bubbles drifted over their heads; their whole bodies were changing colours but not so brightly as their shining faces they were shining because of the water that was trickling out of their eyes, it trickled sometimes out of his mother's eyes, she said it was tears. And they were saying things to him he could see their mouths moving, but he couldn't make out what they were saying for the cries from all the bubbles bursting in the high wind, there wasn't a moment now when one wasn't bursting, and the light from them was flashing down in many colours through the thickly streaming bubbles underneath and was touching the bodies of the people all over, landing and gliding, like the light on the fish in the water, but it was the light moving now not the fish; but it was making the fish look as if they were moving, so the nearer he came to them the harder it was to see which of them was which, and the hands they were all holding out to him were gliding about like the lights skidding over them so he couldn't find one to hold to.

But they found him, they found and held to both his hands and halfway up his arms, and before he knew what was happening they were lifting him up out of his boat and carrying him in amongst them and the colours were flowing all around him. Then they set him down in the midst of them and let him go.

But they were still so close around him that he couldn't see anything but their bodies; and right over their heads the bubbles were so dense he couldn't see the sky. And he couldn't reach up to the bubbles and burst them and see the bright light flash over everything and hear the strange cries because all the people were much taller than he was. He could only reach as high as their eyes and touch the silver tears flowing out of them and watch them dry on his fingertips and disappear. In his mother's tears there were very little rainbows, it was the sun shining in them she said; but the rainbows were big here they were gliding all around him.

The people were moving now and carrying him with them though they weren't touching him, the space around him was always the same. They were moving along boards, it must be boards laid on top of the thin stumps he could see water between them. But it was getting darker, the light was growing less all the time, the bubbles overhead were growing denser and denser, they were packed together so close now they were like the cloud his mother told him about that poured water out of it, rain; and the colours were flowing more slowly over the bodies of the people round him, so he could see them better than at first, he could see where the body of one ended and another began, even when the same colour was drifting over them both. And he could hear their voices better as well because the cries from the bursting bubbles were muffled now by the cloud of bubbles, they were even quieter than when he first began to hear them. And he had more room to walk in because the path seemed to be wider and to be growing wider all the time, and the people were moving back; but it was still a path of boards and he could see through it in places to water underneath it, so it wasn't as if he was on land which his mother said he shouldn't be, boards were as much like a boat as like land, and his mother hadn't said he wasn't to go aboard any boats, even big ones.

There was a grey rock just ahead of him. The people seemed afraid of it, they were all gesturing with their hands and trying to guide him away from it, what was there to be afraid of in a rock; he put out his hand as he was passing it, and touched it. And just as he felt that it was soft, a hand reached out of it and seized him by the wrist, and the people nearest him began a moaning which spread away through the crowd. The stone uncurled into the body of an old old woman, all dry and wrinkled and grey. She was holding her other hand over her eyes.

"Where are you going?" she asked.

"I don't know," he said. "They want me..."

"It's the king. It's for the king," voices behind him began saying. "To make him well."

"Can you?" she asked. Her hand on his wrist was cold.

"I don't know," he said.

"Don't mind her," the people behind him said. "Don't mind her at all. She can't hurt you." She pulled him closer to her until he was right against her old grey body and he could feel the very slow beat of her heart.

"Look at me," she whispered, and lifted her hand away from her eyes, and he saw they were fringed with thick white eyelashes and were white themselves and un-blinking.

"She's blind, don't mind her, she can't do you any harm," the people behind him were murmuring.

"Give me something," she said.

"Don't give her anything," the people said.

51

"I haven't got anything," he said. "Except..." he added, remembering his one earring, and his hand rose to
touch it under his hair before he thought. The old woman
laughed.

"Would you give me that?" she asked.

"I can't. My mother told me not to give it."

"You gave the other."

"I didn't. A black bird stole it. A raven."

"You gave it to a beautiful girl."

"I didn't. I..."

"But you won't give this one to me?"

"I can't. I promised my mother."

"Then keep your promise," she hissed, and her hand
loosened from his wrist and fell limply into her lap and
her head drooped down until she looked like a rock again
with her long hair straggling over it like dry grass.

The people were all standing back from him and they
were all looking at him. In a big half-circle. And in the
other half-circle there were what his mother said were
houses when she drew them for him in the sand. People
lived inside them she said. One of them was bigger than
the others, much bigger, and it had wide board steps leading up to a big open door. And it was out of the door, and
out of the windows on each side of the door, that all the
coloured bubbles were gushing; they were small there but
they swelled in the air and they were so many that they
filled all the air over the heads of the people and the roofs
of the other houses and all around the tops of the grasses
which were higher than the roofs of the houses, they were
growing up everywhere through the boards and out of the
water where there were no boards, they were pushing right
up into the dense cloud of bubbles so all their tops were
lost in the midst of them; the cloud of bubbles was so thick
now that the light was all gloomy and the drifting colours
were dark, and the sound of the highest bubbles burst-

ing in the open wind was like a steady whimpering. The people were coming close to him again, and they were smiling at him uncertainly and gesturing with their hands towards the big house with the open door. The tears on their faces had all dried.

"If you'll only just look at him," one of them said.

"If he sees you, he'll be better."

"At least go inside."

They were behind him and on both sides of him, and had made a path the only opening between them, which led from him to the wide steps of the house.

"Please. Please," they said. "It's nothing for you," And as he began to walk towards the house they smiled happily, and all followed after him right to the steps and up them, and in through the door into a big room where he could see hardly anything but millions of tiny coloured bubbles.

"He's there," they said, and some of them were pointing. "That way. Keep going."

He walked into the bubbles, where the bubbles were, but they weren't there then, they all pulled back from him. He kept walking and they kept pulling back, just beyond his reach, until he could see a big square shape in the corner of the room, and out of it millions of bubbles as tiny as grains of sand were gushing.

"There he is," they were murmuring from behind him, but not close behind him now. "That's his bed, he's lying there. Only go to him. Only touch him. He'll be well then. If you touch him he'll be well."

He made his was towards the bed, and the nearer he came to it, the more the bubbles multiplied and foamed, and the brighter they became; and they were crowded together so thickly they were like a solid wall, how could he reach the bed they said their king was lying on?

As quickly as he could he suddenly stretched out both

his hands towards the bed, and each of his fingers touched a tiny bubble and they all burst with tiny piercing lights and tiny shrilling cries. And he laughed. He stretched out his hands again and broke more bubbles, and the sharp light from them darted round the room, briefly brightening the colours of the other bubbles, passing through them like threads of light, and he laughed again, and reached out again, and again, and every time he burst many tiny bubbles with both hands and laughed to see the beautiful light pass through the other bubbles and to hear the sound of the sharp cries until the room was full of them. And he saw the people behind him were all standing still and their eyes were wide, and they were pressed close against each other and against the walls; and some of them had fallen over and were lying out flat on the floor, and even as he looked at them the colour melted out of their bodies and they were as white as the dancing light and then they were clear like water and he could see the bright floor through them and then they were gone. He watched a woman turning clear until she was like sunlight in the water, and the woman behind her was like a glistening fish, a rainbow fish; and then he couldn't see the first woman any longer, and the woman behind her began to turn clear, it was beautiful to see them all becoming clear; they all stood perfectly still and their eyes were still and big and wide as the colour in them faded. And the tiny bubbles now were swirling all round him and touching him without him trying to touch them, and they were bursting and bursting into the beautiful bright light and making it brighter, they were flooding round him now in streams of rainbow colour, and were tickling his body all over as they touched it and burst, making thousands and thousands of tiny brilliant lights, and the sound of them bursting was like a single unending piercing cry, and all round the room the people were melting like bright water into one another and into the walls.

Except one of them. Someone was coming slowly towards him from the doorway. But he couldn't see him properly because of something he was holding up in front of him that was dark and rippling in the lights. He passed close by him through all the swirling bubbles, right to the foaming bed; it wasn't a man, it was the blind old woman. She threw what she was carrying over the million bubbles that were foaming out of the bed, and spread it out until it covered it from head to foot, and the bubbles stopped. The cloth she had laid over them glowed brighter and brighter, and flowed with rippling colours, but no bubbles escaped into the room. And the bubbles which were already in the room drifted away in a moment out of the door and the windows, and the people around the walls who hadn't melted away slowly filled up with colour again and their eyes moved.

"Come, come with me," the old woman hissed in his ear. "Quickly. The blanket's only of woven rushes and will soon break apart." She seized hold of his hand and pulled him after her out of the doorway and down the steps and into the midst of the people, who were all just standing there looking at him. It was brighter than before and growing brighter all the time; the bubbles were rising higher and higher and the sounds of their bursting in the wind were louder every moment.

"Get inside. Inside," the woman screeched at the people. "And close the doors and windows." And she pushed him in front of her and towards them, and they moved back, as if they were afraid.

"Can you see the way you came?" the woman asked him.

"No," he said. But the people moved further and further back and the light grew brighter and brighter abd he saw the boardwalk path between the high grasses.

"Yes," he said.

"Then hurry, hurry," she said. holding to his hand still and pushing him ahead of her. "If the bubbles over us all burst before the new ones break through the rush blanket, it will be the end of us all. Go faster, faster. Run!"

He ran as fast as he could along the board walk and she kept close behind him, holding on tight to his hand, The sound of the bubbles bursting was every moment louder and the white light from them was every moment more brilliant, and the high grasses on either side of the path were growing paler and paler and the boards themselves were growing paler, he could hardly see them now, it was almost like running in the air over the water. What would happen he wondered if he ran right off the end of the platform, not seeing it; and just then she let go of his hand and he found that he was falling, and then he stopped falling and he could feel that he was in his boat again and it was rocking gently.

And then, as he looked around him, he saw colour slowly seeping into all the lily pads, and he thought it was the most beautiful green he had ever seen; and the grasses too were turning another beautiful green, and he could see the planks of the platform again and the thin stumps holding it up, and the old grey woman sitting on it and swinging her thin wrinkled legs over the edge. The bubbles were flowing past over their heads again and the cries of the bursting were only high up in the wind.

"They're not coming towards you, are they?" she asked. Her blank white eyes were wide open.

"What?"

"The bubbles."

"No," he said. "They're all way up there."

"That's all right then," she said, and she smiled. "He thinks you've gone away. And you must now. Or they'll forget what happened and try to bring you back again."

"They looked beautiful," he said. "When they melted

like water and the colours floated all through them. Why did you stop it?"

"Because you were killing them. And if you'd gone on you would've killed him."

"Killed who? What's killing?"

"Him. The man on the bead. The man they call their king. Your father."

"My father?" he said excitedly, standing up in his boat and reaching out towards the platform; but her hand stretched out and touched his shoulder and held him back.

"If he knows you're still here he'll want to come to you," she said. "And he can't."

"Why can't he?"

"He's not strong enough. He would die." Her hand was resting on his shoulder now, it was so light he could hardly feel it.

"Is dying like killing?"

"Yes. Killing causes dying."

"I remember. My mother told me about dying. But I didn't understand."

"Didn't she tell you to be careful of causing it?"

"Yes. But I forgot. I'm sorry."

"It's all right now. The danger's past."

"But couldn't I just go back quietly and see him? The others wouldn't have to see me if you helped me. Couldn't I? Why couldn't I?"

"Did you see him lying there on the bed?" she asked. "Did you see anyone?"

"No. I couldn't because of all the bubbles."

"Then what's the good of going back? The bubbles will still be there. Or they'll burst and nothing will be there. You must go, even my touching you here puts us all in danger. He may feel you. And this is not the way to him. The only way to him is through the Holy Mountain."

"But if he's here?"

"He's not here, not really. This is only a mirage. Look. Look in my eye." She leant forwards until her face was nearly touching his, and she closed her white-fringed left eye; and the blank whiteness of her right eye melted away until it was like a deep pool of blackness in the midst of her thick white eyelashes; and in the pool he saw his father. He was sitting on a polished floor like the floor in the house where the bubbles began, and beside him a woman was sitting, in a long green dress, and their arms were around each other. Then bright specklings appeared on their faces and their bodies, more and more of them, until he couldn't make them out any longer, until all he could see was light speckling the woman's black eye. Then her other eye opened and both of them were smooth and white, and colours glided over them from the bubbles drifting past overhead.

"That was my father," he said. She nodded.

"Yes, it was. So you see he's not here. He's there."

"Who was the lady with him?"

"His ladylove."

"My mother is his love," he said. She laughed softly.

"That's right, my dear. Of course she is. She always is. But he's travelling now."

"Where is he travelling? Where can I find him? Please tell me where I can find him."

"You must find the Holy Mountain first."

"But I can't find it. I've been looking and looking, but I can't find it anywhere."

"Look here," she said, and leaned close to him again and closed her right eye and her left eye cleared into a white-fringed black pool. And into it a ring fell, and out of it light shimmered and swirled as the ring sank deeper and deeper, until he couldn't any longer make it out in the deep black of her eye, and then her eye filmed over again with dull white.

"That was my earring," he said.

"That's right," she said. And he felt her fingers feeling their way up his neck and pushing back his hair and touching his other earring, his only one now. "And this is your earring. And between them they will guide you. They will guide you true."

"How will they?" he asked. But she took her hand away and put her fingers to her lips.

"I can say nothing more," she said. "You must go now. Go." She laid her hands in her lap and her head too slowly sank down into her lap, and her long grey hair trailed over the edge of the platform and wound itself loosely round her dangling legs, and all the rainbow colours melted into her slack grey body.

Matthew sat down in his boat and pushed the blade of his paddle through the lily pads and paddled himself backwards until the old woman looked like a pile of grey grass half-falling off the platform. Then he turned his boat away from her and continued paddling against the current of the stream until he was out of the lily pads, and the bubbles overhead were big and few, and burst with loud sighing cries in the wind. And the sky was clear blue and the sun was right over his head. Floatng around him on the water were the white gulls, looking at him with round flickering eyes. Then they were gone, and there was only the unending golden surface of the lake.

But he continued paddling, hoping that the old woman had set him off in the right direction. He paddled and paddled, never changing his stroke, gazing steadily and hopefully at the glittering horizon for some sign of land. And in his head he saw her hand touch his earring, and touch his earring and touch his earring, until he was about to stop paddling and touch it himself, thinking that maybe she meant him to do that; and then he saw his other earring sinking into her black eye, and then he saw it sinking into the pool on the island where it first sank, and then he saw it, it seemed that he saw it and the light gleaming from it, in the water in every hole he made in the golden surface with his paddle. He thought he could see the light of it curling down and down into the green water until the gold flowed back over the surface. But he saw it in the next hole, and the next; and then a violet fish swam through it and scattered it in every direction, and scattered it again in the next hole, and other fish, all kinds of fish, were swimming now in the green water below him, and the downcurling light was striking each of them and each of their bright scales and was shattering into ever finer rays of curling light.

He noticed then that the drops of water that were trailing from the blade of his paddle weren't any longer opening small holes in the golden surface, but were resting on it and slowly rolling away over it, like smooth clear stones full of light; and they were leaving behind them fine silver tracks on the shining gold, And then the mouth of a fish broke through the gold beside one of the waterdrops, and it rolled over the edge of the hole into the mouth of the fish, which sank back into the water and the hole closed. In many other places now fish were pushing their noses and mouths up through the surface and letting the tiny balls of bright water roll into them. And through his paddle holes he could watch them as they swam slowly down into the green water again, and they were glowing from the light now inside as well as outside, so even when they swam down very deep he could still see them softly shining. And the water was becoming brighter and brighter green as more and more of the fish swallowed waterdrops, everywhere he looked below him now he could see them, like many many soft-coloured lights in the water, so many that he couldn't any longer see much of the water itself in each stroke-hole of his paddle. And they were clustering around his boat more and more thickly so that the water under the gold was shimmering like a rainbow, and they were pushing their noses everywhere through the gold until it was only like a freckling on the rainbow, which grew brighter and brighter as he trailed more and more water-drops from the blade of his paddle into the eager mouths of the fish.

Then he realized that the air around him was growing darker as the rainbow water grew lighter, and he looked up at the sky to see if bubbles were drifting over it again... or if there were any of what his mother called clouds, big grey things in every kind of shade she said, that he would see one day...but the sky was as clear as ever. But the blue of it was darker, and was growing darker still.

And right ahead of him was land. It was land rising up steeply and so high that the very top of it was blocking some of the rays of the sun, and the nearer to it he paddled the more it was dimming its light. And on the water around him flowers were growing now, little islands of flowers, all colours of them. He thought at first they must be growing out of the backs of the fish, but the fish glided under them and among them; and he could see in the light they made swimming down deep in the water that there was no bottom for the flowers to root in. But the flowers were more and more, and nearer and nearer to ghim, there were unbroken banks of them on either side of him now as he slowly paddled towards the high land. The air grew darker and darker as the land high above him ate deeper and deeper into the bright body of the sun. It was violet and then it was purple and then it was deep purple and the sun was eaten almost altogether away, and he began to be frightened. But he kept on paddling between the flowerbanks, the whole time watching the sharp black edge of the high land eating the sun. Until it was gone. And nearly all the light in the air was gone, and he saw that the flowers on the banks on both sides of him were all tightly closed, and all the light left for him to see by was coming from the faint gliding lights of the fish swimming slowly round and round his boat.

Over his head the sky darkened and darkened until all the blue of it was gone and there was only a kind of pale black emptiness he'd never seen before, and he looked and looked. And then, here and there, and soon everywhere, points of light like fine waterdrops began to sparkle in it, and he remembered that his mother had told him about them and that he would see them one day and that they were stars. As more and more of them appeared the sky around them grew blacker and blacker and the stream under him grew blacker and the fish swimming in the stream were like pale glowings sparkled over with the light of the stars. He stopped paddling and laid his paddle in his boat and sat still and gazed ahead of him, feeling the stream carrying him smoothly forward between the shadowy banks, and wondering if he had come at last to the Mountain.

Then he noticed that the stars were slowly blurring and the light from them was melting all through the black sky, and he thought maybe the fish up there had eaten them the way the fish below him had eaten the waterdrops. He couldn't tell one star from another now, all the light in them had melted together and it was stretching as far into the sky as he could see and it looked like big big wings; which slowly drifted down through the air and flowed over the water, where the fish were now only drifting shadows; and they lay gently on his body, wrapping him round and round in soft light. And he knew it was his mother come to him at last, and he floated through the luminous darkness in the cradle of her arms.

Sometime later he felt her slowly going. The light melted away from him little by little and flowed upwards through the air higher and higher, until it was all gathered again into the sharp points she had told him were stars, scattered thickly through the empty black sky. And then the sky itself began to lighten to dark grey and purple grey, and slowly it came down nearer to him as it filled more and more with light and soft colours; and as he gazed up at it wonderingly the stars were dimmed and slowly buried in the soft blue. And the stream grew light, reflecting the sky, and the flowers close by him on the banks were glistening with fine waterdrops, and he could see again the many-coloured fish swimming about slowly beneath him. And ahead of him, almost overhanging him, was the high land, still dark against the blue sky.

Then he saw the first rays of the sun shining into the blue from behind the high land, and he picked up his paddle and paddled towards it, and with every stroke he made he saw more rays pouring into the sky. He continued paddling eagerly, and suddenly he found he was in the sunlight again himself, and for a moment his eyes were dazzled and he suddenly shivered and then he sneezed. And then he laughed, and looked all about him at everything made brilliant by the sunlight. The clear water of the narrow stream was shining with it, and the fish in the water were glistening, and the flowers on both banks as far as he could see were all open again. The slope to his left sloped down gently right to the shore of the bright golden lake far below, and he could see over the lake now for miles and miles, but as far as he could see, to the shimmering silver mirage at the very horizon, it was all unbroken gold. To his right the bank sloped gently upwards, right up to the highest point of the land, which the whole sun was now standing beside and filling the whole world with light. As he paddled slowly towards it, the stream in front of him grew narrower and narrower, until it looked as if only a little way ahead of him the flowery banks closed right together. He was expecting every moment that he would have to stop, and he wondered if it would be right to leave his boat then and walk, but the stream continued and he continued paddling. And the sun shone down on him from higher and higher, until he passed right under it; and then he saw that he was paddling very slowly away from it, and the high land on his right was rising ever nearer to it, until it began again to hide it. The further he paddled the more the land hid the sun, and the sky began to darken to deeper blue, and far below him on his other side the shining lake turned an ever deeper gold, and the colours of all the flowers round him darkened.

When the high land hid the sun altogether he laid his paddle in his boat and let himself drift forward on the stream. The flowers he passed now were closed, the lake below was a glowing brown and the sky was purple, and every minute he drifted further into the shadow of the high land the darkness near and far was deeper. Then the stars began to appear in the sky again and their sharp silvery light glided over the land, making the flowers around him glisten, and turning the lake below him silvery grey. He sat still and felt the stream carrying him slowly forward and listened to the soft brushings of the flowers against the sides of his boat, and watched the stars wheeling slowly over his head, leaving fine, shining trails of silver in the sky; and he thought how beautiful his mother was, and how soft the touch of her light as it glided over his own body.

Then the sky ahead of him began to pale again and the light slowly to increase and the silvery-grey misty shape of the lake far below to brighten. All around him ,near and far, fine points of light began to appear in the air, until the violet sky and the purple land were both shimmering with them; and fine rainbows, like the ones in his mother's eyes, burst out of them and darted through the air, and vanished. On every side of him they arched and faded, filling the air with ever-changing colours as the light grew brighter and brighter; and the sunlight was splashing through the starlight now, and shattering the points of light into millions of tiny fragments, so dazzling his eyes he could hardly keep them open. Then he saw that his whole body was shining with the light of them and he touched himself and he realized that all the glittering points of light were fine waterdrops. They were so dense around him now that he could see only them and the rainbows darting and dancing among them, he couldn't even see himself.

Then he began to feel that he was slowly and gently sinking. The dazzling water around him was the same, but he seemed to be sinking through the middle of it. And he saw that the rainbows were growing bigger, and they were arching more slowly and passing through one another more slowly and fading more slowly. And then the light began slowly to weaken, and all the silver to fade to pale grey, and the glittering of the waterdrops to soften to glistening. The rainbows were arching ever higher into the air above him, and they were ever fewer and slower, and his fall seemed slower and the dancing of the fine waterdrops was slower they were hardly dancing at all the light from them was just melting softly into the grey, and fading and fading everything around him now was grey, even the rainbows were in shades of grey.

He felt his feet touch gently against something solid, and he stopped falling and he stood where he was and looked about him. He couldn't see anything, no shape of anything. The light was dull grey, the rainbows had died. He could barely see the ground he was standing on. But it seemed smooth and firm, so he began walking on it in the direction he was facing.

When he had walked some way the greyness around

him began to grow lighter, and he could see ahead of him and to either side of him better; but there was still nothing to see, there was only the smooth dark ground and the smooth grey air, and nothing in them. But he thought he could just hear a bird singing somewhere above him, somewhere high in the grey air. He peered up to try to see it and he found he could just make out a grey fluttering high up in the air, like the air itself fluttering, and he was sure it must be the singing bird; and as he watched it fluttering he saw it become pale yellow as pale light flowed past it, and above it he could see the pale sky. And then he heard other birds singing nearer to him in the darker grey nearer the earth, chirping and warbling two or three soft notes; every moment and with every step he took there were more of them and their singing spread further and further through the grey air until they were a chorus as far as he could hear and he was walking through the middle of their singing. But still the only bird he could see was the single one high above him, its fluttering wings and body now were brightly lit by the rays of the sun coming from somewhere behind him.

And now ahead of him he could see the shapes of trees. They didn't look very tall, but the tops of the nearest of them were touched with the sunlight; and as he walked nearer to them out of the empty grey, and the sunlight spread lower on their branches, he saw that they were all in flower. And he saw birds perched in their upper branches where the sun was, and he saw other flutterings now in the greyness under the trees and in the greyness around him and he thought those must be birds too.

The smell from the flowering trees was sharp and strong in his nose. Some of the trees were covered in red blossoms and some of them in white blossoms, but the smell was the same and he liked the smell. Then he saw that the ground between him and the trees was cov-

66

ered with flowers, all tightly closed like the flowers on the banks of the stream; they made his feet wet as he walked through them, watching the sun glide slowly and smoothly over the lower branches of the trees and then down their thin straight trunks; and then under the singing of the birds he could hear the buzzing of hundreds and hundreds of bees.

He felt the sun touch the back of his head, and flow slowly down his neck and his back and the backs of his legs, and he stopped walking and watched it flow like golden water over the smooth ground ahead of him, making all the flowers slowly open. And his shadow flowed through the flowers like a long snake right to the blossoming trees; and he saw that they were all the same size and only three or maybe four times as big as he was; and a white one was on each side of a red one and a red one was on each side of a white one, and they seemed to be in row after row after row, stretching off to his left and his right, as far as he could see, like a wall.

There was a man. He was standing in the midst of the first flowering trees and he was looking at him and beckoning to him with both his hands. He had green circles in front of his eyes, like little flat stones, and the nearer Matthew came to him the more they shone and glittered with the sunlight, so he couldn't see the man's eyes behind them.

"Are those your eyes?" he asked when he was right in front of the man; and he reached up his hand to touch the green stones to see what they were, but the man was so tall he could only reach as high as his chest. "They're like fish eyes." The man didn't answer; his head was tipped forward and he seemed to be peering down through the green stones; and then he reached out his hands and his fingers just touched Matthew's face, they qwere very cold. He drew them back. He looked like a young man, Mat-

67

thew thought, but it was hard to tell because something grey was covering his body from his shoulders to the ground. He was very very thin.

"They're glasses," the man said at last, lifting his hands away from Matthew, and turning them this way and that and looking at them.

"What are glasses?"

"They protect my eyes," he said, and he smiled a little. "From the bright day. If you look closely," he said, bending down until his face was very near to Matthew's, "You'll see my eyes behind them."

"Yes, I see them. But they look very dark. Do the glasses make them look dark?"

"I think they are very dark. But it's a long time since I've seen them. It may be the glasses. It may be an effect of the bright light."

"Look, I can see myself as well," Matthew said happily. "There I am, and there I am in the other one. And there the trees are and the flowers and look, there's a bird. Whenever I pushed back the gold on the water it was green too, but I only saw the sky. And sometimes myself, but not very well because the water was moving. And never anything else. Can I try them on?"

"Oh. Oh," the man said, and he seemed frightened suddenly.

"I won't hurt them. Please."

"It's not that, it's... But if you want them, then of course..." He reached up to his ears and the glasses came away from his eyes, which were closed. He held out the glasses to Matthew, turning his head away at the same time and hiding his eyes behind his arm. "Can you reach them?" Matthew took them from his hand and fitted the hooks carefully round his ears and looked through the deep green glass, and laughed.

"It's like being in water," he said. "Look, everything's

moving." All the trees were weaving like water weeds and the light was sliding and rippling among them and the walls of the house were rippling, and the man was so rippling that he slid again and again out of sight.

"No, no," the man said. "They only soften the brightest light to bearing. The light itself doesn't move. It's always one light, isn't it? It's we who are moving." He was rippling nearer now, like a long fish slithering through the water, and one of his arms was rippling nearer still, looking so funny that Matthew laughed again.

"It's like a thin fish," he said. "It's as thin as thin, and twisting."

"Like a thin fish, eh?" the man said. "Like a water snake? It's quite a usual arm really." His rippling hand touched Matthew's ear and removed the glasses and put them back on himself.

"Ah, that's better," he said.

"It was like putting my head in the lake," Matthew said. He looked round at the unmoving sunlit trees and the unrippling man.

"Yes," the man said. "I suppose it was. If I understand. They're one-way glasses really. Quite useful to me in these exceptional circumstances. But only a joke to you." The grey cloth that was covering his body rippled a little, like shivering, as he spoke; the sunlight didn't seem to touch it, or the sunlight that touched it sank into it, the way it sank into the body of the old blind woman. Matthew reached out and touched it. It was very very soft.

"Is it clothes?" he asked. "Is that clothes you're wearing? My mother told me about clothes." The man smiled a little and looked down at himself.

"Yes," he said. "I made it myself. I knitted it. And there are two more underneath it. Because I feel the cold. Do you like it?"

"I don't know. I don't know about clothes. But my fa-

69

ther wears clothes. I saw him in an old man's eye. Do you know my father? Have you seen him anywhere?"

"Yes. Oh yes, I've seen him. I've seen your father. He stayed the night with me and kept my room warm. One night not long back, I don't remember quite when. That's my room on the other side of this wall." Matthew looked where he was pointing and saw that the air beside him was solid and the trees beside him were flat.

"I've painted it to look like trees, but it's a wall. Did It fool you? Did you think they were real trees? I suppose you knew easily enough."

"What's painting?" Matthew asked. "Is it like drawing? My mother drew things for me on the sand on our island. So I'd know them when I saw them. Is painting like that?"

"Yes," the man said. "Painting's like that."

"Where is some?"

"These trees. I painted these trees right here on the wall. I know it's the wrong time of day and naturally they don't look like..."

"Why did you have to paint them when there are so many already?" The man didn't answer. He was looking at him through his glasses, but he didn't answer. His eyes seemed to be blinking behind the glasses, "Did it take a long time?"

"I don't remember exactly. It did in a way. Because I painted a little every day, just at noon. So it took, I suppose, very many days, because I paint slowly. They're really to be seen at noon, you see, not now, not in the morning. For the proper effect. At noon they look..."

"Is this morning, then?" Matthew asked, looking round at all the bright flowering trees. "Is this what's called morning? My mother told me about morning."

"Yes. It's very early morning. The sun has just risen." Behind his green glasses his eyes were blinking more and more, and trails of shining water were trickling down his face.

"Are you all right?" Matthew asked.

"Oh yes," the man said. "I'm all right. I'm quite all right."

"Did my father leave in the morning? Which way did he go when he left?"

"Come with me," the man said. "And I'll show you." And he laid a hand gently on Matthew's shoulder, so cold that Matthew shivered.

"Oh, I'm very sorry," he said, and lifted his hand quickly away. "I'm always cold after the night. I'll warm up as the sun rises. I'm very dependent on the sun. Like a snake, as you said. If I'm too long in cold shade I find I can hardly move. But if you'll just let me rest my hands on your shoulders a little I know I'll soon be warm right through. Will you?"

"You can if you like," Matthew said. "But I want to find my father."

"Yes, yes, I'll show you. Of course I'll show you. Just come this way with me first." And laying both his cold hands on Matthew's shoulders he guided him a little way back into the streaming sunlight. "I just want you to look at my house from this side," he said, and turned Matthew round to face it. But it was gone.

"What's happened to it?" Matthew asked. "Where has it gone?"

"Hold your hands in front of you," the man said, and very gently pushed him forward with his own cold hands, step after step towards the first row of sunlit trees. But long before he reached them the palms of his hands touched a wall.

"There," the man said. "Those are *my* trees." And he guided Matthew's hand along the wall with his own hand, which wasn't so cold anymore, over the trunk of one near tree and the blossom of one further away, and suddenly his hand pushed through into the air and he knew he was at the end of the painted wall though he still couldn't see it, and he laughed. And the man let go of him and spun round and round and flung out his arms, and then fell to the ground all tangled in his clothes.

"You like it!" he said. "You like it? It's my wall for morning light, you see, that's why it works." Matthew slid his hand along the wall in the other direction, watching closely for the end of it, and again his fingers suddenly pushed through into the air, and again he laughed; and the man kicked up his long legs and jumped to his feet and ran to Matthew and wrapped his arms around him, and little streams of water trickled from under the green glasses and over Matthew's shoulder and down his arm, and evaporated back into the air. The man touched one of the dry trails with the very tip of his forefinger, and let go of Matthew and stood back from him.

"You naturally think me very foolish," he said. "It's all illusion, I know. Really only pretence. But it's the best I can do, as yet. Would you like to come round and see the inside of the house? I've hardly anything to offer you, really only bread and water. Would you like that?"

"I know about water," Matthew said. "But all I know about bread is what my mother told me. She said it's for ,eating', but I didn't understand, but she said I'd find out." The man was still standing a little back from him and his dark eyes behind the glasses were looking down at him in a way that reminded him of his mother's eyes when he was lying in her lap and all the lake was shining in them to the bright horizon. "Is it good to eat?"

"I don't know what to say," the man said; and he reached out and took Matthew's hand in both of his own, which were warm now, and led him along beside the third wall of the house, which he could see easily enough was

72

a wall painted with two trees, one red and one white, and parts of smaller ones between them.

"Why are they so dark?" he asked, touching them with his fingers as he passed.

"Because it's north," the man said. And the sun doesn't shine here. It's the most difficult side for me, for that reason. What you're seeing is their shadowy side, at noon. One noon, you know, I stayed too long. And I was so cold I couldn't move the brush any longer. Wasn't that strange? I found I was looking at the wall and not painting it; and then the light was less, much less, and I knew I must go and stand in the sun, but I couldn't move, not at all. But luckily I was just here, at the west end of the wall, so when evening came a few setting sunbeams touched me. And I stumbled round the corner and fell in a heap on the ground and lay there hardly alive in the dark and until the sun was high enough the next day to warm me right through. There we are now, there's the door. But don't look at my work here. It's the wrong time for it, the wrong end of the day."

"They look inside out," Matthew said, looking at the trees on either side of the door, in dark shadow against the sunlight streaming past the ends of the wall.

"I know, I know. Naturally they seem silly to you. I painted them at sunset. And as well as I could. And I think quite well, really. Considering. But of course at the moment they're the wrong way round. Don't look any more, I feel ashamed of them in front of you. And it's cold here in the shade. Come inside where it's warmer." He led Matthew by the hand through the doorway into the house, and stopped just inside the doorway, and Matthew looked about him.

"It's very very big," he said. "How is it so big? Outside it's not big. It's much bigger than the room where the man...where my father was lying bubbling on the bed.

73

She said it wasn't my father, it was and it wasn't. You will show me where I can find him, won't you?"

"I'll show you which way he went," the man said, drawing him forward across the room towards an open door in the very far wall, through which he could see green trees. Halfway there he stopped and drew Matthew's hand forward until it touched something solid that he couldn't see; and he moved both their hands sideways both ways and always they touched the same flat solid, and Matthew laughed.

"It's the wall," Matthew said. "It's the same wall." Behind his glasses the man's black eyes were shining bright.

"Is it good then?" he asked. "Do you like it?"

Matthew reached his hand further sideways to touch a table and a bowl of flowers on the table, and his fingertips again bumped against the wall, and he laughed. And the thin man laughed, and wrapped his arms around him. "Does it make you happy?" Further to his right Matthew saw the table again with the bowl of flowers on it and he slipped out of the man's arms and ran to touch the bowl and the flowers, and fell against the table before he expected to reach it, and the bowl of flowers rocked back and forth and water spilled out of the bowl and lay quivering on the table. And then he saw a third bowl of flowers on a table and he went to touch it too, but more carefully, and bumped against another wall and laughed, and slid down to the floor and laughed and laughed. And then he saw the thin man's eyes behind his green glasses looking down at him again like his mother's eyes, and water trickling out of them and down his cheeks, and he stopped laughing.

"Are you very unhappy?" he asked.

"No," the man said. "No, no." And he wiped his cheeks with the back of his hand.

"My mother said when tears run from people's eyes it means they're unhappy. Where I was before there were people with tears running right down their bodies. You're sure you're not unhappy?"

"Oh yes, I'm sure. It's the opposite, in fact."

"That's all right then," Matthew said, looking at the still shimmering water on the table in front of him and then at the table to his right the table to his left, where there was no spilt water; and then he saw a cat, a grey cat, sitting beside a shallow cave in the wall, with logs in it. He reached out carefully to touch the cat, but his hand only touched the wall.

"The other way," the man said. Matthew looked the other way, past the doorway, but there was only the cave with the logs there.

"There's no cat," he said, disappointed.

"That's the way it is," the man said. "She won't sit there always. She comes and goes. What can I do? I've done what I could, but naturally I've not been able to make every wall a perfect mirror. How could I, here? It's not like where you come from. There are always difficulties. The flowers wither and I have to paint fresh ones. And I have to repaint the trees outside with the passing seasons. Slowly though they pass, for which I'm very grateful; the May has been blossoming now for I don't know how many times of the sun's rising and setting. But it may fall any day. It does no good to expect it won't. Even your coming... And you're only passing through, after all, aren't you?"

"Can I have some bread?" Matthew asked. The man's eyes blinked behind his glasses.

"Oh yes, yes. I'm sorry. I was thinking only of myself" He walked the other way in the room, past the door, and bent down and cut with a knife into a brown mound, and brought a piece of the mound on a plate to Matthew.

"Luckily I baked it yesterday," he said, setting it down on the table beside the bowl of flowers. "I hope you'll like it." He went back to the other end of the room and poured some water into a cup and brought that to Matthew as well. Matthew bit off a piece of the bread and chewed it and swallowed it, and bit another piece and chewed it and swallowed it, and another and another until all the bread was gone, while the young man watched him from behind his glasses with slowly blinking eyes.

"Do you like it?" he asked at last, uncertainly. "Is it good?"

"Can I have some more?" Matthew asked, and picked up the cup of water and touched the rim of it to his lips and let the cool water flow over his lips into his mouth and down his throat. He put the empty cup back again on the table. "And some more water." The man brought him more bread and water and stood by quietly watching while he ate and drank.

"Is that all right? Do you want any more?" he asked when Matthew had finished. Matthew shook his head, and sat still on the floor and gazed slowly around the painted room. Then the painted doorway opposite the doorway he had come in through, and the green trees which filled the painted doorway stopped him looking at anything else.

"Why are they green?" he asked. The man turned his head to look at them.

"Ah, those," he said. "They're old work. I began there when I was first here. And the trees outside then were green. I know they're wrong now, but I haven't been able to see what else to do. Even if they were flowering, they'd still be only the shape of the way back. But what's the shape of the way on? How can I know that? I thought I might paint a fire; but fire moves and I couldn't paint it moving. Then I even thought I might lay and light an actual fire there...isn't that foolish? It was because I was feel-

76

ing so tired, and cold, and day after day there was never any solution. Every day I looked at it and looked at it and I could never think what to do. Except make the fire itself. Which would of course burn and disfigure and even destroy everything which it has been such a labour to build and maintain. And so I left it as it was. And now... I think now..." He was looking down again at Matthew and his eyes were trickling again with tears. And suddenly Matthew remembered his mother saying he would see her eyes in the water, and the man's eyes behind his green glasses were like his mother's eyes under water; and he stood up and reached up towards the man's cheeks, and the man bent down so he could touch them and wipe the tears from them. Then he looked down at his wet hands and watched the tears slowly gather into a shallow pool in each of his palms, and in each of the pools he could see the room reflected, very small, and the face of the peering man in the middle of each of them, very large; and very very slowly both pools turned to steam and were gone. And the man smiled.

"You're not hungry anymore, are you?" he asked in a low voice. Matthew shook his head. "Then I'll show you the way your father went. Only," he said, as Matthew turned excitedly to go, "Will you help me make a wreath first? Every day I make a fresh wreath and hang it over the door. It won't take long."

"All right," Matthew said, and followed the man out of the house. He looked at the rows of red and white flowering trees.

"He walked right through there?" he said.

"Yes," the man said, turning back towards the house and lifting down a ring of flowers from over the door. "I'll show you the direction he took. I watched him go, with the morning light falling on him through the trees, and the shade and the light and the shade. He has a very long stride, your father."

"Did he stay here long?"

"No, not long. He was too restless to stay more than one night, and he went with the earliest morning light. Will you gather me some fresh flowers for my wreath?"

"It's still there," Matthew said, looking up at the place the man had taken the ring of flowers down from. "There's a beautiful fresh one behind the one you took away."

"You think it's beautiful?" the man said with a sudden smile. "I'm happy you think so. But it's only some of my painting, as you can see. I painted it for this time of day, for this moment, so that something…a token, you know?…will be there when the real one isn't. And when the sun is higher it won't look beautiful, you know, it will only look funny. Unmoving paint isn't the same as an unmoving flower, is it? It's only a shift. Everything is only a shift. Doesn't it all seem very tawdry to you?" He was pulling the drooping flowers out of the ring of sticks they were threaded into, and laying them carefully in a little pile on the ground. Matthew picked up several of them together and looked at their tired heads hanging down limply, and laughed. They he stooped down and pulled up some fresh flowers in both his hands and held them up in the sunlight which was streamimg over the roof of the house, and watched delightedly as their heads slowly drooped and hung down over his hands. He laughed and let them fall to the ground. Then he pulled up some others, as big handfuls of them as he could, and held them up and watched them droop, and flung them down and pulled up others further from the door, and others, and smiled happily and laughed. The man followed after him, gathering up all the flowers he flung down, until his thin arms were full of them; then he carried them back to the doorway of his house and pushed them into a bucket of water and sat on the ground beside them and began threading them into the ring of sticks on his knees. Matthew stopped pulling up the flowers.

"Which way did he go then?" he asked, looking at the row of red and white trees a little way in front of him, and the row behind it and the row behind that, all of them bright with the morning sunlight. "Show me which way he went. Please show me." The thin man looked up from his work.

"You're facing the way he went. Just there he passed in among the trees. But don't follow the avenues looking for him, follow the winding of the wild rose bushes. The avenues are only for me."

"What're avenues?"

"They're the broad straight roads leading back through the flowering trees."

"There aren't any broad roads," Matthew said, peering in among the trees. There was a beautiful smell in the air near him, like the smell where the beautiful woman was dancing.

"You don't see them? No, why would you see them, they're nothing to you. But from where I'm sitting they run away like the spokes of a wheel, right to the blue mist at the horizon. That's not as far as they go, but it's as far as I can remember. I came along them once."

"All of them? You came along all of them?"

"I must have, since they're there. But perhaps I didn't, I can't be sure. Since they're all the same. But the trees are bigger further out, I remember that. And I sat awhile in their shade, and I wasn't cold."

"Will I grow bigger then too?"

"I don't know. I never knew anyone before to go the other way. Except your father. But I think he stumbled here by chance. At an angle, you know. He looked dazed, and talked of finding someone of whom I've never heard. If you follow the trail of wild roses I'm sure you'll find him at last."

"But what are they....wild roses?"

79

"Can't you smell them? There, right at your foot there's a small bush." Matthew looked down and saw a small bush with pink flowers with five petals and yellow centres, and out of them the beautiful smell was flowing.

"I know those flowers," he said, bending down quickly to pick one. "They were growing where I lost my earring. Ouch, it pricked me." He shook his pricked hand and drops of blood flew onto the grass.

"They have thorns," the man said. "You have to be careful."

"Will I find my earring too if I follow them?" Matthew asked, carefully picking one of the roses and bringing it to his nose to smell. "It was an island where they were and there was a beautiful woman and she kept appearing and disappearing. Will I find her too if I follow the wild roses?"

"I don't know. I don't know anything about that. But you'll find your father at last. I think he can't be very far. I think it wasn't long since he passed by here. You may find him anywhere; in a house, or in a field, or sitting by a river. Will you bring me that rose you're holding?" Matthew took him the rose, which was already looking limp, and he threaded it carefully in among the other flowers, and bent over the wreath and laid his thin cheek against it, and smiled.

"I'm going now," Matthew said.

"Yes, I know," the man said, looking at him through his big green glasses and smiling still. "Thank you for passing through here. Thank you."

"You won't cry anymore, will you?"

"No," the man said, but behind his glasses his eyes were beginning to blink faster.

"Well I'm going then," Matthew said, and he turned and began walking towards the trees.

"Yes," the man said. "Good-bye."

Matthew came to the rose bush again, and from it he saw another, and another. He followed them in among the thin straight trunks of the flowering trees, through row after row of them, red and white and red, and in all of them was the soft buzzing of bees. The sun rose higher and higher in the sky, and he saw that a few of the petals were beginning to drift down through the trees as he passed under them, fluttering down to the grass and flowers, some of them coming to rest a moment on his shoulders and his feet. Then, as more and more began to fall, and glided silkily down his arms and legs, he became more and more happy and excited, until at last he began to run. He kept watch on the rose bushes, which way they were winding, but he ran this way and that among the trees, and when he came back to a rose bush he leapt over it and kept on running, and the petals trickled down all over his body, and clung to his feet which were wet from the wet grass. They were falling so thickly around him now they were like the snow his mother had told him about when he was nestled in her warm arms; but they weren't cold as she said the snow was cold. But they were falling so thickly he could hardly see the trees he was running among, only the straight dark trunks of them appearing out of the petal and disappearing, and the ground was all red and white from the blanket of petals, and the rose bushes were mounds of red and white petals, and he couldn't any longer feel the grass but only the petals, cool and silky against his feet; and the air was now so swirling with them that the red and white of them were all blurred into pink, as pink as the roses he couldn't any longer see. But still the smell of the roses filled the air he was running through, and was the same in whichever direction he ran, it seemed to be without beginning or way or end, and he remembered the beautiful woman he could never quite see. And then he realized he didn't know any longer where the rose bushes

81

were which the thin man told him to follow, he couldn't see anything at all around him except the blurred swirling petals, and he stopped running and stood quite still.

Slowly the petals falling around him grew less and less, until they were all on the ground, as deep as his ankles, and the air was clear again, and he saw that he was standing in a small opening among the trees. And the trees were different, they were in different shapes now, big and small and twisting and bent, and they all had small green leaves. And when he looked at the ground around him again, the petals had all melted the way his mother said snow did, and he saw that he was standing in the midst of rose bushes covered with pink roses; and for awhile he stood where he was in the clear sunshine, breathing hard from his running and wondering which way to go.

Then he noticed what seemed to be a narrow path through the rosebushes, winding out of the opening and in among the trees, and he followed it. At first the trees were very thick around him and their shade was nearly everywhere, only in small places were there patches of sunlight, and all the roses were dark pink in the shade and their yellow centres were dark gold, and the air was so heavy with their beautiful smell he hardly knew where he was walking. But then gradually the trees began to thin out and the sun began to spray through their leaves, and he passed through open spaces where it poured down warmly on him out of the clear blue sky; and the roses were paler and more glowing and the smell of them was stronger still. And then there were even fewer trees, only several very big ones, and all among them the flowering rosebushes covered the ground, except for the narrow winding path he was following. And the sun was as high in the sky now as it always was over the lake where he was born,

He heard a sudden noise that sounded like a voice or voices over to his right, and he stopped and looked that way over the sea of roses, but he couldn't see anything but them and the very few very big trees for as far as he could see over the gently rolling land. He started walking again, but before he'd gone any distance he heard the voices again, men's voices; they sounded near enough to see, but still when he stopped he couldn't see anyone. The path was winding up a shallow slope and as he made his way up it he was sure that from the top he would see people, because their voices now were a steady sound just ahead of him.

But at the top there was no one still. There was a fence made of thin logs, blocking his path, and beyond the fence was a big open field, just earth with many many straight small ditches in it, and he remembered his mother telling him about ploughed fields, that was what they would look like, and making one for him in the sand. And he remembered the man saying his father might be in a field; and he could hear the men's voices louder than ever off to his right, so he kept walking between the rose bushes beside the fence. Until there weren't any more, only a few scattered ones, so he stopped.

Then he saw two animals beside the fence on the other side of it, big animals, they looked like what his mother drew and called horses, and the men's voices were coming from right beside them; and he was suddenly sure that one of them must be his father's voice, because the rose bushes had come to an end, maybe his father was just there at the edge of the field. He began to run along beside the fence towards him and the nearer he came to the horses the louder the voices were, and he could see under the horses' bellies to where men were sitting in a circle in the ploughed field. But when he ran past the horses heads, which they didn't even lift from eating the long grass by the fence, the sound of the voices stopped and the men he had seen were all gone, there was only the empty field.

No, there was somebody lying in the long grass at the edge of the field. It was a man, the body of a man, wearing clothes. He was lying on his side and he was facing the other way, but the clothes he was wearing were like the clothes the man he saw in the old man's eye was wearing, it must be his father. And he must be asleep, he thought, because his breathing was so slow and steady. But when he came right to the fence, and pushed his head between the thin logs of the fence, the man stirred and his breathing became faster and not so steady, and he remembered that his mother had told him that he must be careful. So he didn't move at all for a minute, waiting for the man to grow quiet again. But he didn't, his breathing grew quicker and quicker, and his muscles now were twitching and jumping and strange groaning noises were coming out of him.

There was a man on the other side of him, where had he come from, he wasn't there before. He was all in black, even his head was covered in something black, so he couldn't see his face, what was he doing? He had sticks in his hand and he was bending over his father, he was pushing one of the sticks into the ground, right between Matthew and his father, why was he doing that? The stick was growing bigger, and leaves were growing out of it, and branches with thorns all over them, it was growing into a rosebush. The black man was pushing another stick into the ground beside the first one, and another and another, he was pushing them into the ground all around his father's body; and they were all growing branches and leaves and flowers, and they were growing bigger and bigger and closer and closer together, so he could hardly see his father any more in the middle of them.

"What are you doing to my father?" he shouted. "Leave him alone." The black man didn't answer him. He didn't even look at him. But he backed away from the rose bushes into the ploughed field; and as he backed he began

shrinking. He shrank and shrank, right into the earth of
the field, and he was gone. Matthew stood where he was
for a long time, looking through the fence at the rose bushes growing over his father; and then at last he stretched his
hand through the fence and touched the petals of one of
the roses, and tears began to trickle out of his eyes.

*

Fenwick screamed and fell back in his chair, covering
his eyes with his arms against the brilliant light which was
pouring out of his globe. From the shelter of his eyelashes
and his thick cotton sleeves he watched the light flood
through his room, illuminating it to incandescence, dissolving everything in it into bright dancing particles, and
burst forth from all the windows into the cool, early morning air. He felt about with his faraway feet for one of the
legs of his desk, and on finding it pushed himself and his
chair backwards and sideways. The chairlegs screeched
against the floor and the chair itself with the force of his
pushing nearly tipped over; but it held upright and he was
no longer facing towards the dazzling globe on his desk,
and with a further push he was facing full away from it.
He could feel the light coursing over his back, making his
skin tigle and his hair crackle and stand on end, but not
dissolving him altogether he saw with relief, for a giant
throbbing shadow of himself was dimming the brilliant
wall he was facing; only the middle of it was gone, where
the window was, out of which the light and his shadow
both were flowing, out over the red-tiled roofs of the
town, lighting them to the brightness of bonfires. From
the roofs the light was flowing only upwards, for below
them the upper walls of the houses he could see were almost black by contrast, as if the shadow only, his shadow,
was flowing downwards, darkening the air in the great

85

square to the inky blackness of a great well; while the sky over it, the sky everywhere, was filling with mounds and mountains of clouds, white and grey and black, and the light was flooding into the midst of them like water into endless canyons, and now among them was beginning to pulse and throb with a steady rhythm, as if it was losing a little of its velocity.

It was throbbing in the clouds more slowly, how much time had passed? It was flashing in white balls of light in the clouds, and dying for an instant and bursting forth again and again and again, with each time an instant of darkness between, like black sheet lightning, the inside-out of the rain-bringing storm they had been waiting for so long. If only it would be a real storm, if only it would bring rain. He listened, through the whispering, crackling flow of light past his body, for any sound of thunder. And he heard in the furthest distance, but rolling slowly and brokenly nearer, a deep rumbling, gathering together, exploding and fading, fading. And more rumbling, from other quarters, bursting and rolling slowly through the brilliant air. The noise of it every moment was louder, it was breaking out of the bursting light and tumbling down upon the town, rolling over all the roofs and in through all his windows, into the midst of the incandescent light around him, bursting against his body, bombarding his ears.

He found his strength coming back to his body. Slowly. His arms and legs felt nearer him and he found he could move them almost normally. So he lifted himself slowly and carefully from his chair and, sheltering his eyes from the piercing white radiance of the globe, stumbled towards the window which faced directly out over the plain. He knelt against the window seat and gazed over the plain towards the far line of jagged hills and Black Melk's castle sitting atop them, while the unceasing light poured over him and out of the window.

In the plain immediately below, the men who had just been setting out for the fields were halted where they found themselves and were gazing up at the sky filled with highpiled clouds flashed through with sheets of lightning and now bolts of lightning, ripping out of clouds and into clouds, crackling like fire to end the world, searing his eyes with jagged red lines like the jagged red line around the silhouette of Black Melk's castle. But it wasn't Black Melk's work, though they would doubtless think it was. It was work against Black Melk, the beginning at long last of the turning of the tide.

None of the lightning, not even of the sudden jagged bolts, was striking at the earth. Not yet. But it was growing in intensity and frequency by the moment, and the thunder was growing in wildness. He closed his hand round the rose hip at his throat and thought that he must go to the rose garden before it was too late, even though it meant leaving Maria alone. But his strength was so little, the light had bleached it away. And what if Black Melk…? The men below were all looking up at him standing in the window, as if they wanted guidance. They were appearing in the sharp intervals of light and dark, and in the light their faces were so bleached he couldn't distinguish them. He would look the same to them. But they would know him by his position in the window. Was he in silhouette from the light flooding past him from the globe? From where they were they couldn't see the globe, but could they see the flooding light? Or only the lightning, and himself in the window flashing white and black and white? The first of them were beginning to make their way back towards the town gate. They were frightened, naturally they were frightened. They wanted shelter and protection. He must go to the rose garden.

Cautiously he stepped back from the window and backed round his desk in a semi-circle, his back always to the dazzling globe, until he was facing the door. And Maria beside the door, sitting on the floor with her back against the wall and her legs straight out in front of her, her teeth chattering and her eyes staring, as if burnt blind; and her mug of grey milk slopped in her lap. He walked slowly across the room through the streaming light, articulating every movement of his legs in his mind, feeling sure that if he relaxed for an instant he would scatter into atoms, until he reached her and bent down to her and closed her eyes with his hand. Then, gingerly, he took the sticky mug from her hand and set it on the floor and slipped his hands under her body and laid her on her back on the floor, and set a folded piece of cloth between her teeth. When he stood up again he found that his own teeth were chattering and that his body all over was prickly and cold from a fearful sweat, and within his flesh all his bones were tingling. How would he be able to go to the rose garden if he remained so weak? The light was too strong, too loose, too formless for his grasp. And the time seemed wrong, it felt too soon, he felt unready, fearfully unready. But William was nearly at the wall.

Then he felt, from its whispering flow over his body, that the light was almost imperceptibly ebbing. The lightning and thunder were every moment more extravagant and terrifying; the air from his very body to the furthest heavens was in quivering torment from them, and within it a wind was rising; and below, in the deep square, people were running and stumbling in panic; but the light from the globe was dwindling. Very very slowly. And as it dwindled it softened a little. For whatever cause, he was grateful; and he found his body obeying his wishes a little more easily.

The wind was rising swiftly, he would have to close the windows. He made his way haltingly,, through the still barely endurable brilliance of the light, back to the window overlooking the plain. As he unhooked the window frames to close them, a sudden gust of wind pulled them sharply from his grip and banged them against the wall, and one of the doves in their cage under the window seat suddenly flapped its wings. He forced the windows closed and bolted them, and saw the men crowding in against the gate below, the last of them now, holding up their faces to have them checked off by the gatemen in the flashing light, struggling to keep their footing in the swirling wind; there would be no spies among them, since the storm for once wasn't of Black Melk's making. Behind them the wind was driving whirlpools of dust along the road, through alternating brilliant white and jet black, and through the sad fields where the sparse green of the crops was only beginning. They would amount to little as usual. Further off, the air was already heavy with swirling dust, so heavy that even with the continual flashes of lightning the sharp hills on which Black Melk's castle was standing were barely distinguishable.

His room itself was now shaking with the gusting wind inside it; the leaves of his books were blowing about and his papers were scattering on the floor, and Maria's black dress was fluttering feverishly her body. He crossed to the other windows and with the exercise of all his strength forced them closed.

And the air in the brilliant room was suddenly and oppressively still, and felt moment by moment more painful to him as the almost unbroken flashing of the lightning and crashing of the thunder beat upon the walls from every side. And Maria's body began to twist about on the floor.

But the light from the globe was still dwindling. He thought it would in a minute even be within his powers to look at it. In another minute, another, surely now, just now...

89

He staggered backwards, holding his arms over his eyes, which had burning black balls of flame at their centres. But he had survived the glance, he was still in the room. If the light continued its slow dwindling he would be able soon, surely, to survive even gazing; it was time to draw the curtains to hold the light within the room.

Stumbling across the floor past Maria's body, writhing below him in red and glittering blackness, he dragged and pulled together the long heavy curtains of the window facing towards Black Melk's castle, that must be the first direction from which the light, now that he could bear it himself, must be withheld, and Maria protected; as he closed them he felt the light soften, and its reflection from the dark wool bathe his branded eyes. As he pulled the eastern curtains together he felt it mellow further and found his normal sight returning. He could see Maris's body quite well now, and it appeared quieter, as he stepped over her, crossing to the west window; the black and red fire was rippling over her body but no longer in his eyes. And as he pulled the heavy western curtains together against the view of the roofs of the town, he could see their red tiles clearly, he could see the outline of each of them sharply, he could even see some spots of deeper red on them, signs of the first splashes of burst raindrops, would they be the first of many? That would be a miracle to confound Black Melk.

As he made his way to his fourth window, beside the door, his sight was so restored that he cpould see down into the flashing brilliance and gloom of the square below; and the light from the globe was dwindled almost to a sunset light as it flowed caressingly past him and, like water, overspread the rainfreckled roofs of the whole town, some of it now even trickling like water, as through holes in the air, like fine glistening waterfalls down into the deep pool of the square. Which was empty except for a cluster of cats in the middle, huddling tightly into themselves and against each other, their wide fearful eyes with every flash of lightning shining like jewels. And around the square, in the shelter of doorways and archways, the faces of the upward-gazing people gleamed like white stones. He pulled the curtains vigorously together and the room was almost gloomy: the light from the globe had diminished to barely more than a soft glowing, and the lightning flashes were like pale ghosts on the curtains. But the thunder rolled and crashed through the room as heavily as before.

He crossed the floor to the east window and lifted the lid of his trunk; then, alert against any fresh outpouring of light, he lifted the glowing globe from his desk with both hands and carried it with all the care he knew to the trunk and lowered it into the silks and linens stored there, and wrapped it round with them, and lowered the lid of the trunk and locked it; and except for the ghostly patterns of light pulsing through the heavy curtains the thunder-filled room was dark. He made his way carefully past Maria's body, which was now quiet again, and slipped out of the door, closing it quickly after him, and locking it.

On the landing the lightning and thunder flashed and crashed about him, and on the skylight raindrops were shattering like fine glass. He wrapped his cloak well about him and descended the stairway swiftly, only halting a moment when he came to the first floor, to listen for the soundes of the raven through the sounds of the storm. Its croaking was loud and full of fear, and it was striking against the wall with its beak almost in a frenzy, but there was nothing he could do to calm or comfort it. He shook his head and trailed his fingers helplessly against the bars and continued down the stairway to the ground; and out into the howling wind which was swirling in the square like a great whirlpool. It was of such force that he could make his way through it only by holding onto walls and windows and doorways...where people were still huddled, and seemed paralyzed; their faces were perfect flashing mirrors of fear. They didn't seem even to see his passing. And at the centre of the square the cats were still clustered; it must be that the whirling wind was holding them there.

A woman just ahead of him, a youngish woman she seemed, with her loose hair half-wrapped round her face, was reaching out with both hands towards the middle of the square, or across it, and even through the wind and the thunder he could hear her shrieking. But she seemed blind to him fortunately, perhaps it was the lightning; he ducked past her under her outstretched arms. If he were delayed in any way the power would go to Black Melk; and the rose garden then would hardly live, and all their pale blue eyes would be paler still.

And William might even this moment be arriving... He strove to quicken his pace at the thought, turning into the street leading off the square, where the wind was more restricted and he was able almost to run. Overhead, the lightning flashing in zigzag bolts from cloud to black cloud was lightening his way, making the rain-splashed cobblestones glisten. There were no people now to be seen, and the houses they would be sheltering in on either side of the street were shut up as tight as those which were empty.

The old palace loomed up on his left at last. He unlocked the high gates and locked them again after him and made his way across the slippery cobbled courtyard. He unlocked the great front door and closed and locked it after him, and made his way across the dusty floor through the mirror-flashings of the lightning, and up the broad dust-carpeted stairway, with no footprints in it but his own, to the great double doors of the throne room. He threw back his cloak and pushed the big key into the lock, while around him the muffled thunder rumbled, punctuated by the soft sounds of big raindrops landing on dusty floors near and far, under holes in the rotting roof. It was difficult to hold in his mind that William was almost at the wall, but it was so, it must be so. If the light had come, William must be coming. How could it be otherwise?

*

William stood at the foot of the high wall, and looked up. The dark green branches of the cedars resting on the top of the wall were dripping cold rain on his tired and aching body and blocking out the sky. He couldn't tell the time of day. The light was grey.

He reached out his hand to the lichen overgrowing the wall. It was wet, grey and wet. He pressed his hand against it and all the water in it trickled over his wrist, as cold as ice. There was no opening in the wall, so far as he could see, not far; it stretched to left and right unbroken, closing off his way.

Left or right, it didn't matter. He turned left, and began pushing his way through the soaking underbrush close to the wall. But there were brambles in the underbrush, more and more of them, and his going was slow. They caught at and tore his skin within his clothing, and in trying to escape them he stumbled and fell and they tore his arms. At last he had to retreat some way from the wall, back into the dripping forest, where there were only ferns and bracken and other soft growth. He walked and he walked, but the wall never changed, it was as high and solid and as grey with lichen as ever. And his tiredness was so great he began to think his knees wouldn't hold him much longer.

Then he saw a gate in the wall. It was as high as the wall itself and it was thickly woven with brambles, and in front of it there was a broad mound of brambles as high as himself. And beyond the gate, as well as he could see through the railings and brambles, there seemed to be greater light, even a little pale blue sky. He stood still a moment to quiet himself, to still his heartbeat in its weariness and sudden expectation.

He wouldn't be able to push his way through the brambles; they were too high and too thick and too many. He looked around behind him in the deep-shadowed forest and saw a fallen log close by. He tried it with his fingers, his fist and his boot; it seemed only half-rotted. So he slipped his hands under it, pushing them through the soft earth, and wrapped his arms round it and pulled and strained with all his strength to wrench it up out of the ground. Suddenly half of it, three times as long as he was, broke loose and he lost his balance and fell down beside it. When he'd caught his breath he wrapped the log in nis arms again and dragged it over to the brambles and slowly and laboriously, foot by foot, raised it to an upright position. Then he pushed it over, and it fell right across the brambles, half-crushing them to the earth, and its further end came to rest against the gate; and he walked cautiously and safely along it himself to the gate.

But the gate was shut tight, and its railings were closely interwoven with brambles as high as where the cedar branches were resting thickly on its top. But the brambles would help him to climb; so he started climbing, finding handholds on the railings, and made his way quickly upwards. The brambles tore at his clothes and his skin, even the skin of his face, however he tried to avoid them, but they gave foothold to his boots. He climbed until his head touched the cedar branches, and the rain in them trickled all over his body, cooling the sharp wounds of the brambles. He climbed in among the cedar branches, and found the spiked tops of the railings with his hands, and hoisted himself over them in the dripping gloom, and climbed down the other side of the gates until he was free of the cedar branches. The brambles still caught at his clothes and skin, but he hardly noticed them now for the sudden caressing softness he felt in the air; and when he was some way still above the ground he leapt free of the gate and landed, and tumbled head over heels, on the earth; which was hard and unyielding, not like the forest floor; it crunched under the impact of his body, and winded him.

When his breath was back he opened his eyes and looked up from where he was lying. The sky overhead was a pale blue, with small fleecy clouds drifting slowly across it, and sunlight was lying warmly on his wet and stinging body. He sat up and looked around him.

He was in what appeared to be an overgrown garden. The weeds growing about him were as high as his head, and were mingled and tangled with bushes of every kind of rose, in bud and young flower and dying and dead flower, and dense with dead branches: so woven and bound into each other that they were like walls or hills of roses and weeds beside him. But just where he was sitting there seemed to be a kind of fine gravel path, overgrown only with small weeds and moss. He stood up to see better where he was, but the rose bushes further back were as tall as he was, and other shrubs and saplings were taller, he could make out nothing beyond them, only the pale blue sky over them.

He began to walk along the gravel path through the weeds and the gentle sunlight, gazing round at the roses of every colour and kind, breathing in deeply the scent of them, sweet and sharp at once, feeling his body heal of its bramble wounds and weariness in the softness of the air. A yellow rambler overarched the path. He crouched almost to his knees to pass under it and its sharp thorns.

Then, as he was bending, he stooped to the ground, seeing yellow petals falling about his head and come to soft rocking rest on the earth. He touched the curved inner side of one to feel its silky surface and watch the sun glide back and forth about the shadow of his finger. But the shadow was very faint, the shadow of a shadow. He held his hand close over the petal and still it glowed with light, little less than the others. He held his hand out in front of him and looked at it; it was nearly as bright on its under as on its upper side. It must be the air, he thought, standing up, it was so soft it diffused the shadows to nothing, and held the light. It made him feel very easy and walk very slowly through the fallen petals of every kind, fresh and faded and dry, red and pink and white and deepest yellow, tangled in all the weeds and scattered all over the overgrown path. He tried at first not to step on them, but did step on some of them, and apologetically stepped back, and stepped on others, and suddenly laughed low to himself, and knelt down in the path in the midst of some weeds cutting with their pungent smell into the billowing scent of the roses, and laid his face down among whatever petals happened to be lying there, and whatever weeds growing; and remained some while unmoving, feeling the warm sun on his back and his calves and the cool damp of the ground seeping into his knees. The only sound was the murmuring of insects.

Then, of a sudden, there was the noise of something hard and sharp, and not far. He lifted his head and listened. The sound was ahead of him somewhere, beyond a winding of the path. He stood up and began to walk towards it. It might be another man making the noise. It was long since he had seen another man. He followed the winding of the path, which crossed with other winding paths, all of them equally deep and narrowed with weeds and wild rosebushes pressing in on him from both sides, many of the bushes grown so high, and with flowering shoots reaching up still higher into the pale sky, that he could see little more about him than in the forest. But the sharp sound was ever a little nearer. At every crossing and fork he halted and hesitated and listened, and followed the direction of the sound. Until he came upon it, rounding a curve in the path where, still half-hidden by the roses, he saw a man with a pair of shears in a narrow glade. The shears were giving off soft darts of sunlight, and the roses of the bush the man was pruning, deep-red roses, were tumbling over and falling in a scattered heap among the weeds and long grass. William approached the man carefully, wanting not to startle him, but the man abruptly turned towards him and saw him, and his eyes and mouth gaped wide, and he dropped his shears and before William could stop him he was running away, twisting and turning through the high weeds of the long glade until he was gone; and there was no sound in the glade but the unchanging buzzing of the bees.

William looked at the rosebush, which was cut almost square, and at another beside it, like it, except that it was more of a triangle and the roses or parts of roses left on it were the colour of pale violets, and then stooped and picked up the shears. He had hardly straightened when the other man reappeared, running swiftly towards him; on coming up to him he stopped, looked him in the eyes with his own big sky-blue ones, pulled the shears out of his grasp and ran off swiftly in the other direction. William watched him go, and waited, wondering; and after a short while, very short, he saw him reappear, and halt, at the bend he had a few minutes ago come round himself. Timidly, almost fearfully, he came forward along the glade; his clothes were old and worn and torn.

He wasn't a young man; his long and matted hair was grey, and the flesh of his beardless face was grey, and his lips were lined and sunken. Only his great pale eyes looked young. He held out the shears with both hands, offering them.

"No," William said. "I was looking at them only." The man didn't seem to hear. William shook his head. The man lowered the shears. But he didn't lower his eyes.

"Is this your garden?" William asked. The man's eyes blinked slowly, but he didn't answer. William gestured with his arm in a broad arc at the roses all around them and pointed with his other hand at the man, and looked questioning. The man suddenly smiled, and then suddenly laughed, a shrill belllike laugh; then vigorously shook his head, so that his long hair scattered about, and pointed over William's head in the direction he had first run; and was just taking William's arm to turn him round to face in that direction, when his smiling ceased as quickly as it had begun, and fear overspread his face like a cold mask and he backed away a couple of paces, staring at William's forearm.

"What is it? What's wrong? What's wrong with me?" But the man didn't answer; and it seemed he couldn't answer, it seemed he was both deaf and dumb. But it was evidently the long, blood-encrusted scratch on his forearm which was holding the man's unwavering gaze.

"It's just a scratch," he said, speaking slowly, maybe the man could read his lips. "It's nothing serious. Just from the brambles at the gate. It doesn't hurt. And it's almost better." It must have been the deepest one, for other smaller scratches had almost disappeared. "The air here makes them better. I think it must be the air." The man wouldn't look at him, he wouldn't take his eyes from the scratch. So William covered it with his other arm. "There, it's gone," he said. "Gone away." The man looked easier and his expression of fear slowly faded, and the cloudiness in his eyes faded, until they became again as pale and clear as the sky above them. And he smiled again, and pointed again past William in the direction he had first run and in which it seemed he now wanted them both to go. He touched William's shoulder with a strange light hand and passed him, and led the way along the path, glancing back every other moment with an anxious look and a mild smile, carrying his shears in the crook of his arm. Then a rosebush, heavy with small coppery roses, caught at his tattered clothes while he was looking back, which seemed to frighten him. He pulled free of it and was caught behind by another. Fear overspread his face and fearful noises began to gurgle in his throat. William reached out quickly with his unscratched arm, hiding the other behind him, and jerked the back of the man's worn blue tunic free of the thorns, and the man looked at him in wonder. After that he no longer looked back, but only where he was going; and although the bushes in places were growing so close together that there was barely room to pick their way between them, and he seemed time and again about to be caught again by the thorny branches, time and again he escaped them, lifting them aside with care and strange precision, even smiling now as he paused beside them or under them, even holding them back for William to pass, and never using his shears to make their passage easier.

As they followed the meanderings of one path and then another, the man never hesitating at any fork or crossing, though the sunlight and shadows were so diffuse that William couldn't make out even in which direction they were generally tending, the paths very gradually became broader and the weeds smaller and sparser and the fine gravel of the path less and less overgrown with moss and fine grass. But still all around them the rosebushes were in a condition of neglect, intertangled and laden with dead flowerheads and thick with dead wood. There were short footbridges now, soft with moss, crossing over slowly flowing rivulets choked with flowering waterweeds and so overhung with wildrose bushes that they were lost to sight in the distance of a yard. The man pointed down at each of the streams as they passed, and then pointed ahead of them, in the direction they appeared to be going and, sheltering his face with the arm holding the shears, he made a high arching gesture with the other and smiled a sudden brilliant smile and then as suddenly frowned and looked fearful, and then smiled again and frowned again, and again, each time more mildly, like the sun dappling the earth under trees on a windy day, until the rivulet was well behind them. The pale gravel was now crunching sharply under William's boots, and the small weeds and mosses in it were few; but the edges of it, under the rosebushes, were thickly strewn with petals, most of them dry and shrivelled, with only here and there fresh glossy ones resting on their curved backs and glowing in the soft sunshine.

The man was walking more slowly and it seemed more cautiously. And when he glanced round his eyes were clouded and his lips were set in a firm line. Looking beyond him, William could see that the path was opening out very gradually, and at the same time curving round to the left. The further they walked the slower the man walked, until he wasn't walking at all, but was only lifting and lowering each foot in turn, standing on one spot. William stopped behind him, though the path was easily wide enough for two abreast or three; but the man was familiar with the place and he wasn't, and it seemed that there was some danger. There was a new kind of perfume in the air; very faint, perhaps very far, not the scent of any rose.

The man, without looking round, was waggling his fingertips at his side as if to urge William forward; and when William was beside him, turned his head a little way towards him and seemed to be trying to smile, but his lips wouldn't move and his nostrils were flaring and his great pale eyes were wide and still. He waggled his fingers again as if to urge William to continue along the path and then, as William was passing him, he began to shuffle his own feet backwards. William continued walking around the broad opening curve, and withing a few strides found himself facing an open meadow. He looked round for guidance from the man, and saw him backing steadily off, with his hand half-raised in front of him and his fingers still waggling in what seemed now like farewell. Then he was gone and William was alone.

There seemed nothing to be feared in going forward that he could see, or to be gained in going back, so he walked to the edge of the meadow, and saw that it was a broad grassy avenue, like a green river, bordering the garden and stretching away as far as he could see to left and right. But beyond it the garden continued, or another garden began, for he could see roses of every colour and kind, and paths leading in among them from the avenue; but all much more orderly, as if tended by many hands.

What was the danger then, he wondered, stopping at the end of the broad gravel path. All around him there was peace. The sunlight was warm and gentle, the air was soft, and sweet with the scent of roses and with the other, sweeter scent, still very faint. The broad grassy avenue was freckled with wildflowers and crossed by many narrow brooks; and at intervals sheep, tethered to stakes, were quietly grazing. He stepped onto the avenue, onto the soft springy earth, and two or three of the nearest sheep raised their heads, but their gaze was mild and unafraid. He passed them by and in a few more strides was in the further rose garden, on a path of fine gravel, finely tended, beginning with a row of russet bricks at the edge of the grass. As in the garden behind him the roses were of all colours, but here they were all carefully trimmed, so carefully that every bush was at its peak of perfection, without deadwood or a dying flower, yet without any sign of trimming; and there were no fallen petals, fresh or wrinkled, on the fine gravel path, nor on the short grass on either side of it, nor even on the red earth under the bushes themselves. The colours of the roses were so much more intense than in the garden behind him, and their scent and the other scent so much stronger, and the murmuring of the bees among them so soothing to his ears that he could hardly feel his feet touching the gravel path. But he could hear them, like a slow regular beat, as they carried him through the unmoving apparently unchanging stillness of the garden.

Some way ahead of him he could see a man on the grass beside the path, kneeling it seemed, yes kneeling, he was on his knees beside a large square cloth and he was gathering a scattering of petals from under the nearest rosebush and laying them on top of a small pile on the cloth. He thought he might frighten the man as he had frightened the other, he thought he ought to approach him more slowly or even halt his approach altogether, but his ears were filled with the sound of the unchanging rhythm of his boots striking on the fine gravel. The man would hear them, any moment he would hear them, yes he was looking around and his face was full of alarm. He was an old man, whitehaired and whitebearded, and the features of his brown face were deep in wrinkles; but he was clean and his clothes were clean. His startled blue eyes glanced this way and that, and suddenly and swiftly he gathered the four corners of his cloth together and stood up and shouldered the bundle and ran away along the grass beside the path, and then turned in among the roses and was gone. When William came to where he thought the man had disappeared among the roses, between a scarlet bush and a purple, he looked to see him, but there was no trace. There hardly seemed space for a man to pass between them.

He continued his steady pace until he came to a cross-path, as straight and well-tended as the one he was on, and looked both ways along it as he crossed it. As far as he could see, which seemed to be as far as the horizon, there were rosebushes of every shade of the rainbow; and crossing the crosspath at intervals, and crossing his path, were fine streams, glistening in the soft sunlight. In the distance in one direction he saw a gardener kneeling on the grass beside a square of cloth, but it wasn't in the direction the other gardener had gone. Then ahead of him he saw a third gardener, bending down to a brook beside the path, turning aside a little earth dam with his spade, to let the water from the brook flow in among the rose bushes. Again he thought he ought to stop, but knew that he wasn't stopping, and the man turned round sharply and gasped and gaped, and repaired the dam quickly with his spade and ran off stooping through the rose bushes. He too was old and whitehaired and wrinkled, but beardless. There was no sign of him as he passed where he had been.

The perfume within the scent of the roses, the sweeter perfume he had first smelled in the further garden, was much stronger now; it fumed in his head like bright mist, coming between him and his eyes. But he could see as well as ever. He could see for what appeared to be many miles along the gravel path ahead of him and the gravel paths which crossed it, each one as straight as a line hung from the sky; and the roses on each side of them shaded one into the other in a regular and repeating series, so that the passing of his gaze from one to the next was like from one musical note to the next in rhythmic undulations from him all the way to the horizon, where they blurred into the enveloping blue of the sky. And near him he now could see between the rose bushes, for they were further apart; and he could see quite a number of gardeners as well, tending them, gathering their fallen petals and removing dead flowerheads and ill-growing branches, and opening and closing earth dams in the clear and glistening brooks. There was no longer any grass: every rosebush was standing in a diamond-shaped space, marked out with bricks laid edgeways into the earth, dividing the earth from the yellow gravel. And through the gravel ran the sparkling brooks, in perfectly straight lines, beside his path and perpendicularly across his path and diagonally across his path. He stepped over them, one and another and another and another, his legs walking and walking without his will. He couldn't hear his feet any longer, he couldn't hear anything any longer, the sweet perfume was so strong it was excluding all sounds and all other smells. The roses now seemed separated from him by an invisible wall; and the gardeners seemed separated as well, they seemed not to be aware of his passing, unless they chanced to look round; then he saw himself for a moment in their clear blue eyes before they leapt like startled animals and ran away.

He was in an avenue now of standard roses, great globes on tall thin stems, rows and rows of them to each side of him, their colours passing almost imperceptibly from hue to hue in regular rhythm; and even the gardeners who saw him now became only glassy-eyed, so still and staring that he could watch himself passing them. They all stopped what they were doing as he passed them, they were all turning and gazing at his passing, a line of them to either side of him, almost as many of them as there were standing roses. He continued with unchanging pace along the broad avenue, his mind drifting in the sweet perfume, which seemed ever stronger and sweeter, feeling his legs and arms moving like the legs and arms of a man made of wood.

Far ahead of him the horizon was shining. It was shining white, bright white. The colours of the roses were fading and the pale yellow of the avenue was fading and the soft blue of the sky was fading into the white. It wasn't so very far. Every moment it was nearer. It looked like a great radiant circle of white, a sun of white. It was growing more intense and brilliant by the moment; and sharp, darting reflections of it were darting against his body out of the gardeners's staring white eyes. It was more and more difficult and painful to look at but he couldn't not look at it the perfume was swirling in his head in light-dazzled mist he was nearly...

It was a lily, a lily of dazzling light. It was the perfume of the lily in his...

What had happened? His eyes were filled with searing blackness and he felt himself turning round and round and round. And in his ears was a sound like a voice, a man's voice, pushing into his head from both sides; but he couldn't make out any words, what was he saying? He was saying no lily. No lily. No lily. It's perfume was faded it was flowing away out his nose; and he could breathe in the scent of the roses again and hear the humming of the bees, and feel the soft air against his skin, and even see the soft blue sky, the black was only a tall narrow shape in front of him.

It was a tall thin man, a grey-haired man, peering at him with grey eyes half-closed.

"What lily then, eh? What lily?" he asked, his thin lips faintly smiling. His hand was at his throat, where he was fingering something small and red. William couldn't answer at first, his voice seemed locked inside him. Then it burst out suddenly, almost in a shout:

"Behind you." The tall man's thin lips smiled a little more distinctly. "Behind you," William said again, in a lower voice, in what sounded to his ears like his normal voice. The tall man gave a quizzical look over his shoulder, and stepped to one side. Behind him was a clear pool of water, out of which a tall slender fountain was rising.

"Is that your lily?"

William stared at it in surprise. It looked a little like a lily, and the fine spray of its crown was glistening silvery-white as it fell back into the pool. But the smell of it was fresh and clear, the smell of water. The lily...

"There could be no lily here," the tall man said, sinking down and seating himself on the stone parapet which surrounded the pool. "The roses would die if a lily were allowed in their midst. Or the lily would die. They cannot live together. Come, sit beside me here. Rest yourself. You will be needing rest. And they," he said, glancing at all the gardeners gathered in quite near them who were gazing at them both with unblinking blue eyes, "Will be reassured if they see you sitting quietly with me. They need reassuring. They are easily troubled. And you are a phenomenon in their unchanging lives." He was himself looking steadily at William with his keen grey eyes, which made him vaguely uneasy. But he sat down beside him on the parapet; and at the same moment the man let his hand fall from the little red ornament at his throat, which seemed to be a dull wrinkled stone.

"A hip," the man said, trailing the hand which had been fondling it in the water of the pool, as if washing it. "A rosehip. Years old now. Naturally it is wrinkled. It was the first intimation I had of your coming. Did the fool show you the way?"

"There was a man who seemed to be deaf and dumb. In the other garden. The wild one."

"Yes. The fool. We call him the fool." His eyes flicked in the direction of the gardeners. *I* call him the fool. He works in that outer garden. Not well."

"He seemed afraid to come to this garden."

"Did he?" A faint shadow flitted over the man's face. "Yes, that's so. He is afraid."

"I think maybe it was the smell of the lily that made him afraid."

"There is no lily to smell."

"His nostrils were flaring."

"Fear itself would make them flare."

"I suppose so."

"Rest a moment," the man said, looking at William steadily. "Don't speak. Rest." His keen gaze slackened then and his eyes became almost blank, and his head slowly swung away until he was gazing at the garden beyond the gardeners, unmoving except for his hand trailing in the pool behind him, gently purling the water. The fine gravel of the avenue was glowing pale gold and the blue of the sky seemed to be resting softly against it, and all the globes of roses on their slender stems seemed in all their colours part of the sky, and all the gardeners gazing, their eyes like blue holes in their heads, seemed part of the sky, living in it as if it were water; and in the furthest distance there was only the sky. As William gazed as the man gazed and the gardeners gazed he felt peace such as he had no memory of feeling ever before. And gradually, one by one, as he gazed, the gardeners turned away from their gazing on him and stooped to their work where they found themselves, raking the gravel, looking through the rose globes for the smallest fault, or wandered off through the roses which stretched away in avenues in every direction from the fountain.

"Ah!" the man beside him said abruptly, and turned to look down behind him. "There we are." In the pool a golden-orange fish three times the size of his hand was resting against his fingertips. Just as William saw it it swam towards the centre of the pool under the waterdrop-freckled surface, and as it swam colours began to flow out of the jagged fin on its back. They rose up through the water and as they broke the surface they formed into a brilliant rainbow, which arched itself as high into the air as the fountain and back again into the pool, coming to rest on the back of another fish, and arching again. The man was waving his other hand to the few gardeners who were still nearby to approach nearer.

"They like to see this," he murmured. "It's the only time I can persuade them to come to the edge of the pool." The rainbows now were rising and falling everywhere out of the glittering surface of the fountain-splashed water, wherever a fish was swimming; some of the arches barely skimmed the surface, others rose even with their eyes, and others still rose through the falling spray as high as the fountain itself. Some of the gardeners were standing at the very pool edge and their wide blue eyes were rflecting the rainbows.

"You like watching that, don't you?" the man said to them. They made no answer. "They don't hear a word I say," he said to William, and again a shadow flitted over his lean face. "Not that it matters, of course, not that it matters. They have been here so long they can't hear anyone, if there were anyone else to hear. The fool didn't hear you, did he?"

"I don't think so," William said. "We talked a little with our hands."

"Did you?" the man said absently. "Yes, it is very long since... Very long." He stretched his hand under a near fish and tickled its golden belly. It shivered as if in pleasure and turned its belly half towards him and swam slowly back and forth against his fingertips, while the rainbow springing from its back shivered as well, becoming all quivering colours almost melting into each other as they rose higher and higher in the air, through the spray, above the spray, high above the fountain into the soft blue

108

sky, its rising brightly reflected in the wide tear-brimming eyes of the watching gardeners.

"Well. That's enough of that," the man said in an abrupt, cold voice, and withdrew his hand from the pool; and all the rainbows at once ceased. And the gardeners stumbled back from the pool with numbed faces and sudden fear in their eyes, and flaring of their nostrils. "It's only a game, however pretty. Fit only for their big blue eyes. They don't know that the sun will soon be setting. They don't know anything at all. Don't put your hand in the pool."

"I...I'm sorry," William stammered, looking down at his fingertips nearly touching the surface of the water. "I wasn't aware..." He pulled his hand back to himself.

"If you want to wash, you can wash in the streams," the man said, pulling a small bottle from within his cloak and holding it in the pool to fill it. William looked round at the streams flowing out of the pool through five evenly placed holes in the circular parapet containing it.

"I didn't want to wash," he said. "It was... But I am very dirty. It's a long time I've been travelling. With only the rain to wash me. Days and nights and days. I don't know how long..."

"It doesn't matter," the man said, rising to his feet. "You're here now. At last. You can wash in the town, if you still feel dirty. Come, we must be going. The sun will very soon be setting." William looked up at the sun which was as high in the sky as when he came into the garden...not far off noon, but whether before or after noon he couldn't tell...and down at the man's grey-gold shadow on the fine gravel: which was squat and dwarfed, not a quarter his standing height.

"I mean in the town," the man said. "Come." He corked the bottle he had filled with water and slipped it into a pocket within his deep green cloak and wrapped the cloak round him and settled its cowl loosely over his grey head, and set off through the standing roses, following no discernible path among them. William followed after him, nodding goodbye to the nearest old gardeners as he went; but they didn't nod or make any other gesture in return. Their mouths were almost invisible in the lines and wrinkles of their old old faces, and their pale blue eyes were as unmoving as looking-glasses, reflecting his passing.

"Pay them no attention," the man said over his shoulder. "Their minds are as empty as their eyes. Keep close behind me. It will be easy to lose me, and I haven't time to spend finding you again. And I haven't waited so long only to lose you so soon. Keep your eyes steady on my back." William did as he was told, following the man's weaving course through the roses, breathing in the delightful scent of them, which was as ever varying as the colours of them varied, one blending into the next; seeing only the drifting of the colours past the outer corners of his eyes, as if they were all flowing out of the intense dark green of the man's cloak close ahead of him, so dark that it seemed at the same time to be swallowing all the light it passed through.

"I'm stopping," the man said. "Lay your hand flat against the flat of my back. And don't look around." William did as he was told. The cloak was velvet, as soft as anything he had ever touched, softer than the softest featherdown. He felt himself drawn after the man, and the roses now seemed to be flowing out of the cowl of his cloak as well, for the air above him was of the same flowing colours as on both sides of him; and the colours grew slowly deeper as if the light was growing less. And less. The man's cloak was so dark now it seemed pitch black, and the roses were dusk roses, the light was becoming night. He could no longer see the man at all, nor even any passing colour, nor any light at all. But still the man

110

was drawing him forward through the blackness, and still there was the scent of the roses. Fainter. And still fainter. That too was gone. Still the man drew him on through the featureless dark.

At last, when they didn't seem to be anywhere, the man stopped.

"We have arrived," he said. "Don't move." William could feel the muscles of the man's back moving against his palm, and could hear a faint clicking of keys, then the clear sound of a large key being pushed into a keyhole, and turned. And a door it seemed was pushed open, for there was a smell of dust and old wood rising about them.

"It's a stairway," the man said. "We're going up it." They climbed three steps and the man turned round on the steps and leaned forward, William's hand following his back, and pulled the door to behind them and locked it. Then they climbed more steps, many more, before the man stopped again and William heard him fumbling in the dark with his keys again, and then felt him bending down to fit one of them into a keyhole. When he straightened again he was lifting something, for his back muscles were tense and rippling against William's hand. And a dim light diffused around them. The man lifted William's hand away from his back, and lowered what appeared to be an immense hinged chair back to the floor, and stooped and locked it in place.

"There," he said, straightening and stretching, and removing his cowl. "We have arrived safely. We are all right, we may say." They were in a great room that light was flowing into from tall windows, all of them opaque with dust. The room was empty. The light was a pale-pink light, a grey-pink light.

"The dust is grey," the man said. "The light is red. We had better hurry, I think there may be trouble." He led the way across the great room, along a path of footprints in

111

the dust on the floor, to high double doors which he unlocked and one of which he opened, and closed and locked after them.

"Nothing is safe," he murmured, and led the way to the head of a broad, shallow-stepped stairway, and down the long flight of it to a lower floor, where the light was stronger and redder, and the dust was fretted and worried into ripples by a seeping wind. They crossed a wide and high hallway and stopped in front of a great door flanked by two tall windows, both of them broken and boarded over. The man unlocked the door and gestured to William to stay where he was while he himself cautiously pulled the door open and peered round it. Then he slipped out, gesturing to William to follow, and they were in a broad cobbled courtyard, closed on the further side by high railings. The light around them was mauve and the cobbles were purple and the sky was clear red. The man locked the door quickly and glanced about in evident unease as he led the way across the courtyard to the railings and opened a gate in them and let him through. As he was closing and locking it behind them, a door in one of the tall houses across the broad street opened a little and a woman's head appeared between it and the jamb; and disappeared and the door closed as the man turned round from the gate.

"A woman…" William said uncertainly. The man glanced sharply across the street, at the door and at the doors of the other houses in the terrace, all of them drab and crumbling and greyish-mauve, with many windows boarded up and more broken. Here and there a shard of glass was as bright as fire. The man's searching gaze rose to the uppermost floor of the house where the door had opened, where there were curtains behind closed windows.

"Was she young?" he asked.

"Pretty young. I think. I couldn't see her well. Her hair was red." The man nodded and turned away.

"Not so young as she looks. Come along, before someone else sees you. Her word alone won't be enough."

They made their way along the street through the reddish-mauve light, under rows of dead trees between blackened houses all boarded up; except here and there one gaping at the door and windows and filled with fallen rubble. They turned into another, narrower street, where the high houses were so close together above them that the light deepened to purple between them. The man clucked his tongue uneasily.

"Too red. Much much too red. We're in for trouble. And it hasn't rained. Look at the dust silted against the doors. I thought it would rain. Why did I think it would rain?" He was looking around now in a distressed way, but not cautiously. And when they passed a thin, sallow woman standing in one of the few doorways which were not boarded over, he seemed untroubled to see her. She smiled like a ghost and bobbed her head as if to please him and seemed about to say something, to ask something, when they had left her behind.

"It doesn't matter if they see you now," he said. "You might have appeared from anywhere now. They won't know. The gatemen will know. But nobody speaks to the gatemen." They were passing other people now, women and children, and a few old men, all standing or sitting in doorways, all nodding politely to the man as he passed them, all flicking careworn glances at William. Three or four children were playing listlessly in the street, rolling a ball back and forth along it, watching the wobbling track it made in the dust. At a crossing with another, broader street, where still more of the houses seemed lived in, though as black and decayed as elsewhere, a young woman was standing and weeping, her hands hanging down

113

limply by her sides and the trails of her tears on her sunken cheeks glistening pink in the intense red light.

"Please. Please," she said. The man stopped beside her.

"Yes? What is it? We have little time."

"It's my baby. My boy. The cats scratched him. In the storm." The man looked angry, and the red light so reflected from his eyes that they seemed to be flashing fire, and he turned away from her to go along the broader street. She reached out a hand to his cloak; but before she touched it he glanced down at her hand, on which there was a scar like a long welt, and it fell back limply to her side.

"The cats were all in the middle of the square," he said, not looking at her, looking along the street. William gazed at her wet black eyes, which were shining like gems, and at the fine violet streams flowing from them.

"My baby was with them there," she said. "The wind rolled him with them. I only put him down a moment. The gatemen took him away. Don't let them kill him."

"It is the scratching which kills, not the gatemen," the man said coldly.

"I know. I know," she said. People were gathering now from every side, gathering in close. "He wasn't scratched bad. I know he wasn't scratched bad."

"Did you see him after he was scratched?" the man asked, still looking away along the street. She looked down at her feet, fumbling with her dress.

"I... I..."

"The gatemen, they took him off smart," an old man said, bent over a cane and shuffling in close to the man as if to whisper something private. His hands on his cane were crosshatched with fine scars, pink in the red light. "When the wind died the cats ran every which way, and there was just this poor squalling mite alone in the middle

114

of the square. They reached him before she did."

"That at least was lucky." the man said.

"Oh, she didn't touch him, you may be sure," A middleaged woman said, wisps of her grey hair blowing about her face, and a knobbly round scar on her left cheek, and another on her throat, as bright as carbuncles in the red light. "We held her from that all right."

"I'm glad not everyone has taken leave of his wits," the man said. "Now if you'll just let me through, I have work to do. This weather is very dangerous. Don't expose yourselves more than you need."

"He was my only baby," the weeping woman said. William watched one of her tears fall from her chin fall like a tiny glittering red stone and shatter on the stones of the street. The people moved back, letting the man and himself pass through; their faces and bodies were red in the direct light and purple in the shadows.

"You're still young, you may have others," the man said, without looking back. "And he mayn't die," he added, though he seemed to find it difficult, or distasteful. "The branding may save him." The people they were passing through, into the broader street, were some of them nodding their heads at that, and a few were shaking their heads, and most were doing neither, but merely standing still.

When they were clear of them all, and nobody was near them except one or two very old men or women visible here and there on doorsteps, or leaning on the sills of open windows above their head, the man began to walk ever more quickly along the middle of the street, and seemed to be in a near-paroxysm of suppressed rage.

"I vow again and again never to speak but the truth," he said at last fiercely, between clenched teeth. "And again and again I break my vow. The branding will *not* save him. It is too late and he will be too much scratched." Even as he spoke a slow tolling from a bell not far off rolled into the street, and the old people began to cross themselves. Behind them there was the sudden sharp shriek of a woman and, looking round, William saw the people at the crossroads gathered close around the woman who had been weeping, holding her. Her hands were stretched above her in the air.

"They are holding her arms to prevent her harming herself," the man said, without looking round. "People like her think only of themselves."

"If she's lost her only child," William said uncertainly, uneasily. Her screaming was searing his ears; and the tolling of the bell was going on and on; and an old man they were passing was crossing himself without cease.

"She isn't alone in that," the man said. "Very far from alone. We must quicken our pace; the men are beginning to come in from the fields."

Just ahead of them the street ended in a great square, and in it were people, all of them it seemed men, who were standing about here and there, as if they had no particular other place to go. They glanced at the man as he swept by them, but their glances were incurious. They kindled a little when they saw William, but died again to blankness when they saw that he saw them. The face of every one of them was badly scarred, and all the scars were brighter red in the light than the flesh around them, which looked grey and tired, whatever their age; and their eyes looked tired, and dull. None of them nodded or showed any measure of respect for the man as he passed them, cutting diagonally across the square; but any man in his path moved out of it. William followed close behind his outflying cloak.

When they reached the far side of the square, the man slowed his pace a little. Then, gesturing to William to keep following him closely, he led him a short way along a narrow street to a doorway without a door in a tall, narrow house. Within the doorway was a stairway winding upwards into the deep red gloom; and at the bottom of the stairway were four big tubs which stank of garbage, and on their heavy wooden lids a dozen cats were sitting.

"It can't be helped," the man muttered in passing, it seemed in some kind of apology. "The raven must eat." He started up the stairway, the hem of his cloak brushing against each step, and William followed close behind him. As they reached the first landing, a noise of heavy knocking began somewhere down the dark corridor which was closed off from the stairway by a grill of close-set bars. It continued as they continued climbing the stairs for four more flights, at each landing passing a corridor where footprints wandered away through the dust into the dark; but in the stairway itself the red light grew brighter the higher they climbed. At last they reached the top landing, where only a broad skylight was between them and the clear blood red of the sky. The landing was strewn with cushions and rags, and beyond them was one door. The man unlocked and opened the door, and pushed his head cautiously into the room beyond.

"Stay here," he said over his shoulder, and disappeared into the darkness of the room, which little by little lightened, until it was as blood-red as the landing, when the man reappeared and beckoned William in.

"Be careful of her," he said, indicating a woman lying in the middle of the floor, and closed and locked the door. "Go and sit by that window. I have work at this one first." William made his way carefully past the woman, who was young and whose black dress was so thin and worn that her breasts were almost bursting from it at each breath. And they were such beautiful breasts that he had to make himself look away or be no more than a beast of prey.

"Sit down and look out over the plain," the man said from the opposite window, where he was gazing down into the square from which they had come, and seemed to be counting, or checking. "That will cool your ardour. As it has theirs. Well, at least they all appear to be genuine this evening, despite the protective colouring of the air. Are there many still coming in from the fields?"

"I don't know if it's many; maybe a dozen. They're helping one of them. There's something wrong with him." He looked round as he spoke, and his eyes fell on the woman again, and seeing the slow movement of her body with her breathing he couldn't make himself look away.

"I said look over the plain," the man said sharply, striding over her body towards him. "There is danger enough, and dying enough, without your making conditions worse. That man they are so kindly helping is a spy."

"He's bleeding," William said. His side is all red with blood. It even looks like it's flowing out into the air."

"Blood doesn't flow in the air," the man said, looking at him sharply as he reached with one hand behind him and rummeged in the nearest drawer of a big desk, and reached up with the other to a rope dangling beside the window, and pulled it. Above them a sharp-toned bell began to ring, and directly below them two burly men appeared out of the shelter of the wall and stopped the wounded man and the two men helping him. "Blood flows on land or in water. It can't flow in air."

"It looks like blood," William said. "What is it if it isn't blood?"

"It's nothing. There's nothing there," the man said, as if with only part of his attention, gesturing down to the two upgazing men, apparently guards, so that they separated the bleeding man from the two who were helping him. "It's a trick of the red light. A trick of Black Melk's." He gestured again and the burly men together shoved the bleeding man so that he staggered backwards and fell to the bare ground.

"As you will see," he said, catching the last rays of the sun in a little round mirror he was holding in the palm of his hand, and directing them onto the fallen man, who burst into flames and within an instant was gone. William stared down aghast at the traceless earth, seeing out of the corner of his eye the man polish the surface of the mirror against his cloak and lay it back in the desk drawer. The guards hurried the last of the men within the walls of the town and closed the gate with a heavy crash of wood against wood.

"You killed him," William said, and felt his skin prickling with confused anger and fear. The man glanced at him with a curiously mild eye.

"No," he said. "Not at all. He was never alive."

"But I saw him. And the other men were carrying him. And the guards pushed him so he fell. He must've been there."

"He was well made," the man said with a thin smile. "Black Melk knows his trade. But would you vanish in flames if I trained sunlight onto your body?"

"No. I don't think so," William said, eying him uneasily. "I'm not sure."

"You mean you're frightened." His smile was wider but still thin. William nodded, ashamed, but still uneasy. "You needn't be. I know you're no servant of Black Melk's. I've been watching you and waiting for you for a very very long time. And besides," he said, gesturing out across the broad plain, As you see, the sun has just set. We reached here just in time." Behind him the woman moaned, as if she was waking. William wanted to look at her; perhaps she wanted help.

"Hold onto yourself," the man said. "You can't help her. She must come to of herself. Look across the plain. Right across. That's right. Do you see that jagged line of hills right at the horizon?" William nodded. "Do you see

119

where they are a little higher than elsewhere? Directly across from us." William nodded. "Do you see how the red of the sky intensifies at the peaks just there, almost like a fine line of deep red?" William nodded. Behind him he could hear the woman moaning more loudly, and the soft sliding of her body against the floor. "That's Black Melk's castle. On normal days, and at night, the red line around it is clearer. There is a red line, a very fine red line, too fine for most people to see, enclosing everything of his. Which is why red days like these are particularly dangerous, because it is that much more difficult to see the red line around the spies he sends into our midst. And in fact only I can see it. They look exactly like us except for the red line; which he has never been able to eliminate, and which in the nature of things he never will eliminate. That ,blood' you saw flowing into the air was only a leaking of the red line. Which is a kind of fire. Black Melk's fire. It's a trick he tries from time to time, hiding it as blood; and coming late to the gate, so that if it had been a moment later there would have been no sunlight to destroy him. I'll have to keep watch on those two men who were helping him," he added, half to himself. "Maybe they were brave, but maybe they were traitors."

"Isn't there anything at all left of him?" William asked, peering down through the fading light at the grey ground where he had exploded.

"What should be left? There never was anything. All Black Melk can make are glamours and fireworks. You don't think he can make men? Even the flames were a glamour, a bit of his melodrama. Designed to frighten people with his power. I must light a candle now against the dusk and the coming dark. Don't look round."

William sat unmoving on the windowseat, gazing out over the plain, over the drab fields and broken-down fences and scattered derelict houses to the far jagged hills where the red line was clearer now against the darkening sky. Then the man appeared at his side again, holding a slim white candle with one hand and cupping its yellow flame with the other.

"Isn't it a beautiful flame?" he said in a low voice. In each of his eyes was a flame reflection; and the flamelight on his face made it look strangely gentle. "It is the purifying of fire. It makes Black Melk afraid." He set the candle in a tall candlestick by the window, and fitted over it a freshly washed and polished glass, and gazed silently for some while over the grey plain as the dusk slowly deepened.

"So you see," he said at last. "What his glamours and spells have done to our land. Which was once so fruitful. And which now, day as well as night, is grey and darker grey and black, from the peoples' faces to the earth. Even their clothes, as perhaps you saw, are in only the dullest colours, barely colours at all. Though only she," he said, gesturing to the young woman behind them in the room: who was quiet now, whose breathing even was so quiet that William couldn't hear it through the murmuring of doves somewhere nearby. "Only she actually wears black. It's her privilege. For them it's merely a fear of any colour which might catch Black Melk's attention. You must be very tired."

William blinked, and realized that his head had fallen forward. He wasn't sure that he hadn't for a moment or two been asleep. It was the soft murmuring of the doves he thought which was making him so drowsy. They must be overhead on the roof.

"I've been walking a long time and a long way," he said.

"That's right," the man said. His face was gentle and blurred with the dusk and candlelight. "Sleep then. The doves will help you sleep."

"I don't think I'm going to need any help," William said, and his eyelids drifted down over his eyes and his head lolled back against the windowframe. He felt his body growing warmer and lighter, and he was beginning to drift out of the window on the caressing air, drifting among great trees heavy with flowers the air was heavy with perfume...

Then he heard the woman's breathing sharpen into irregular gasps, which passed like knives through the trees and the doves' murmuring, and he found hinself sharply awake. Opening his eyes a cautious crack, he saw that the man was standing near him still, but was half-turned away from him, and was just removing from within his cloak the little bottle he had filled in the pool in the rose garden. He uncorked the bottle and lifted up the hem of his cloak, and crossed the room to where the young woman had been lying, and William saw that she wasn't lying there any longer, but had woken and had pushed herself back to the far wall by the door and was sitting with her back against it and her legs straight out in front of her and her hands woven tightly into each other in her lap. And she was staring fixedly and fearfully at himself. The man stooped to the floor beside her and picked up, with clear distaste, a mug which was standing there. Immediately she began to make fretful noises, and frowns passed over her face like squalls on water.

"All right, all tight, I'm not depriving you of your precious milk," he said in a low voice, giving the mug into her clutching hands, and watched her a moment in silence as she lifted it to her mouth and greedily drained it; and William watched a fat drop of milk glide over her chin and down her throat and trail over her swelling left breast, and another disappear in the soft crack between her breasts. Then the man saw him watching, and strode back across the room and planted himself in front of him so he couldn't see her any longer, while both his long hands enclosed the water bottle as if to hide or protect it.

"Will you give her no peace?" he said. "You'll bring on her sickness again. She is still very near to it. Look away. Look that way."

William looked where he was told, towards the window facing east, out of which he could see more of the grey plain, and the deep red tiles of roofs of houses in the town, and the first star just pricking through the purple sky. And still, out of the corner of his eye, he could see the man, see him lift up the corner of his cloak again and pour onto it a little of the water from the bottle, and cross the room back to the young woman; but he couldn't see her, he could only see the back of the man bending over her. And her loud and irregular breathing slowed and eased, and disappeared again into the soft watery murmuring of the doves. Far outside the window the ruins of three houses were being slowly buried in the deepening dusk. Then the man blocked them out, and most of the window as well, as he unlocked and lifted the lid of a trunk under it; and out of the trunk a very soft glow mysteriously flowed, gently lighting his long bony face. William stared at it shining through the little bottle and all around the man's hand holding the bottle; he leaned towards it, he wanted to go nearer to it, to… The man closed the lid of the trunk and locked it; and looked round at William with searching eyes.

"You will say nothing about the water, will you?"

"What is there to say?" William asked. "No, I won't."

"That I brought it out of the garden. ‚What garden?' they will ask; and then they might try to find it for themselves, to find some water for themselves, and we would all be in great danger. One or two of the more daring…and there are one or two, as you saw earlier," he said, indicating out of the window beside William the place where the bleeding man had burst into flames, "Might try to break into the garden. Which would be the end, the end that Black Melk is waiting for and encouraging. One way to the end." The corner of his mouth lifted in a slight, bitter smile. "There are, of course, many ways." Then his smile vanished and his whole face became troubled and he turned sharply to look in the direction of the young woman. William kept himself from turning to look at her by fixing his attention on the ever deepening purple of the sky beyond the eastern window, but he could hear her breathing again, loud and irregular, and the beginnings of whimpering; and he couldn't stop the tingling of his skin.

"Did you look at her when I wasn't watching you?" the man asked suspiciously.

"No," William said. "I wanted to, but I didn't. It's very hard not to look at her." The man looked very uneasy.

"The water usually calms her. The water *always* calms her."

"She's looking at me," William said. "I can feel her looking. It's burning my face."-

"I *know* she's looking," the man said irritably. I can't stop *her* looking. I can't stop her doing anything. Perhaps if I stand between you..." But it didn't seem to make any difference. Her breathing became more and more laboured, and more broken with whimpering and groans. And her hands or her feet began to hit against the floor, unrhythmically.

"Both her hands and her feet," the man said in a hissing whisper through his teeth. "They will develop a rhythm, they always do. It will be worse when they have a rhythm. She will drive herself into a paroxysm and another coma. A night coma is the most dangerous of all. Black Melk is waiting out there for just such an occassion. I think you had better go from the room."

"Where will I go? I don't know where… I've only just come…"

"It doesn't matter where. Outside. Wherever you like. You can't leave the town, because the gate is barred at sunset. Just don't say where you came from." He reached forward suddenly and grasped each of William's upper arms in each of his long thin hands. "Stand up and circle round to the door. I'll keep between you and her for whatever good it may do. Quickly now, quickly! We've only a moment. And don't whatever you do catch her eye with yours."

Together, the man holding William tightly by both arms, they circled round the darkening room from the little light of the candle to the door; which the man then hastily unlocked and opened just wide enough for William to slip out. When he was on the landing the man pointed down the stairs and shut the door again quickly and hard, and William heard the key turning in the lock.

Then he didn't know what to do, and he suddenly felt very tired and wanted to sleep, and looked at the rags piled and scattered on the landing and thought he might sleep among them; days and days seemed to have passed without his sleeping, and the great trees and the rain and the roses were all in his head together with the dry plain. Then he found he was already going down the stairway though he couldn't remember starting down, and the noises the woman was making faded the further he went; but the less he heard her the more he saw her, all the way down into the deepening purple gloom: her beautiful body sweating and trembling, her thighs swelling out against the floor, her throat rippling and throbbing as she swallowed the milk, the swelling of her lips and the dark fear in her eyes. He reached the barred hallway of the first floor, and stopped and lightly touched the bars with his fingertips, just to feel them. They were smooth and strangely warm.

The stink of the garbage from below was very strong, and around him on the landing balls darker than the darkness moved and were cats. There was no sound of knocking, no sound of anything now, but his own footfalls on the wooden stairs.

But as he stepped off them onto the stone floor of the entranceway, the little light there was was abruptly blocked out by two big men standing in front of him. Their faces were so in shadow that he couldn't make out their features, but it was clear that they were both looking at him search-ingly, and for a moment nobody moved. Then, as if by or-der, they stepped back together and moved apart so that he could walk out of the house between them, and they both nodded to him respectfully, and he realized that they were the guards he had seen from the man's window; but their clothes now were different, they appeared to be of some thick coarse cloth, and they were wearing heavy leather gloves up to their elbows. When he had passed between them out into the narrow twilit street, they closed together again and went into the areaway at the bottom of the stairs and lifted up one of the big tubs of garbage and started up the stairs with it; and the cats on the stairs began to whine and growl. Suddenly one of the cats screeched, and the voice of one of the men burst out:

"Fuck off out of here, you filthy beasts." There were sounds of kicking and of cats scrabbling and yowling, and one landed at the foot of the stairway and limped away around the doorjamb and along the narrow street, keeping close to the wall; and others came running, fleeing after it. Suddenly there was the sound of knocking. William stood stock still. It grew louder and wilder, and through it he could hear a squealing noise which he thought must be the railed gate being opened; and then there was a croaking, louder than any hundred crows could make, which went on and on and on. At last he heard the gate upstairs slam shut, and the guards hurrying back down the stairs. They flung down an empty bin in the entranceway and settled its lid on it, and were hurrying, almost running, out of the doorway when they saw him watching them, and stopped abruptly in their tracks and straightened themselves, and walked slowly past him, their faces white and gleaming with sweat, not looking at him as they passed him, but continuing straight into the square and across it. The noise of the croaking and the noise of the knocking had stopped as suddenly as they had begun, and cats were creeping back cautiously towards the entranceway.

Aimlessly, not knowing what else to do, William walked after the men into the square. It was so deep in dusk now that he could barely see the buildings on the far side of it, only a candlelit window here and there and the silhouette of their roofs against the deep red western sky. There seemed to be very few people standing about now, only a shadow here and there, a man by himself. Or a woman. There was no sound anywhere, or movement. He stood still and gazed at nothing for he didn't know how long, feeling dead dead tired.

"Seems you're pretty close to him," a voice said suddenly, behind him. He turned about sharply. Three figures, three men, three old men it seemed, were close beside him, in the shelter of the wall; all three with their eyes fixed on his. "Seems to us. Since they treated you so respectful."

"The gatemen, he means," another one of them said. "They ain't so respectful with us." The third man began a little chuckle which ended in a cough.

"That's for sure. They ain't that," he gasped. "They ain't respectful."

"You're an old friend, are you?" the first man asked. His voice was strangely soft and silky. Willliam felt uneasy, not knowing what to say.

"He's not so friendly with everyone, is he? Is he, boys?" The other two shook their heads. The first one gave William a big wink. "The Protector, I mean," he said. "Our Protector Fenwick. *Mr.* Fenwick. Fenwick the Good." The third man began giggling uncontrollably, until the first man stopped him by standing on his foot.

"He certainly ain't friendly with us," the second man said. "With us it's: ,Do as I say.'"

"But we're of no account, no account at all," the first man said. "And we mustn't ever forget it. Are you lodging with His Highness personally?"

"I… I…" William stammered. "Y…es. That is, I don't know exactly."

"There she goes, God bless her," the second man said, looking past William. The third man was looking the same way and fluttering his fingers in a wave. Before William could look round himself, the first man leaned forward and rested his old hand on his forearm. It was badly scarred, or burned. His face too was scarred, William could now see, and the faces of the others equally.

"What he's done to her he can do to you," he whispered in his strange silky voice. "So watch out. He's always putting the fault on others. She was as lovely a child as the sun ever shone on. Before he ,protected' her."

"Who was?" William asked. "Who do you mean?" He turned to look where all three of them now were looking, and saw the shape of the young woman from the man's room…Fenwick's room, if Fenwick was his proper name…crossing the square towards its far corner. Her sickness had quickly passed.

"Who is she?" he asked. The three old men all looked at him sharply and suspiciously, and the first of them dropped his hand from his arm.

"I thought you was a friend of his," he said.

"An old friend," the second man said.

128

"An old, old friend," the third man said.

"But you don't know who Maria is," the first man said.

"I never saw her before today," William said. "She was…he said she was…going to be sick, if…"

"*He* said," the first man said. "Never mind what *he* said."

"*He* says what it suits him to say," the second man said.

"Can you tell me where she's going now?" William asked. She was already two-thirds of the way to the far side of the square.

"Going? Going? Who knows where she's going?" the first man said.

"She goes where she goes," the third man said.

"She goes to the graveyard," the second man said. "She goes to the old palace."

"She don't go in there," the first man said.

"No, she don't go in there."

"It'll be the graveyard at this hour," the first man said.

"Why?" William asked. She was nearly at the far side of the square. She was like a dark shadow in the dusk. Soon she would be gone.

"Why?" they all asked together, and moved back against the wall, as if they wanted him to be further off.

"To see her father, of course," the second man said.

"To see his grave," the first man said.

"Because he's dead, he's dead, poor girl," the third man said in a singsong voice and seemed ready to weep.

"Is that why she's in black, then?" William asked. But they didn't answer. Their eyes were still fixed on him, but they were sidling away along the wall.

"I think I'll go after her," William said suddenly. There was no sign of her now across the square, but if he ran he might catch up to her. And she might tell him what was happening, she might make it not so strange.

"No. No," the first man said, his silky voice full of fear. "Don't you do that. You better not do that."

"I have to," he said. "I have to." And he started running across the square.

When he reached its furthest corner and saw nobody, neither her nor anyone to ask, he stopped. But there was a narrow street leading from the corner, which seemed the only way she could have taken, so he began running again, along it. Still he saw no one, though here and there through shutters he could see yellow gleams of candle-light. Then he saw a square patch of light ahead of him in the street, like a carpet, and he stopped just before it; and beside him was an open window, and candles burning in the room beyond the window, and an old white-haired woman in a rocking chair just inside the window. She turned and gazed at him with old grey eyes, white at the edges, and continued gently rocking.

"Are you looking for something?" she asked, in a soft voice much younger than her face.

"Maria," he said, breathing hard from his running. "They called her Maria. Did you...?"

"What are you looking for?" the woman asked again mildly. As she rocked, the light of the candles played over her wrinkled face and reflected from her smooth white hair in pale fairy lights on the walls of the room.

"I said... Maria. Did she...?"

"The cemetery? Do you want the cemetery?"

"I'm trying to... Yes. Yes, I want the cemetery," he said loudly, leaning towards her and resting his hand on the window sill beside her. "Which is the way?"

She nodded, and continued rocking. The fairy lights were dancing all over the walls and ceiling of the room. He felt his eyes being dazzled. Then her hand rose through

130

the lights and pointed along the street.

"Follow it," she said in a soft whisper. "It goes there."

He pushed himself away from the window with all the strength of his arm and stumbled back into the middle of the street, and began running along it as fast as his legs would carry him. It weaved and wound one way and then another, and the surface became ever rougher; and the day-light was altogether gone and there was no light in the street and the glimmering lights behind shutters were fewer and further between, until there were none at all; and again and again he stumbled in potholes where paving stones were missing, until the street was no longer paved at all, and he realized from a wind blowing across him that the houses had come to an end and he was outside the town altogether. And he stopped, remembering that the man, Fenwick, had said that he couldn't leave the town, because it was walled, and the gate was barred. But under his feet the road was of earth, and he could just make out empty land to either side of him. The wall then must be further off.

He began walking, trying to catch his breath from his running, and had hardly walked twenty paces when he saw her, standing beside a square column, almost in front of him. As he slowed his walking she pressed back against the column, staring at him fixedly, and sank slowly down towards the ground. She began to whimper, as though she thought he would hurt her.

"No, I won't..." he began to say, gently and hesitantly, but his breathing was still heavy from running. "I only want to..." He reached out his hand slowly to touch her and lift her up again, but before he could reach her her hand had flashed out and her nails had scratched all the length of his forearm. He started back in shock and she crouched lower to the earth, and her whimpering was half growling.

"Please," he said. "There's nothing to be afraid of..." The smell of her body was rising to his nostrils and spreading like fire through his own simmering shivering body. "I only want…" Her other hand flashed out and scratched his other arm, and sand suddenly flew up from the ground, stinging his face like needles and blinding his eyes. He staggered back from her, covering his face with his arms, and by the time he could see again through his streaming stinging eyes, she was gone. There was only the bare square column in front of him, which he leaned against for support; and he saw then that a gate was leaning against it as well, and that a few feet off another such column was lying on its side, and he realized that he was at the entrance to the cemetery. Beyond the gateway he could see the silhouettes of stones and monuments in the gloom; and beyond them, rising to three times his own height and stretching left and right into the night, was a wall. He listened awhile for any sound of Maria moving, but there was none. There was no sound at all; and he knew he wouldn't be able to find her if she didn't want to be found, since she was at home here and he was a stranger. So he turned about and walked slowly back into the town.

As the black shapes of houses began to appear on either side of him he looked for lights behind their shutters, but there were none, they seemed all deserted. And they closed the darkness around him, so he couldn't see even a foot in front of him. He stumbled again and again into potholes, and he could hear what he supposed were rats scuttling in the street near him, but he couldn't see them or anything else. Then, without warning he bumped into a wall…a shuttered or boarded window it was, and his hitting against it loosened a pane which he heard shattering on the floor inside. He backed off from the wall and stretched out his arm to guide himself along parallel to it with his fingertips; but he'd only gone a few yards before he stumbled over a loose rock and fell to his knees, and couldn't find the rock again when he stood up. Then a moment later he bumped into it, or another, and he could feel the brickwork of a wall with his fingers, and the frame of a window or door; and then, backing off from the wall while still touching it, he backed into a wall behind him. It seemed he had stumbled into a narrow lane. So, touching both walls to guide himself, he made his way slowly and cautiously along it. The further he went the closer the walls came together, until they were almost touching his shoulders; though still he couldn't see them, whichever way he looked there was only blackness. He turned himself sideways to continue further along the lane, until his foot touched something big and soft, something lying in the lane and blocking it, which made him shudder and stop. And at the same moment, ahead of him, somewhere ahead, he heard music; faint music, but cheerful: the sound of a fiddle, and of people singing. Not seeing what else he could do, he gritted his teeth and stepped onto the soft bulk and walked on it, sliding his way between the walls that were now so close together they scraped against his chest and back, and filled his nose with their smell of decay. It couldn't be a body he was walking on, he told himself, it was too soft, if it was as soft as that it would be rotten, and stinking. He would never be able to smell the walls if he were walking on a rotting body. But still the feeling of it under his feet was nearly making him retch.

Then the walls came to an end and his feet touched clear hard stone again, and whichever way he stretched his arms his hands touched nothing. And the cheerful music was nearer and clearer. He set out, cautiously and haltingly, like a blind man, in the direction it seemed to be coming from; and soon came to a wall again, and guided himself along the wall, and came to a corner and heard the music more clearly still, it was nearly all singing with only a thin fiddle in the middle of it and it sounded now very close. He guided himself around the corner and along the wall, feeling his way past windows and doorways; and saw at last a weak light in the dark ahead of him. It seemed near, and the singing seemed equally near; and then, before he was quite expecting it, he was upon the light, it was shining on his hand out of a steamed-over window, and the singing was flowing all around him. He thought it must be a tavern, and turned the handle of the door beside the window and pushed it open and put his head inside, and the singing and the fiddleplaying abruptly stopped.

All the people gathered in the room were looking at him, their faces flickered over by the candles burning throughout the room, and by the blazing fire set into the chimney in the opposite wall; all unspeaking and unmoving, except a fat, middleaged man sitting on a stool by a great barrel, who was filling a jug from the spigot in the barrel and who was nodding to him slowly as if encouraging him to come in; and a woman, younger than the man, who was carrying a jug and mugs about on a tray.

"Is this a public tavern?" he asked uncertainly; and then saw, sitting side by side in the corner just beyond the window, two burly men, dressed like the men he had seen at the foot of Fenwick's stairway, but with different faces. One of them had a white cat on his lap and was stroking it, and both of them were watching him with particular steadiness and attention. Then their gaze suddenly sharpened and they reached down beside their stools and picked up a pair of heavy gloves each and slipped them on. The one man lifted the cat very gently and placed it on his stool as he stood up, and they came over to William together with a heavy tread.

"Your arm," one of them said, reaching out a gloved hand.

"Let's see your arm," the other said. "Your other arm." They took hold of an arm each and together drew him into the room. Instinctively he drew back.

"It's just an inspection, don't worry," the first man said.

"It's already dried," the second one murmured.

"When did it happen?" the first one asked.

"When did what happen? What's the matter? I haven't done anything."

"The scratches on your arms," the first one said. "When did they happen? Are they fresh?"

"They weren't there when he came down the stairs," the second one murmured. "The others would've told us. Wouldn't they?" He seemed suddenly very uneasy. The people in the room were beginning to shift about and to mutter in low voices to one another.

"Are they very recent?" the first one asked, his tone gentler than before. "I have to ask, I'm sorry." The second man let go of the arm he was holding, and stood back and seemed in confusion.

"Yes," William said. The muttering among the people was louder.

"How long ago?" He seemed to be embarrassed now at still holding William's arm. "Please understand my position."

"I don't know. A quarter of an hour. Maybe half an hour. It was dark." The murmuring among the people grew loud and excited. The man let go of his arm and both of the men backed away from him, nodding their heads respectfully, almost bowing.

"It's not been dark half an hour," an old man on a tall stool nearby said. "Not really dark."

"Come in, dear sir, come in," the fat man by the barrel called out. "Make room for the gentleman in our midst there." All the people in the tavern were now gazing at William with admiring interest, and a bench big enough for three was suddenly bare and waiting for him across the room, not far from the fire. As they continued waving to him to sit there, he did what they wanted; and the moment he was sitting, facing towards the fire, the woman with the tray of mugs came to him and offered him one brimming full, and the men around him grinned and nodded, and the fat man by the barrel gestured to him that he drink it straight down. He held it out towards them all in greeting, and saw that their attention was particularly on his up-held arm, on the scratches on his arm; and two people, a man and a woman, were bending over his other arm, peering at it carefully, cautiously. He brought the mug to his mouth and drained it at one draught, as they all seemed to want, and almost immediately sparks began dancing in his blood throughout his body and his head. Around him they were all smiling. The woman with the tray was smiling as he held up his empty mug and she filled it from the jug until foam was flowing lazily over its lip.

"Was it a cat? Was it a cat,eh?" an old man asked, leaning across from his stool and pointing at the scratches on his arms. He had a long white scar like a twisting snake running right down his thin neck from behind his ear. Beyond him, beside the fire, was a youngish woman in a long blue cloak. With red hair. Deep auburn hair.

"They're the worst danger, you never know when they'll use their claws. Like that poor baby," another man was saying, nodding and nodding his head, and glancing covertly at the gateman with the white cat on his lap, stroking it with an ungloved hand.

"Showing off how brave he is," someone said in a whisper. Beside the red-haired woman, between her and the fire, was another woman, very old, her face all fine wrinkles, her eyes almost white, her blue cloak making one with the cloak of the young woman.

"It was Maria," he said. All around him they fell silent and he felt them drawing back. They were looking at him askance, mistrustfully. Was the red-haired woman the

136

woman he had seen as Fenwick led him out through the railings? Her bones were fine and her skin was so white it was as if the sun never saw it. She knew him. She remembered him: her clear green eyes were gazing at him unfalteringly. "I didn't want to hurt her. I didn't have any idea of hurting her."

"Of course you didn't," the fat man by the barrel said cheerily. The woman was leaning close to the old woman beside her and was plucking at her cloak and whispering into her ear. The firelight was glintimg in her loosely coiled auburn hair.

"And the scratches have healed, haven't they?" the fat man said. "The blood's clotted anyway. So what's there to fear?"

"Well that's true, that's the main thing," someone else murmured, and the woman with the tray continued making her way about the room, pouring beer from the jug into everybody's mug. He watched the glinting golden stream pour into his own mug, and all around him the talking began again.

The old woman by the fire was beckoning him with a bony white hand to come towards her. He didn't know what to do. Around her hand light from the candles and the fire seemed to be playing; no, not just around her hand, around everything, everything was shimmering with the light, it must be the beer in his brain, it was making him feel warm and good. He drained his mug and reached it towards the woman with the tray, and as she poured more beer into it from the jug he rested his free hand on her hip, and then let it slide down and around until it was resting on her warm swelling bum. Around him people were chuckling, it was a good thing he was doing. The woman put the jug on the tray and lifted his hand away, but she wasn't in any hurry and she was smiling. Later maybe she would be free.

The old woman was still beckoning him to go to her. And the young woman too was beckoning him now, a ring she was wearing glittered out of the pale light round her hand. He stood up to go to them, and felt the room sway a little, and felt hands here and there on his body, holding him steady, and made his way the few steps to the fire, holding his mug in front of him and watching to make sure he didn't foolishly spill any of the beer. In front of the women was a low stool, which the red-haired woman patted with her ringed hand, smiling at him a slight, pale smile. He sat down on the stool, more heavily than he intended.

"My mother wants to see your arms," she said. Her voice was fine and sweet, like the smell of roses. "If she may. But she is very short-sighted. Indeed, little short of blind. If you will hold one of them very close before her..."

He raised his left arm and she brought her fingertips to its underside, they were as cool as snow against his hot skin...and guided it towards the old woman's bleary, nearly white eyes. Tiny sparks were glistening on her old skin and on her daughter's fine skin, and on his own skin, on his bare arm held out in front of her old white eyes. He thought it must be the firelight as well as the beer; further off it was making people look blurred and bleached. The old woman bent her face nearer still to his forearm, until her nose was nearly touching it, and peered at the scratches and seemed to be smelling them; and then gave a sudden gasp or sigh and fell back in her chair. And her daughter gave him a faint, shimmering smile, and withdrew her fingertips from under his arm. And his arm, as if of its own accord, drifted slowly downwards in a glistening glow until it touched the cloak covering her legs, and rested there, his hand hanging loosely over the side of her thigh.

There was uneasy murmuring behind him, he was doing something wrong. But the woman was still smiling down at him, and her cloak was soft and comforting against his arm. It must be very warm to wear, he thought, her body inside it must be very warm. His own body was sweating, the fire and the beer were heating his skin from both sides. The woman was enclosing his arm with both her hands, how could they be so cool, she was lifting it from her lap. In mid-air she released it, so that it fell again, all sparkling, and he watched it fall and drift towards the floor; and was thrown off balance just as it reached the floor, and his other hand spilled half the beer from his mug. Near him, behind him, people were still muttering strangely. He watched the beer flow a little way over the dark floor before sinking into it, leaving only traces of foam behind. At the same time he felt his stool being pulled backwards, and looked round to see two men leaning forward from their bench, pulling him with strong hands; and another man, an old man, who looked he thought like one of the old men who had spoken to him in the square, was wagging a finger at him.

"You've no right to've done that," the old man said. "Touching her like that." With one glowing hand he seemed to be trying to hide his mouth and his words from the women. "You can't go round just touching anybody you want."

"I thought she wanted it too." She was still looking at him, she had never stopped looking at him, and the expression in her green eyes was as clear as before. She wasn't angry with him.

"Wanted it or not, who knows about that? She didn't want it here. Not like that. Not just easy." Her skin was so white and shimmering and the gaze of her eyes so unwavering that his own eyes were beginning to water; and his sweat was prickling his whole body.

"She's not just anybody, you know," one of the men behind him said in a low, deep voice. "She's gentry. It's only her condescension that she comes here at all. That, and her mother's liking a good fire."

"It's only when they come that we has a good fire," the old man whispered, close to William's ear, his voice husking and sparking inside his head. "I'm very glad of it myself."

"Her being so old, you know," another man behind William said. He thought he should turn round to face them, but he couldn't bring himself to take his eyes from her emerald gaze. Her fine lips were faintly but steadily smiling now; and beside her there was a little stretch of empty bench, just room enough for him to sit on. It wouldn't be so hot there, he would be sheltered by her from the fire; and she would like it, he was sure that she would like it. But the moment he tried to stand up the room swayed about badly and he felt hard hands on his arms pulling him down onto the stool again.

"It's very hot here," he said. His tongue was too big for his mouth. They were giving him very strong beer. The landlady was standing beside him again, holding out the jug. He held up his mug and watched the frothing, glistening beer gush into it; and lazily explored up her leg under her skirt with his other hand. She smiled and didn't seem to mind. But she was pulling away, his hand was being pulled away; no, it was the men behind him they were pulling his stool around, he couldn't find the woman's green eyes they were lost in a sea of faces gliding past his gaze all shining and sparkling the scars on their faces were gleaming white.

"She's the one not got any scars, you saw that?" one of the men said, the one with the deep voice, his black eyes glancing warily sideways.

"And her mother," the other said. The red of his thick

curly hair was like the red of her hair in deep shadow. "That's gentry. That's what gentry is. That's why he's scared of them, your friend up there." He waved his hand over his head and bright sparks flew out of it in every direction. "Your friend Fenwick. Because they remember better than any of us how things were in the old days. Before the big burning. In the old king's days. When the fields weren't just beds of nearly ash."

"We all remember some," the deep-voiced man said, his heavy black eyebrows frowning over his black eyes. "But they remember better. That's the reason they haven't got any scars. That's what I think." William wanted to turn round and look at the woman again, but the men were holding him by a big hand each on each of his shoulders. And beside him the old man was still close to his ear.

"The old woman's so old she even remembers the king before the last one," he whispered. She used to talk about him. I remember. I remember her talking well. But she hasn't now in a long time. It's my guess she's waiting to die and she can't. But she will, eh? There's nobody who don't die. And then her daughter'll be the only one of their kind left." A thin, middle-aged woman, leaning against the red-haired man's shoulder and gazing at the fire, slowly nodded her head.

"If he don't get rid of her too," the black-eyed man growled. "He don't like people remembering. If they remember, maybe they'll talk, and he don't like people talking. He likes things quiet. Dead quiet." The room was quiet; but a long way from the room there was a knocking.

"He makes out he's doing it for us, but he don't care a pimple for us," the red-haired man said. "He don't care any more for us, I'll bet, than Black Melk himself does." He was beginning to look uneasy, and the people nearby were looking uneasy, and the far knocking was louder. It was like the knocking in Fenwick's house, the raven's knocking. The old man was making small crosses on his breast with his fingertips.

"You oughtn't to say his name like that," he said, and glanced at the gatemen in the corner.

"*I* don't care if I say his name," the black-eyed man said, looking about him proudly and raising his voice. "Black Melk. Black Melk. BLACK MELK. It's only another of old Fenwick's tricks for keeping us down. If you ask me, the two of them are hand in glove." All around the room people's shining heads were turning this way and that, and their bright faces were trembling like the candle-flames, even the big faces of the gatemen. The two men close in front of him sat with their mouths closed tight, and their fingers on his shoulders were digging deep into his flesh. Then the knocking ended. And the people were still again, and began talking again.

"It's eating now," the old man said. "It'll be quiet now till it's hungry again. Like every night. It eats and eats."

"It eats enough for all of us," the red-haired man said. The woman at his shoulder was nodding and nodding her head. "If it ever gets out, it'll eat us ourselves. That's the day he's waiting for, you mark my words."

"It was wrapped right round him," the woman leaning against his shoulder said in a thin voice. Her hands in her lap were thick with criss-crossing scars. "Like it was holding him when he was holding it."

"She saw it when it was small," the old man whispered. "When she was just young, and working there for him."

"It was as big as he was," she said dreamily, gazing steadily at the fire. "And its wings were wrapped so about him you could hardly see him. He told me to face the wall and not move. But I saw it. I saw its black wings and its round bright eye. The day he carried it down to the big room."

142

"I just want to warn you," the black-eyed man said, and his grip on William's shoulder tightened. The scar across his nose was dazzling white.

"We both want to warn you," the red-haired man said, and together they pulled his face nearer to their own, until their breath was hot against his hot and prickly skin, and they were one hot blur of sparkling against his eyes.

"You better watch your step," the red-haired man said. "Maybe you're his friend now, I don't know. Maybe you're even ready to tell everything we say to you to his gatemen. But you better be careful and look where you're going and…"

"Don't trust him," the black-eyed man said fiercely.

"What about a bit of music, then?" a woman's voice said from close behind William; the landlady's voice he thought it must be. "What about a dance? The young man might like to dance a bit. He looks like a dancer. What about it?" William thought he might well like to dance a bit if somebody played a tune, but the two men continued holding his face close to their own.

"She's one of his hirelings," the black-eyed man growled. "Don't listen to her."

"You saw what he did to our mate," the other man said. "We saw you looking. You were up at his window."

"You mean outside the gate?" William said, pulling back from them enough to focus on their shining faces. "The man who was bleeding?"

"It could've easy been branded," the black-eyed man said. "It wasn't a big wound. His sickle only caught in his arm and tore his skin a bit. Scratched it, that's all, just scratched it. Like happened to you. Only his was still bleeding."

"He don't like wounds of any kind," the red-haired man said. "We tried to cover it up a bit so it wouldn't show, but he saw it. So these big hulkers of his piled him on the fire like he was a bunch of sticks."

"What fire?" William asked, pulling himself back

143

further to drink a long draught out of his mug. The two men drank from theirs at the same time, but their eyes stayed fixed on his face. Their faces and faces all around them were so bright and shimmering that he could hardly make out their features. Beside him the old man seemed to be trying to reach his ear to say something into it.

"What do you mean, what fire?" the black-eyed man said, wiping the foam from his mouth with his arm. "The fire outside the gate. They keep it piled up ready. One of the hulks lit it and the other kicked him onto it. I thought you said you saw?"

"Keep your distance from these two," the old man was whispering right into his ear, holding onto it with both his hands. "They're in trouble already for trying to bring a spy into the town. Maybe they didn't know what they were doing. Or maybe they did. Either way the gatemen over there've got their eyes on them pretty steady."

"He was a real good worker too," the black-eyed man muttered. "And with a wife and a little girl. Who'll look after them now?"

It was only his arm," the other man said. "It would've healed sure with branding." Brilliant tears were trickling down his reddish cheeks. The other man put a consoling arm around his shoulders, but he was weeping too. In the corner beyond them the bright faces of the gatemen were like moons shining at their backs, and in the lap of one of them the white cat too was like a moon.

"I would like to hear a song," a voice said, the voice of the green-eyed woman, reaching him through the blur of noise in the room and in his head, ringing in his head like a fine bell. The men's hands had fallen from his shoulders, so he turned round to look at her; she gave him a slight smile and his heart beat faster. "And I would like to see the young man dance. If he will. And I know my mother would like it, as much of it as she can experience." Her

144

mother's head was resting against the strut of her high-backed chair and her white eyes were gazing blankly up at the lights and shadows drifting back and forth over the ceiling. "If you don't mind playing, Mrs. Grainger."

"I don't mind," a woman said from the other side of the fire. William could hardly see her for the brightness of the fire. "I'd be glad to play a tune. Glad to hear one. Glad to hear one's wanted."

"It will do him good to dance," the green-eyed woman said, her gaze steadily on William. "He has come a long, a very long, way. Have you not?"

He didn't know what to answer.

"He has been where no one has been for years," she said. He began to find something fearful in her unwavering cool green gaze, but he couldn't look away. "Have you not?"

"Where's that, eh? Where?" The old man beside him asked sharply, and around him in all the blurred faces there seemed to be sudden questioning. Did she want him to answer? Was she going to say she had seen him coming out of the palace? There was no expression in her eyes or her face.

"I...I've been walking in forests," he said hesitantly. "And by the ocean. On sand by the ocean. I don't know how long ago."

"Did the air ever smell of roses?" she asked softly, her voice a cool trickle of water in his head.

"That's a good one," the old man said, chuckling. "Did it ever, eh? Did it?"

"What do you mean?" he asked, glancing uneasily about him; all their fire-and-candlelit eyes were shining brightly. "I don't..."

"She means," the deep-voiced man behind him said, resting a heavy hand on his shoulder, "Was the air ever nice to smell? Like it's not here."

145

"She means," the old man whispered in his ear, "Are you old enough to know what roses are? Because not a one has grown here for years and years. Before the old king died we used to have feast days with roses. I remember them. That was a very different time. There was dancing in the square then, and big dinners with plenty of food for everyone. But not after the old king died, and all the bodies had to be burnt in big piles..."

"Please could we have a tune," the green-eyed woman said, and the room fell silent; and the woman on the other side of the fire lifted a very small fiddle to her chin and made a few trial passes with her bow.

"If you can call it dying when you're *made* to die," the deep-voiced man said abruptly and loudly, close behind William's ear. "Your friend up there, your friend Fenwick, he knows about that. And if he got my mate today, it could be any one of us tomorrow." He was leaning with his whole weight now against William's back and his breath was hot against William's ear. Whoever catches his ill-will. It could be me. Or you."

"Not him," the old man said sharply. "Not if he don't bleed."

"Please Mrs. Grainger," the green-eyed woman said, her gaze never faltering from William's hot face; the fiddle broke into a lively jig tune, and people around him began to tap their feet.

"If he don't bleed, he's safe," the old man said, his voice rising and becoming shrill, and his finger poking the shoulder of the man slumped against William's back. "Or if he heals. Like we can see he does. Nobody's going to burn him if he heals, what's the need? Your mate, he was dripping all over the ground. Plenty of people saw it. You leave me alone now, you leave me alone!" he suddenly screamed, as the man pushed him almost off his stool with a heavy hand. The tapping of people's feet was spreading all over the room and the big man by the big barrel was clapping his big hands and William could feel the vibration in his thighs of his own tapping feet. The man behind him seemed now to be sobbing against his back.

"I'm only saying what's so," the old man said. "You want him to bring the disease inside the gates? So we all catch it and we all bleed to death?"

"It was only a scratch," the man behind William said. His voice was as heavy with weeping as his body.

"Scratch, my eye, it was a great gash."

"It could easy have been branded."

"That's for *him* to decide," the old man said. "That's what he's there for. He knows better'n we do what can be branded and what can't." William's hands were beating time on his legs. His whole body was beating time. He wanted to dance and he could see from their shining faces around him that they wanted him to dance.

"We know what *you* are well enough," The other man close behind him muttered at the old man. "We know why she gives you drink when she don't give it to us. Because you're a favourite."

"And we know who you're a favourite *with*," the deep-voiced man added fiercely.

"It's not true. It's a lie, it's a lie," the old man shrieked, and began striking with his thin fists against the nearest man's shoulder. The woman was playing her fiddle at an ever quicker tempo, and the stools and the benches were all rocking and the floor of the room was shivering with the beating of feet and hands, and everywhere he looked William saw shining eyes willing him to dance. Even the gatemen were uneasily tapping their toes and heels; and the green-eyed woman's mother was tapping her finger-tips on the wooden arms of her chair. Only the green-eyed woman herself was still, steadily and expressionlessly

147

gazing at him, faintly smiling, her hands lying still in her lap and her feet resting still on the floor.

"Dance! Dance!" both men behind him whispered sharply in both of his ears, and the weight of the one was gone from his back; and the people's enhaloed heads fell away towards the floor and his head rose up like a spring towards the ceiling and he knew he was standing, he was standing high above all of them and they were all clapping in rhythm with the dizzying pace of the fiddle, and his feet flew into the air and he danced. The room swayed around him and the flames of the fire and the candles danced and flickered and the floor felt like the wall and he danced up and down it through the dizzying, skidding lights and shadows, the fire was way below him and the woman with the fiddle was below him, he was coming near her he was nearly touching her, her face was sweating and her mouth was laughing. Beyond her, beyond the fire, the green-eyed woman was so still she was blurred, he saw her and he saw her again, but she was always blurred, her ivory face was like a little mist between her goldred hair and her blue cloak flowing into her mother's, around them both the flames of the fire were lapping.

He saw Maria. She was black in the bright light. Where was she, he had lost her. He saw her again, she was crouched by the door, by herself. She was staring across the room at the fire. He danced between her and the fire, throwing out his legs they seemed as long and straight as stilts, there was the sound of a bench falling over or a stool, and some laughter, he danced back and forth between Maria and the fire, but she didn't see him she only stared at the fire. His shadow passed over her face, it was gone, it was there again. She didn't move. He tried to dance nearer to her, but there were people between them; he danced away to the right and up the wall and over the ceiling, all the people were raising their hands in

148

the air clapping and clapping, and stamping their feet. He danced down the window close to her, but the people were still between them, they were all standing facing him and clapping and smiling but they wouldn't let him through they were as thick as a wall, he danced away from them towards the fire, the greeneyed woman was altogether in mist, he leapt into the air and over the fire and there was a gasp and all the air in the room vanished into their lungs and came out again in a great wind, all the candleflames swung about wildly on their wicks.

Someone was passing between him and the dancing flames and shadows. It was a man, he was dancing too. And where he passed the people were uneasy for a moment and blurred like the green-eyed woman, until he danced away from them and they began clapping again, and they clapped louder still as he danced towards them himself, and they laughed. But wherever the other man danced there was a shape of stillness and silence, circling the room like a shadow. They were both turning round and round as they danced, and the other man's face was always turned away when he was facing towards him and he couldn't change his own turning he was turning so fast now his arms were flying out from his sides and his beer mug was flashing with the flickering lights; he danced round all the walls of the room and on the big barrel by the back wall, far below him the landlord and landlady were clapping, the landlady's arms were encircling the landlord's neck. He danced down the swelling side of the barrel and stretched out his mug to her for refilling but he couldn't reach her she swayed and glided this way and that, she was laughing and the landlord was laughing everyone was laughing he danced round and round on the spot in the midst of them, spinning the light and shadow on all their faces flat against the walls of the room.

The mug in his outstretched hand struck against

something and there was a faraway tinkling sound; and the playing of the fiddle stopped. And the clapping and stamping died away, and he staggered about the swaying room, trying to keep himself from falling through all the spinning lights. He could see that his mug at the end of his still outstretched arm was broken, and foam was trickling out of it and falling slowly to the floor, as the walls swung back and forth, hung with white and shining faces and sharp candleflames. Then he saw another mug, also broken, also dripping foam lazily over its broken rim. And blood as well. The blood was welling out of the other man's knuckles, every moment more and more thickly. It was the man with the black eyes; they were gazing blankly and seemed to be glazing over, and his body was swaying more and more.

"Hold him somebody."

"Somebody hold him."

Voices were whispering and murmuring and urging. But nobody moved. Their eyes were all on his still outheld hand, from which the blood was now pouring in a steadily flowing stream.

One of the gatemen was standing up, with the white cat in his arms. He set it gently down on the floor and pulled on his heavy gloves and pushed his way through all the unmoving people; and the other gateman followed after him. The face of the black-eyed man was lily-white and his legs were beginning to sag. One of the gatemen seized his outstretched arm in both his hands and held him standing. The carcass of the mug slipped from his fingers to the floor, shattering and scattering in bright pieces. People sheltered their faces with their arms. The bleeding man's head suddenly lolled loose against his shoulder.

"Are you all right?" the other gateman asked William in a low voice, and examined his hand and removed his broken mug and set it carefully on the floor. "He's all right," he said to the other. "He's not even scratched."

"We've got to get this one out quickly," the other one said, and the two of them half-carried, half-dragged the man along a broad lane which opened between them and the door as everybody drew back either way as far as he could. Except Maria, unmoving on the floor by the door, with her head in her hands, still gazing enrapt at the fire. As they circled round her to go out of the door, a candle over her head sputtered, and the bleeding man gave a sudden cry of terror and seemed to be trying to hide himself from the flame.

"He's far gone," a woman behind William said. It was the landlady, gathering mugs onto a tray. She stooped to pick up his broken one from the floor. The people were all moving towards the door now, all of them quiet, those who could walk straight helping those who swayed with every step. The redhaired man was sobbing and holding onto the shoulders of two men who were guiding him steadily towards the door. Nobody was passing nearer the drops of blood on the floor than he had to, and at the door they went out in single file, watching where they stepped. Already the tavern was nearly empty.

"You want to sit down a minute?" the landlady asked him. "Till they're all gone?

"What did I do?" William asked. "Did I do it?"

"You didn't do anything, love. He shouldn'ta been dancing. Dancing's not for the likes of him. As it is we're lucky: a lot of people besides him might've been hurt."

"What're they going to do with him? Where're they taking him?"

"Eh? Oh, they'll try branding him. To see if they can stanch it. But it's my guess they won't manage it. Don't you want to sit down?" Over beyond her the green-eyed woman was standing up at last, and was helping her mother to stand. The swaying room was ablaze with red flames from the fire and yellow flames from the candles.

"I'm all right," he said. "I feel fine." The greeneyed woman was walking towards the door, guiding her mother with one hand through all the stools and benches, and with her other raised to her white cheek, touching her cheekbone... She looked at him and looked away, and he saw that her gaze was no longer clear, but strangely misty. Then, as she neared the door, and looked down at Maria as if she wanted to say or do something, and then looked up uneasily at the candle hanging over Maria's head, he saw a thread of red, of blood red, trailing down between the white fingers pressed to her white cheek.

He wanted to speak to her, to say...he didn't know what he wanted to say; and anyway his voice wouldn't work, and then she was gone. And he felt his legs growing soft under him and he knew he was sinking to the ground. The air felt as thick as water and he drifted down through it until he came to rest gently on the floor. It felt soft. The landlady from high above him was saying something, but he couldn't make out any words. The broken pieces of his mug or the other man's mug were only a little way from him, rippled over by light and shadow. Was it his fault there was blood trickling through her fingers? The pieces must be from the other man's mug because they were rosy red with blood they were glowing red like soft fire, like fire slowly dying. Beyond them the white cat was crouched, looking at them too, and its pink nose was twitching. He reached out his hand slowly and carefully towards the nearest piece, to touch its warm softness.

"Watch him. Watch him." A man's voice said from near and far, and a broom came between him and the glowing red edges, and swept his hand back to his body. And the cat screeched as if kicked.Then he could hear the broken pieces being swept together as he felt hands pulling at his body, lifting him up into the air. It was the

landlady who was sweeping. It was the gatemen who were
holding him up on his feet, with their gloved hands. The
landlord was going slowly and haltingly about the room,
leaning on a stout stick and snuffing out the candles with
wet fingertips. Moment by moment the light was dying.
And the fire was dying, it was already low. And Maria
was looking at him at last. She was staring, her black eyes
weren't blinking, and her hands were twisted tight into
one another in her lap. He tried to smile at her across the
dying light, but his mouth seemed too slack to move.

"Where'll we take him?" one of the gatemen asked
the landlady. She glanced up from her sweeping. Her face
looked tired.

"Everywhere's much the same for sleeping it off," the
landlord said, and with a soft hiss the last candle went out,
and the only light in the room was red firelight; which
made Maria's eyes shine like coals, and her worn and torn
black dress shimmer like satin on her slowly breathing
body.

"The stable's best," the landlady said. "Take him
there." And as they nodded, and were carrying him past
her towards the doorway, she suddenly smiled at him and
reached up and patted his shoulder.

"You mustn't think it's your fault," she said. "It's nobody's fault. It's the way things are." He couldn't answer
her, he couldn't even nod or shake his head or smile; his
body was like jelly in the hands of the gatemen. As they
carried him past Maria, stepping carefully through the
splattering of blood on the floorboards, she followed his
passing with unblinking black eyes.

Then they were in the street, they were carrying him
along a street. An empty street, black and pale white from
the stars and small puffs of white cloud reflecting the light
of the moon. He couldn't see the moon. They carried him
towards the far end of the street, meeting no one, passing

153

no one, not speaking to each other or to him. But just before they reached where it opened out into the big square, they turned in through a high double doorway and laid him down just inside it on some straw. He could smell cows, and hear them from deeper inside the stable; and he could see the big empty square through the doorway, like a blurred checkerboard from the drifting shadows of the many small clouds. He felt he was drifting too.

There was a clattering noise on top of him and he started awake. Animals were passing almost over his head, only a little darker than the first grey morning light. They were gone, and a man with a stick after them, driving them into the square. There were other animals still in the stable, some of them softly lowing. His head was heavy and aching. He laid it down again on the straw.

He started awake again, and couldn't think why. Around him everything was still. The cattle were many more now in the square, over toward the gates, and the light was stronger and tinged with rose. And the sky was blue.

"Oh, curse that Black Milk," a girl's voice said. He lifted his head and saw her only a few feet away, sitting on a stool and milking a bony cow. She looked very young, her breasts just beginning to grow, and very cross. Suddenly she kicked over the bucket into which she had been milking the cow; and the milk, which looked grey in the grey light, flowed over the hard earth towards his feet. He lifted his feet and she saw him, and she leapt up like a scared animal and ran out of the stable. He waited, but she didn't come back, and the stable was quiet except for a cow here and there lowing; and the square was quiet, and his eyelids drifted down over his eyes.

He heard soft giggling, and half-opened his eyes again, cautiously. The sun was risen, it was shining on the upper parts of houses in the square, and the gates were open and the last of the cattle, all thin and grey, were being led out through them. The giggling was coming from two pretty girls standing close together and whispering in the street, just outside the stable doors. They were glancing again and again at his groin as they giggled, and he realized that his cock was hard and that it showed. And the lovely sounds of their giggling and their whispering, and their young faces in the reflected early light were making it harder still. Then, of a sudden, they stopped, and he saw through his lashes that they were looking into the stable beyond him; and then they were running away, they were gone. Slowly, stealthily, he turned his head to look where they had been looking, into the shadowy stable. The thin cow was still standing there just as before, but the bucket beside it was upright now, and full to the brim with milk, which still looked grey; and Maria was standing beside the bucket, and she too was looking at his groin. His moving head didn't bother her, or move her steady gaze. In strange unease, feeling she was looking right inside him, he twisted himself round to hide his groin from her eyes; but still she was looking at his body. Her hands were dripping with milk and her face and arms glistening with fine sweat, and a lock of her black hair was trailing down the side of her throat and between her dress and her right breast. Would she let him go to her? He felt himself hanging and quivering between wanting her and fear.

A sharp whistle pierced the air, and she glanced up in alarm. He looked round and upwards to see where the whistle came from, and saw only blank windows, some closed and reflecting the clear morning light, others open and empty. Then, right across the square, at the highest window of all, he saw Fenwick. He was leaning out of the window and peering down at him through a telescope, and gesturing with his other hand. For him to go up there. Why? Why was everything what he wanted? And he couldn't go right away even if he would, his cock would show like a beacon. But it seemed that Maria was going…was the whistle for her?…she had picked up the bucket, slopping over some of the milk, and was standing in the doorway. If he reached out his hand he could just touch her bare leg. Just gently, just stroke it, it was so beautiful. But before he could decide to, the whistle blew again sharply, passing through him like fine harsh wire, and Maria moved to the far side of the big doorway, as if in a kind of trance. Fenwick was watching his every move; he was gesturing now to him to get up, he wouldn't let him alone probably until he went up there where he was. Well, he thought, he might as well, he couldn't quite see why not; so he pulled himself to his feet with the help of the wall, and then stood free of it while his brain rocked painfully in his skull, and his cock to his surprise slid quickly down into softness. Fenwick was still watching and waiting. He straightened himself and stepped out into the street, turning to look at Maria as he went. but she was gazing straight ahead of her, at nothing.

He walked into the square, surprised to find himself so steady on his feet, and began walking what seemed the great distance across it. He angled past men making their way slowly and quietly towards the open gates, with tools on their shoulders, on their way out to the fields. Most of them looked at him askance, as if they didn't know who he was. A few, who had maybe been in the tavern the night before, nodded at him, but uneasily, and with a glance overhead, as if they feared Fenwick's seeing them nod. He nodded at them in return.

As he started up the stairs of Fenwick's house he heard the low croaking of the raven. Then just after he had passed the first landing it stopped; and he heard feet behind him, muffled heavy feet, and he turned and saw Maria on the landing, carrying the bucket full of grey milk. She stopped when he stopped, and waited; and when he turned from her and continued up the stairs, he heard her feet following after him; flight after flight she followed, to the top landing under the skylight, where Fenwick was waiting in a loose dressing gown with a frying pan in his hand.

"Quickly," he said, and pulled William by the arm into his room, and slammed the heavy door behind him and bolted it before Maria reached the top of the stairs.

"That will give us at least a moment," he said. "While she drinks some of her filthy milk. Would you like two fried egs or three? Or four? I have quite a few." William looked at him suspiciously. Why was he shutting Maria out?

"Four," he said. "Or five. I'm hungry." Fenwick's pale grey eyes were looking at him keenly. "It's a long time since I've eaten."

"Very well," Fenwick said. "Five it will be. While you're waiting for them, go and sit on the floor by the doves, and befriend them. So they won't be afraid to come to you when I send them." He turned away and settled the frying pan on a charcoal brazier in the window overlooking the square. What doves? Where were the doves? He seemed to think he could tell everybody what to do, and do what he liked himself.

"There." He pointed across the room. "Under the window seat." There was some kind of netting stretched from under the seat to the floor, and shadowy shapes moving behind it. "Didn't you see them before?"

"I heard them," William said, and crossed the room and eased his body to the floor beside the netting. "I thought they were outside." They were cooing softly, which was soothing to his aching head. "How do you mean you're going to send them to me? Send them to me

157

where?" His eyes were just on a level with the windowsill, so he couldn't see the plain, but only the jagged row of hills at its far edge, and Black Melk's castle atop them; looking like a row of sharp uneven teeth resting on the sill. Rising above them was a heavy black cloud, and the fine red line between it and the castle was very clear.

"There," Fenwick said. "To Black Melk's castle; or on the way to his castle. But around the other way. Where he doesn't expect an attack. I'll explain the whole plan when you've eaten."

"Why will I go?" William asked. "Why will I?"

Fenwick didn't answer. It seemed he answered only what he wanted to answer. William pushed his forefinger through the netting of the cage beside him and stroked the head and neck of a pleased dove. Another was pushing against the first to be stroked in its turn. Above the far castle the clouds were building slowly higher. The loudest noise in the room was the eggs sizzling in the pan.

He could smell the eggs, they were near him. He glanced round and up and saw Fenwick looking down at him with an unwavering gaze, with the frying pan in one hand and a plate in the other.

"Don't you trust me?" he asked, and his voice was strangely low.

"Well, I…" William began, embarrassed. "I don't know… I don't know you."

"They have been speaking against me, of course. That's their nature and their need. Do you believe them?"

"It's not that, it's… I don't know why I'm here. I don't even know how I'm here. Why am I here? What am I doing here?"

"You came through the rose garden."

"I know. I can remember. But I… I was in the forest by the ocean. Where's the ocean from here? It feels very far from the ocean."

158

"Do you think people often come here through the rose garden?"

"I don't know. How do I know? My head aches. Can I have the eggs?"

"They never do. Never. How can they? The forest is deep and thick. Even for you I have waited many years." He tilted the frying pan over the plate and the eggs slipped onto it and he handed them to William. "And then, when I could hardly any longer believe even in the possibility, the light burst out of my crystal ball, and electricity filled the sky, and you climbed into the rose garden. Ah, you'll need a fork." He pulled a fork from his dressing gown pocket and wiped it on his sleeve and handed it to William, who began eating the eggs greedily.

"Here's some bread," Fenwick said, pulling a thick crust from the same pocket. It's only a day or two old." Then he remained standing there, gazing out across the plain, while William ate.

"And now," he said after a minute, in a low voice, "Black Melk is gathering his forces together to use all that electricity against us when the occasion arises. Which may be at any moment. A moment when Maria is ill. What did they say against me?"

"What?" William said, swallowing a lump of bread halfchewed to answer. "They didn't say anything exactly. I mean, I don't remember anything exactly. I don't remember much at all. It's bloody stong beer they drink here." But his head was feeling much better. "They wanted me to dance, and I did."

"There are many spies among them," Fenwick said in a flat voice. "Black Melk's spies. Babies he filched away years ago and trained up, and infiltrates now back in among the people. And I can't detect them like the spies he makes himself, because they're just like anybody else. Except in their opinions. They're always fomenting trouble. Did they say it was my fault that the old king died?"

"I don't think so. But I don't remember…" There was something, somebody said something, somebody whispered… "They were blaming somebody all right, some of them were, but I didn't always make out if it was you, or Black Melk."

"Ah,"

"But they seemed scared, most of them, even to say his name."

"Yes," Fenwick said. "They are. For fear that they may make him materialize. Not that it's his real name. But it's a convenient name. Some years ago the milk of certain cows turned grey, or even black, the moment it emerged into the air from the udder. I don't know why. Something they had eaten, I suppose. The whole plain is grey, it's not really surprising that the milk should sometimes be so as well. But they blamed him," he said, looking across the plain with narrowed eyes. "Wrongly, for he doesn't waste his time with foolish games. And somehow they evolved that name for him. And nobody will drink the milk when it's black or grey. Except Maria, who will eat or drink anything."

"Yeah, well it was him they were blaming, some of them," William said, uncertain and uneasy, wiping his plate with the last of the bread. "For the most part."

"And for the other part? They blamed me. But for what?" William could feel his eyes peering down at him sharply. "You're sure they didn't say…or suggest, or faintly hint…that it was I who caused the death of the old king? Their beloved old king?"

"I don't think they did," William said. "But I don't remember. There're only pieces here and there I remember. Floating pieces." He could feel Fenwick waiting, waiting and watching him. The doves had all fallen silent. "What they seemed to feel, maybe said…yeah, somehow there was a feeling that...you've got everything and they've got nothing."

"Everything," Fenwick said flatly. "Ah. And what exactly do they mean by that? These luxurious apartments? If I did kill the king...which I didn't, nobody killed him, he died all on his own...I gained very little from it."

"I guess. I don't know," William said. "But I know they're scared of you. *They* think you got something."

"What is it then? What is it?" Fenwick asked sharply.

"I don't *know*. But it felt like they're more scared of you...some of them...than they are of Black Melk. Maybe because you're here. And he isn't"

"He isn't yet. That's what they don't know. Anymore than they know that I'll soon enough be gone."

William didn't say anything. He couldn't see what there was to say. The doves beside him were murmuring again, for more attention. He put his fingers through the netting for them to rub their heads against. Fenwick abruptly reached down and took the empty plate from his lap. Across the plain the cloud was higher and blacker, and the jagged red line was sharper. The feel of the doves' heads was like satin against William's fingertips, and their croodling was like satin and water to his ears.

"When did he die then? he asked, after what seemed quite a while. "Was it a long time ago?"

"The old king? Yes, a long time."

"What did he die of?"

"He was ill. He was never really well. And at last he died. Maria was only a baby." Something in the way he said it made William suddenly suspicious.

"Whose baby?" he asked.

"His," Fenwick said. "That's why I closed her outside. So I could tell you without her hearing me tell. Since it might trouble her to hear, and that could... Not that I think she does hear. But she can. If she will."

161

"You mean she's the princess and she doesn't know?" And he tried to touch her, he tried to...

"How do I know what she knows?" Fenwick said with sudden heat. "In that dark cavern of her mind, where only serpents slither? I've never hidden it from her. She knows where to go to her father's handsome memorial in the cemetery. The people stand back from her wherever she passes. I presume she is aware of being in some manner apart."

"They stand back from you as well."

"They stand back from what I have that scares them, as you say; whatever that is. they stand back from her right."

William sat where he was, unmoving, and watched the far black cloud billow slowly higher and higher in the windowframe, and saw her standing by the column outside the dark graveyard and standing in the stable and crouching in the tavern; and he thought he could hear a faint knocking, either faint and far or very faint and near. He turned and looked at Fenwick.

"But if the king her father is dead," he said, slowly and unsurely, feeling his body prickle with embarrassment and shame at his wanting her body, "And she's his heir, she's not the princess, she's the queen."

"She is not yet of age," Fenwick said. "And has not yet been crowned. I still have the keys to the throne, as you have seen. But when she is of age, I will surrender them, if matters then are as they are now. And go." Then his eyes narrowed and glinted, and his whole thin body seemed to stiffen. "No," he said. "*Not* if matters then are as they are now, not if the raven is unready to fly. For then it would not be a day, not an hour, after my going, before Black Melk swept into the town on silken wings and proclaimed *himself* the true heir. And Maria his bride. They would have no means then of combatting him, for all the means they have are in here," He tapped the side of his head with his fingertips. "And they would necessarily go with me, as there is no other vessel here in which I could leave them. My books, for what they are worth, they can have. But where is the cup to hold the sunlight?" He turned away from William and gazed some while in silence down into the big square, from which mingled morning noises were rising and filtering into the room.

"When will she be of age?" William asked, trying to keep his mind clear of visions of her body, but it was difficult. The billowing black clouds reminded him of her. The murmuring of the doves reminded him of her. And the soft knocking was against the door of the room, it must be her hand.

"Soon. Too soon. She has grown so quickly. And the raven, latterly, so slowly. Because of his already so great size. That is why we must try this other way, before the people come knocking at my door, saying that she is grown...they will, you may be sure, have been counting the days...and that it is time for me to go. They are waiting for that day, all of them are waiting, both those who favour Black Melk and those who fear him. Because in their eyes I have no right here, no right at all, none." He was looking at William with sparkling eyes.

"They didn't say that to me," William said uneasily.

"They say or they think it, it is the same. They say, or think, that the true king is dead and the true princess and successor is enslaved and I am a usurper; so naturally Death will be abroad in the land." He stopped speaking suddenly and gazed fixedly across the room and over William's head out of the window giving onto the plain. From where William was sitting the black clouds now filled the whole space of the window, except for the jagged row of hills and the red-lined castle at the very sill. The knocking at the door was growing louder.

"Is it true?" William asked in a low voice.

"Is what true?" Fenwick asked blankly, gazing blankly. "Death is certainly abroad in the land."

"That you're a usurper?" Fenwick glanced down at him briefly, then returned his gaze to the black clouds beyond the grey plain.

"It is not true," he said quietly. "I am only a caretaker. I know I am only a caretaker. For the time of her minority. And I am not abusing her, though they will not believe it. Things are not what they seem. I don't make her sleep on those rags on the landing, she wants to sleep on those rags on the landing. And what she wants to do, she does. I have nearly no control over her whatever. It is only just within my power to prevent her controlling me."

"Is that her at the door?" William asked. The knocking now was loud and steady. Fenwick nodded. "Why can't she come in now?"

"She will come in, you may be sure of that. When I can bear it no longer. But I have something to show you first, to prepare you. Keep stroking the doves," he said, as he crossed the room to the east window. "Make them your friends. When you are travelling you will need them to trust you if we are to remain in touch." He bent down to the trunk under the window and opened it, and reached his hand into the soft glowing which flowed out of it, as soft as the dove's head against William's fingertips, and gently lifted out a globe of glowing glass which he held in both his hands and carried to the desk and placed with great care on a small wooden stand. The knocking on the door was still louder. It sounded as though Maria was kicking it. Fenwick glanced round in passing irritation.

"Now come and stand here," he said to William. "Close beside me. So that you will see what I see."

William stood up and walked through the light, into it, towards the globe; feeling it spread through his body

164

like cool sweet water. But the whole room was now rever-
berating with the knocking, almost as if the raven from
the dark hallway below was beating against the door.
It seemed that Maria was now flinging her whole body
against it; and heavy as it was it was shivering on its hinges. Fenwick was watching it with narrowed eyes.

"Well," he said at last with a faint shrug, "There is
clearly no alternative. If she sets her heart on something…"
He crossed quickly to the door, and unbolted it and pulled
it open in one movement; and Maria, who was just flinging herself against it again, stumbled into the room and
fell down, and the bowl she was carrying slipped from her
hands, spilling most of the greyish milk, and slops which
were floating in it, all over the floor. Fenwick looked down
at the mess in disgust and kicked the door shut.

"Be quiet then, and sit there," he said, pointing to the
wall beside the door. She scraped some of the slops back
into the bowl, and crawled to where he had told her to sit,
and crouched there, cradling the bowl in her lap and dipping her fingers into it and putting the slops in her mouth.
Dribbles of grey milk were trickling all over her chin and
soaking into her dress on her breasts and her belly.

"Don't look at her," Fenwick muttered to William.
"Look in the globe, give all your attention to the globe
and, because she is evidently more used to you than she
was, we may escape." Then he seemed to see for the first
time the scratches on William's arms; he lifted the one
nearest him to examine it more closely, clucked his tongue
and let it go.

"The gatemen told me they'd examined you," he said.
"I told you not to approach her too nearly."

"I didn't mean…" William muttered, very low; feeling
ever more uneasy at her being only a few feet away from
him; looking with all his strength at the light which was
blurring the edges of the globe, trying to hold his mind

there as well. But still he saw her stretching her body and slowly turning and twisting round in the light. As if it was water.

"You might have said it was a cat," Fenwick said.

"Why should I lie?" Fenwick glanced at him sharply, then shrugged.

"Yes," he said. "I see that. But it told them the more clearly that you are from nowhere near here. The gatemen, of course, were very impressed, even frightened."

"By what?"

"By your blood so quickly congealing. By it's congealing at all. No one else's does. Except Maria's. And mine of course. But hers is nature, mine is but an act of mind and will. Do you see anything in the globe?"

"Just light."

"Just so. Keep looking." William kept looking, and slowly the light began to be more misty, and then to billow like clouds, thick clouds like those piled high above the hills at the far side of the plain, but luminous. And then in the middle of them a mountain, narrow and steep, began to appear. Slowly the luminous cloud around it dissolved, and trees and stone walls and people began to be visible. The mountain was terraced with fields, green fields, scattered with flowers. But Maria was making noises, groaning and sighing noises, and he was sure she was making them for him.

"Don't look at her. Don't think of her. Ignore her wholly," Fenwick said in a low, cold voice.

"What does she want?" With every sound she made the mountain and all the fields on it quivered inside the globe.

"She wants your attention. She's offering you some of her food. Don't turn your head. Keep looking into the globe. She is trying to destroy your attention. I said don't turn your head," he said with sudden fierceness, and

166

gripped William's arm in a steely grip. Her cries were more and more insistent and pathetic, and in the mists which were closing in again on the mountain William thought he could see the glistening of her body.

"You can't eat what she eats, even if you would," Fenwick said, his mouth close to William's ear. "She's as omnivorous as the raven. What she is offering you now she has probably pulled out of the tubs of garbage below. She will eat anything which takes her fancy. She once spent an afternoon eating all the ants in an anthill. I've seen her eat a live frog. Its hindlegs first. I saw her lips close round its pathetically squealing head." The mountain in the luminous mists was so quivering it was nearly shapeless, little more than a shadow in the light, and the trees and walls and people were invisible. The shadow was twisting in the mists like a soft body, like a woman's body, turning and twisting and glistening with sweat.

"No, no, no," Fenwick hissed in his ear, but he couldn't stop himself, he turned his head without even willing it and looked across the room at Maria. She was still sitting against the wall, but both her arms were outstretched towards him, offering him her bowl, and her swelling breasts were straining against her poor worn black dress and her throat was rippling with the eager grunting and gurgling sounds she was making and she was staring at him with burning black eyes.

"You must refuse," Fenwick hissed in his ear. "She is not so simple as she seems. She is of the blood royal. She will draw you in deeper and deeper. And you are unready. Her desires are stronger than you will be able to bear. Refuse. Refuse. Refuse."

Without knowing what he willed William felt his head turning slowly from side to side on his unmoving neck, his eyes never leaving her eyes; and suddenly her mouth burst open in a terrifying scream and she flung the bowl

167

to the floor where it smashed and scattered. She screamed and screamed, and rose up on her knees and began tearing at her dress and her body with her nails.

"Don't move. Stay where you are. There's nothing you can do," Fenwick said, holding William's arm still in his iron grip. Maria tore at herself until her dress was only black tatters scattered over her flesh, and her arms and breasts and belly were covered over with long red welts and scratches, and blood was spattered and trickling all over her body.

"Don't move," Fenwick said, as tense beside William as a taut wire. Maria's mouth was still wide open with screaming and her body was wracked with it, but the sound of it was dying away.

"We may just..." Fenwick said, his head turning towards the window, his eyes alert. Maria's arms fell down loose at her sides and hung there limply; and slowly her whole body drooped and sank down to the floor like boneless flesh, and she lay there in a heap, with her eyes and mouth wide open, facing the ceiling where the soft glow of the globe was playing like light on water.

"I think we may have..." Fenwick whispered.

And then, all at once, the room blazed and shuddered with simultaneous lightning and thunder, and William and Fenwick were thrown apart and nearly thrown to the floor; and through the blackness gl;ittering in his eyes William saw the globe of light bounce out of its rest and roll slowly away across the desk. Just as it reached the far edge, Fenwick's long fingers closed round it and retrieved it. And his eyes fixed in anger on William's face.

"There. *Now* do you see?" he said bitterly, his hand reaching up to the bell-rope. "*There. Look!*" Still half-blind from the lightning, William looked where Fenwick was pointing out of the window over the plain, at the ground just outside the gate. There in the earth was

168

a pitch-black hole with a plume of smoke rising out of it; and in the near plain more lightning bolts were striking into the earth; and the thunder of them was crashing like breaking waves into the room; and the black clouds now filled all the sky he could see from any of the windows. Fenwick was pulling vigorously on the bell-rope and the bell above them was clanging loudly and wildly, and men were running as fast as they could, and some were driving thin cattle at a run, out of the fields and towards the gate.

"If you hadn't looked, you wouldn't have had to refuse," Fenwick said in cold anger. "So now we have the whole weight of Black Melk upon us. Next time perhaps you'll do what I tell you. And stay where you are," he added sharply, as William moved nearer to the window. "Stay near the globe."

The lightning now was searing the air everywhere and burning deep into the grey earth, burning it brilliant white then glowing red; and black smoke billowed from each hole up towards the black sky. The men had abandoned their tools wherever they were working in the ashy fields and were pressing against one another to enter the gates. Behind them, in long straggling lines, the cows were being beaten and driven home. Fenwick watched the gateway through the flashing lightning and the sudden blackness which fell between the flashings, peering down through slit eyes, his hand ready on the bell-rope, until men and cows were all inside and the gates were slammed shut.

"At least his spies are easy to detect in this sharp light," he said, turning away from the window. "Which he knows, so of course he doesn't send any. Because he knows me. Look at the globe. This will be a storm such as you have never known. Keep your eyes only on the globe." He made his way around the desk from the window to William's side, holding to the desk as he came. The whole building now seemed to be staggering from the bolts which were falling all around it, so swiftly upon one another that the thunderbursts were almost unbroken; and everywhere in the room things were falling over, books and objects of all kinds were falling off their shelves. William worried that Maria would be struck by something, lying unprotected on the floor; but he didn't dare look at her against Fenwick's harsh instruction. He kept his eyes fixed on the globe, which was bouncing about in its rest; but the light within it was so obscured by the jagged flares of lightning that even there he found he was seeing only fleeting and distorted reflections of the room. And he was suddenly afraid.

"What if it...?" he began, but his voice was lost in the thunder bursting and rolling around them. Fenwick pointed with his long forefinger at the globe, then rested his hand, but very lightly, on William's wrist. Gradually, very gradually, the soft light within the globe began to increase, and the reflections of the room faded as the light blurred the surface of the glass. And the crashing round him of the thunder seemed a little less. The light in the globe became more and more radiant and began again to billow like clouds with their own light; which dissolved like gossamer and again the mountain was revealed, just as before, rising in green terraces from a misty valley. Which was not a valley, William then saw, but clear green water encircling the mountain like a moat; and in the water bright fish of all kinds and colours were swimming. The terraces rose in rings upwards, all of them deep green and deep in flowers, with sheep and cattle grazing on them, and with more flowers tumbling down the stone retaining walls between them; and with trees, some in blossom and some in fruit; and men, some working and some standing still, under the trees. Between the terraces paths wound upwards to the very peak of the mountain, where a castle stood, its great gates open and banners of many colours

170

flying from its battlements, and people passing into it and out.

"All that he has taken from us," Fenwick said in a low voice, startling William. Without his noticing it the lightning had diminished to wild flashing round the far-off walls of the room, chased by a low rumbling and grumbling thunder. "Keep looking in the globe," Fenwick murmured, in a voice oddly calm. "It's the only way to defeat him and his dangerous games. Are you willing to go and find him?"

"I don't understand," William said. "Where do you want me to go?"

"There. To his castle, which you see there. I can't go myself, I must stay here and defend us from this side. And no one else can go, because they all bleed, even the gatemen for all their brave swagger. In that land they would trickle away into the earth in a moment. Will you go? It is, as you see, very pleasant and approachable from that side. And if he is not soon reached then all life here, land and people, all, will cease. Will you go?"

"How do I go?" William asked. He was willing to go. It looked a beautiful land to go to. It was hard to believe that it was only on the far side of the far hills.

"Oh, you can't go across the plain, he would see you in a moment. You'll have to go round. When it's dark. Will you go?"

"I'll go," William said. "If I can, I will." Women and children were coming out of the castle gates, the women carrying baskets. They were making their way down the paths towards the terraced fields. The children were running and playing. The men were looking up from their work. The lightning was now flickering round the room in an unbroken flickering circle.

"If you can reach him there," Fenwick said, "All that he has and has shut up for himself alone will again be ours. And the plain will again be as it was when Maria's father...the old king as they call him; not that he was old...was still living. Unimaginable time. Nearly unimaginable. We must not let it go, we must not let the fine thread break."

"But why did he die? If he wasn't old."

"You have asked me that before."

"You didn't answer. Not why he died. Not why."

"Yes," Fenwick said in a voice very quiet and gentle. On the uppermost terraces the women and children were approaching the men. "I didn't because it's difficult. Difficult to answer. But you are looking now at why he died. He couldn't look at it himself, not as we are. Perhaps that was the trouble. He could only stand in a high window of the palace and look out across the plain, fearfully, from the moment, one sunrise, that it first appeared on top of the far hills: Black Melk's castle. Soon he couldn't do even that. He retreated within the palace, gradually closing off room after room. The queen tried to help him, to restore him, but she grew ever weaker herself, poor frail thing. I remember her as a mere wraith drifting aimlessly about the palace, as if trying, half-trying, to find the room into which he had last retreated; until one day she seemed to float like a feather down the great stairway, the stairway down which you came yourself yesterday afternoon; and light as she seemed in falling she was dead and broken when we picked her up at the bottom. And after that no one said he saw the king alive. And after his fine oak casket was buried, with great ceremony, the people cowered fearfully against the very walls of the palace; and the shadow of Black Melk stretched ever further across the plain."

"And Maria?" William asked. The men on every terrace were laying their tools against the overgrown walls of the terrace above them, and were sitting down with their women and children in the dappled shade of the trees.

"I brought her here. To protect her. Because the plague was then upon us, and no one knew where it would end. Wounds and sores were opening in unbroken, undamaged skin, and were pouring blood which nothing at first could stanch. Anyone who touched a wound caught the plague, anyone who even saw a wound seemed to catch the plague. People shut themselves in their houses. But they sickened and died there too, and their bodies were dragged into the streets and carted outside the walls. By brave men and women, who died as well. The streets were brown with bloodstains, and all the drains and gutters were dark red. People died in their thousands. And their white drained bodies were piled together and burnt, there, just outside the walls, below these very windows. Under my direction. And my sight. I have slept little since, and when I do I still see and hear and smell those bodies burning through the length and breadth of my mind."

"How did it end?" William asked, looking at a family under a tree which was heavy with golden fruit. The father was drowsing with his head against the tree trunk and his hands laced over his belly; the mother was cutting up fruit into a bowl and the children were taking pieces and eating them and licking their fingers. He almost felt he could reach out out his hand and...

"It hasn't ended," Fenwick said. "Some people, those few in the town now, or their parents, the remnant of the many, responded to cauterizing if cauterized in time. Branding, it came to be called: a sign of their survival. Some of them have scars of it all over their bodies. And if any one of them is wounded and not branded it will soon spread to the others. And in a matter of days they will all be gone, and there will be only a dry, dead wind fretting at doorways. And Black Melk will have won."

"When Maria is queen..." William began. A woman

173

was cradling her baby in her arms, bending over it and crooning. Another was lying beside her husband.

"Don't think of her," Fenwick said, a little sharpness coming back into his voice. "If you think of her now it will be the destruction of everything. The town will be stricken into fragments by the storm. She is not ready to be queen. She may never be ready. Not that I mean," he added more softly, "That I am satisfactory myself. Far from it. It is all I can do to hold the line. And all they can do to bear me." Children, both boys and girls, were making their way down through the terraces, some by the winding paths, some by jumping down the terrace walls, to the lowest wall of all, which rose sheer out of the emerald-green moat; which reminded William of the woman with the emerald-green eyes. The glinting of the fish in the water was like the sparkling of the fire in her eyes.

"It is, I suppose, because they can't see themselves in me that they fear me," Fenwick murmured. "If you look at yourself in a mirror and see only the room around you but not yourself, you are afraid. Aren't you?"

"It can't be done," William said.

"It can be done. I can do it."

"And they can do it? What do they do then?" The fish, all colours and sizes and shapes of them, were swimming curiously but cautiously towards the lines of the children which were trailing like fine golden threads into the green water.

"When they see only the room? They turn their backs on the mirror. Or they try to break it. Or they try, the brave ones, to continue standing in between, and not bleed. One or two have tried that. The woman who saw us coming out of the palace…"

"She bled," William said. The fish were biting at the bait on the lines and the children were drawing them in one after another out of the water, laughing and calling.

The fish were flashing brilliant colours against the grey stone wall as they thrashed and struggled against the hooks.

"When? How?" In his voice there was a note of alarm.

"In the tavern. A shard of one of the mugs must have struck her on the cheek. I don't know whose mug. I hope not mine. I saw the blood trickling like a thread through her fingers." The bright fish were wriggling on the green grass. The children were gathered delightedly around them.

"She will die," Fenwick said.

"But it was hardly a scratch. And they said she has no scars. Because she's gentry." The children were trailing their lines down into the green water again.

"Being gentry was no bar against bleeding," Fenwick said drily. "Most of them died, despite their closeness to the king. And the knowledge that gave them, the knowledge of the rose garden, the memory. But if he couldn't live, how could they? She has held on a long time, she and her old mother; but the memory of the rose garden must be only a pretty mist now in their minds. And you noticed. I suppose, how she, as well as her mother, likes to have her hand metaphorically kissed."

"She is extremely beautiful," William said. The clear green water was alive with brightly coloured fish darting about the fine golden lines, and the green terrace was dancing with colour from their wriggling and flapping bodies. The children were in a laughing ecstasy of delight.

"She will die," Fenwick said. "When we go out, I expect we will find her by the well, craving water. And it is almost time to go out; Black Melk's storm is beginning to fail." A light wind was stirring the surface of the green moat, and rippling the leaves of the trees on all the terraces up to the gates of the castle. Men were opening their eyes to look up at them, and women were beginning to look about them in mild anxiety, as if to find their children. The lightning was still circling and crackling round the walls of the room, but with longer and longer spaces between the lights.

"Let the mountain go. Slowly. Just let it go," Fenwick said. The surface of the moat was now all ruffled silver, hiding the fish, and the children were rolling up their lines and looking up the terraces to where their mothers were standing, waving and calling. The bright fish on the grass were still, and were slowly losing their colour as a mist drifted up out of the moat and flowed over the terrace. The children were running, and laughing as they ran, up the winding paths to the higher terraces. Their fathers too were calling them now. The silvery mist was rising swiftly after them, overflowing terrace after terrace.

"We have held him off yet again," Fenwick murmured. The lightning was now bursting in soft explosions, each softer than the one before, in the room around them. The shimmering mist had drifted over all the terraces, veiling them and the people on them. Only the castle was still visible, floating on the mist as on a glistening silver sea, with its gates still open and people passing within the gates. Then, as the mist rose up around it, they slowly closed. And the lightning ceased, and the thunder rolled away, slowly and heavily, to the furthest reach of the dark and cloudy sky. In the globe there was only a soft pearly light. Fenwick sighed softly.

"Every time is a miracle," he murmured. "I always expect to be overthrown. Don't move from where you are for a moment. She is awake."

Before he could stop himself William looked past Fenwick and saw Maria. She was standing in the middle of the room, gazing at the glowing globe. Only a few shreds of her dress still hung about her, but her welts and scratches had faded away, and her face was calm and clear. Fenwick was watching her closely.

"She has never looked at it before," he said in a low voice. "That is to say, she has never looked at it with such interest. Or with any interest at all. I've tried in the past to show her pictures in it, even pictures of you, when you were in the forest or by the ocean; but they had no more meaning for her than they would have for a cat. Something, some pattern of light and shadow, did once catch her attention, and she reached out her hand to try to touch it; but when the glass stopped her fingers she looked puzzled, and then her interest died altogether away." She was coming towards the globe now, stumbling through the debris which the storm had shaken onto the floor, and was peering at it, looking both uneasy and entranced. As William was at the beauty of her near-naked body.

"It is the Light," Fenwick whispered in William's ear. "Since the Light, the globe has continued to glow even when it is at rest."

"What light?" William asked. Her body seemed to be giving light, it was glowing with light from the glowing globe. She was standing near him, much too near him. He gripped his thighs with his hands to hold himself still.

"She was in the room when it burst out. She sank into a fit, but it seems that she remembers."

"What light?" William asked. He couldn't hold himself still forever.

"The light that made this storm."

"I thought Black Melk made the storm." It was difficult to think. It was difficult not to think of pressing his body against hers.

"He did. He stole the light from the clouds where it was resting. Because she was in a coma. If we can't use it, he takes it. And uses it against us."

177

"I don't understand," William said. His mind was full of his own pumping blood. Then he felt Fenwick's fingers against his cheek, patting it and then pushing against it, so firmly and steadily that Maria passed out of his sight and the room passed in front of his sight and he was gazing out of the window at drifting indistinguishable blackness.

"It doesn't matter. You need not understand," Fenwick said. "So long as you will do what you said you would. For you see the need before you."

The drifting blackness slowly separated into columns, many many columns, and William saw that they were columns of thick black smoke spiralling up from the earth to the low dark clouds, spreading like the crowns of fountains as they reached them, and flowing against their undersides. Around the base of every column was a pitch-black hole, and around the hole for many yards the earth was so burnt that the poor thin shoots of green that the earth had supported were burnt away to nothing. And the circles were so many and so close that they intersected one another, leaving only diamonds of different sizes of pale scattered green. Fenwick gave a small sigh.

"It will be the same all around the town," he said. "Though we have managed to save the town itself. Will you help me heal the wounds?"

"I don't..."

"Just help me," Fenwick said, his voice suddenly weary and flat.

"I'll help you," William said, turning towards him from the window, keeping Maria at the very corner of his eye. Fenwick nodded, and a thin smile flickered at his lips; and he closed his hands over the globe, so that they were bright red from its light, and lifted it from its rest and carried it back to the trunk, watching carefully where he put his feet among the fallen rubble. Maria's eyes followed him, followed the globe, watched him lay it gently in the

178

trunk. Her body was still, but her face was troubled, and her lips were trembling. William held tightly to the desk with both hands to control his body.

Fenwick lifted out of the trunk a large shallow white bowl, and some fine black material which he draped over his shoulder; and then closed the trunk and locked it. And Maria's face cleared. When Fenwick came to the desk with the bowl, William saw in the bottom of it the bottle which he had filled with water from the fountain-pool in the rose garden. Uncorking the bottle, Fenwick poured the water into the bowl, which was so translucent that shadows of the rippling water played like pale flames over the desk underneath.

"They think it's magic water," he murmured. "Which I have said a spell over. Which is as good an explanation as any. The bowl is of alabaster, a relic of the good old days they never tire of recalling. To their minds, that is; would they could recall them to the earth by mere longing." He laid the empty bottle in a drawer and shook out the black material and draped it around Maria's near-naked body. She let him, and she let him tie it at her waist with a piece of her old dress which he picked up from the floor. And William breathed more easily.

"She is very quiet," Fenwick said, lifting the bowl from the desk with both hands. "I have never seen her so quiet. Perhaps after all there is some real reason for hope. Will you open the door?"

William made his way to the door through the rubble, mostly of books, passing so close to Maria that he could feel the warmth of her body, but managing somehow to continue. He pulled the door open and Fenwick, nodding to Maria to follow him, crossed the room and passed out onto the landing. Maria looked at William and looked suddenly alarmed.

"You'd better come first," Fenwick said to him. And

179

when he did, she seemed calm again, and followed.

Holding the bowl in both hands with evident care, Fenwick led them down the stairs in single file, William in the middle. When they neared the landing of the first floor, Fenwick walked with great care, picking his way through the many crouching cats. Far along the barred corridor the raven began to make knocking noises and strange strangled cries.

"It has been frightened," Fenwick said over his shoulder. "There has been no storm so violent since...since it arrived here itself. And that was a wind-storm." He rachetted the toe of his shoe gently against the close-set bars as he passed them. "Just to let it know I know it's upset. It likes attention, of course, having to spend almost the whole of its life in solitary confinement, in a room barely big enough any longer for it to spread its wings. Poor bird. It is in its way most beautiful. I'll show you to it later. I mean, I'll show it to you." Maria, as she passed the bars behind William, stroked her knuckles back and forth against them; and the bird's cries died away. Fenwick glanced round fleetingly and then continued down the stairs between the crouched cats to the front doorway.

Immediately outside the doorway the street was empty, but a little way beyond it, to left and right, people were closely gathered, watching for Fenwick it seemed, and troubled; all of them kept back by six gatemen, three abreast across the street in each direction. Fenwick began walking in the direction of the square, and the gatemen ahead of him guided the people back in a semi-circle, and the gatemen behind him followed after him, holding the people back in a semicircle. But the people pressed hard against them, with fearful faces yearning towards Fenwick and the alabaster bowl, which was casting reflections of the shivering water onto the lower part of his body and the flagstones; they pressed so hard that the gatemen were forced to join hands against them and make a complete circle around Fenwick and William and Maria as they made their way slowly right across the square, the people ahead of them being steadily forced backwards, and the gaze of all the people fixed on the alabaster bowl; and the people themselves all strangely silent.

As they neared the far side of the square, William saw patches of sunlight on their faces, and then felt it momentarily on his own face, and glanced up at the sky to see that the cloud had paled and thinned and was breaking up, and scattered rays of sunlight were pouring through. And in the air around them was some sweet perfume, sweet and sickly.

Then he saw that something beyond the people ahead of them was separating them into two parts, and the nearer they came to the side of the square the nearer the point of separation came, and the sicklier the perfume became; until only the gatemen in front of them enclosed them on that side. Beyond the gatemen was a well, with a heavy lid on it, and the bodies of two blackcloaked people on their knees beside it. Beyond them and the well the crowd was closing together again in a deep circle.

"Let us through," Fenwick said, and the gatemen in front of them parted hands and moved beyond the well to hold back the crowd there. Fenwick looked at Maria, and seemed to be waiting for her to turn and look at him; but she was gazing steadily, unblinkingly, at the two people kneeling by the wellhead. At last Fenwick turned to William and held out the bowl to him. The surface of the water was glistening silver, and on the flagstones at their feet long thin flames of pale light were fleeting back and forth.

"Take it," Fenwick said, William took it into his hands. The alabaster was cool and smooth against his palms. There seemed to be a sudden catching of breath among the surrounding people.

"Hold it with extreme care," Fenwick said. "No one has ever held it but myself and Maria." He pulled his bunch of keys from the pocket of his dressing gown and searched through it until he found the one he wanted, and unlocked the padlock holding the bar down over the lid of the well. Two of the gatemen removed the bucket sitting on the lid, and the bar and the lid itself; and there was a low sound, like a sigh and a groan, from all the people. And the two crouched figures began simultaneously to slide their hands up the wellhead as if seeking blindly for its rim. Both their hands and their arms were sheathed in long grey gloves. Maria's gaze never left them.

"Hold them back," Fenwick said. The two gatemen who had opened the well pulled leather gloves onto their hands and seized each of the two crouching people by the wrists; whose heads swung up in sudden alarm and whose hoods fell from their heads, and William saw that it was the green-eyed woman and her mother.

"I told you that they would be here," Fenwick muttered. But they were much changed. The wound on the cheek of the green-eyed woman had healed over, but where it had been was a big blue-black bruise, so big that it was forcing her eye halfclosed. Another bruise was twisting her mouth into a crazy onesided grin, and a third was stretching out one of her ears. And her skin wasn't white, but blotched black and red. And the face of her mother beside her was as smooth and blue as a ripe plum from what looked like little bruises all over it, swelling it to twice the size it had been the night before, and hiding her eyes completely. William felt sick to his stomach. The tongues of pale light were quivering on the stones and his feet.

"Hold the bowl steady," Fenwick said sharply, almost in his ear.

"She was so beautiful. What has happened?" She didn't seem to see him, or anyone; she was stretching her

182

body, against the gateman's grasp, towards the open well. The people wouldn't look at her, it seemed that it was of her and her mother that they were frightened; they were all gazing at the alabaster bowl in his hands. But Maria was looking at them, and approaching them step by slow step.

"They are bleeding internally," Fenwick murmured. "Can't you smell it? That sickly perfume leaking out of them is poisoning the air. Little by little, unless they die, it will poison the whole town. They will have to be dealt with." He gestured to the gatemen with a flick of his hand and they dragged the women harshly to their feet. The daughter's long red hair tumbled loosely down her back, and her good eye passed round all the people, who shrunk back as if burned. When her look touched William he felt his body quivering, and the bowl shaking in his hands.

"She is very proud," Fenwick muttered. "And strong. But it isn't enough." Her mother had begun to whimper and groan, and saliva was trickling out of her bruised blue lips. The sickly smell flowing from them both was very strong. Maria was still very slowly approaching them, as if she didn't know who or what they were.

"Take them away. And don't let any part of them touch you," Fenwick said to the gatemen. "And breathe only as much as you must." The crowd was falling back from the gatemen and the women, pushing against one another almost in panic to give them as wide a passage as possible. The daughter, looking neither right nor left, walked quietly behind the gateman holding her by the wrists, but her mother fell groaning to the ground and her small body had to be picked up by the other gateman and carried at arm's length between his big gloved hands.

Maria was following them. The crowd stayed parted for her to pass between them, walking as if in a trance; and was closing behind her.

"Go after her!" Fenwick said urgently to William. "If we lose her we lose everything. Offer her the bowl." William set off after her with long strides, but steady, careful not to let the water slop over the rim of the bowl, and the crowd drew back again to let him through. Towards the middle of the square he caught up to her, and circled round her, keeping well off from her, until he was between her and the women, in the trail of the sickly air left behind them. He stopped and stood there silently, and held out the bowl. The clouds overhead had so broken up now that the paving stones round them were gleaming with sunlight; which was glistening like gold on the surface of the water in the bowl and casting its reflections through the bottom of the bowl onto the stones in long liquid snakes. Maria approached to the very edge of the bowl, as if not seeing it; until the reflected sun was dancing all over her face and filling her expressionless black eyes with sparkling; then she stopped, and seemed to see the quivering water as if half-waking from a dream; and slowly lifted her hands from her sides and slipped them under the bowl. Her hands touched William's hands and he felt electricity from them tingle up his arms and spread like wildfire through his body. Her eyes looked startled. He drew his hands away and she was holding the bowl alone. The light on her face and dancing in her eyes was almost too bright for him to look at; then suddenly it was gone, as she turned away from him without warning, and walked back towards the well, her black hair and clothing like a hole in the sunlight; and the people parted for her to pass. He followed closely after her, for fear they would come together again behind her and not let him through.

Fenwick was waiting at the well. Maria stopped and stood beside him, gazing steadily and in fascination at the shivering golden surface of the water.

"What will happen to them?" William asked. Fenwick looked at him blankly.

184

"To whom?"

"To the woman and her mother."

"Ah. Ah yes. They will be cared for. I'll ask you to draw up the water, since you are young and strong and I am neither. And to fill all the buckets they have brought; which are, I'm afraid, very many."

"How will they be cared for? Will they get well?" Fenwick gazed at him, slowly blinking, for a moment.

"I doubt it," he said. "They are too proud to heal properly. Their memory of the rose garden keeps their skin from breaking open, so they can't be branded; and yet it's too faded and worn a memory to make them well. Their longing for water is a very bad sign, a certain sign of the advance of the disease. That, and a fear of fire, which the gatemen will be testing. Please," he said, holding out the rope of the bucket, "Draw the water. The earth is more important than those women. We must heal it."

The people had closed in round the well and the fear had faded from their solemn faces, and all of them had buckets at their feet. William took the rope from Fenwick and lifted the bucket, weighted on one side with a small horseshoe, over the lip of the wellhead and lowered it into the well down, down, down, until, just as it seemed the rope wouldn't be long enough, the bucket touched the water. He let it tip and fill, and drew it up hand over hand, feeling the cool air it brought with it flow past his face, and emptied it into the nearest bucket of those gathered round. He lowered it into the well again and drew it up full again of clear and trembling water, and emptied it into another bucket, and lowered it again and drew it out again and emptied it again, and again and again, until he had long lost count and his arms were weary and his back was aching and the stones by the well were glistening with the water he had spilled; and still there were empty buckets waiting.

And then there weren't, and Fenwick's long fingers suddenly wrapped themselves about the rope just above the handle of the bucket as he was about to lower it once more into the well.

"You've done," Fenwick said, squeezing the rope so tightly that water flowed out of it in sunlit tracks over his knuckles. William stood back from the well and straightened his aching body, and saw that the sky overhead was a clear blue, and the sunlight resting on everyone round him, all of them unmoving, was clear and even. Fenwick gestured to two of the gatemen, who came forward and fitted the lid of the well, and the bar, back in place, and set the bucket upside down on the lid. Fenwick watched them appraisingly and then locked the bar in place. Maria hadn't moved, she was gazing still at the barely quivering golden surface of the water in the bowl in her hands.

"It's the only duty I've been able to teach her," Fenwick murmured almost in William's ear. "She is very suited to it, because she is so steady on her feet. She never spills a drop." He touched her very lightly on the shoulder, which seemed to rouse her; and then gestured to two other gatemen, who made their way through the quiet crowd, opening a path diagonally across the square in the direction of the main gates; towards which the continued at a marching pace, into the light of the midmorning sun which flared round their bodies.

"Follow us close," Fenwick said, moving off along the path opened through the crowd, with Maria beside him. William followed them between the unmoving people, each one of whom, men and women, of all ages except the very oldest and frailest, and the youngest children, was holding a bucket full of water. As the three of them reached the open square, the two remaining gatemen closed in behind them and followed closely after them to the gateway, where both gates were being pulled open by the first two gatemen. Fenwick and Maria, with William following, walked out onto the bare plain outside. Almost immediately Fenwick stopped, and Maria stopped, and William stopped behind them, at the first black hole in the earth, out of which a thin column of smoke was rising into the windless air. Behind them all six gatemen stood abreast in the gateway, closing the people within.

In every direction William looked, for a long way out from the walls, thin columns of black smoke, like the trunks of strange tall trees, were rising up from the plain to the blue sky, into which they melted. Amongst them here and there were real trees, but they were all leafless and most of them were broken. Fences were broken too, and ends of railings were bleeding pale smoke. Most of the earth itself was charred black. Fenwick sighed.

"We have had storms before," he said. "Many storms. But none like this one. He has taken all the power which should have been ours. Well, there is nothing for it now, we had better begin."

He raised his hand over his head, and the gatemen let a woman through with a bucket. She came forward quietly and set it on the ground beside him and stood back a little, waiting. He pulled back the loose sleeve of his dressing gown and dipped his fingertips into the water in the alabaster bowl, momentarily breaking the still, sun-struck surface, and let the water drip from his fingers onto the rippling surface of the water in the bucket. Instantly the water became still; and then, out of the centre of the surface, a perfect ring emerged and rippled smoothly to the rim, followed by another and another.

"Empty it into the hole," Fenwick said, half-turning towards William, who lifted up the bucket, and saw that his lifting didn't disturb the perfect rings flowing in unceasing smooth succession from the centre of the surface to the rim. He tipped the bucket over the hole, and watched the water pour out of it in a glittering tube of concentric circles, which splashed and shattered against the sides and bottom of the hole. There was a hissing sound of fire being quenched, and the smoke dwindled and ceased; and in its place steam gushed up out of the hole, and within the steam, like an arching backbone, a slender rainbow arose, up and up towards the blue sky. Behind him William could hear a low sighing from the people.

"Give her back her bucket," Fenwick said. "We have much to do." His voice seemed further off. William looked round and saw that he was standing with Maria beside another hole; he must have lost himself a moment in watching the rainbow. He gave the woman her bucket and she passed back through the line of gatemen; who let a man, old and bent, come through them in her place. He carried his bucket towards Fenwick and set it at his feet and stood back. Fenwick dipped his fingers in the bowl and let them drip into the bucket, and the same momentary stillness of the surface occurred, followed by a regular outflowing of rings. At his indication, William picked up the bucket and emptied it into the hole, and just as at the first hole the fine column of smoke ceased as the water quenched the smouldering fire, and a fine rainbow arched upwards in the midst of rising steam. Again something held him there, because he heard Fenwick's voice again telling him to give back the bucket, and saw that he and Maria were standing by a third hole, and he hadn't seen them move. He gave the old man back his bucket and he watched Fenwick drip water from the bowl Maria was holding into the bucket another, younger, man brought forward, and he poured the glittering circles into the hole and saw the rainbow and heard Fenwick's voice and gave back the bucket and watched the drops fall like stars through the air and shatter on the surface of the water, stilling its trembling, and he picked up the outflowing rings and poured them into the midst of the rising smoke and saw it turn from black to white and burst into all colours rising up in front of him, so close to his eyes it blurred in his eyes and he heard Fenwick's voice and he gave the bucket to a man who drifted backwards through another drifting forwards and he glided over the ground after Fenwick and Maria and saw sparkling waterstars falling and falling and falling and slipped his hands round the bright rings and poured them into the open blackness and the rainbow rose up around him and through him and everywhere he turned rainbows were rising and people were gliding and drifting among them and holding their babies in the midst of them, the babies were glowing with a soft golden light.

"You must help me," a voice said, drifting in through his ears. He looked through the rainbows around him. There was no one near him. "Help me." Something was touching his body, weighing against his body. Something was white and shining through the rainbows. It was coming nearer and the weight on his body was heavier. "Help me."

It was Fenwick's voice. And he could see Fenwick, he could see his shadowy shape close beside him, closer than the rainbows; it was his hand weighing like lead on his shoulder. And the white shining was the alabaster bowl just in front of him, glowing with the sunlight. Behind it, holding it, Maria was like a column of darkness.

"I can't continue alone," Fenwick said. His voice was dry and weak. His long thin face was white and drawn. Beyond him and Maria, between them and the gates of the town some distance off, thin columns of smoke were rising from the burnt earth as thickly as a thickly planted wood.

"We are almost there," Fenwick murmured. Confused, William turned to look about him, and saw that all six gatemen were drawn up in a row behind him; and behind them, beyond them, the people were all spread out among the holes from which slim rainbows were arching upwards towards the sky. As far as he could see along the walls of the town and a long way out onto the plain, rainbows were standing where there had been columns of smoke. And the earth was no longer black and charred, but a rich brown, even at the gatemen's feet.

"For the moment," Fenwick said weakly. "For the moment only. He will attack again. And again. Hold my right wrist in your hand."

William took hold of his fine, trembling wrist and it seemed to give him some strength, for he lifted his other hand away from William's shoulder; and nodded to the gatemen, who let an old woman through with her bucket.

"Guide my hand over the bowl," he said, and when the woman had set down her bucket he dipped his fingers in the little water which remained in the bottom of the alabaster bowl and, guided by William. held them above the bucket. But his hand was trembling so that one or two drops missed the bucket and landed on the charred black earth beside it, into which they seethed angrily and made little white craters, dry and white, their edges as crumbly as powder.

Keep back from them. Keep back," Fenwick said with sudden sharpness. "Keep the people back. Make them go around," he said to the gatemen. "You must hold my wrist more firmly," he said to William. "Now pour the water into the hole." William let go of his wrist and poured the bucket into the hole; and then, before he could properly watch the rainbow rising, he felt Fenwick's hand on his arm, drawing him away, drawing him towards the next hole; where he held Fenwick's wrist so firmly that the water trailed smoothly from his fingertips to the waiting bucket. And then at the next hole, and the next, turning column after column of smoke into a rainbow, through which all the people of the town passed after them; until they reached the gates of the town again, and beyond the gates were the first rainbows...paler now, paling even as William looked at them...which had sprung out of the earth when they had set off around the town in the morning. And it was now afternoon, and the sun a darker gold. William held Fenwick round the waist as he seemed about to fall, and guided his wrist to the bowl Maria was ever impassively carrying, never looking away from the surface of the water which was now only a small golden disk at the bottom, and which on the earth below was a dark disk in the middle of a large pale circle of light, threaded through by the shadows of her fingers; and lowered his wrist until his fingertips touched the water, and raised it and swung it over the waiting bucket of trembling wellwater, and watched the bright drops fall from his long fingers and still the water to perfect rings. While he poured the water into the very last holes, Fenwick stood by like a dry and rootrotted tree, waiting for a wind to fell him; and when the last column of all of smoke had been quenched and a rainbow was arching out of its hole, and they were standing beside the gateway, he seemed as near dead as alive.

"Carry me," he said in a voice little more than a husking croak. William lifted up his light and trailing body and carried him in his arms through the gateway into the town.

"To my room," Fenwick murmured feebly. William carried him along the side of the square and into the narrow street leading off it and into the entryway where the cats were sitting quietly on the lids of the tubs, entirely covering them with their closely packed bodies, and up the stairway. Behind him he could hear Maria's heavy following feet. As they passed the first floor, there was a knocking from far along the corridor, but not loud, and it stopped as they continued upwards. At the topmost landing, in the clear afternoon light, Fenwick moved for the first time in William's arms, looking round as if waking, but his eyes had never been closed.

"Let me down," he said in a soft whisper. William set him gently on his feet and watched while he searched slowly and meticulously through his keys until he found the right one, which he gave to William to open the door. Maria stood behind them the while, holding the bowl as ever in both her hands, gazing down at the few remaining drops glistening in the clear light against the palely glowing whiteness of the bowl. As William stood back from the open door, Fenwick gently lifted the bowl from Maria's hands, which she continued to hold out in front of her, fingers outspread, as if she didn't know the bowl had gone.

"Sleep," Fenwick said, nodding his head to the pile of rags on the landing. "Sleep." She didn't move, but gazed still at the bowl. Fenwick turned from her and went into his room.

"Come in," he said over his shoulder to William as he set the bowl down on his desk. "Leave her. Close the door behind you. She will sleep. She always sleeps after we heal a storm." William went into the room and closed the door.

"Bolt it," Fenwick said from the window overlooking the plain where he was standing and gazing. "And come here." William bolted the door and crossed the room and stood beside him in front of the window. "Sit down. You will need to rest before your journey this evening." He didn't feel tired, his whole body was tingling awake; he felt clean and almost shining. But Fenwick was so white and drawn it seemed he would fall to the floor if he didn't rest.

"It doesn't matter about me," Fenwick said. "What I

can do I have done. For this moment. Sit down. Rest."

William sat down on the window seat. Under him the doves were cooing gently. Out on the plain below, rainbows were still rising high into the air from the watered holes, like bright columns joining the earth to the blue sky...except from the nearest holes, directly below the window, where they had poured the first buckets of water and where the fire was long quenched and the earth was now so soft it had crumbled into the holes so that they were only shallow depressions, in the bottom of which green points of grass were just beginning to appear.

"There never was a plain like it," Fenwick murmured, his eyelids drifting down again and again over his eyes, and his bony hands clutching the windowsill for support. "Though it is difficult now to remember that it was so... rich. When I was a boy. And my...brothers and...I....... played in the fields and the lanes and the...the trees. Those stumps you see and burnt logs. There were...walnut trees and chestnut trees and...and....oak, oak trees. Oak trees. Gone now. Apple trees. And wells...full of water, all full. Now we have two, two only. One on this side of the square, for everyday, and the other one for these....particular occasions. And of course the...water in the......rose garden." His knuckles were white with the tension of holding onto the windowsill, and his face was so drained and expressionless that William expected at any moment to see his legs buckle and his long bony body crumple half on the window seat and half on the floor.

The light was changed. It was red now on Fenwick's face. William moved his head to see better, and found that it was resting against the windowframe, and that his neck was stiff. He must have fallen asleep.

"Are you rested?" Fenwick asked, still gazing out of the window across the plain. It seemed he hadn't moved. But the alabaster bowl was no longer on his deak. William straightened and stretched, and stood up and stretched again.

"Yes," he said. "I think I am." His feeling of nearly shining had faded almost entirely away.

"Good. In a very little time we must go."

The red light of the late sun was flowing across the plain like a flood of fine red water, in which the rainbows, all faded and dwindled now and many altogether vanished, were swaying back and forth like ghostly rushes. Just below the window, a little way out from the walls, three of the gatemen had fixed a stout pole into the ground and were now engaged in fixing another. everyone else it seemed was inside the walls.

"What are they doing?" William asked. Fenwick appeared not to hear him. Two of the men were holding the stake upright and the third was shovelling earth into the hole around it.

"What are they doing?" William asked. Fenwick sideglanced at him and seemed troubled, and returned his gaze to the plain. William waited.

"It is for the two women," Fenwick said at last, coldly, absently. "It will perhaps cure them. That is the hope."

"What are they going to do?"

"They will take them to those stakes at first light. And leave them there throughout the day. In the sun."

"But why? What have they done that…"

"To heal them, I said. To try to heal them. Since their wounds are too deep inside them to be branded. Perhaps the sun will break their wounds open, it's possible. Though I fear they're too proud. Come, we must go now. The sun has touched the horizon. When it has set Maria may wake….like a cat, her eyes seem to open with the coming of the dark. Which troubles me when I think of it. It is as if… Well I won't think of it. We must go. If she is awake she won't let us go, she will fear you will not come back.

194

It is a fear I have myself for that matter, a little fear. But in her it will reach from one end of her soul to the other. Come, we must go very quietly." He released his grip on the windowsill and moved back into the room. The light outside was deepening into soft purple, staining the gate-men and the stakes and the soft damp earth they were pil-ing and tamping down around the second stake. She was so beautiful and so fine and her mother was so old.

"You can't prevent it," Fenwick said in a thin whisper from across the room. "They brought it on themselves. Come along. Come along." He pulled back the bolt and quietly opened the door. William followed after him out onto the landing, where the light was a clear violet. Maria, wound into a pile of rags, was snoring softly. Fenwick locked the door and, with his forefinger to his lips, led William down flight after flight of dusty steps into deep-ening purple darkness.

As the neared the landing of the first floor, the raven began its knocking.

"Won't Maria hear?" William murmured uneasily, as Fenwick bent forward to unlock the railings which closed off the gloomy corridor. "And wake?"

"She is used to the raven's noises, she will absorb them into her dreams. But if she had heard you..." He lashed out suddenly with his foot, kicking one of the cats nearest the railings, which sent the others scuttling away up and down the stairs. "Quickly now," he said, and pulled open the railing-gate and slipped through, pulling William af-ter him, and closed and locked the gate again before the cats dared to glide back. The knocking of the raven was louder, and the strangled croaking as well. They seemed to come from a long way down the corridor.

"You're not frightened, I hope," Fenwick said, as they walked into the darkness, their footfalls muffled almost to silence by the thick dust.

"No," William said. He didn't think he was frightened. But his senses were all alert. "What's there to be frightened of?" Fenwick's face, barely visible now in the dark, seemed to be carrying a fine smile.

"Of the raven, I mean. They are all frightened of it. Even now, hearing its knocking, they will be standing or sitting still, and listening. It is a big raven, you realize, a very big raven. Which they know from all the tubfuls of scraps, their scraps, it eats. I'll need your help now with those, if you will."

William nodded in the darkness, and they continued walking along the corridor until the croaking and knocking were so loud that the stale air around him was pulsing against his skin. Cautiously he reached out his left hand and touched the wall beside him; it was throbbing with the blows being rained on it from the other side. The croaking was like sawing on his temples and the stink of stale and rotting food was clogging his breath.

"Here we are," Fenwick said, in a sudden loud voice, almost a shout, almost in his ear. "We'll just have a look at it first."

William couldn't see or hear what he was doing, but suddenly a panel opened in front of him, just at the height of his face, through which a purply grey light filtered into the hallway, gently lighting Fenwick's sharp face beside him. At the same moment the croaking of the raven rose suddenly to an earsplitting screech and he saw it, only a few feet from the opening; he was looking into its huge crimson throat. Involuntarily he started back. The raven continued screeching, its sharp tongue quivering to a point out of the depths of its throat, and it struck again and again with its wings against the quivering wall between them.

It can't get out," Fenwick shouted, holding William fast by the arm. "The opening is thickly glassed and grilled." The raven turned its enormous head a little to one side and looked at them with one huge unwinking copper eye; its feathers were glistening purply-black in the purple light flowing weakly from the six tall opaque windows at the end of the great empty room. Suddenly it stretched out its wings until their tips stretched the far side walls, and closed its beak and struck it with all its force against the wall in front of them, shuddering it almost to splitting.

"It's very hungry," Fenwick shouted. "We must feed it at once."

He searched hurriedly through his keys in the poor light, while the raven battered the wall with its beak from the other side, until he found the one he wanted, and led William a little way along the hallway to where a big tub was just visible, and pushed the key into a knob protruding from the wall.

"Now," he shouted, close to William's ear, through the blows raining on the wall beside them, "I'll pull back this sliding door and you push the tub into the room. It will be very hard to push. You will need all your strength. Are you ready?" William set his shoulder against the rim of the tub, and held his breath against the stink of rotting food inside it, and when Fenwick abruptly pulled back the sliding door, he pushed as hard as he could. But the tub hardly moved. Wind whistled round its edges, tearing at his clothes and buffetting his head, and it was only by the greatest straining that he was able to push it forward inch by slow inch into the opening. When it was just more than halfway in, Fenwick pushed the sliding door as close against its side as he could, but still the air screeched and whistled through on both sides, driving against him like a gale. He ground his teeth together and exerted more strength than he knew he had, and pushed and pushed against the wind, and Fenwick steadily closed the sliding door; until, in a moment, it was over: the tub was in the room and the sliding door was closed, and there was only the muffled soft wet sound of the raven ravenously eating.

William sank down to the floor, and rested his back against the other wall of the hallway, and Fenwick sat down beside him. Around them the purply-grey light spreading from the square of the glass panel very slowly diminished.

"It arrived in a wind, you see. After a fashion," Fenwick said, when William was breathing easier. "In the only storm we have had which was the equal in violence of the storm this morning. But it was a wind-storm. I may have told you already. I find that I forget. But not the raven's arrival, of course; not important events like that.

"Its mother came first. She blundered into my room one morning very early...as ravens in their cunning pretend to blunder...while I was sitting up in bed waiting to see the first comforting rays of the sun. I managed to catch her and cage her, realizing that she was an agent of Black Melk's...as many ravens are. But that was a mistake, as matters turned out, turned as I didn't foresee. From the moment of the cage closing on her...the very cage indeed where the doves are now: she was a raven of ordinary size...I could feel the wind rising in all four quarters of the plain, and I knew tha Black Melk's anger was building; but didn't know... The wind rose higher and higher, building all day in intensity, yet holding off; and the raven herself sat quietly in the cage, apparently indifferent, even peaceful. And then, by ill fortune, just at twilight, Maria toddled into my room. How pretty she was then, and her black eyes were full of light.... I don't know even now what happened, I suppose it was some maleficent magic of Black Melk's, but she approached the raven sitting quietly in the cage, I remember seeing her cross the room, and her little arm outstretching, her little hand outreach-

198

ing....and the next thing I knew she was in a fit, foaming at the mouth, the first of all her fits. And the winds burst out of the heavens upon us. I held her tightly in my arms and crouched on the floor throughout the night, while the windows all round us shattered and almost every object then in the room blew out of it; and houses everywhere in the town were broken or even thrown down. Until at last, with the first blush of daylight, I crawled to the cage, I don't know how, with Maria still in my arms, and opened it. And the raven walked slowly out of it as if there were no wind swirling wildly around us, and opened her wings and drifted up into the air and glided out of the window into the morning twilight. And the wind ceased as suddenly as it had begun; and Maria stirred in my arms and opened her eyes. Oh, her eyes: they were dull black, all the light was gone out of them, gone. And so they have remained. And will remain...how can it be otherwise?...until Black Melk is overcome.

"But then," he said, staring steadily at the dim opposite wall of the hallway, "I saw that resting on the floor of the cage was an egg, a small purplish egg, almost exactly the colour of the light at the moment. I remeoved it carefully from the cage and held it in my folded hand to keep it warm, and to keep it from Maria's sight, since I didn't know how it would affect her. As she had then become she might easily have swallowed it, or sat on it, there was no longer any judging of her actions. That same morning I had a female swan brought up to my room, and devised quarters for her as comfortable as possible. and she was content; she sat on the egg for hours on end, days on end...I brought her food, of course...and when the egg broke open and a most unusually ugly creature appeared from its midst, with purply-black flesh and a flat shapeless beak and eyes like black studs, looking centuries old, she cared for it devotedly. Until it was fledged, with glossy black feathers, and already as big as she was, and the wind began." He stopped speaking, and beyond the barely visible wall opposite there were sounds of the raven's great beak scraping against the sides of the tub.

"What wind?" William asked at last.

"The wind you felt just now. When you were pushing the tub into the room. It began at first as only a mild breath, a breeze, flowing out of the ugly creature; but soon increased in strength. The swan was bewildered, and found it ever harder to approach her foster child. The raven too was bewildered, and hopped towards her, and the wind from it drove her further back. Every day the wind was stronger, as the raven grew with every day. Until it became impossible for the swan any longer even to approach it. I set up a screen in the room, with glass panels in it so that they could at least see one another, but soon even that failed to serve. I came back to the room one day to see the raven in the middle of the floor, croaking pathetically, and the swan in the air beyond the open window, beating her wings wildly in an attempt to regain entry, but quite unable. At last the unfortunate bird exhausted herself; her strength failed and her head fell away on her long limp neck, and she spiralled down to the ground, into the midst of quite a number of people gazing up. They took up her body and buried her reverently; and I'm afraid their resentment of the raven dates from that day. Because the swan, you see, was the last of the flock remaining from the days of the old king. They used to wander freely about the town, and people took them to be a sign of good times. When the times were gone, that is, they so took them. It was fitting enough, of course, if the times were gone, that the swans should go too. But they blamed the raven. And me.

"Soon enough after that I couldn't easily sustain the wind from the raven myself. Books and papers blew out of my room, even a chair; and I could see it would get worse, much worse, for the raven was still growing. So while I was still able, I took it in my arms…it was frightened, it is very strangely gentle…and carried it down here, so it would have room to grow, because this is the largest room near to my own, having been once a ballroom. Indeed, I can remember well enough when there was dancing beyond that very wall…when I was young and the women's skirts smelled of sweet powder and crushed lavender, and high over my head the chandeliers were dancing fire. The old king himself was then too but a boy." He fell silent, gazing still in the direction of the wall, which could no longer be seen, for the light had failed almost altogether. Beyond the wall the raven was silent also.

"Why? What for?" William asked at last, as the silence went on and on. He felt Fenwick beside him start very slightly.

"'Why?'" he asked. "Why what?"

"Why have you got it here? Why have you kept it here? What's it for?"

"Ah," Fenwick said very softly. "That. That will come. When you return I'll tell you. If you return. I hope you return," he said, his hand touching lightly and fleetingly on William's knee and his voice as fleetingly gentle. "I'll show you the purpose then. Now we had better be on our way." He stood up, and after a moment William heard his fingers tapping and stroking against the opposite wall, not far from the floor, until he evidently found what he was looking for, for he was still.

"You had better move from there," he said. "A few feet to your right, or you may be hit." William stood up and moved aside. At the same moment he heard Fenwick pull back the sliding door and a high wind scream out of the room, and something heavy, which he supposed was the empty tub, crashed into the wall just where he had been sitting. Fenwick slid the door closed again and the wind died as suddenly as it had risen, and William could hear him threading his fingers slowly through his keys.

"Who usually pushes the tub in?" William asked, suddenly wondering as he heard Fenwick lock the sliding door. "One of the gatemen?"

"Oh no. They are quite unable. Or quite unwilling, which is the same thing. It is the full extent of their courage to carry food up from below and dump it here in the tub, with the raven knocking and crying beyond the wall. They are no different from the others, only a little harder-skinned, say a little braver. But they would no more heal of bleeding than anyone else. I did once try to persuade them to help me with the feeding, but they glided away from me like loose shadows."

"But somebody must help you," William said. "You couldn't…"

"Maria," he said in a low voice. "She is the only one unafraid. I suppose you might say she is beneath fear. She has never seen the raven since it has been here, she has only heard it and, I suppose, smelled it. But one evening, long ago now, I came upon her crouched by the railings in the midst of the cats, peering into the corridor. And she so whimpered and clung to me that I let her come to the feeding, and then help me push the vat in, and then, not long after, push it in all by herself. She is very strong. And the wind seems to… Well that's curious about the wind, I'm not quite easy…. Still, I expect there's nothing curious really. Come then, we must be going." His wandering voice became brisk and William heard the little panel close, though he saw no change in the darkness, and a moment later he heard it being locked. "There. That's all in order. Give me your arm. The moon will very soon be rising,"

They walked along the pitch-dark corridor, their feet muffled by the dust, away from the way they had come.

Fenwick seemed to know the way by heart, leading William...who stumbled now and then...down flights and flights of steps, always down, and along other corridors and into spaces which felt like rooms, or high halls, and the sound of their feet echoed softly back from far walls, and then again from near walls. They walked and walked through the silent darkness, and neither of them spoke. Until at last Fenwick stopped, and held William's forearm tightly in his grasp, and seemed to be listening.

"It's quiet," he said, after a few moments. "The moon hasn't yet risen. Stand just as you are." He released William's arm and seemed to be looking for something in his clothing. Then he reached his hands up over William's head and William felt him lowering around his neck some dangling object on a string. It came to rest a little below the base of his throat.

"What is it?" he asked. "Can I touch it?"

"If you want. It's a pentangle. Where you are going you must guard it as you would your life. If you lose it I will be unable to help you. You will be lost yourself. But so long as you have it I will be able to keep watch over you and guide you as best I can, and keep Black Melk's attention on me, on us, so that you may approach his castle unseen. But make for his castle, only his castle...will you remember? If you see signs of him elsewhere, ignore them, they are only his misleading glamours, designed to entrap you. Only the castle itself."

"And then? When I reach the castle?"

"*If* you reach the castle, it will then be soon enough to tell you how to proceed. I will see you in my globe, and a dove will come with instructions. And I will wait for your return in the rose garden. But whatever you do, whatever happens to you, don't lose the pentangle."

"I won't," William said. "I'll keep..."

"Shhh," Fenwick said. They both stood still and listened; but William couldn't hear anything except the whispering of his blood in his ears.

"It's all right," Fenwick said after a moment. "The moon still hasn't risen," William heard him threading through his keys, and then the sound of a big one being fitted into a keyhole just beside them, and turned. The lock sounded stiff and rusty.

"Help me pull the door open," Fenwick said. William found the handle and they turned it together and pulled on it together, and slowly the door creaked and eased out of the jamb, and around it flowed air so fresh and sweet that William's whole body seemed to open to it and breathe.

"Go," Fenwick said. "Go quickly." He stayed in the shelter of the big door himself as he pushed William around it, and immediately closed the door heavily behind him; and William found himself in the middle of the night.

He heard the key turn in the lock, but he didn't turn around. Without thinking, half-drunk with the sweetness of the air flowing through his body, he began walking in the direction he was facing, threading his way through close-set trees he couldn't see, feeling their thin trunks with the palms of his hands, and their branches lightly scratching against his face and shoulders; and gradually he became aware that he was seeing them too, all around him, all stiff and straight, all very faintly lit on their far side by a light which was moment by moment growing stronger. And he realized that it was the first light of the rising moon.

He continued walking, slowly and steadily, over a carpet of deep leaves, soft and noiseless from rain and dew; so thick it seemed they had been gathering for years, and as if they had not until now been disturbed. The perfume in the air was flowing from the trees through which he was passing, from their blossoms which brushed past his face, all silver and black from the moonlight; and above his head their crowns rose like pale clouds between him and the clear black sky. He walked through them unhurrying, even it seemed to him ever more slowly, and there seemed no end to them. The moon rose very slowly, almost blinding his eyes in the glimpses he had of it through the glistening clouds of blossom, and he began to think as if from faraway that he was no longer walking through the trees at all, that he was merely standing in their midst, for the black and white patterns were no longer moving past him or around him, there was only the very very slow change of light and shadow following the glacial rising of the moon. Then he had a sense that all the clouds of blossom around him were rising on their black and silver trunks; or he was falling. If he was falling it was very slowly, and he could almost remember falling so before, though not when nor why, and he felt untroubled, he was only drifting like a loose petal down through the silvery light; the flowering trees were ever taller, but still the scent of their blossoms bathed his whole body.

He seemed to have come to rest, he seemed to be lying outstretched on the ground, on his back, and overhead the circle of trees were edging a circle of night like a window; into which was swelling the brilliant upper edge of the rising moon, so brilliant he couldn't look at it, his eyes sought rest in the clear black sky, in the silvery blossoms, in the pattern of their straight black and silver trunks like a striped wall all around him. He could feel his body rising and falling with his breathing, and being gently touched here and there with petals falling onto it, rocking a moment and coming to rest. One was rocking coolly against his throat.

He wasn't alone. Someone was coming towards him, slowly, across the moon-silvered ground. A man. He seemed to be walking blindly with his face upturned to the moonlight; and his hands upturned, they were as silver as the ground; in a few more steps it seemed certain that he would walk or stumble over William's far-stretched legs, like long thin logs on the bright ground. But just as he reached them he stopped, and slowly straightened his head until his eyes, flashing an instant like beacons as they caught the slanting moonlight, were looking down at William's legs and his whole outstretched body. He looked for what seemed a long while, his face black and featureless in the dark of the moon, and half his body dark, and the other half bright silver; and it was strange how it was not troubling, but peaceful, the man seemed peaceful. He bent forward at last, slowly, and let his long thin fingers trail experimentally over William' unmoving leg. Then something caught his eye, something it seemed at William's head, for he was approaching along his body, bent half-over, his face as low as his waist and his long thin beard nearly touching the ground. His face came closer and closer to William's face, until he could see that it was an old face, with black lines and creases in the dark-shadowed skin, and moon-sparkling eyes almost buried in wrinkles; his beard now was trailing over William's chest.

It was the pentangle he was drawn to. His shadow suddenly covered it, snuffed out the moonlight glowing on it; which made him start back, so that the moonlight caught it alight again. He moved to one side so as not to cover it again with his shadow, tentatively reaching out at the same time with his right hand, as if to touch it. But then, when he had nearly reached it, he withdrew his hand behind his back; and his encaverned black eyes were full on William's eyes, and William suddenly felt his blood run cold.

"Don't be afraid," the man said. His voice was like far music, passing through veils. It made William's body shudder. "There is no danger." But it felt as if there was danger; he remembered Fenwick's warning as he left, and became fearful that the man might take his pentangle, at which he was gazing once again. He tried to move his body. His legs and arms were as heavy as fallen trees, but with a great effort he managed to lift them, and then to lift his head. At which the old man stepped a little back, and glanced at the ground roundabout and then at the silver-flowering trees over their heads, and stepped back further. Something was troubling him.

"You can't stay here," he said abruptly, his voice breaking through the veils like a single sharply plucked string. "Look at all the petals you're causing to fall." William sat up, his body feeling as if he was raising it out of the earth itself, and looked around him and saw that the ground near him was covered with fresh petals, and that his body was covered equally, and that those on his chest were sliding and tumbling into his lap. Even as he gazed about him, the petals from the near trees were falling ever more thickly to the silver ground.

"Please. Stand up," the old man said, his voice now imploring. "You can stay in my cabin, In my cabin it will be all right." He gave William his hand to help him get up from the ground; and his grasp was strong and his arm was strong, so that William found himself rising upwards as effortlessly as he had fallen; and when he was standing, more than a head taller than the old man, he couldn't feel his own weight on his feet. Which made it difficult to walk. But the old man drew him somehow, and he let himself be drawn, right across the bright silver glade to its far side, where the old man reached into the close-set trees and turned something and pushed with the flat of his free hand, and the space between two black-and-silver trunks just in front of them swung away from them; and the old man drew him through what appeared to be a doorway into what appeared to be a dark room.

"There. You can sit there," the old man said, releasing him and pointing to the floor just inside the door, just beyond where the moon was lighting the floor. "There's a pallet to sit or lie on, as you like. Sleep if you like. I must go now and do my work. Please don't come out of the cabin. If the petals fall, all the work I've done will be in vain."

"Maybe it's their time to fall," William said uncertainly, apologetic.

"No. No. Oh dear, no. It's not their time. It was your breathing which was causing them to fall. Look over there where you were lying, how they are like a mound around the shape of your body. If you had continued there just this night long, all the trees would have come into leaf by morning, and by noon it would be high summer, even coming to harvest. How would I maintain my work then? How? I don't mean it's your fault. It's not your fault at all. It's nobody's fault. But it's the way things are. I would have to change all my paintings. It would mean beginning again from the beginning, and I'm far too old, really I am. The very little I've managed has taken all my long life. You won't leave the cabin, will you? Please say you won't. Look how they're still falling everywhere."

"I won't move," William said, settling himself down in the dark on what felt like a thin pallet. "I didn't mean to cause you…" The old man nodded and turned away, and hurried out of the cabin into the moonlit glade, where after a few steps he stopped. Then slowly, very slowly, he bent forward and let his arms hang down limply, until his fingertips touched the ground, until his palms were flat against the ground. His head hung down between his arms and his beard trailed over the earth. Then equally slowly he lifted his arms upwards, as if he were letting them be lifted, and his body slowly straightened until he was standing upright in the full moonlight, with his face and palms upturned and shining silver from the light, as William had first seen him, but quite still. And while he stood so, the twinkling of the falling petals around the glade became ever less, until it ceased altogether and the air was as clear as the sky overhead, and even the petals on the ground had faded like waterdrops into the earth.

Then he began walking across the glade. Upon reaching its centre he made a slow complete turn on the spot, and continued to the far side, where he began slowly wheeling round and round, his face and the palms of his hands still turned to the moon, as if he were dancing into the edge of the glade under the silvery trees. For a while William couldn't see him for the front wall of the cabin, then suddenly he passed close in front of the door, still turning very slowly and as if in a kind of trance. He disappeared again from sight, and appeared again following the farther edge of the glade to where he had begun circling it, where he continued circling inside his first circle, still turning round and round but, it seemed, a little faster. He disappeared, and passed the cabin door again and disappeared, and reappeared further round the glade, and began a third circle inside the first two, and now his turning was clearly quicker; the moonlight was spilling off his upturned hands and face, casting fleeting lights all through the glade and in through the doorway of the cabin. William felt them strike his skin like fine icicles, and retreated deeper into the cabin. The old man was turning now so quickly that his beard was flying out horizontally in front of him and his scanty white hair was flying out behind; but still his hands and his face were held steadily upturned to the dazzling white moon, and the arrowing lights they cast were multiplying, skidding and bouncing all over the glade, so that it was itself dancing with light upon the still moonlight, and the wall of black-and-silver trees everywhere around it was everywhere broken through with glittering arrows. William could hardly bear to look at the man any longer, he was turning so fast; he was all scintillating light. But when he closed his eyes he could still see him spinning in the glade, through a softening spiralling of colours; and he couldn't keep his eyes closed, they seemed to open of themselves: the arrowlights stung into them but they wouldn't close, all he could do was protect himself by peering through his threaded fingers. The old man was spinning now like a top, round and round in the middle of the glade, flashing millions of bright needles in every direction; he was becoming silvery-grey, and paler silverygrey, and silver, he was only silver he was silver light he was light, stinging light... William's eyes were flowing with water, it was trickling through his fingers, blurring the pain of the stinging; but still the pain was too great, more than he could bear he would have to close his eyes he couldn't...

"Good morning."

He started, and opened his eyes. It was daylight, and the old man was a dark bent shadow between him and the bright doorway. In sudden apprehension, he clutched at the pentangle, what if the man had taken it while he slept? But it was nestling against the base of his throat.

"Did you sleep well?" the man asked. How could his voice be so like music? There was some other light in the room, some light from the back wall lighting the man's face, and glowing on a pair of big green glasses covering his eyes. There were heavy curtains hanging in the middle of the back wall and the light was shining through them. There must be a window there, receiving the first of the sun.

"Yes," William said. "Very well." What was the fear stirring in his stomach? They was nothing fearful near him. The man was very very old, older than he had appeared by moonlight; his skin was a web of finest wrinkles, and he was holding himself up with both hands on the head of a cane. The room was pleasant and clean and orderly; it was curious that each of the walls was painted with furniture or objects which were near or against other walls, so it seemed at first to be completely symmetrical, but it wasn't fearful. But Black Melk's castle in Fenwick's globe didn't look fearful either, and it was. He kept his fingers wrapped round his pentangle, and the fear in his stomach grew.

"You needn't be afraid I would take it," the man said. He seemed almost translucent in the light flowing in through the doorway. The pale grey shift he was wearing was thin and worn and hung straight down from his shoulders to his ankles. "Or even try to take it. Without your consent, no one could take it."

"I was told not to lose it, whatever happened," William said uneasily, defensively. Every note of the man's voice seemed to sharpen the pain in his stomach. He wished he would move back. And not look at him, the light through the curtain was making his eyes sparkle strangely even through his green glasses. "It's to protect me where I'm going."

"Are you looking for your son, then? At last?" the old man asked, bending down closer to William, peering at him from behind his green glasses, while the strange music of his voice resounded in William's head and through the whole length of his body.

"My son?" he asked, and his own voice felt unsteady, unstable. "What son? I haven't got a son. I've been sent to find the far side of Black Melk's castle. Nobody else could be sent, because only I…"

"He is looking for you. He passed here on his way out. He is looking for you day and night."

"But I haven't got a son. I've never had a son." She

211

was gone beyond the forest, beyond the ocean, she was gone from him, long gone...

"He went with her," the old man said, barely murmured. Why did he want to stand so close, it was becoming hard to breathe. "And she gave birth to him, to your son. Where were you then?" William felt his sweat stinging his skin, and the smell of it was strong and sharp in his nose. She was standing by the edge of the ocean, waiting for him, her hair hanging loose to her waist. She was fading, the light on the ocean was melting her.

"I couldn't find her," he said. "She was gone. She left me on the shore alone."

"Where did you go then?"

"Into the forest."

"Why?"

"I didn't know where else to go."

"Were you looking for her?"

"I... I was looking... At first I was looking..."

"What colour are her eyes?"

"Her eyes? They're blue, blue as the... No, they're grey, grey as a dove's wing... No, they're..."

"They're green," the old man said, his voice like the trilling of a bird, which set William's nerves shrilling. As green as the ocean. As green as these glasses I'm wearing. How can you expect to find Black Melk, as you call him, if you can't even remember her eyes? How can you ever expect to see your son? It was in seeing these glasses that he saw her again. He wore them and he laughed. And I wept. And you couldn't even remember their colour."

"She left me," William said. "It wasn't my fault. I loved her. I remember thinking how I loved her."

"Then why was she not there when you returned to the shore of the ocean? Why was there only sunlight on the ocean? Why were you not with her when she died? Your pentangle will protect you for an hour or a day, or a year. But not at last. What particularly is it to peotect you from?"

"From Black Melk. So I can reach his..."

"You said you were looking for Black Melk. How can you find him if you are protected from him?"

"I'm protected so Fenwick can guide me. So I can help the people bring their land back to health. Because Black Melk has..."

"You won't find him," the old man said.

"Why not? If I..."

"Because he doesn't exist. If you remove the pentangle you'll see that he doesn't exist." William closed his hand tighter around it, and felt the cramps in his stomach spreading up into his chest and down into his groin. The air around him was hot; the old man must be making it hot; behind his green glasses his eyes were all fine sparkling and his voice was like a throbbing silver wire. "He's only an invention, an invention of your own, to give yourself somewhere to go."

"But I've seen what he's done. And Fenwick told me..."

"You invented Fenwick too. He doesn't exist."

"I *know* he exists. I've talked with him. I've helped..."

"Let me show you something," the old man said abruptly, and backed away from William; and the air flowed freely and coolly around him again and he could breathe in deep draughts of it.

The man was gesturing to him with his cane.

"Stand up and come here beside me." He didn't want to, but the man was offering him the end of his cane and he found that his free hand was grasping it and holding on as the man pulled him up and up through the air; the cramps in his stomach were as sharp as arrows but he held onto the cane, and found himself standing close beside the old man, almost touching him. The little air between them was so hot it was almost on fire. It was the old man's body which was so hot, it was making the cramps in his body sear him like fire. He could hardly stand straight.

"You see that curtain, covering the opposite wall?" the old man said. William nodded. The sun shining through it seemed stronger than before. The old man's hand lightly holding his wrist seemed to be burning his flesh. "Behind it I've painted a picture of your son. Many years ago now I painted it. When i was a young man, when I thought I had made considerable progress in my work, particularly as he had deigned one daybreak to walk into this glade where I... Though he was only passing, it was a passing moment, he was on his way through to look for you. Still, I painted what I could in the years after, what I could remember. It was nothing at last, hardly even a hint of what he was... But still, it may help you somewhat, somehow..." He stepped forward, and reached forward with his cane, and with the end of it he jerked back the curtain, and the sudden light in the room was so blinding that William screamed before he could stop himself, and fell in a heap on the floor. His head was throbbing with shapeless light, which seemed to be trying to burst in every diection out of his skull, and his whole body was burning like fire; until he felt coolness begin in the middle of his forehead, which spread throughout him like a cool stream quenching the fire. It was gone, gone as quickly as it had come; and the blinding light seemed to be gone. Very cautiously and fearfully he opened his eyes. The curtain had fallen back in place, and the old man's fingertips were withdrawing from his forehead. How could they be so cool when his body was so hot? The pain in his stomach was melting and melting, and his eyes were inexplicably filling with tears.

"And you are looking for Black Melk," the old man said, and his voice sounded so sweet that William's tears flowed down his face. "As you call him."

"I couldn't help it," William said, his voice breaking in sobs which he couldn't control. "I didn't mean to leave her. It was she who left me. I loved her..."

"What will you do if your son finds you while you're wandering? If he suddenly comes upon you? If this mere painting of him is more than your eyes can bear?"

"I didn't know he was even born." His tears were flowing into his mouth. "She left me just when I was coming back to her."

"I'm not speaking of your wife," the man said. He seemed to be bending kindly over him. His voice was kind. "What you've done you've done. I'm speaking of your son. What will you do if he comes upon you? If you turn a corner, if you pass a tree, and..."

"I couldn't help it," William said. "Half the time I couldn't see her. If I wan't touching her I couldn't remember what she looked like. Or even where she was. I don't know how I wandered off. It happened. I wandered days in the forest while the filtered light danced round me and I forgot to eat or sleep. And I forgot her, I forgot her altogether. It seemed to be chance only when I found her again by our house on the beach. And even while she cooked food for me and I spooned it into myself, I heard the ocean caressing the pebbles and saw far far out on it where the sunlight was dancing. I didn't mean to leave her alone. I loved her. I loved her at moments. At moments I didn't know anything except her."

"Those moments were when he was born," the old man said in a strange singing whisper, and his hand reached down and touched William's hand, and it was neither hot nor cold; and he held William's hand and pulled on it gently but so strongly that Wiliam found himself rising with no effort of his own to his feet, And the old man then seemed very small, and weak, as he peered up at him through his green glasses.

215

"What am I to do?" William asked, his tears still trickling uncontrollably from his eyes. "I'm not fit to do anything. She will never forgive me. How can I find her now and ask her to forgive me, if she's dead?"

"Look at my eyes," the old man said, and lifted both his hands to his glasses and removed them from his face. And William's heart almost stopped beating at the sight of his eyes: they were like small black holes in the very air.

"Do you see?" the man said, quickly replacing his glasses, and the music of his voice stilled William's wildly beating heart. "You're not less than I am. Or than anyone. These eyes saw him only through these glasses, not otherwise. And you see what they have become. So beware of him in your wandering, your searching." Gently he turned William round and led him out of the cabin into the early morning light in the flowering glade.

"But where will I search?" William asked. "Which way? And what for? For him?" The old man was peering steadily up at him through his glasses.

"No," he said at last, gently. "You would never find him, not now. And you must shelter yourself from him, for now, lest he find you. You had better continue searching for Black Melk's castle."

"But you said there is no castle."

"But you say there is," he said, and suddenly smiled. "So go and find it." He let go of William's hand and pointed across the glade with his hand. "Go that way. From just there where you can see the wild rose bushes. Do you see them?"

"I can see some lilies," William said. His tears were dry now in his eyes and on his cheeks, and the burning and the pain were gone from inside his body; and the air in the glade was so soft and sweet, and the voice of the old man was so like a beautiful song, that he suddenly didn't want to go anywhere, but only to stay where he was.

216

"You can't stay," the old man said, still gently smiling. "You must go. You will see the roses when you are there, they are growing just beyond the lilies, which grew from where his blood landed when he pricked himself on the roses. And then you will see a little stream. Follow it. It will lead you some part of the way. Now go. Go. Don't hesitate, and don't look back. You'll not see me if you look back. Go quickly."

William couldn't stop or stay himself, he was walking before he knew it across the sunny still glade to its further side, toward the lilies. But when he reached them they were wilting, their white trumpets were melting and dripping onto the soft earth. Into a pool of water in the earth, he could hear the drops splashing within the grass. Then he smelled and saw the wild roses, a ring of them, and heard the trickling of a thin stream in their midst; and then he was among the blossoming trees in dappled sunlight and all around him petals were falling; and then in what seemed only a few moments, only a few long strides, all the trees around him were in leaf, and the stream beside him was swift-flowing and clear.

With every stride he took the stream broadened, and the trees were fewer; until there were hardly any at all near him. The grass was deep and thick, and the stream beside him was now a broad and shallow river; and it was curving, it appeared, ever round to the right, so if he continued following it he might well end up back where he had begun...

Begin by following it, the old man had said. Only begin.

So he stopped and looked about him. The sun was beyond the river, already sinking down into the western sky. The land beyond the river seemed like the land on his side, rolling grassland with only the odd single tree. But also there was a far hill, towards which the sun was setting. A conical hill, just like the hill he had seen in Fenwick's globe. It was so far off he couldn't make out anything but its shape; but there seemed to be a jaggedness at its peak, which could be a castle. And because of a trick of the light the whole hill seemed to be resting not on the land but on a glittering lake. He gazed at it for some while, and found that the sun had set further towards it, and that the toes of his boots were touching the water at the very edge of the river. That must be his way, he thought and walked into the water until it was halfway up his legs. It was very cold, but it didn't grow deeper, and it gurgled and glittered around his legs as he slowly walked over the smoothpebbled bottom.

"He's all right so far, we may be thankful for that," Fenwick said. Naturally Maria didn't answer, but it was some faint cheer, he thought, that she would stand there beside him quietly. The longer he could persuade her to do so, the further along they would get with their piling the wood round the base of the stakes.

"You see him, don't you?" It almost seemed that she did see him, but of course she didn't, it was too much to hope. "You see the light flashing and flickering around his legs/ That's water he's walking through. The water is catching the light. You see it?" She didn't appear to, her eyes were as dull as always; but it was considerable that she continued to look at the globe, it was much more than she had ever done before. She even seemed interested in it in a general way. "You can see the light shining on his hair as well. You see that? You remember that, do you? You remember his hair, how the sun makes it shine. Surely you remember?" The stink in the room from the women was almost unbearable, the sickly sweet stink of rotten blood, even Maria seemed aware of it, from the way her nostrils were now flaring. It would be highly unfortunate if the smell should draw her away from the globe before the gatemen had lit the fires. He must do everything possible to keep her attention fixed on the globe. He held his clove-apple out to her nose, holding his own breath the while; but she shied away from it. Her nostrils now were flaring more than before and she was making a grunting sound through her teeth. Or whimpering, it was impossible to know what sound it was, what meaning it had. He placed himself on the bank towards which William was walking, so she would be able to see his face.

"There. There he is. He's coming towards you. Look how his face is warm red in the setting sun. Isn't he beautiful? You remember him, don't you? He hasn't left you. Look, he's coming right to you." Her grunting or whimpering was more intense, and her breathing was beginning to be unsteady, uneven. Surely she wasn't going to have a fit... "Look at his face, he's smiling. You see? His lips are smiling. And the light in his eyes is soft and rosy, you see how the light is warming their natural blue? You see? Look closer, come closer, that's right." He took her gently by the arm and drew her slowly closer and closer to the globe, where only the upper part of William's body could now be seen. "There. Don't be frightened. There's nothing to be frightened of." She was breathing very eratically and her whimpering was quite alarmingly loud. And her face was quite horribly distorted. It was the greatest misfortune that the air should be so putrified by the stink of those two women even after a whole day of being bound to their stakes in the sun. They were proud and unchanging. Unwilling to change. They would cause the death of everyone in the town rather than yield their sense of their privileged selves. And their memory of the rose garden, their memory of their memory. When they were gone, no one would long remember, it would be only a tale for a cold evening, a fairy tale...

"Be quiet, my dear child. It's William. It's only William. You remember him, don't you? He's looking at you. You see his eyes looking at you?" She saw him. Or she saw something, she was reaching out to touch the globe with her hand. He reached out to pull her hand back.

"No, no, you mustn't touch the globe, you'll come between him and his sunlight." But she was too strong for him, catching him so by surprise; her hand was almost upon the globe and William's startled face was plunged into deep shadow. "No, no, please, you mustn't..." But he couldn't stay her hand, her whole body was driving her towards the globe, both her hands now were struggling with his to grasp it and her strength was like a mountain's to his own, she would crush William in an instant, the darkness he was already in was almost as great as the night.

He would have to let him go.

He released himself from the riverbank back into the room, and the globe became clear empty glass, only very faintly glowing.

"He's gone, my dear," he said. "Gone away." Her struggling stopped. Her hands in his remained tense, but still, and she seemed to have stopped breathing altogether. Then slowly, as she continued to gaze at the empty globe, both her hands and her body relaxed, and he released her and she stood quietly staring, at nothing or at her memory of William, with her nostrils only very gently flaring.

She was crying. Tears were overflowing her eyes. He couldn't remember her crying, he was sure she hadn't cried, since the day she saw the raven's mother; but she was sobbing now, her sobs were wracking her breast and throat and bursting out of her mouth, and tears were pouring down her cheeks; and still she was standing like a rooted tree in front of the clear globe, which through all her tears she couldn't surely any longer see,

"No. Please. Please don't cry." He didn't know what

220

to do. And they would hear her; everyone was waiting below for the fires round the stakes to be lit. They would hear her, and they would be sure that he was the cause of it and his authority would be further undermined. "He'll be back. I'll bring him back. It was because you would have hurt him, and I couldn't otherwise protect him. You might even have killed him. I know you didn't mean to, I know..." It was useless. Nothing would stop her sobbing. "I'll bring him back. I promise you. But you mustn't touch him." But she would touch him. She would try to touch him. And he would have to protect him by dissolving his image and she would weep and...

There was a cry from outside the window. He glanced down over his shoulder at the two stakes set up below. The gatemen had lit the brush around one of them and were just now lighting the brush round the other. Another cry passed through the gathered crowd. Oh dear. The mother was beginning to scream.

William stumbled onto the low grassy bank of the river and fell on his knees, his eyes still blinded from being battered down into the cold water by the sudden hard darkness. His head throbbed painfully as if it had been struck in many places at once. But the pain passed quickly as he knelt there, and he was aware of a wind blowing around him, and he stood up to see where he was. The cone-like mountain was there still, but it was very far off, and very black from the sinking sun throwing it into silhouette. He had better begin his way towards it at once, he thought, though he wouldn't be able to walk far before nightfall.

The wind was fitful; it rose, tore at his wet clothes, and died. The grass he was walking on wasn't green any longer, and the flowers had mostly gone to seed. There were even patches of hard bare earth. But there were houses not far off, two or three; but they looked empty. And broken, with gaping holes where their windows were, and roofs long fallen in.

He passed near one of them. Nettles were growing all round it and its walls were crumbling and rotten, and no one seemed to have been near them, within or without, for years. A broken bucket was lying by the door, and near it were the dried bones of a big bird, maybe a chicken. The weeds his feet were crushing smelled strong in the russet sun.

Some way ahead of him, just atop a rise in the land, was a group of houses, a village, silhouetted against the sky. They seemed as derelict as the farmhouses, but he lengthened his stride to reach them before the fast-sinking sun set beyond the far conical hill. It was easy to walk now, the ground was dry and caked and almost bare of any weed; but it was dusty, and the wind swirled the dust round him, so that he had to shelter his eyes.

The village seemed empty. He came into it along a narrow street, along which the last red light of the sun was streaming. The houses and shops on both sides of it were shuttered, and the shutters were mostly broken. Some were creaking and banging in the wind. He thought he saw two people at the corner of a side street, but there was nobody when he reached it, the light had fooled him. But there was somebody else, right ahead of him in the street, this time there was no mistake. He hurried after the figure, it seemed to be all in black, it was walking away from him in wind-billowed clothes. He overtook it and touched it on the shoulder.

"Please, can you tell me where I…" It was a woman. It was a nun. Her white wimple was close-fitting around her full, sun-reddened face. She smiled and the sun glinted on her gold teeth.

"She is waiting for you," she said. The wind was swelling and flapping all her garments.

"Who is…? where is she…?"

"There. Over there." She raised her arm and pointed to a tall house standing in its own grounds at the edge of the village. Its windows were all tight-shuttered.

"But who is...who is she?" he asked uncertainly, with a queer rising of fear. But she only smiiled at him more broadly, knowingly.

"Now, now," she said, and patted his arm. "None of your games. Off you go." Then, waving her fingertips, she turned away from him and was gone down a narrow lane he hadn't seen. He looked after her as she passed between low crumbling walls, to see if she was surrounded by the fine blood-red line Fenwick said surrounded all Black Melk's servants, but the light was too red around everything.

He swung round to look at the tall house; the wind seemed to swing him, he had to hold himself steady against the swirling gusts of it. Again he couldn't see if a red line surrounded the house; but anyway, he thought, if it was a trap laid by Black Melk, it would at least be a way of coming to him; for all his walking the conical hill seemed no nearer than when he had first seen it at the river.

He walked slowly towards the house through the dying light and stopped outside its gate and pulled the rusted chain of a bell on a spring. When nobody answered, he pushed the gate open and walked up the broken-flagstoned path, strewn with dead weeds and windblown rubbish to the house itself, and around it to the other side. Brown dry leaves blew out of half-dead trees and were caught in dusty cyclones and scattered, and lay still as the wind suddenly and momentarily ceased. The weathercock on the roof above him was squalling and silent by turns.

At the back of the house was a sandy yard, strangely pock-marked as if by a recent scattering shower of rain. The slanting light was deep red, but the sky overhead was now heavy with dark grey clouds. The windows on this

223

side were shuttered as well, but over his head he heard a creaking, and saw one of them opening, and a key begin to slither down against the crumbling plaster of the wall. It came to rest on the dry sand. He stooped and removed it from the hook by which it had been lowered, and walked to the door and unlocked it; it opened easily and swung back smoothly from his hand.

The hallway within was bare except for worn and torn carpets lying over the dusty black-and-white tiled floor; he walked along it to a flight of stairs, and up them to the first floor, where the wind was whining at the closed shutters, and he could hardly see for the gloom. He walked up the stairs to the second floor. It was lighter there; the shutter on the landing was half-broken. A pot of geraniums was sitting on the windowledge, dripping water down the wall. And beside the window was a half-open door. He approached it and stood in front of it a moment, waiting to see if anything would happen; and then he tapped on it with the key.

"Come in," a woman's voice said, a beautiful low voice. He pushed open the door and went into a dim room, where he couldn't see well. But he could smell the woman, her body and the perfume she had touched on her body. And he could see her sitting half in shadow by the shuttered window.

"Shut the door," she said. He shut it and stood beside it and waited, breathing the scent of her in and out.

"You found your way easily enough," she said, and she turned her head towards him from the window, and the last rays of the sun glinted on her dark hair and bloomed on her full smooth cheek.

"A nun told me..." he said.

"Oh," she said. "Did she?" With a little gurgling laugh. And she beckoned him closer with one hand, which gleamed strangely with horizontal bands, were they rings?

He approached near to her and the heavy scent of her flowed in him like a dark warm wind. The light was dying. He laid the key on a little table beside her.

"Take my hand," she said. He took it. It was warm and soft and large, and heavy with rings.

"Take them off," she said. He began slowly slipping them one by one from her fingers and laying them on a velvet tray on the table.

"And now the other," she said, lifting her other hand. The light was as little as light in deep water. The rings were like sunken rubies. He slipped them one by one from her fingers, they seemed unending, and laid them with the others on the velvet; and held her hands together to his lips and kissed them, and kissed her bare full arms, and her shoulders and her throat, and her soft, full, half-parted lips.

"You have not undressed," she murmured, and touched her lips softly again to his. He didn't understand, the smell and feel of her were too much for his brain, too much for his body. "You have undressed me, but you have not undressed yourself." Then he saw his pentangle lifted on the palm of her hand between them; even in the dusk it was glistening. He felt a cold pang of fear pass through him, but her body so close to him warmed it and blurred it. He breathed in her sweet breath.

"Will you not undress?" she asked, and the music of her voice melted his fear away. His body was throbbing now against hers. Her great deep melting eyes were asking, asking.

"Yes," he said. The feeling of his own voice in his throat made him shiver. "Yes. I will." She was smiling, in the dark she was smiling, she was smiling in the glistening of the pentangle. It melted in bright drops through her fingers and he sank down with her onto her bed.

"Ohhhhhhh!" Fenwick moaned. "He is lost. We are all lost. No, no, please my child, you mustn't approach so close." He extended his arm as a barrier between her and the globe. She leant against his arm and stretched her own arms and her head yearningly towards the globe, so dark now that nothing could be seen in it under the quivering reflection of the candleflame on the surface of the glass. But evidently she knew that William was still there in the arms of the woman, making love with the woman. Her whimpering was pathetic, poor girl, it must be very painful for her to see him so quickly and easily accepting the embraces of another. How could she understand? There was nothing which he could say or do which would console her: William was gone; without his pentangle his eyes would be dilated, he would wander aimlessly in the broken world, forgetting her and the rose garden and Black Melk's castle and everything else. He would wander lost until he died; however he might die. Maria's whimpering was becoming weeping, but at least so far it was quiet. But the night itself was so quiet they might still hear her below if any of them were still gathered around the dead fires. If only a wind would rise and carry the smell of burning out of his room. Though the mother's screaming would always be in his head, whatever the wind, whatever the weather. And the daughter's unending silence. That was all he was left with now, and Maria's weeping, when everything had seemed, at last, so wellfavoured.

What had gone wrong? What had he himself done wrong? He touched the fingers of his free hand to his throat, where the rosehip was no longer. Fallen into the darkness in a moment. How had it so easily happened, what there was now no mending?

He might still send out a dove or two, he thought, hearing their soft croodling through Maria's weeping, but would William know them, would they know him? He was

deep in Black Melk's land and Black Melk would overcome him; and then, when it suited him, he would glide
in here and take Maria. Poor dear thing, she was weeping
uncontrollably now, with her arms wrapped round his arm
and her head lolling limply against it; which was shooting
pains at bearing the weight of her, but the was nothing else
he could do. Everything had suddenly come to nothing.

William awoke and looked around him. The light was
pale grey. He moved and the bed under him creaked. He
tried to sit up, and he managed to sit up, but his muscles
cried out in pain. He could feel insects, very small, crawl-
ing over his skin under his clothes, and stings from them,
or from something, which set him scratching his body
all over. The lumpy bare mattress under him smelled of
mould. He stretched himself until the cramps in his muscles were less, and he stood up from the creaking bed and
walked slowly to the window to breathe the outside air.
He stumbled, and saved himself from falling by pressing
his hand flat into the thick dust on the top of a table by
the window.

He pushed open the shutters and looked outside. There
was a fine rain falling, and bare and broken trees, sharp
black where the rain had wet them, against grey fields and
a grey sky. He put his head out of the window and turned
his face upwards to let the rain wash it a little.

It wasn't like the rain in the forest. How had he left the
forest? And come here? Wherever he was.

He had come to a wall, he remembered that, rising out
of the bracken and brambles to the lowest branches, wet
and dripping, of the cedars. He had touched the wall. And
then? The fine rain was cool on his face, but inside his
head it was dry and hot. And his bladder was in swollen
pain; so he leaned his thighs against the wet windowsill
and pissed out of the window, smiling at the relief of his
pain and at the bright yellow arching stream, the only co-

lour in all the landscape. He watched the stream weaken and die, trailing over the windowsill as he stepped back, and over the dusty floor to his feet; and he realized, now that his bladder was easy, that his stomach was in gnawing pain, as if it was very long since he had eaten. And it was long, as he remembered: he had been days in the forest without proper food; and who knew how long he had been here in this room? The dust was thick everywhere and there was no sign in it that he could see in the poor grey light, of his own entering footsteps. It smelled as if it had been empty for years. It was even empty of all furniture except the dustladen table beside him, with only the print of his hand spread out on it, and the sagging old bedstead, and a wardrobe with its doors hanging open and all the shelves broken down. It was no place to stay, he thought, wherever it was; and he crossed to the half-open door and went out onto the landing at the head of the stairs. The window there was grey with dust and the only sign of life was a dry and cobwebbed flowerpot on the windowledge. The stairs were so broken, some of them even missing, that he wondered how he had made his way up them. Cautiously, holding to the walls and rotting bannisters, he made his way down them, down two floors to the gloom at the bottom. Ahead of him in the hallway was only deeper gloom, but from behind him some light was flowing; so he turned towards it and made his way over the rubbly and creaking floor to a doorway across which a broken door was sagging, and stooped through it; and found himself in a desolate yard, with rubbish lying everywhere, and somewhere a stink of something rotting. At the far side of the yard was a brokendown stone wall, and beyond the wall he could see the shape of a church steeple against the drab grey sky. Where there was a church there would be houses, he thought; and they would give him food, or work for food; so he made his way across the yard through the fine rain, and over the broken wall and into the flat grey fields; which looked as though they hadn't been tilled for years, the ground looked hard and baked, as if it was very long since it had last rained, the surface of the earth was so smooth that the rain made it glisten in the grey light. He walked through them for a long while, and his hunger was ever greater, gnawing at his belly like rats, before he could see the body of the church below the steeple, and the roofs and then the walls of the houses clustered round it; and he felt sure that it was a living village, even though the fields he was walking through were so dead. There were trees now, here and there, and they weren't all leafless, though their leaves were drab brown and were hanging from their branches with little life.

Just as he reached the village, he saw a bird. It was in the crotch of the tree just beside him. It was a big bird, it looked like a pigeon, and it looked as if it was somehow wedged in the crotch, with its tail towards him, unable to escape. If it was so it would be food. Stealthily he crept up on it and stretched out his hand and seized it, and wrenched it out of the tree. Its head fell limply over his wrist and maggots crawled out of it onto his hand, and the stink of it nearly made him retch. He flung it to the ground and wiped and scraped the maggots from his hand; and heard thin cackling laughter behind him.

He turned round. An old man, old and withered, was sitting on the doorstep of the nearest house as if oblivious of the fine rain. Had he been laughing? He wasn't laughing now. Nobody was laughing.

The old man looked well enough fed. Maybe he had food to give. William approached him, and was about to wish him goodday when the man, peering up at him with sharp black eyes, stretched out a begging hand and pointed with his other to his mouth. Was he dumb? He opened his mouth with his fingers and showed his rotten teeth and wagged the scarred stump of a tongue. And before William could say or do anything, he abruptly spat at him. William staggered back, and as the thick spit trickled down his legging he heard laughter again, the same laughter. He looked round sharply and saw an old woman on crutches in the middle of the street, facing his way. Both her eyes were dull white like eggs. But she knew he was there, she was beckoning to him with her fingertips, and she was still softly laughing.

As he started along the street towards her, doors of other houses opened and people came out of them; they all watched him as he passed them and their eyes were hostile. Some of them spat. From behind them children came running, they came running right up to him; and some of them spat; and some of them threw stones, and darted away. He didn't know what to do. People were moving in closer to him from both sides of the street, and most of them now had sticks in their hands and were looking at him more and more angrily, and were making noises like low growling; and the children were still throwing stones which were bruising his body, and shouting, and singing songs whose words he couldn't make out. The woman on crutches was almost hidden away from him now, he could only see her white eyes at moments between people's shoulders. They still weren't blocking the street in front of him, so he walked faster before they did; but they were moving in nearer and nearer and their growling was louder and their sticks were all raised in the air ready to strike him.

Just as he thought they were going to begin striking him, he ran. Ahead of him there was still a narrow way open, and he ran along it, and it continued open and they didn't begin to strike him. But they were spitting at him from both sides and all their faces were filled with anger and hate.

He was suddenly at the end of the village, there were no more houses. Except one. Right ahead of him, standing by itself. And the people were so close on either side of him that he couldn't run any way except towards the gate of the house, a high iron gate, which was shut. But just as he reached it, it opened; and when he had run through it it shut again behind him, and he found himself alone in a large derelict garden with bare and broken black trees; and ahead of him a shuttered old house, three storeys tall, to which the gravel path he was standing on led; and at the door of the house, half-open, a woman in maid's uniform was beckoning him urgently to hurry. He was breathing hard.

"You may be just in time," the woman said, standing aside as he reached the doorway and walked past her into the dark hall. There was a sound, from somewhere upstairs, of faintly tinkling bells. Like running water. He tried to slow and still his breathing, it seemed too hot and loud for the house.

"Don't just stand there," the maid said. Her face was thin and bony, and her body. "You must hurry. Up the stairs. Quickly. Right to the top."

He climbed the stairs, which smelled of polish and were gleaming in the dim light, past the first floor and up the second flight and onto the upper landing. Ahead of him a door was halfopen and the silvery tinkling was coming from the room beyond. He entered it. His breathing sounded louder than ever. The room was darkened with curtains against the day, but he could see a great double bed in the middle of it, and a figure, a woman, lying on the bed in her nightdress. The tinkling was coming from her.

He approached slowly, uncertainly, and stopped just at the edge of the bed, and stood there unmoving, gazing down at the woman, until his breathing was quiet and his heart was quiet and the only sound in the room was of the very faintly tinkling bells. The woman's long white hair overspread the pillow and the sheet and even trailed over the side of the bed. Her face was old and withered, the oldest face he had ever seen. Her eyes were closed and her breathing was so low that he didn't know if she was breathing at all, until she startled him by speaking.

"Kiss me," she said. He didn't see her mouth move. "Kiss me. Please kiss me." Her lips were sunken into her jaws. Her skin was dry and tight against her bones. "Kiss me." He bent low over her and kissed her where her lips should be, and the silver bells rang a sudden quivering peal, and then were silent.

"Well," a voice said flatly, the voice of the maid. She was standing in the doorway. He stood back from the bed in embarrassment and unease. "You've done it, have you? Well then, we haven't very long before the jackals hear the silence and climb over the walls. Help me remove her nightdress."

She approached the bed briskly and bent over the old woman and pulled her long noghtdress away from her feet and her legs as thin as old sticks. And William saw the bells and heard them softly tinkle; they were small and silver, and one was fastened to each of the old woman's toes. The maid removed them one by one, laying them together in a little bag of soft white fur. The sound of their tinkling grew thinner and thinner, until there was only one bell left, on her big right toe. Then that too stopped.

"They'll have heard that," the maid murmured. "It will keep them at bay for awhile." She laid the bag beside the old woman's feet. "Lift her up so I can slide off her nightdress." Uncertain and uneasy, almost afraid, William slid his hands between the nightdress and the old bony body and lifted it up, surprised at the weight of it; and the maid pulled the nightdress carelessly over the

232

dead woman's head, leaving him gazing down at her grey wrinkled body, whose flseh seemed to absorb the light around it. It was hard to keep looking at her, she seemed to be sinking into darkness inside herself, she seemed to be shrivelling inwards.

"You'll have to wash her," the maid said, rolling up the nightdress and dropping it over the head of the bed. "I haven't the time. I have my own life to think of." William nodded, gazing the while fixedly at the old woman's body. The darkness in her seemed moment by moment to be increasing. He could feel the light from the room flowing past him on both sides like water, like vapour, and flowing unendingly into the dark of her body.

"Here it is then," the mad said. He started. It seemed she had gone and returned, for she was setting a bowl of gently steaming water on the floor beside him. She was putting a pice of soft cloth into his hand. She was no longer wearing her apron and cap, and her hair was hanging in a long plait down her back. "Wash her from head to foot," she said; already she was leaving the room again. "I must go and pack my things. Don't delay. Time is very short." He listened to her heels striking sharply on the wooden stairs as she went down them, and his hand holding the cloth sank into the water in the bowl and rose out again and up the side of the bed while he watched it, and slowly approached the nearly black body on the bed, and touched it. And electricity throbbed through his whole body. His hand moved the cloth slowly over the old woman's belly and bird-like breast, and her old flesh began to shine in the light flowing round him and into her, and he could see a ladder of bright ribs inside her skin. His hand was trembling, his whole body was trembling; the cloth slipped from his grasp and over the side of her body to the bed. He continued washing her with his bare hand, dipping it into the bowl and stroking it gently over her flesh, dipping both hands and stroking her with both hands; her flesh was as soft and clear as a girl's, and glowing softly now where it was wet. He bent closer and closer to her, his eyes were filled with the pearly light of her glowing his lips were wet from her cool wet flesh he kissed her body again and again, his face following his caressing hands over her breasts her throat her glowing arms, the bones under her skin like diamonds. He laid his face against her face it was cool and gleaming, his own face slid away down her body following his gliding hands they were at full arms' stretch towards her feet, his face was resting against the cool of her groin, the water was caught there in a glistening pool his breath was ruffling it, it was casting off millions of lights like fine diamonds.

"All right. That's enough. That will do." It was the maid's voice. She was standing at the foot of the bed, looking at him with bright sharp eyes. She was dressed for traveling. Slowly he drew his arms back from the old woman's legs and raised his body from hers, pushing himself upwards with all his strength away from her, feeling his hands and arms and face and all his upper body burning and seething from the touch of her. And even as he drew back he saw her pearly flesh dim and darken and grow dull. It was grey again, grey and wrinkled and dry.

He saw his hand rising from the bowl on the floor beside him, with a few last drops glistening on its fingertips, moving back through the air towards her body.

"No," the maid said sharply. "No more. No longer. She must be wrapped now in her sheet." His hand was suspended in midair, he couldn't make it go or come. The drops at his fingertips swelled and swelled.

"No," the maid said. "No." Why was she so alarmed? He only wanted to touch, just touch. Her body and his body. The maid's hand reached out and seized his hand and wiped off the drops and let his hand go and sheltered

234

her own against her breast as if something were wrong with it, as if it were in pain, like a bird with a hurt wing.

"It's nothing," she said flatly. "What does it matter?" She turned to the tall mirror in the wardrobe door and began to fix a hat on her head. But with one hand only, the other hand. "Stitch her into her sheet. The thread is there beside the bag with the bells." He saw it, and reached out to it, tried to reach out to it, to do what she said he had to do, feeling her eyes looking steadily at him out of the mirror; but his body was hard to control. He couldn't seem to make it move as he wanted. It seemed loose and boneless.

"Keep trying," she said. Her reflection in the mirror was unmoving. "That's right," she said, her voice tense and sharp, harsh against his ears. "Watch me, keep your eyes on mine. Now move your hand. From the shoulder. Push. From the elbow. Push. Twist your wrist. Lower your arm, More. More. Open your hand. Lower your arm. Close your hand. Close it. There. Do you feel the thread? And the needle buried in it? It is sharp and bright. Take it to you." He saw his hand in the mirror, coming back to him under the maid's keen watching eyes, and he felt the bones in his body hardening and his muscles stretching and tense.

"Now draw the sheet over her. The one she's lying on. From the far side. Don't look at her. Look past her." He couldn't not look at her. He saw both his hands travel beyond her and stoop to the sheet like far birds and lift up the sheet in their closed beaks and draw it over her towards him until she was covered, until only her shape under the sheet was visible and the light stopped flowing past him and into her. As it stilled it grew dim.

"Now sew her into it," the maid said, looking at herself now not at him, seeing if her hat was sitting well and properly on her head. "Leave the end at her feet until last."

He drew the ends of the sheet together and began sewing as best he could, beginning at the corner nearest her feet and working his way up towards her head.

"Stop there," the maid said quietly, when he was halfway along; and she carried a little table from behind him over to the bedside. There were many rings on it. All kinds of rings. Beautiful rings. He was about to reach out to pick up a glowing ruby one, when her hand came between him and the table. Her hand was twisted, and red and raw as if burnt; it was the hand which had caught the waterdrops. She pulled it back to herself sharply, and pressed it as if trying to hide it against her breast; and with her other hand she picked up a ring.

"I'll hand them to you," she said. "That was always my work. They must go on her fingers. Or they'll be stolen by the jackals sneaking in here with the first failing of the light. Draw her hands out from under the sheet. The far one first." One by one she handed the rings to him, and pointed to the old fleshless finger on which he was to place each of them; until all the old woman's fingers were laden with four or five or six rings each and the table was bare.

A drop of water landed on the table, in the centre of it, splashing to its edges. Glancing up, he saw that the maid was weeping. Another tear was just falling from the end of her nose. He reached out an uncertain hand to touch her, if that would help her; but she shied away.

"Leave me, leave me," she said quickly, drawing in her breath sharply, her twisted hand enclosed by her other hand, both of them held close against her thin breast. There's nothing you can do for me. It doesn't matter. She never cared about me. She took my work, every day of my life. And she gave me nothing. And she's gone, gone forever. What am I going to do now?"

"I don't know," William said.

"They'll be here soon. I'm too old to start again from the beginning. Who will want me at my age?"

"I don't know," William said. But she wasn't listening to him, she was only talking to him. Her bright weeping eyes were fixed on the dead woman's ringed hands.

"Not one," she said. "Not even one. All my life I worked for her and not even one has come to me. It's as though I never began. Oh cover her, cover her hands and sew her in. If they come and she's uncovered, they won't leave her a thing. Sew her, please sew her, sew her in."

Gently, his own fingers tingling at the touch of her, William laid the dead woman's ringed hands back beside her dark body, and drew the edges of the sheet together again and began sewing again, to the top corner of the sheet and along the top edges, past threads of her white hair, until they were closed tightly together, and only at her feet was the sheet still open.

"Leave her now," the maid said from behind him; and there was the sudden tinkling sound of the bells. Startled, William glanced round, and saw her standing motionless by the window, gazing out at the black and broken trees; with the bag of bells cupped in her hands. Her voice was quiet and flat. "Go down to the garden and dig her grave. In the far corner under the big tree. There's room there." She shook the bag and the bells tinkled softly again. "They haven't yet dared to break into the garden. And they won't so long as they hear the bells. You'll find a spade under the stairs. It's been waiting a very long while for this day. Go now. Dig deep. I'll stand guard up here."

William made his way down the dark stairway to the ground floor and found the spade under the stairs and carried it outside and towards the far corner of the garden. It was raining steadily now, and so heavily that by the time he reached the high wall around the garden water was trickling out of his hair over his face and down his neck. He placed his foot on the edge of the spade and pressed it into the earth, which was soft and yielding, easy to dig into. Then it wasn't so easy, it was dry and hard; but he went on digging, piling up the earth in a mound. Soon he had to stand in the hole he had dug to dig it deeper, as the light failed and failed. He thought he heard the bells ringing from time to time, far and faint, but he couldn't be sure for the sound of the rain on the black trees around and on the earth and on his body and on the water already gathering in the bottom of the new grave. He kept on digging until he was as deep in the ground as his own waist and the light was a dark grey. Then he climbed up the slippery mud of the sides of the hole and laid down his spade and walked back to the house through broad puddles of shallow water. As he entered the house he heard a door somewhere close, it seemed to be the door at the other end of the hall; and as he mounted the stairs he heard a gate outside clang shut. And in the old woman's room there was only the old woman's body on the bed, the maid was gone. He walked to the bed and saw that the white fur bag in which the maid had placed the bells was again resting at the foot of the bed. But it was empty. And from within the sheet, as he touched the dead woman's legs, came the faintest tinkling of bells. The maid had evidently made her ready, and had left the rest to him.

He slid his arms under the dead woman, and lifted her up to the sudden tny pealing of the bells, and cradled her in her sheet in his arms, and carried her out of the room where the light was nearly gone and down the stairs where it was altogether gone, feeling her belled feet dangling against his thighs, so making them tremble that he had to fix his mind on each step to continue walking. And the hallway below was harder than the stairs, his legs seemed to be melting under him from the soft touches of her tinkling toes; but he reached the door, and opened it and carried her out into the heavily downpouring rain.

Ahead of him the earth was like a black stippled lake in the grey light. It was too far across it to the grave. His legs would never manage it. His knees would give way and he would sink down into the water. But he started across, and managed step after step through the water, and somehow reached the grave; and lowered the old woman's shrouded body into it, to a last wild silvery peal of bells before the water in the grave covered and silenced them; and her body in the sheet was only a twisted white shape half-sunk into the long pool of rain. He dug the spade into the soft drenched mound of earth beside him, and closed his eyes and let the earth fall in a heavy clod on her body. He shovelled in more clods, and more and more, until he was sure she was well hidden from his sight. He looked down into the grave then, and there was only wet earth and water; and he continued shovelling earth in until the earth was a mound above the earth.

He heard voices; and a sudden unreasoning trembling fear swept through him. He threw down the spade and ran to the wall, and jumped to catch the top of it and pulled himself over it, and half-fell down on the other side. He could hear more voices through the rain, growling and muttering. He picked himself up and began running away from the wall. It was almost dark and the rain was streaming down unceasingly, but he could see still darker, huddled shapes moving over the flat land from every direction towards the house. But they didn't seem to see him or they didn't care about him, all their intent was on the house. And after some while, when he stopped running at last to catch his breath, and turned round on the spot where he found himself, he couldn't see anyone or anything, he was alone on the rain-drenched plain.

He was cold. The rain pouring over him was cold, and where the old woman's body had touched him he was most cold. He began walking through water and mud and long downbeaten grass, through meadows it seemed, but long abandoned, even the walls were gone, except for loose tumbles of stone here and there. He thought there must be a moon, for there was some blurred whiteness in the sky beyond the steadily falling rain, and by its weak light he saw the shape of a house now and then; but each one when he reached it was broken open and roofless, its windows like dead staring eyes, offering no lodging or even shelter.

There was a figure ahead of him, not far ahead, which seemed to be angling across his path, and which seemed from its size and way of walking to be a woman. She might be able to help him, he thought, she must at least know where she was, and where he could soonest find food and shelter. She was walking quickly and away from him, if he didn't hurry he would lose her in the dark. He began to run, splashing sheets of muddy water at every footfall, and she heard him for she turned her head toward him, and began to run herself.

"No, no. Wait!" he called after her. But she continued running away. He ran after her faster, and came to the cobbled road on which she was running, and ran faster still, and soon overtook her.

"Please," he said, panting. "I only want..." She turned round sharply and he saw that it was the old woman's maid. Her long red hair was wet and matted against her bony face and shoulders, and her black eyes were full of apprehension. She didn't seem to know him.

"I buried her. They didn't come before..."

"What do you want? Leave me alone," she said, almost in a scream, backing away from him.

"Don't you remember? You told me to..."

"Get away, get away. You killed her and now you want to kill me."

240

"No, no, I only want… Please, I only…" He stretched out his hand towards her, gently, and moved a little nearer to her. Something glinted in her clenched hand.

"Keep back," she hissed. "Or…" It was a needle, a long needle, the needle he had used to sew the old woman into her sheet. Before he could move back she had struck him with it in the middle of his chest. Once, twice, three times.

"There. That'll teach you," she said. "One for each of us." And she was running away again through the rain. He stood where he was, watching her go until he couldn't see her or hear her, until there was only the unending rain. The three places where she had struck him were burning like fire, his whole body was burning like fiery coals from his wounds, and the rain falling all around him couldn't reach him, he couldn't feel it, he seemed to be walking through falling fire. He felt up his burning body with his burning arms, towards the wounds in his chest. His shirt was torn open, he must have torn it open. It was soft as if it was wet but it was dry to his burning hands. He felt over his burning chest with his hands, there was a mound in the middle of it where the wounds were; he screamed before he knew he had touched one of them, and balls of flaming light burst in his eyes and he didn't know anymore if he was walking or…

He was walking. And the rain was still pouring down around him, but not on him. His body throbbed with the fire of his wounds as he walked and walked along the straight cobbled road and nothing changed.

Then, straight ahead of him, he saw what he thought was a shaft of sunlight, and he stopped in his tracks. It was gone. Probably it was only lightning. It was there again, in nearly the same place, it was sunlight. And another shaft near it, and another, finer, falling to the ground from as high in the sky as he could see. He began to walk again,

241

faster. There were more shafts of sunlight and they were nearer. And there were trees among them rising tall and straight from the ground, more and more trees the nearer he came and more and finer beams of glistening sunlight. His wounds burned his body almost to searing with every stride he took, but he drove himself on; if it was the forest again, if he had found it again everything would be all right, the rain would fall on him again and his wounds would heal in time and he would find his way; and he would find her. He was nearly among the trees, and wherever the sunlight glided down among them to the earth there were still golden pools; he drove his burning body faster and faster through the pouring rain, splashing and stumbling and nearly falling again and again.

He could hear the waves of the ocean, they were breaking like a bell tolling on the shore, it must be just beyond the trees if he could make his way through the trees he would be back on the sand at the edge of the ocean it couldn't be far the tolling of the waves was heavy and deep in his ears he would throw his burning body into them and they would cool him the ocean would cool him.

One of the rays of light touched his body, and the sudden tearing pain of it made him scream and wrap his arms over his burning chest, which made the pain worse the throbbing arrowheads of his wounds drove fire into the depths of his body so great and painful he couldn't stop screaming. He stumbled to his knees. The great trees were close around him now, but the rain was as heavy as ever, and the sunlight was in mere threads trailing down to the ground. He watched them warily.

She was in the trees, in the threading light in the trees. She was full of child and she was going away. He tried to call her but he couldn't there was no voice in his throat. She was further away and it was so dark he could see her only when she passed through the fine threads of light, if he didn't go after her he would lose her again. He forced himself to his feet and stumbled after her, fearful of the weaving threads of light, watching them to avoid them. He lost sight of her, then he saw her again not so far away; but the threads of light were too many and too close to him and his fear of them made him stop, and she was gone again. Then he saw her again, nearer still, but she was still going away and looking away, she was so round and heavy with their child it was a wonder she could walk so easily, why wouldn't she look at him why was she always going away?

He was nearly to her. She was moving but she didn't seem to be moving away; he was nearer and nearer, the threads of light were trailing down all around them but not between them, he opened his burning arms and stretched them out to her, and around her, and drew her gently in to him. She was calling out she didn't know him, in the dark she couldn't see him, he pulled her in against his body. The rain was pouring down heavier than ever and all the threads of light were gone the rain was blotting them out he held her body close against his own, she was whimpering and moaning but she was wet and cool, and the burning in his wounds was beginning to die.

Why was she so bony? He peered down at her in the neardark. Her hair was grey. Her face was thin and grey. It wasn't her face, or her body, it was another woman, a stranger, thin and old, with eyes expressionless from fear.

No, not from fear. From death. Her head toppled over against his arm and her body sagged against his body. She was cool and wet, he wrapped her closer to him to ease his burning, to feel the rain landing on her. But the rain seemed to be melting her, her body was melting away to nothing inside her clothes.

She was gone. He let his arms loose and her clothes fell to the ground in a little heap.

The forest was gone; around him were only a few black and broken trees. And his wounds were flaring up again in his chest, and the rain wouldn't touch them or any part of him.

He saw her again. She was rising through the rain, something was lifting her up, only a little way from him. And he could hear the ocean, its waves breaking, it wasn't far. He stumbled through puddles and over stones towards her, over sand, hard sand, he could hear its fine crunching under his fiery feet. She was sinking down again in the rain, she was gone. No, she was rising up, she was rising higher and higher into the darkness. She was riding on the ocean. She was sinking down on the wave, on the far side of the wave, it was lifting her again, her bright red hair was floating round her head the wave was curling at its crest under her little boat and her arms were enclosing her fullness, she was sliding down the far side of the wave. It was breaking, the high foaming lip was swelling ever larger, it was about to break over him. He stumbled back over the sand as fast as he could and reached out for a bleached halfburied tree and held to it fast in the dark as the wave poured down in solid water over his head. It would cool him, in a moment it would cool him, surely it would cool him... What was that screaming?

It was a girl, a thin girl, whose shoulder his hand was tightly clutching. He willed his hand to let go of her and watched it let go. Slowly, like a shell opening. And her screaming stopped. There was no ocean, no waves; nor her on the waves, she was gone, long gone, gone forever. There was only the rain and the dark, and the thin frightened girl, her black eyes big in her little white face, fearfully watching him. He bent down and picked her up from the mud where it seemed he had pushed her, and gently wrapped her in his arms against his burning chest. She let him, she lay limply in his arms, how cool she was against his body he could feel her wetness flowing over his wounds, the whole cool length of her body against his own. He rested his lips against her wet white throat and trailed his tongue over its silvery smoothness, her black eyes now were soft and melting. The warm water flowing between them was gathering at his swelling groin.

Her heart was beating slower, and slower. It stopped, and he could feel her still body melting away inside her clothes, until his arms were wrapped only round the rain, and himself. He opened them and let her clothes fall to the ground.

The wound in his chest burned fresh fire, and all down the middle of his belly he could feel a line of searing flame. He tore the rest of his shirt open and saw that his wound had burst and was oozing thick blood from its centre down its chest and belly. He touched the blood with his fingers and it seared them as it was searing his belly. His wound was bubbling and overflowing, burning him from his throat to his groin; the flesh of his belly was erupting in pustules and his groin was burning so fiercely that he could barely walk; but he couldn't stand still. He staggered through the rain over the muddy ground, clenching his teeth with all his strength to keep himself from screaming; his legs would hardly move, they were burning from his blood flowing down them, but he forced them on and on through the dark; if only he could find another living body to cool him for a moment only for a moment...

His outstretched hand touched a wall. He rested both hands flat against it, leaned against it for its wetness and its coolness, pressed himself against it. And in front of his eyes it opened, and a woman's face looked out. A small neat face, with eyes as dark as the dark. He stretched his own face towards it.

"Just let me kiss you." His lips would hardly move to say it. His throat was a crackling whisper in his ears.

"Just rest my lips on you. Just touch you. Please, please."
She backed away from the window, shaking her head, and
pointed silently to his right. And the window closed. And
there was no sign of it in the wall.

But off to the right he heard a door open, and he stumbled towards the sound through the rain, guiding himself
by the wall; fearful that he would stumble away and lose
himself, the wall seemed his only hope, and the woman
beyond the wall. She was standing in the open doorway,
beckoning him in. He reached out a hesitant hand to touch
her arm, to draw her against his burning body.

"No," she said, in a little voice, a girl's voice. "Not me.
My mistress is waiting." She turned and led him along the
dark hallway and opened a door at the foot of the stairway,
into a large room full of candlelight.

A woman was lying on the floor, on a thick rug, in a
glowing green dress. She was looking at him with clear
green eyes and her arms were outspread in welcome. The
door behind him closed. He walked towards her over the
thick soft rug and stood over her a moment, all his oozing
wounds like fiery spikes in his flesh. She wasn't wet from
the rain, how would she cool him? But she was smiling,
beckoning. He sank onto his knees, his body screaming
with pain, and pitched forward against her, and her body
was soft and cool, as cool as water against his burning
flesh. He wrapped his arms round her and held her close
and all his burning throbbed against her and swelled in
his groin he pressed harder and harder against her cool
sweet-smelling softness. She yielded and yielded and he
pressed ever harder, ever fearful that she would vanish
like the others but she was still close against him and he
forced himself deeper and deeper inside her, and his burning pain died down as he lay on her limply breathing the
scent of her damp throat.

A drop of water fell onto her bare breast and trickled

over her shoulder onto the rug. Where had it come from?

"From the ceiling," she murmured, her voice very low; she was lying with her arms and legs outspread, gazing at him with empty green eyes. "The rain hasn't ceased. Would you like to eat?"

"I don't know," he said. "I think so. It's long since I've eaten." All his wounds, on his chest and arms, and all over his belly and his groin and his thighs, were oozing. And burning again, he could feel them burning, but in the distance, like fires far off in the night. Fine trails of blood over his skin were breaking it here and there, and even as he looked down at himself new wounds were opening. She was ringing a silver bell.

"Food for him," she said when the door opened and the little maid appeared in it. He leaned forward and kissed her throat, and licked with his tongue where it moved as she spoke and swallowed. His wounds were burning nearer. He lifted himself up a little and laid himself down on her silky yielding body and felt it quivering against every one of his wounds which burned hotter and hotter but the pain was pleasure he could feel them oozing against her silkiness, hot fires against her watercool flesh, he pressed his fiery groin against hers and into hers deep deep inside her all his fire burning in the watery coolness within her, until he melted and flowed and lost all sense of his own shape; and slipped away from her and rolled over on his back on the soft rug.

She was looking down at him with her great green eyes.

"Here is your food," she said. A dish piled high with fruit was lying beside him, The maid had come and gone. "Eat," she said, taking a pear and touching it to his lips. The smell was almost more than he could bear; he bit into it and felt the flesh melt in his mouth and the juice trickle down his cheeks, she was licking at the juice as it trailed

247

from the corner of his mouth, her bright hair was trailing over his face her body was settling softly over his body she was pressing the pear still against his mouth its juice was flowing in a river down his throat her tongue was in the juice in his throat his wounds were pushing and throbbing against her body he was forcing his way upwards between her slippery thighs pushing his way into her she was rising and sinking over him sliding and slipping on the hot oozing of his wounds her face sliding against his and licking the sweet juice of the pear he burst inside her all water and fire; slowly she slid away from his body like a loose flowing stream.

Her fingers were gliding softly over his belly, caressing his wounds. The more she caressed them the more the fire in them gathered deeper into his groin swelling it again to throbbing hardness she was licking each of his wounds with her silver tongue the great wound in his chest burned like a furnace under her licking all his wounds were burning driving fiery pain deeper into his body his groin was throbbing with pain and fire her soft lips were kissing all round it and her body was sliding over his body again he was buried under her and breathing with her breathing his tongue in her mouth and all his body throbbing with her body he throbbed and throbbed inside her and his great wound overflowed between her breasts his searing blood was flowing over her bright silvery skin.

But the rain was falling on her and washing it away, it was splashing all over her body her hair was in wet dark-red dripping ringlets. The maid, bent and grey, was standing in the doorway. She was gone. The door was closed.

The rain was splashing all round them on the thick wet rug. She was holding his head in both her hands she was drawing his head to her groin his burning body was sliding over her body he was lying over her with his face against her sweet groin his tongue was sliding into her his wounds were flooding hot blood over her he was sliding and slipping on top of her body he was pressing deeper and deeper into her throat she was flowing out into his hot mouth his tongue was licking over her bright bloodstained belly his mouth was filling with his own blood and soft rainwater he nuzzled against her bloody breasts and her throat kissing and licking her already rainwashed skin his blood flowed in the rain his hot tongue touched her tongue and pushed deep into her mouth his body was slipping on top of her body on hot blood and cool water he was burning hard against her pushing deeper and deeper into her his wounds were throbbing blood against her silvery softness. He burst inside her, throbbing and throbbing all he could feel was her unending cool body.

She wasn't moving. He held her close against him, kissing her throat her eyes her lips, but her eyes and her lips were softly closed, taking his kissing not giving. In sudden fear he laid his hand on her wet body below her breast; but her heart was beating, she wasn't dead. Rain was splashing all over her body, washing away the blood from his wounds; which was still oozing out of his body onto hers, trickling from his groin onto hers, there was a pool of blood there where he sheltered her body from the rain. She opened her great green eyes and gazed blankly up into the rain. He bent forward, uncertainly, to kiss them.

"No," she said, her lips barely parting. His blood was splashing afresh on her breasts and belly. "Lift me." She was stretching her arms up towards him. He wrapped his around her and carefully and gently lifted her up until he was standing with her cradled in his arms. His wounds were still staining her with his blood.

"It doesn't matter," she said, her lips very slightly smiling. The rain was pouring through the ceiling onto them. "Take me outside."

He carried her across the room, his feet squelching in the drenched rug, kissing her gently as he went, fearful of what was to happen. As he pulled open the door it fell off its hinges and toppled over onto the floor. Beyond it in the hall the maid's body was lying, in a pool of water at the foot of the stairway, bloated with water; and a dead pigeon was lying beside her face, its limp head against her old nose. He stepped over them and walked along the hallway through the rain to the open front door, and carried her outside, holding her as tightly as he dared, kissing her cheek and her forehead and her long wet red ringlets, his fear growing every moment greater.

She wanted to be carried further, onto the open ground which was ankle deep in water and stippled by the downpouring rain. She was smiling and her green eyes were full of dark rainlight.

"No," he said. "No. Please." But he kept walking, carrying her over the water; and saw her lips and her cheeks, and her breasts, grow brighter and clearer, more and more like water themselves; and her whole body grew lighter and lighter in his arms... "No. No!" The rain was glistening within her body as well as without. "Don't leave me. Please don't leave me. What will I do without you? What will I do alone? How will I live? Oh please don't leave me." She was gone. He was holding nothing, his arms were envelopping rain. He wrapped them round his own bare body.

The rain was falling so heavily that he could barely see. He let his arms slide loosely down his sides and began to walk numbly in the direction he was facing, splashing his way through the shallow water. It didn't matter which way it was, all ways were the same.

He walked on and on and on. Nothing changed. The rain poured down around him. There were no people or houses or walls or trees. Sometimes there was a rock, and he thought he might sit and rest; but he didn't, he kept on walking.

It was a long while and he was very tired before he realized that although his wounds were still oozing blood, the fire within them had died. And then, a moment afterwards, he saw a flickering of light ahead of him, and the big wound in his chest quivered suddenly with fire, throwing out sharp needles of pain. The light died away and the pain died, and he continued his slow shuffling through the shallow water and the dark grey light. Then he saw the sparkling light again. It seemed nearer, but wasn't just where he was looking, but danced at the corners of his eyes. And all his wounds, big and small, throbbed with a fiery needle pain, and his blood streamed out of them down his chest and arms and belly and legs.

The light was more and more, but he couldn't see where it was coming from. It was sparkling and flashing everywhere in the midst of the rain; and with every flash his wounds throbbed fiercely and he could barely keep himself from sudden screaming. Blood was now pulsing thickly out of the wound in the middle of his chest and the fire in all his wounds was increasing moment by moment. The light was increasing too, it was dancing about him, circling round him, now near the ground now over his head, he weaved and ducked to avoid it as it appeared to be darting and diving at him, his whole body now was aflame with pain and streaming fiery blood, the light was everywhere at once now the raindrops were glittering with it he couldn't be sure he was walking forwards he seemed to be staggering backwards he seemed to be turning round and round the light was spinning round and round he could barely breathe for the searing pain in his body.

He fell to his knees and water sprayed up around him in rainbow fans; and his knees and his legs felt some far coolness filtering into them from the water. He fell forward on his chest, outspreading his arms to the water, feeling it ripple round his body, far off from the searing fire inside him, but slowly flowing nearer. He treid to force himself deeper into the water to make it cover his whole body he could still feel the light burning against his back; he pressed his wounds against the soft drenched earth and felt the cool of it very slowly filtering into him. But the light was more and more brilliant, it was flashing on and through the water against his closed eyelids, it was burning deep into his head and back it was flaring against his wounds right through his body they were bursting again in explosions of searing pain he couldn't bear it any longer it was more than anybody could bear...

Something had happened. The light was gone. He lay unmoving, alert for its return, feeling the pain of his wounds slowly subside; and then, when there had been no light for what seemed a long while, he cautiously opened his eyes. One of them was underwater; the other was in the air, in darkness, cool darkness. Very cautiously and slowly, afraid the light might burst again out of the dark at any moment, he turned himself over on his back.

A big man was standing over him, his legs spread wide apart and his arms raised round his head. Around his body light was still flickering, but his shadow was as dark as night, no light crept into it. And suddenly, before he could make out what was happening to him, William was gathered up like a child into the man's arms and sheltered there against his big body from the light; and was being carried over the watery ground; and the light even beyond the man's body was growing dimmer and dimmer, it was now only the faintest sparkling.

There was a wagon, and the man was laying him gently down in the back of it, on what felt and smelt like mounds of wet hay, and left him there. The rain seemed less, but it was still splashing on his bare body, washing off the mud

252

and blood. He saw with a pang of fear and quiverings of pain that there was a flickering light still above him; but it didn't touch him, it was held away from him by two rows of trees whose branches were tightly interlaced overhead. The man was climbing up into the front of the wagon and the wagon was beginning to move it must be pulled by a horse, or two horses he thought he could hear two. He lay limply on the hay, feeling suddenly very weak and weary, letting himself be jostled about by the steady bouncing of the wagon. The further they went the weaker he felt, his body was loose and his mind bounced about with it on the soggy hay. The intertwined branches overhead went on and on. He slept or thought he slept and woke and the branches and the bouncing were the same. But there was no flickering light beyond the branches, or anywhere, there was only the grey gloom and the steady light rain.

There was a thump on the hay beside him and the wagon stopped. He lifted his head to see where the man was, and saw him beside him on the hay, his head upside down by his own head, his dead eyes open and staring up at his own. He could see the black lacings of the branches reflected in them; and then he saw his own face reflected, white and distorted, and his own eyes staring at himself, and he gathered just enough strength to lift his hand to the other man's face and close his eyes. Then he lay for what seemed a very long while on the mouldy straw in the unchanging grey light, waiting for his strength to grow. It seemed he slept, for he was wandering and stumbling and then he was lying again on the hay, and again wandering and again lying on the hay. At last he felt that his strength was enough, and he pushed himself up until he was sitting, and slid off the end of the wagon and stood up. The dead man was lying on the hay like a big scarecrow. He walked along the side of the wagon nearest to where he was lying, and reached over the side of it and gently and hesitantly poked his chest. It was soft. And his clothes were rotten, his fingers went right through them; and there wasn't any body in them, he felt all over the clothes with his hands, they seemed to be stuffed with rags. And the head was a cloth bag full of straw, the cloth was broken and rotting, the man was a scarecrow. Bending over the side of the wagon he lifted him up, holding him as tenderly as he had himself been held, and carried him down the side of the road and between the trunks of the interlacing trees and across the waterlogged land until he came to where a pile of rocks rose above the raindappled water. He laid him one its surface and he floated; but little by little, as he laid the rocks on him, he sank. He couldn't bring himself to lay a rock on his face, but the water was deep enough to cover it. Wisps of straw drifted away over the surface.

He walked back to the wagon and unhitched the horses and led them to the rear of it and pulled the old hay near them so they could eat it if they wanted. they were very thin, just skin and bones. He left them, and walked along the road the way the man had been driving him, under the interlacing black trees. He was weary to death and wondered when his legs would give way under him and thought he would keep walking for as long as they held.

The trees came to an end and the rain poured down heavily again, drenching his bare body. Cold rain. He walked through it steadily, following the road between flooded fields stretching away to either side of him like unending grey lakes. When the road came to an end he walked across the land itself, through water up to his knees, hardly able to keep moving for weariness; but still his legs didn't give way.

He saw to his left what looked like dry land, land higher than where he was walking, and turned his steps to push his way through the water to reach it. He climbed up on it and saw that it was only a mound in the middle of the unending water; but there was a kind of lean-to on it, half-rotted away, where he could rest he thought, and his legs suddenly gave way under him and he fell to the ground. With the last of his strength he dragged himself into the shelter of the little overhanging roof and curled himself into a ball for warmth.

Light was flowing around him and over him. It was soothing, soft light. He rolled over and stretched himself. The light was flowing out of a doorway some way off, and in the doorway was a figure in silhouette from the light flowing around it; a small figure, like a child, which he seemed to be beckoning him to go towards it. He arched his back and raised himself from the soft grass where he was lying, lifting himself through layer after layer of soothing light...

"Good morning." He opened his eyes. There was a smell of burning leaves, and something palely smoking swinging back and forth in front of him. Beyond it the pale grey water spread away and away, just as when he had lain down to sleep, but it was as smooth now as glass, reflecting the pale grey sky. He couldn't even make out where they met. The rain had altogether ceased.

"Good morning." It was a woman's voice, as soft as a whisper. An old woman's voice. He suddenly remembered he was naked, and sat up and covered his groin with his hands. He couldn't see her well, she was in silhouette against the water and the sky, but he could see that she was holding out a hand to him; so he gave her his, still covering his groin with the other, and let her help him to his feet; and saw her face then, it was old and lined, very old, and came up only to his chest; but there was strength and her hand and arm. Her eyes were like pale honey, enwebbed in fine lines, and her old lined lips were very faintly smiling. She was wearing a long pale grey robe, and around her waist a very fine gold chain.

"There's no need," she said, nodding to his hand on his groin; but he couldn't bring himself to lift it away. Shaking her head a little and smiling still...so that he suddenly wanted to stoop and kiss her forehead or her old cheek, or her badly plaited pale-reddish grey hair, but didn't dare... she took his hand again and led him through a doorway he hadn't seen when he lay down to sleep, swinging in front of her a little smoking saucer.

It was dark within the doorway, and smelled of burnt candlewax. She led him along a hallway and stopped at the end of it and opened another door, and light poured in over her. She drew him through the door and let go of his hand, and closed the door behind them.

"Here we are," she said. It was a large courtyard, paved with broad flagstones. Overhead the sky was the palest grey, with light enough in it to cast a pale shadow of her as she shuffled slowly across the courtyard in her old slippers to a wellhead in the middle of it. Around the walls were beds of vegetables and flowers, and against the walls trees were trained, fruit-bearing trees, they were even now bearing fruit. Pear trees they were, and apricots. The old woman had lifted the lid from the well and was lowering the bucket into it.

"Here, I'll do that," he said, and felt immediately that his voice was loud and harsh. She was loking at him, and he realized that he had uncovered himself in starting towards her, and that he would have to uncover himself again to draw the water.

"No, no," she said, like a whisper of air. "It's my own work." She threw in the bucket and drew it up hand over hand, and seemed to draw it easily; and there were little flutterings of light, like butterflies, all around her. She lifted out the bucket and carried it away towards a deep wooden bath under the only freestanding tree in the courtyard, a young tree with smooth grey bark and round green

256

fruit: a walnut tree. As she poured the water into the bath light danced up and down her grey robe and glittered over everything near. She brought the bucket back to the well and lowered it again. He came closer to the well himself, to see the water better; as she pulled up the bucket he saw brighter and brighter reflections of light dancing on her hands and face, and the surface of the bucket itself, when it reached the top of the well, was almost too bright to look at. And it wasn't from sunlight, the sun was still half-lost in the high hazy cloud. He backed off a little, a little fearful.

"No, no," she whispered. "Don't be afraid. It's only because he is passing through it."

"Who is?"

"Who? Oh, I don't know that. But it's been like this for some while now. And it's all the same water, isn't it? Wherever it is. So if he's passing through it somewhere, it must shine everywhere. Mustn't it? The sun shines every-where, doesn't it?"

"Except where there are clouds," he said. There seemed to be clouds forming overhead now. Low clouds which all looked alike, all smoothly round, he'd never seen such strange...

"Then the clouds shine," she said softly, lifting the bucket from the mouth of the well. "Inside." The clouds were shining now, they were like glistening circles filling the whole of the sky, like rain that wasn't falling...

They were gone; as if a wind had blown through them, scattering them like bubbles. There no clouds of any kind now, only a soft and gentle sunlight.

The lid was on the wellhead. He looked about him for the old woman and saw her sitting on the ground beside the bath and a full bucket of water, with her hands in her lap; and she was wearing a white apron. When had she put on an apron? She was looking at him and gently nodding, and smiling, her whole head glowing from the sunlight and the light in the water in the bath beside her.

"The sky was weeping," she said softly. "I saw it once before. Only once. You will see…" He realized that his arms were both hanging loosely at his sides and that he was uncovered. He laid both his hands at once over his groin.

"There's no need to protect your body from me," she said. Her golden eyes were glistening with the light. "Or me from your body. I am very old. And you are very beautiful. Come and bathe yourself."

"I only meant not…" he said embarrassedly, moving towards the bath, letting one hand fall free of his groin.

"No need," she murmured. He let the other hand fall free. She lifted herself to her feet and smoothed down her apron. There was a light fresh air by the bath. She was looking up at him, watching him, and her old face was gently smiling.

"That's the scent of the walnut tree," she said. "Isn't it beautiful? I always take my own bath under it because it smells so fresh and sweet. And I burn a few of its dry leaves in a dish morning and evening, I walk about with them so that everything can smell them. I even go right outside with them, that's how I found you. Oh, I'm sorry," she said, and her fingertips touched his arm very lightly, and she looked suddenly as shy as a girl. "Here I am talking and talking, and you must be wanting to take your bath. And I'm sure you must be hungry. I've been alone so long, you see." And before William could think what to say she had turned away and was shuffling across the courtyard, her faded grey hair shining in the sunlight. He watched her to the far side of the courtyard, where a black pot was hanging over a low fire. He watched her stir what was in the pot, and then sit down on the stones beside it.

Beside him the water in the bath was still faintly rip-

258

pling, and the light from it was rippling up his body. Hesitantly, feeling too dirty and clumsy for the bright water, he lifted one foot and slowly lowered it into it. It was very cold. But then it wasn't cold, it was like cool silk against his skin. He stepped in with his other foot and lowered himself down into the water, blinking against its dazzling which seemed to be making his very body bright. Suddenly he remembered his wounds, and searched for them on his chest and arms and belly and groin and thighs; only the first great triple one was still apparent through the glowing of his skin; and even as he looked at it, and the water trickled over it, it faded away.

The old woman was carrying a small table to the wellhead and setting it down beside it. She was laying it with bowls and spoons. He found the soap at the base of the tree and soaped himself from head to toe, and poured over himself the full bucket of water she had left beside the bath. It was like a waterfall of silky light. He stood in the bath, still holding the empty bucket, and for a little while he couldn't seem to see. Then, through the smell of the drifting woodsmoke, he breathed in the aroma of the food she was preparing, and his stomach rumbled.

"Are you ready to eat?"

She was standing beside the bath, looking up at him. Her honey-coloured eyes were full of dancing lights from the water still tingling on his body. He nodded, and smiled uncertainly she seemed so full of light; and suddenly bent down to her and kissed her old cheek. Her face creased into a radiant smile.

"It's only soup," she said, in a voice so low he could barely hear her. "Perhaps it won't be enough."

"It will be. I know it will be," he said, hardly knowing what he was saying, unable to take his eyes from her shining old face, just able not to bend and kiss her again, and enfold her in his arms.

"That's good then," she said, turning from him and shuffling back towards the fire. It was like light turning from him.

"What do I do about the water?" he asked, only wanting her to turn round to him again.

"Pour it out where it is," she said, without turning round, still shuffling away. "It will flow among the plants and water them."

He stepped out of the bath onto the smooth stones, and tipped all the water over them, and watched it flow like melted sunlight over them and along shallow runnels in the beds where her vegetables and flowers were growing, flowing along ever narrower runnels until it had soaked everywhere into the earth.

She was waiting for him. She was by the little table, holding the fire-blackened pot in one hand and motioning him with the other to one of the two little benches set at the table. He went and sat down where she wanted, and she served out the thick steaming soup with a big wooden ladle, much in the bowl in front of him, little in the other bowl. She set the pot down on the stones beside them, and before he knew it he was spooning his food greedily into his mouth, and then before he knew it the bowl in front of him was empty. He looked across the table at her, embarrassed. Her soup was still untouched, and she was looking back at him with steady eyes. She glanced down at the pot beside her, and again at him, her glowing old eyes questioning. He nodded, and gave her his bowl as she reached out for it. She filled it again to the brim and gave it back to him. This time he could taste the soup, lentil soup all thick and brown, but again he had hardly begun before he had finished. He laid his spoon beside his bowl and sat quietly with his head down.

"Don't you want any more?" she asked gently. He shook his head. But when he lifted his eyes to look at her, hers were looking unwaveringly at him and her expression was troubled. He nodded his head and gave her his bowl with both hands, and she smiled. He ate the third bowl slowly, and when he had finished it he had eaten enough. He laid the spoon beside the bowl and sat still and silent.

"Do you want any more?" she asked. He shook his head, and her face was untroubled; she laid her spoon beside her own empty bowl and laid her hands in her lap. The air was still and the sunlight was gentle and warm and all the flagstones were pale yellow, and he didn't want to move.

"Is it later?" he asked. She was sitting opposite him still, with her hands folded in her lap, but the pot was gone from beside the table and the table itself was bare. And the light seemed still gentler, and the flagstones more golden yellow.

"Yes," she said.

"Is it later again?" he asked.

"Yes," she said. Her eyes and the courtyard were the same violet gold. The sun seemed to have set. Slowly she stood up, smoothing down her grey robe.

"I don't want to go anywhere else," he said. "I want to stay here," She smiled.

"I'll prepare your bed," she said.

He felt her touch him on the shoulder and looked round. It was nearly dark. There was a smell in the air like the smell of the morning, of burning leaves. The little saucer was swinging beside him on its chain, billowing pale smoke.

"Breathe it," she said. "It will give you peaceful sleep." He breathed it in deeply.

"Come," she said. "Your bed is ready." He stood up and followed her along a path through her garden. Against the far wall was a little narrow bed.

"There," she said.

"But... It's yours. Isn't it yours?"

"I will sleep on the ground," she said. By the tree. I am old, it doesn't matter about me. But you must be strong tomorrow." She leaned forward and kissed him in the middle of his chest, just where his wound had been. "Now sleep," she said, and turned and shuffled back along the path to the middle of the courtyard. He lay down on the narrow bed and gazed up at the stars in the clear night sky.

She was standing beside him, just at his head. He couldn't make out if it was light or dark. There was a pale dancing light gliding and flickering over her body and over the ground near the bed, and like pale silver on the undersides of the leaves and fruit of the trees; he saw then that she was carrying a bucket of water.

"Are you awake then?" she asked in a whisper. "I'm just watering. I'll soon be done. It will soon be morning."

She poured the bright water slowly and carefully around the roots of a pear tree trained against the wall beside the bed, and went back to the well to draw up more water. Her face and upper body were like bright moonlight as she drew it.

The light in the courtyard was pale and even, and the darkness had faded from the sky. She was standing by the well and she was beckoning to him. He got up from her bed and walked to her.

"We must go before sunrise," she said. Already the sky overhead was pale blue with morning.

"Go where?" he asked. She smiled, and took his hand in hers and drew him after her across the courtyard to a small door beside her cooking fire. She opened it and he followed her through it, stooping not to strike his head.

Beyond it was only darkness, but she seemed to know her way through it by heart for she drew him unfalteringly forward. The further they went the more light there was in the darkness, soft and pale and apparently from somewhere ahead of them. And he could see that they were passing between what appeared to be pillars, a row on each side of them. Then, with the light ever stronger, he saw rows beyond the near rows, and rows beyond them. And they weren't pillars, they were the straight trunks of trees; and their branches, he could see now, were all in leaf and bearing round green fruit.

"Walnuts," she whispered. "They're all walnut trees. Mine comes from here."

The light was strangely peaceful, like the light in her courtyard, like the light which poured up from her well; and every step which he took nearer to its source, which seemed still a long way ahead of them, made him feel strangely stronger. It flowed over him, through the green of the trees, like a kind of blessed water.

"We're near now," she said, her low voice like a ripple in the green light. "We're really quite near."

Suddenly a sharp flash of light made him blink; it struck the trunk of a tree beside him, lighting it fleetingly to incandescence, and glanced away among the endless rows of trees. Uneasily he looked to her for guidance, but she was looking straight ahead in the direction of the flowing light. Another fleeting flash shot past him like an arrow, and another and another. They struck against trees all about them, and exploded in white dazzling. He became more and more uneasy. But she was quietly walking ahead of him, it was almost as if she didn't see the flashes.

"You'll see it in a moment," she said. "In just a moment now. It's been waiting for you a very long time." She was still drawing him forward over the soft earth between the closer and closer trees; he couldn't stop himself being drawn, but his arm was tense, his whole body was tense, and with every burst around him of the white light it was tenser.

A flash struck him on the forehead with the force of a hammer, and the whole forest was spinning in light and spurting fire.

He was lying at full length on the ground. She was bent over him, looking down at him, and her eyes were full of confusion.

"Oh dear, oh dear," she said. "Oh dear." What was wrong, what had gone wrong? Over her head the arrows of light were flashing past in their hundreds and the heads of the trees were bursting into briliant white light, and when the light left them they were pale grey.

"Can you stand?" she asked. Why were her eyes so troubled and sad? He couldn't seem to speak to answer her, he couldn't seem to make his mouth move; but with the help of her slowly pulling arm he was able to rise to his feet.

"Stoop," she said, pulling down on his arm. Keep your head as low as mine and look at the ground and you'll be all right. Oh, I'm sorry." Tears were trickling out of her eyes now and down her old cheeks, what had he done to make her weep, he couldn't bear to see her weep. She turned her head away from him and pulled him slowly after her through the brightening and brightening greenish light, as the flashing white light burst and burst and burst just over their heads. Soundlessly. there was no sound at all.

"Stop," she whispered urgently, her hand tightening on his. "There it is. You can look, but keep down." Ahead of them, not far ahead, was a gigantic black tree stump; and from the top of it the myriad white spears of light were flashing. And they were darting in the honey green of her eyes as she looked at him. Her tears seemed to have dried, but her face looked all sorrow.

"What have I…?" he began, but couldn't go on. She gently shook her head.

"It's not your fault," she murmured. "I misunderstood. I brought you to take your… But it wasn't you. It isn't you. It's because I've been so long alone." She smiled faintly and her tears began again to overflow her eyes.

"Please," he said. "Please don't…" She turned half away from him towards the great black stump.

"He will come," she said softly in the bright flashing silence. "He will come one day. And it will be there, waiting for him."

"What will?" His voice was like a soft raven's croak.

"The ring. His earring, resting there on the top of the stump. That's what's making the bright lights. It didn't at first, not when I first saw it. It was only like a glowing then, in a little circle around it, so gentle I could hardly see it even from the very edge of the stump. I came here every day to look at it, and watched it grow stronger. Until, as you see…" She began to pull her hand away from William's hand. He held on to it tighter.

"I have to go there," she said.

"No," he said, his body trembling with sudden fear.

"I have to," she said. "For you. For what I've taken from you. In my foolishness." And her hand slid out from the middle of his like water, and she backed a few steps away. "Wait here," she said. "Sit down on the ground and wait."

Trembling with fear for her, he did as she told him; and watched her as she began walking towards the great black stump. The ground rose as she neared it, and her head was nearer and nearer the silent flashing spears of light. She sank onto her knees and crawled towards the stump, lowering her head further and further as she crawled, until she was practically flat on her belly, and her hands, so far

265

as he could see through the dazzling light, seemed to be touching the black side of the great stump itself, and to be clawing their way upwards to its incandescent lip.

A piercing shaft burst in a fountain of blinding light against the very top of her head, sending her tumbling backwards down over the sloping earth. She rolled almost to where he was sitting before she stopped.

"No. No!" she whispered, her voice carrying like a shout in the bright silence, as he half stood up to go to her. "Keep down." She stood up herself, and brushed down her grey robe with one hand. She seemed to be holding something in the other. Both of them were as white as snow, and her hair was as white as snow, and her forehead.

"Come," she said, and walked past him back in among the trees. He followed her, stooping as he followed, keeping his head well below the flashing and bursting spears of light. Soon they were fewer, and then fewer, and then there were none, there was only the light around him which he remembered as feeling so peaceful. It felt peaceful now. The old woman stopped and turned and looked at him. Her white hands were cupped together in front of her.

"Lower your head a little," she said softly, and he realized that he was standing straight. He bent his head and shoulders toward her, and she slipped her hands round his neck; and when she removed them, and he straightened again, he saw what looked like a glistening waterdrop resting against his chest. It was cool against his skin.

"It flowed out of his earring," she said, her voice the barest breath. "The last time the sky wept, the only other time. It flowed to the edge of the old stump, and hung at the edge, and the light has been flowing into it ever since. It will protect you wherever you are going. Don't lose it." Her hands were undoing the fine gold chain at her waist.

"I'll guard it with my life," he said.

"Yes," she said, and stooped down to the hem of her

266

grey robe and pulled it up over her head. Her old body underneath was naked.

"Take it," she said, holding it out to him. "Put it on. You will need it against the heat of the sun, where you're going. Come now, put it on." He took it by the hem and pulled it on over his head and shoulders. It was as light as a feather and as soft as a feather, and fitted him perfectly. She drew the chain round his waist and fastened it; and stood back from him and looked steadily at him, and in her eyes was a concern for him he could hardly bear to see.

"What is it? What have I done?" he asked, wanting to hold her in his arms. She backed a little away, and tears brimmed again in her eyes.

"No, no," she said. "It was my own folly, putting your life in danger. Merely because you were naked, and outside my door. And I thought you had come to claim your earring." Her tears were trickling slowly down her old face. What was stirring in his mind? Water, and something rising out of the water. Rainbows, a cone of quivering rainbows. Her shrunken lips were all wet with her tears. Bright fish were swimming in the rainbows.

"What could I know?" she said. "Solitary here as I am. And I nearly caused your death." Her tears were slower, and she was wiping her cheeks with her white fingers.

"Black Melk's castle," he said. "I've just remembered. I'm looking for Black Melk. He lives on a big pointed hill. Everybody is happy there. I've remembered." She smiled at him as she had smiled when he kissed her; and all her tears had gone, except for three shining trails down her old wrinkled body. She reached out and patted his hand very gently with her white fingers.

"You'll find him now," she said. Then her face clouded. "I was so afraid I had taken your strength away from you, and your journey so far from done."

"How will I find him?" he asked. "Do you know where his castle is? Do you know which way I should go?"

"No," she said, shaking her head. "But there's little I do know, so it doesn't mean anything that I don't. I'm sure you'll find it all right. I'll take you to the edge of the forest." Her fingers patting his hand wrapped gently around it and she led him among the trees through the pale green light. There was no sound of any kind except their feet on the earth. All the trees were the same, all walnut trees, all young and straight. After a while she stopped.

"Here we are," she said. The forest looked the same.

"Straight ahead of you," she said, pointing, and released his hand.

"Go," she said in the softest whisper. "Fare well."

He stepped forward between two near trees, and light fell upon him in a brilliance so dazzling that he instinctively threw up his arm to shelter his eyes. But it was only sunlight, hot and strong, and his eyes quickly grew used to it. He let his arm fall and peered ahead of him. An open steaming plain began a little below the level of where he was standing, and stretched away to the horizon. He turned round to see the forest where he had been, to see her just once more before going. But there was no forest, there was nothing but a rotting lean-to, and beyond it the plain again, stretching to the horizon. He looked about in every direction. They all seemed much the same. Here and there were broken walls, a broken house, a broken tree; and everywhere a fine heat haze was rising up like a veil.

Then he saw, at the very horizon…it seemed he saw, he rubbed his eyes and looked again and it seemed sure that he saw…a conical hill which appeared to be floating just above the surface of the land. And on top of it a gleaming tower. Or castle. Black Melk's castle! And he was only two or three hours away! Holding his gaze upon it so that it shouldn't escape him, he made his way down the shallow slope of the mound where he was standing and began walking with a light and eager step across the plain towards it.

The earth was still soft and spongy from the rain. His feet sank into it and were cooled by it; and a warm mist rose out of it, drawn by the hot sun. As far as he could see the earth was mantled in mist, and so thickly that he had to trust to fortune that there were no sudden pits or ditches on the way he was going. The conical hill rose above it, but he was uneasy that the mist would rise yet higher and hide it. He was uncertain about it anyway, the further he walked, that maybe it was only a mirage; because it didn't seem to be resting exactly on the earth, but on a silver stream flowing along the horizon. But probably the stream was the mirage and the mountain was real; so far at least the mountain was staying fixed in the position in which he had first seen it.

The sun rose and rose and was ever hotter, until it was right overhead, and then began to sink slowly towards the mountain. The warm mist continued rising all around him, but as the light grew slowly gentler and the heat milder, the earth under his feet felt firmer. He no longer sank into it. And from time to time he touched the smooth surface of a broad stone. But when twilight spread over the land from behind him the mist was still shrouding it. He could see the silhouette of Black Melk's castle, tall and jagged on top of the hill, against the pale green sky, but it was still at the horizon; and the green of the sky slowly darkened until he couldn't see it, until there was no line of any kind between the dark sky and the dark earth. So he stopped where he was, for fear of wandering in circles without the hill to guide him. He sat down on the ground, facing towards where he had last been able to make out the hill, and gazed up at the stars glittering coldly in the black sky.

He was cold and stiff. He opened his eyes and stretched himself. The mist rising round him was cold, and a fine sliver of moon, just risen, was fading in the bright morning sky. There was a hole in the earth on each side of him, as big as his hand, and his hands were the co-lour of the earth. Why had he done that? He stood up and stretched himself again, and pushed the earth back into the holes with his feet. His thin grey robe was drenched with dew. He shivered.

Black Melk's castle was just where it had been, atop the hill at the horizon; bright and shimmering, like water itself, from the first rays of the sun. He shivered again, and began walking towards it again, through the mist and the birds murmuring on the ground in the mist and the birds singing in the sunny air above him. The mist grew less and less, un-til it was rising hardly to his ankles, and the ground against his feet was firm, at times even hard. And the further he walked the harder it became, and the fainter the mist. As the sun rose ever higher and its burning beams poured over the gently undulating land, and over him, he was glad of the protection of his thin robe against it.

By noon the mist was gone and the earth was hard and dry, and warm against the soles of his feet. And to either side of him as he walked steadily towards the high hill... higher now than before, much higher, but still far off...were remains of farms, derelict houses and sheds, and bones of animals halfburied in the earth. He found that he was walking along an earth road, which brought him after a while to a village where all the houses were empty, their windows and doors broken in; and the remains of a long lean dog in a doorway, the fur and bone of his head lolling just over the threshold. Then the village was behind him and the bare earth road was hot against his feet and rose in dusty puffs around him with every step he took; and in his ears the noise of insects was sharp and shrill, and he could no longer hear the singing of the birds. The sun was burning hot and heavy on his body and the air was hot and harsh in his nose and lungs.

He was thirsty. He found a little pool of water in a hole in the earth and scooped it into his mouth with his hands, hot though it was, and sour. But before long he was thirsty again and he couldn't find another hole with water, only dry holes or holes with a little damp earth, soft to his fingertips, at the bottom. The sun seemed held in the middle of the sky, he seemed to have been walking through noonday for hours, and the only sign of water anywhere now was the high hill which seemed never to be any nearer, only bigger and greener, and Black Melk's castle on top of it, rippling against the burning blue sky like a huge fountain.

He walked down a slope of bare, cracked mud to the centre of a basin which had been a pond, but even at its centre the water had sunk away into the earth or evaporated into the air, there were only deep dry fissures and dry weeds, and dying frogs. Some were already dead, and black and dry; some seemed only a moment ago to have rolled over, showing their milkwhite bellies to the sun. Two or three of them were still green. But even as he looked down at them, sheltering them from the blazing sun for the moment with his own short black shadow, the green grew dull and blackened and they rolled slowly over on their sides and their loose hind legs trailed in the little breeze like dry grass; and ants crawled over their bellies.

A snake slithered past in front of him, black with fine yellow rings. Its head was weaving about as if looking for prey, but it didn't seem to see the frogs; it made its way up the sloping side of the dry pond and was gone. But some way further on he came upon it again, or one like it, dead, and its eyes sunk into its head; and a thin crow with dull black feathers was pecking at it listlessly, not even lifting its head as he passed by.

He walked more slowly now, for the earth was harsh and burning against his feet. He stopped time and again; and started again, drawn on by the sight of the fountain-castle on the high green hill, ever higher and greener, awash and sparkling with what seemed to be streams of bright water running round it in rings. And as the sun at last began to sink beyond it and the sunlight very slowly reddened and weakened, and the air grew hazier with myriad specks of drifting dust, the shadow of the hill and castle flowed nearer over the land. He urged himself towards it over the fiery ground, and reached it just as the sun seemed to be forcing its huge red body into the body of the castle; and urged himself on even more quickly then, while there was still light and the heat was dying, running over the rocky ground where nothing but bare thorn bushes seemed to grow, while the hill rose ever higher over him. He ran through the twilight as it deepened and deepened into darkness and the air was ever milder against his face; until everything was so dark he couldn't see the earth he was standing on, and the stars in the black sky were glittering everywhere over his head, even where the mountain had been, as if it wasn't. He stood awhile, panting to regain his breath, feeling smooth warm stone under his feet; and then sank down to the stone and sat still.

As he gazed up at the slowly wheeling stars he felt the air cool and cool and cool against his hands and face and feet, though his thin robe still sheltered his body. And he began, little by little, to feel afraid. The stone under him was only a bare black table and the night above him was pouring away from him unendingly, ever more black and empty, to the empty stars, beyond the empty stars; if he started to fall... That was why he had dug the holes in the earth the night before, to hold onto it, to hold himself from falling into the open night. But the earth under him now was stone, why didn't he think of it when he sat down on it, it was too hard for his hands and he would slide easily off it. He felt over the stone around him with his hands, searching for any crack or hole, but there wasn't any. And it wasn't safe to move, to look for earth, he could more easily fall off if he was moving. He closed his eyes against the unending blackness and tucked his feet under him and each hand into the armpit of the other arm and rested his chin on his shest. But he couild see the night inside him, and the pale dead light of the stars, and his fear swelled. He threw back his head and opened his eyes and looked up at the outside black night; and for a moment he felt better, but then worse, he felt perched over the void on his smooth rock and it seemed to be slowly tilting he would slide off it and fall through the endless black...

Around him it wasn't black. Right around him. Not quite black. There was some soft light, very faint. Which wasn't the stars. Or the moon, there was no moon, he was between the old moon and the new. The light was faint on the stone around him, and not so faint on his robe, or on his feet and his hands; it was strongest, almost as strong as the blurred light of a glow-worm, just at his chest. He gazed down at it in wonder and fear; and then remembered, how had he forgotten, the drop of water the old woman had hung at his chest.

Carefully, very carefully for fear of hurting it, he slid his hand inside the neck of his robe and enclosed the waterdrop, and drew it out and cradled it in the palm of his hand in front of his face. It looked like a pearl with light inside it, and all over its surface were the minute reflections of the stars in the black sky. As he gazed at it, entranced, the light it shed seemed to spread into his hand, bathing it softly, and to pass up his arm under the veil of his sleeve; and his other hand was glowing where it was resting on his knee, and his feet were glowing, and all around him the smooth pale stone was bathed by the gentle light. And his fear died. He watched the stars wheel over the surface of the waterdrop-pearl, and the black night around him felt suffused with a pearly light, and he felt at peace.

There was light in the sky also. He lifted his eyes from the waterdrop-pearl and saw that the night was fading, that he was sitting in the twilight before dawn. He watched the light spread slowly through the sky, hiding the far stars and filling the black void with blue. As the sun itself rose, striking first against the high bright castle of Black Melk, and slowly sliding like gold down the watery green hill, he slipped the waterdrop back inside his robe and lifted himself to his feet and began walking again; but slowly, unhurriedly: the beginning of the hill seemed now very near.

It wasn't so near as it seemed. He walked and walked and still he didn't reach it, though it reared up ever higher before him. while the sun rose in the sky behind him and poured its burning rays down upon everything around him, standing or fallen: dead trees and fence-posts and broken-down dwellings. There were many dwellings, many more than he had seen before; as if the castle had drawn back from them and left them to the burning sun. They seemed almost aflame in the sun; and the earth they were standing on, and he was walking on, was as hot and smoking as coals. But his feet felt it only as from far off, for the waterdrop seemed to be bathing his whole body with a film of cooling water.

A dead pigeon on the ground burst into sunbright dust as he passed it, and drifted slowly away on the faint wind. A stump crumbled in the same way, and a tree and a house, even stones seemed to be breaking up in the blazing heat; and balls of glittering dust were drifting slowly past him, bigger and bigger balls of dust. Beyond them and above them the great green hill was glittering and trembling, and

274

seemed every moment brighter, and he began to be uneasy that even it would burst into dust.

One of the balls of dust, a hazy globe as high as he was tall, drifted gently against him and around him until he couldn't see anything but millions of sparkling motes. Something touched him lightly on his back, something else brushed against his leg, and his arm, and seemed to come to rest there, clinging to his robe, but he couldn't see what they were. Then the globe of dust was gone, and he saw that light twigs, silvery and beautiful, were caught here and there in his soft robe. Others, as light as feathers, as thistledown, were drifting past him and catching in his robe and resting there; and the dust balls were more and more and were rising higher and higher in the air, and on touching each other burst into fragments blazing with sunlight. But the sunlight was being dimmed, the balls of dust and twigs were thicker and thicker in the air, the sun was already blurred and the green hill was blurred he could hardly see that it was green at all, it looked more like dull silver, and the pale orange sunlight around him was every moment paler. He continued walking towards the foot of the hill, he could feel the pearly waterdrop at his chest drawing him towards it; but slowly, ever more slowly, through the burning air around him, and the sudden sharp lights of the dust balls bursting. His robe now was so thickly encrusted with pale twigs that he couldn't even see it, it was as if he were covered in glistening feathers, the air was ever more filled with them they were collecting in his hair and landing and resting on his forehead and cheeks, so soft he could feel them only when they quivered with every explosion and the sudden sharp lights which touched them like needles; and touched his skin, pricking it sharply. The air was now so thick with them that he couldn't see any trace of the hill ahead of him, and the light around him was like burning twilight, through which the bright needle-lights flashed and flashed

275

and pierced through the silvery twigs deep into his flesh, even through the waterlight which was flowing from the waterdrop-pearl all over his skin.

He could no longer move. The thick matting of twigs had bound his arms to his sides and encrusted his robe round his legs in a thick cocoon. But the sharp explosions and the needle-lights were fewer, and then fewer still; and everything round him was still, silent and still, and the only light was the pearly reflected light of the waterdrop resting against his chest.

There was the sharp sound, in the distance it seemed, of metal against metal; a quick sound and often repeated, and it was coming slowly nearer. And with its coming nearer, the light was increasing again; but not the light of the burning day, a pale gentle light. The sound was over his head now, close over his head, and there were pale blue holes in the silver around him. The sound was everywhere around him and was quicker and quicker and the pale light was gliding through the blue holes, and green holes, and now he could hear somebody breathing.

It was a man; he could see his shadow on the silver, he could see parts of the man himself through the holes. He was a young man, and he was cutting away all the silver branches with a pair of shears. The light was pouring in all around him now, soft pale sunlight, and the sky overhead was pale blue. The young man's face was alight with his work, and his shears were flashing here there and everywhere, cutting and cutting at the branches. They were no longer silver and dead, they were stiff and thorny, and some of them were pricking him where they touched him: they were rose branches.

The young man's shears flashed just above his head and behind his head, and suddenly his head was free. And the young man stared at him in alarm and staggered back and nearly dropped his shears. And William remembered him, and looked about him and remembered what he saw: he was in the rose garden again. All around him were overgrown rose bushes and trailing roses of all colours and hundreds of scattered petals among the long grass and weeds, and three bushes close to him cut into sharp geometrical shapes. The man was gazing at him with great blue eyes; and he wasn't young, of course, he was old, it was only his blue staring eyes which looked young. His fear seemed to have passed and he was approaching the rosebush again with his shears raised and open. He was even smiling, he seemed to remember who he was.

He was cutting again at the rose bush, but carefully and slowly, not at all as before, and the whole while he was smiling, and his white face seemed to grow ever brighter; and before William was expecting it, the rose bush had fallen away from him and he was standing in the open, in the soft rosescented air, and the old man was standing close in front of him and was gazing at him steadily and seemed half in a trance. He wasn't gazing at his face, but at the middle of his chest; and as he gazed the shears he was holding slipped from his hand and fell with a soft clatter to the earth.

It was the waterdrop he was gazing at, it seemed he could see it through the grey robe. He was lifting his hand towards it now, it was coming nearer and nearer, and his blue eyes were gazing steadily and his whole face was alight. But his hand stopped just a few inches away, it seemed he wanted to go further but didn't dare; his open palm was upraised as if to catch the pearly light. And William was suddenly aware that all the flesh of his body was stinging, that it wasn't any longer cooled by the pearly light; was the stinging then from the rose thorns? It seemed that there were no marks of blood on his face or hands, for the old man wasn't at all afraid.

"Do you want to see it?" he asked him gently; then remembered that he was deaf, and gestured to it and unfolded his hand away from him. The old man nodded, his face radiant. So, with great care, William slipped his hand under the neck of his robe and reached for the pearl-waterdrop; and his hand touched something sharp. In sudden fear he closed his hand round it, and it seemed to have many sharp points. He drew it out and opened his hand, and saw that it was a pentangle. Like and not like the pentangle the man...Fenwick...had given him before he let him out through the heavy door, where the other man was, in the moonlight, who said Fenwick wasn't. And then he lost the pentangle with the woman, how beautiful she was her eyes were like honey, no the old woman's eyes were like honey it was she who gave him the waterdrop, the pentangle was glistening on his palm like water in sunlight.

The old man was stretching his fingers nearer and nearer now to touch it, he seemed to be straining both toward it and away from it at once, his blue eyes were clouding and clearing and clouding. She told him not to lose it, he remembered, and a sudden cold fear ran through him, and the old man's eyes clouded nearly grey and his hand drew back. Which was so painful to see that William reached out before he could stop himself, and took his old hand and held it, and drew it to the pentangle lying in his other hand, until they touched. And the smile on the old man's face was so beyond bearing that he found he couldn't move or even breathe, until the old man of his own will slowly withdrew his hand from the pentangle, and his gaze as well, lifting his great blue eyes to William's face.

After some time, he didn't know how much time, much or little, he saw the old man turning away from him, backing slowly away from him, gently gesturing that he follow. He let go of the pentangle, let it rest against his chest outside of his robe, and took hold of the old man's outstretched hand and let himself be drawn gently through the sunny glade and into a narrow winding path, through the flowing scent of roses.

The old man led him skilfully along the narrow overgrown path and other overgrown paths, gesturing with his other arm that they were going and going, and glancing back from time to time with a smile like the light of the early sun. Like the time before, they crossed over rotting bridges over weedchoked streams, as the way slowly broadened and was less wild and overgrown; until they were again on the curving path which led to the dividing meadow and the carefully tended garden beyond. As they approached the meadow the same sweet perfume reached William's nostrils through the scent of the roses, and he felt the old man's hand tighten in his; but his old feet didn't falter even when they stepped onto the grass of the meadow itself, or when they stepped off it onto the fine yellow gravel path of the inner garden.

There the perfume was ever more intense, flooding through the fresh sunlight scent of the roses; but he found that his senses weren't yet overpowered by it, he could smell it, this far, and the roses at once. And he could still feel the skin of his body stinging.

They came to a gardener kneeling on the grass by a rosebush, gathering fallen petals. Expecting him to be startled and frightened, he was about to say something to calm him; but there wasn't any need, when he turned round and saw them he didn't move to run, he stayed where he was, gazing at them with empty blue eyes, and only when they had passed did he rise to his feet, and follow after them, leaving his square of cloth, with its little heap of petals, lying on the grass where he had been working. They passed another gardener, a woman she seemed, though she might have been a very old beardless man, who looked on their slow passing as the other had, mildly and without moving, and followed after them.

The way was broad now and straight, and so were the clear brooks bubbling past them on either side, flowing towards the meadow and the outer garden; and crossways they came to were equally straight, running to the pale blue horizon in each direction, in his mind as well as his eyes, for everything was the same as the first time he was there, the sky and the sunlight were the same, the undulating colours of the roses were the same, shading from hue to hue, and the scent of them was as fresh and clear. Only the gardeners were different, because they weren't frightened of him they only gazed nearly blankly at him and the old man holding fast to his hand; and were following after them, already they were a considerable number behind them. And still the intense sweet smell which wasn't of the roses or of the brooks or of anything he could see, but which was much stronger than the rose scent and which had so overcome him at his last arrival that he wasn't in control of himself but could only walk ever forward like a kind of puppet, wasn't now overcoming him, or the scent of the roses, or the soft bubbling of the brooks, or the murmuring of the bees.

The roses were all like trees on slender trunks now to each side of him as far as he could see, and the gardeners were very many and were leaving their work and following after them almost like sleepwalkers as they passed them, their big blue eyes shining and still; and ahead of them the whiteness in the sky just at the horizon, which had seemed to be a great lily but was really a fountain, was beginning to appear. The old man was clinging to him now more closely, holding onto his arm with both his old hands, so that he felt he was almost carrying him over the fine yellow-gravel path; and his old clear eyes were staring fixedly at the pentangle. The white was more intense with every step they took, and the roses to each side were paler, and their scent was fainter though still clear through the intense sweetness of the perfume flowing towards them in waves from the whiteness ahead of them, now almost around them for the path was white and the sky was nearly white and even the stems of the roses were white and the gardeners moved like white shadows among them and flowed out of them and into the parade of their fellows following him and the old man, surely in a moment he would see the lily, or the fountain, for even the old man beside him was like a white shadow the only colour anywhere was in his own hands and feet moving through the incandescent whiteness, and his pale grey robe, and the pearly pentangle glowing like a rainbow on his chest.

"Stop there. Just there," a voice said gently, very gently, the merest breeze at his ear. He stopped and stood in the middle of the whiteness, and slowly beside him a shadow deepened in the brilliance, deepened and deepened and took the shape of a tall thin man. More and more colour washed into the near glaring whiteness, and the man was clear and the light around him was as clear as morning, and every grain of yellow gravel at his feet was clear. He was Fenwick, and he was gazing steadily at the pentangle at his chest. The colour was flowing all around them now in bright waves, lapping against the white, washing around and into the man clinging to his other side; a few steps furhter off the gardeners were appearing, their blue eyes first, as the colour flowed away and away, and the roses reappeared in deeper and deeper yellows, in golds and coppers and crimsons and even purples, and the sky was a soft pale blue. And he found that he was standing by the parapet of the fountain, and spray from its high crown was finely splashing him, and still he could smell the perfume of the lily.

"Wash in it," Fenwick said softly, waving a hand towards the pool beneath the fountain.

"But… You said… I thought you said nobody…"

"Wash," Fenwick said again, gentle but insistent. "The danger is past now. For you."

He could feel the old man on his other side clinging to him in fear of his life; and as he lifted his foot in obedience to Fenwick to step over the parapet into the pool, the old man began to tremble violently and to claw across his chest towards the pentangle. He was gurgling and weeping, and digging his fingers into his flesh.

"Give him to me," Fenwick said, and reached out a long hand and took hold of one of the hands of the old man and slowly drew him around William's body to himself, and enclosed him in both his arms. "Now wash yourself. He will be all right."

He stepped into the water; and then, as the fountain splashed down over him, panic stuck through him like lightning as his body began to sting again as sharply as when the old man cut him free of the rose bush, and his hand rose to clasp and protect his pentangle-waterdrop for fear it would melt and he would lose it as he had lost the other. But it was itself laden and glistening with fine waterdrops and was as hard and sharp as a jewel to the touch of his hand; and from every part of it fine rainbows were darting into the gushing fountain and passing down through it into the pool and the golden fish which were slowly swimming there. He could hardly feel the water itself, but he could see it purling about his feet as he walked and let the fountain spray over him.

"Remove your robe," Fenwick said. Obediently, without thinking, he tucked the pentangle inside the robe, and stooped to its hem and drew it up over his body and his head; and let it fall away from him into the pool, where it drifted just under the surface like a long grey fish.

His whole body was trickling with blood, it was bright

red with blood, flowing from hundreds of tiny holes. In alarm he looked round for Fenwick, and saw that all the gardeners were staring at him and their mouths were agape with horror. But Fenwick was smiling, and was stroking the matted grey hair of the terror-stricken old man in his arms.

"Wash yourself," he said again, and William rubbed his hands all over his body; his blood flowed over his hands with the water and into the water, it was flowing fast out of every tiny hole and there seemed to be no stanching it, already the whole pool was bright with it and the golden fish were purple in the midst of it and the water flowing from the five outlets of the pool into the garden was the colour of the deepest red rose. He began to feel dizzy, and unsteady on his feet, his whole body seemed to be swinging loose; and the fountain seemed higher than it had been, it seemed to be pouring down on him from the sky itself and it wa glittering every moment more brightly. Fenwick seemed to be speaking to him, to be calling him, but he couldn't make out what he was saying his voice was like a far tinkling bell.

There was someone else in the fountain. It was a woman, he was sure it was a woman, she was just to the side of him just beyond where he could see her, she was dancing round him, as he turned she danced round and round he couldn't quite see her she was always just beyond where he could see, but he could feel her he could feel her arms circling round him and round him they were washing his body her touch was as soft as light she was gliding over his flesh with her hands her arms all her sweet body, the perfume of her was too great he couldn't stand he was melting down into the water...

She was gone. He was standing where he was, and all the stinging of his body had died away and all the blood was washed away and the pool was only the colour of the palest rose. And his pentangle was still glistening like a rainbow on his chest.

"Come," Fenwick's voice behind him said in a whisper. "Come out."

He looked about him. The gardeners were still all standing round in rows, all gazing at him with wide blue eyes; but their fear had faded away, they seemed quiet and still. And the old man now had his arms about Fenwick's neck and was kissing his cheek. Unsteadily, still feeling the woman near him, he lifted his foot to step out of the pool.

"Bring your robe," Fenwick said. He found it resting against his other foot and drew it up out of the water, and brought it with him out of the pool.

"Lay it on the ground," Fenwick said. "It will soon dry. As soon as you will yourself." He spread it out on the fine gravel, and stood up and breathed the soft air. He felt the sun warming his body and the water trickling coolly over his body and the perfume of the woman inside his body; and the blue gaze of all the gardeners touching him so gently and lovingly that he was unable to move.

He felt a hand touch him on the shoulder, and slowly turned his head to see whose it was; and found the old man standing close beside him, looking at him steadily, with tears trickling down his old grey cheeks like rain. Fenwick was beyond him holding his other hand.

"Don't be concerned," Fenwick said. "It can't be helped. He sees the end. Don't worry, it's of no moment. He sees as he sees." The old man's tears were falling in a flood so heavy that his eyes were swimming blue.

"But why is…? Who *is* he?"

"The old king," Fenwick said softly. "Maria's father." He was holding the old man's hand in both of his own and drawing him slowly back towards himself. "And my brother."

"I don't understand. I don't seem to… I can't seem

to…" He couldn't seem to think at all. The perfume of the woman was flowing through his whole body.

"Not here," Fenwick said gently, loosening his hands from the old man's hand. "It can't be understood here. Come with me, we must go. It's time."

The gardeners were backing slowly away; some of them were moving off among the rose trees, others were following. Almost all of them had gone now, disappeared among the rose trees. The last were going. They were gone.

"They have their work," Fenwick said. "Much more than before, now that the outer garden… Come, we must go." He bent down and picked up William's robe and handed it to him. It was dry. William slipped it on over his head, and left his pentangle hanging inside. Fenwick sat the old man down on the parapet, where he remained unmoving, still gazing at William and the tears still trickling down his old cheeks.

"There's nothing more we can do," Fenwick said in a whisper. "But he will be able to stay here now by the fountain. Until… Until." He turned away from the fountain. "Come. Follow close after me. Though there is no danger now of your being lost."

William followed him through the rose trees, deeper and deeper into the midst of them, and they were growing ever higher over them and closer together and the light was every moment less; until there was no light at all. But they walked on through the darkness until Fenwick stopped, and unlocked a door and locked it after them, and they climbed the long steep dark stairway to the other door, which Fenwick unlocked and pushed away upwards. And they were in the great room with grey light filtering down through the high dusty windows. Fenwick lowered the great chair into place and locked it, and gestured to William to follow him across the room and out of it, and down the broad stairway to the front entrance, out of which they slipped as cautiously as before.

The light outside was pale grey, and there was no one to be seen. The house across the street, where the red-haired woman had opened the door and looked out, was boarded up. But in the narrow streets away from the palace a few people were standing, two or three here, another two there, another one. They seemed aimlessly there, they seemed unnaturally quiet, hardly breathing or blinking, as grey as the light. Only their lifeless eyes followed Fenwick's passing. William thought he remembered the face of one of them, an old short man, and smiled a greeting and half-raised a hand, but the man looked at him as if he were a stranger.

"They have declined," Fenwick said, holding his cape close around him as he walked. "They've stopped breeding, stopped, I think, even making love. Every day one or two more die, and none are born." There were more of them now where they were passing. One or two seemed to recognize Fenwick and moved back to give him easier passage, but the rest only gazed blankly whichever way their heads were facing... "They still work in the fields, poorly, some of them do, are still able. And they die there too, and have to be carried back into the town. The least irregularity and their hearts burst and what blood they have turns to water. It has seemed but a matter of time, of little time, before Black Melk would come and assume the town. But now," he said, glancing at William, his glance like a sharp arrow, gone as quickly as it came, continuing the while along the narrow length of the steadily darkening street. "Since, against my fears, you have returned, we may be able to overcome him first. It will have to be very soon. You will help me, of course?"

"If I can, I will." The people to both sides of them

were many now, but they melted back against the walls like humble shadows, as silently as shadows.

"You can. If you will."

"Then I will."

They passed out of the street into the great square, and across it, through the quiet gloom of dusk, towards Fenwick's tall house. In the middle of the square there was no one, but all around it, in the shadows of the buildings, there were very many shadowy people. And in the narrow street in front of Fenwick's house there were many more. All of them unmoving, as if they were waiting.

He followed Fenwick in through his doorway, and up the nearly dark stairway, to a sudden soft running of cats. Fenwick climbed the stairs slowly, he seemed to find the climb difficult. At the first landing they stopped. A kind of whistling breathing was pouring through the grill beside them from the black corridor, and an overwhelming smell of rotting; and cats were gathered there like smooth round stones.

"He is ready," Fenwick said, drawing in deep breaths and holding tightly to the bannister. "We have only to be ready ourselves." He started up the second flight and William followed him; but with every step he appeared more exhausted. And William didn't know whether to offer him help or not, all he could do was hold himself ready in case he fell back or down. His breathing was ever more as if his heart would burst with the effort, but he didn't stop again, he dragged himself upwards along the bannister, until they were both standing on the topmost landing under the skylight, and the first stars were beginning to prick dimly through dark grey sky. And then without warning he slumped back against William's chest; and stayed there, panting and struggling for breath, while the stars grew brighter and brighter.

"It's my heart," he said at last, straightening himself

and standing by himself, but swaying. "I overstrained it. You overstrained it. It's failing."

He moved off unsteadily to his door and opened it. William followed him. The room was darker than the landing, but the smell of it was fresher, the windows were all open and the door closed out the seeping smell of rotting.

Someone else was in the room, it was a woman, she was silhouetted against the window which faced towards Black Melk's castle. He couldn't see which way she was facing herself and he couldn't see who she was, and just as he was thinking that it must be Maria, Fenwick lit a sputtering candle close beside him and its faltering flame danced in her big black eyes. It was Maria. But she was so changed.

"She has been waiting for your return," Fenwick murmured. "Patiently." He felt fixed to the floor as he stared at her shining beauty. Her eyes were full of light, not just the candlelight, their own light; and her long black hair was brushed back from her high and glowing forehead, and was glistening on her shoulders in the unsteady light; and she was wearing a plain white dress nearly to her ankles. She was unmoving, gazing at him unmoving, and her hands were resting quietly at her sides. His blood was throbbing in his ears.

"She is waiting still," Fenwick said very softly from somewhere beside him, somewhere beyond the candle-light. "She has watched you with the other women and has learned." She had seen him, she had seen him in the globe. What would she think of him? "She is only waiting for you to call her to you."

"She's the princess," he said, half-fearing that he was already moving towards her. "It's for her…"

"She is waiting," Fenwick whispered. "During all the time of your absence she has been waiting. She would

288

never leave me alone here, for fear that I would look in the globe and she would not be here to see you. And slowly, little by little, she became quieter, more gentle; and only watched you, no longer tried to touch you." Was he going to her, he seemed to be nearer to her, or was she coming to him? Fenwick's voice sounded further away, somewhere behind him. "Except once. When you were with the solitary old woman. She began then to cry. But gently." She was so close he was about to touch her, her skin was all shimmering gold. "Her tears flowed down her face like rain and splashed all over the globe...tears of love they were, of course, and I suppose of happiness that you seemed at last to have come through your pain. But I was afraid to leave you so, all dazzled by her vault of tears, so I brushed them away with my hand. And after that day she was quiet and still. hour after hour she sat in the window there, sewing...how she learned I don't know...sometimes gazing across the plain, and sometimes down at...well, that's no matter now. As if in a dream, as if at every moment she was seeing you, was even with you. The dress she is wearing is all her own work." It was moving, it was rippling on her body, she was coming towards him he hadn't moved towards her he was still where he was and Fenwick was where he was. He held out his arms to her and she came to him more quickly the whole room was fluttering with the candleflame and his heart was so beating and his blood was so throbbing...and she was in his arms, her body was quivering against his and he could feel her warm breath against his chest just where the pentangle was resting. Fenwick was saying something, he could hear his voice through the candleflame but he couldn't make out any words, Fenwick was pulling at one of his arms around her body why was he pulling it what did he want him to do now?

He had put the candle in his hand.

"Now go," he said. He seemed to be whispering right into his ear. "Go with her to your room."

"I haven't got a..." Her arms around him were loosening, she was backing away, why was she...?

"She will take you there. She has prepared it, all by herself. On the floor below this one. She will show you the way." She was moving towards the door. He went with her, his one arm still cradling her, his other holding the candle. The door opened, Fenwick must have pulled it open, and they were out on the landing, and they were going down the stairs, her body moving with his body, sliding with every step against his body, she was turning him away from the stairs along a black hallway she was opening a door into a black room she was leading him around the room it smelled all of flowers, or herbs, crushed herbs they were crushing them with their feet, she was guiding his hand with the candle towards another candle its wick rose softly into flame, she was leading him to another and he was lighting it all the walls of the room and the ceiling were gliding with the flickering light and the shadows, she was leading him towards a big white-covered bed by the window, she guided his hand to a candleholder on a little table beside the bed and he set the candle in it beside a bowl of tiny white flowers, and enclosed her with both his arms and held her and held her.

He could hear breathing. Not her breathing or his breathing. The room was full of breathing, slow breathing.

She was turning his head towards the window, it was open to the night sky above and the great square below; and the people were in the square, they were almost filling the square, starlit shadows hardly moving, all their up-turned faces like small pale moons. It was their breathing, rising and falling in the room, he moved through it with Maria she was drawing him to the bed down onto the bed he was drifting down with her enfolded and enfolding her the air was sweet with the smell of herbs and deep with the breathing of the people.

He opened his eyes. The big room was pale with very early morning light. Twilight, the sun was still unrisen. He was alone in the bed. But she was in the room, she was standing in front of the window across the room, looking down, in a loose finespun nightdress, so fine he could see the shape of her beautiful body against the pale light. He left the bed and crossed the floor through the scattered herbs, and wrapped his arms around her and rested his face against hers, and looked where she was looking, at the ground directly below; and started, and held her tighter. There were two leaning and blackened stakes in the earth and two blackened and tattered bodies bound to them, unrecognizable bodies. Maria hardly seemed to be breathing.

"He said the sun would heal them," he said. She didn't seem to hear. "Would perhaps heal them. He hoped the sun would…" In her throat there was a murmuring, a soft throbbing. He kissed her ear and her cheek, and gently caressed her body with his hands. The murmuring in her throat was louder. Her lips were parted and the murmuring was passing out between them.

"I…" she said. "We…" she said, like breathing out small puffs of air. "…take them…" she said. He wrapped his arms close around her and buried his face in her thick black hair.

"Anything," he said. "Anythingsoever you want." Her whole body was quivering with her efforts to speak.

"…down." she said. "Take them down." And she turned in his arms and looked up at his face with her great black questioning eyes.

"Yes," he said. "Yes. We'll take them down."

"Now," she said, and seemed to want to be free of his arms.

"Yes," he said, and let his arms fall away to his sides; and felt his pentangle suddenly cold against his skin. Everywhere in the room the candles were melted away, and the little white flowers in the bowl by the bed were withered and dry. He crossed to the bed and took his grey robe and pulled it on over his head; and saw that she was standing quietly by the door, still in her nightdress and barefoot, waiting for him. When he was beside her she pulled the door open, and a spider's web was torn apart. He followed her into the hallway and down the stairway, through the huddled cats, to the street; and along the street and along the side of the great square to the gates. In the middle of the square a few cattle were gathered, and a few men with the cattle, waiting for the gates to open. On a bench against the wall in the gateway two gatemen were lounging and yawning. Maria went up to the nearer one and stopped in front of him. He immediately stopped yawning and sat up straight, and tried to stand but she was too near to him.

"Open," she said. Both the gatemen looked surprised and frightened at hearing her speak. In the square the men had seen her, and they were coming nearer, they were herding their cattle nearer. Other people were coming across the square, they were coming from every direction, coming as if they knew.

"But…" the gateman said. "The sun hasn't risen. Fenwick will…"

Lifting her arm, Maria pointed to the highest pinnacle in the town, which was just that moment touched with sunlight; a breath like a sigh passed through the gathering people.

"Open," Maria said, and both the gatemen hurried to open the gates, and she walked out through them, and he walked out after her.

"Come," she said to the first gateman, and he followed

after them across the dead, hard ground to the stakes. There was a fine dew glistening on the two charred bodies. She stopped and gazed up at them, at one and then the other.

"His knife," she said, not looking round. "Take his knife." The gateman was already pulling it from the sheath at his belt, he was handing it to him with a little bow of his head.

"You...will...?" she asked, looking round at him. Her black eyes were unblinking. He would do anything, anything at all. He went to the nearer stake and reached up to the black, charred corpse, and felt over it to find what was still binding it to the black, charred corpse, and found a frayed rope and cut it and then another and cut it, and the whole body fell into his arms, with sharp sounds of sinews snapping and muscles pulling loose from bones; and he remembered her fine white skin and her emerald eyes in the midst of all the red and brown faces, and her fine white hands, and the blood in a fine red trickle between her fingers. Or was it her mother he was holding? He didn't look any closer to see, if he could see, but laid whichever it was out gently on the hard ground; and went to the further stake and felt over the body bound to it and cut it free and brought it back in his arms and laid it down beside the other, and looked up at Maria to know what to do next.

"Can you...carry...?" she asked.

"Yes," he said. He could carry them together, there was no weight in them, all their blood and water had been burned away. He handed the knife back to the gateman, who took it without looking; he was looking upwards and seemed uneasy. He was looking up at Fenwick's window, at Fenwick himself standing in the window, looking down on them all.

He stooped down to the two charred bodies and gathered them together in his arms and lifted them up, and followed Maria along a narrow pathway opening ahead of her between the blankly gazing people and cattle, and back in through the gateway. He followed close behind her across the great square, and into the narrow winding street where he had first seen her disappear, and along it, still past gazing people, gazing at her and at the two black bodies in his arms, their four loose legs hitting against his legs, the crowns of their seared heads just under his chin. The people were turning after him as he passed them, it seemed that they were following.

Maria's white nightdress was shining with the morning sun and the houses were behind them, and the cemetery was just in front. He followed her in through the broken gateway and stayed close behind her as she threaded her way among old gravestones and tilting and broken monuments, and long dry tangled grasses, until they reached a kind of opening, where a hole had been dug in the earth; not very deep, but deep enough. A spade was standing at an angle in a pile of loose earth beside it.

"Lay them...in," Maria said. He laid the bodies out on the flattened grass, and climbed down into the hole himself, and drew the nearer body back into his arms and laid it gently on the rough bottom of the hole, arranging her limbs as best he could on the earth, whether she was the mother or the beautiful daughter; and stood up and gathered the other one into his arms and laid her also on the rough bottom of the hole, and arranged her.

Something glinted in the sunlight at the edge of the hole. It was a ring, a ring with a green stone, it was her ring. He picked it up and turned it in his fingers to see it glisten in the slanting sunlight, and laid it in the grave between their bodies, and climbed out. Maria was gazing down on them with no expression in her beautiful eyes. Behind her, and around the grave everywhere, were the grey faces of the townspeople, peering over and around the broken and buckled gravestones, like ghosts creeping nearer and nearer.

"Cover them," Maria whispered. He took the spade and, as gently as he could, tipped earth onto their bodies, spadeful after spadeful until they were covered, until the earth was filling half the hole, until it was flush with the edges of the hole, until it was a low mound over the hole.

"Thank you," Maria said. Her voice was so low and weak that he glanced round sharply. Her eyes were opening and closing and she was swaying where she stood and seemed about to fall. He threw down the spade and ran to her and gathered her into his arms, lifting her from the ground. The people all around were looking at him.

"The baby," a woman whispered. What baby? Maria's head was resting limply against his shoulder, but her breathing was soft and even. Other women were nodding and murmuring. An old woman touched his sleeve.

"Let her rest," she said gently. "Rest is all she needs. Take her home." Around her they were all nodding, men and women, and in front of him a path was opening in their midst, leading towards the cemetery gate. He carried her through them out of the cemetery and along the broken road back into town, and along the narrow winding street back to the square. In the square there was no one except two gatemen in the open gateway, watching.

He carried her in through Fenwick's entryway and up the stairs. The raven, as they passed his landing, croaked very softly, but she didn't stir in his arms, she seemed to be sleeping peacefully. At their own landing Fenwick was standing, but he carried her past in front of him and along the hallway to their room and into it, and laid her tenderly on their bed. Gently he removed her nightdress, stained with the dirt of the poor women's burnt bodies...fearful that he would wake her, but her sleep seemed very deep…and laid her back again on the bed and drew the sheet over the beauty of her body, and kissed her lovingly on her lips. They were so soft and yielding that it was hard to draw away again, and she seemed to be smiling faintly and he wanted to lay his own body down beside hers; but he saw the bowl of withered flowers on the table and he remembered the broken cobweb: they must have been longer, even much longer, in the room than he knew. He backed away from her to the doorway, looking at her the whole way, and only with a great effort of will managed to pull the door closed between them.

Fenwick was beckoning to him from the landing. He went to him.

"Come upstairs," he said. He nodded, and followed him up the stairs and into his room.

"You will be hungry," Fenwick said. He didn't know if he was. He didn't know anything really except the feeling of Maria in his arms. He felt strange in Fenwick's room, it seemed a strange place to be, why wasn't he with her?

"Here you are," Fenwick said, handing him a plate piled with pieces of cold fowl, chicken they must be. He was hungry, Fenwick was right, only at the sight of them his spittle was nearly dribbling out of his mouth. He took a piece in each hand and began tearing ravenously at one of them with his teeth. Fenwick laid the plate down on a table beside him and halfturned away.

"Aren't you having any? he managed to ask through a full mouth. Fenwick smiled wanly. He looked tired, and old.

"No," he said. "Food is of no moment now. Not for me. Is she sleeping?" He nodded, So beautiful she was, sleeping. And waking. Was it true she was with child? With his child.

"Are the women buried?" Fenwick asked, not looking round, fingering a bare cord at his throat. He nodded,

296

his mouth and hands full of chicken. The old man in the moonlit glade said he had a son already. Who was looking for him. He had gone from his mother into the forest, why had he gone? He wouldn't ever go from Maria, he could feel her body move against the sheets he could feel her slow breathing. The cord Fenwick was fingering used to have a berry strung on it, what had happened to...?

"It crumbled away one day," Fenwick murmured, letting his hand fall from the cord. "It's time was past. It crumbled under my own fingers." He shrugged slightly and vaguely, and walked away to the window facing across the plain to the jagged line of hills. At his feet the cage where the doves had been was empty, what had... He stopped eating and looked down at the halfchewed leg in his hand; it was small for a chicken.

"Their time was past too," Fenwick said. "They had served their turn. Or rather, due to the circumstance, they failed to serve. Though you noticed them here and there. I sent off two or three, in the weak hope that they would a little stir your memory."

"There were a couple of dead ones," he said.

"Yes, those were the ones. The climate was too extreme. But they are good food, Eat them." He began chewing on the little leg again, uneasy but very hungry. Fenwick was gazing down at the ground below the window, at the bare stakes it must be, how could he have left them there so long? He could still feel their burnt bodies against his body.

"I'm glad they are gone," Fenwick said. "Are safely buried. Things seem to be coming round, into order. I thought it would be otherwise. You're sure she's sleeping peacefully?"

"Yes. I'm sure." He could feel every sleeping quiver of her body. Her belly was gently rising and falling. Was his son, his child...

"You think I could have done differently. But I couldn't. They were too hard and strong. The daughter was, it was the daughter; she thought she could remain outside here in the town when all her kind followed the king into the rose garden, begged and clamoured to be let follow him into the rose garden. Where they are still, as you have seen. It being the only place safe from the plague. Which broke out with his going. They wanted, too, to be near him, they were loyal, and they couldn't quite see living without him. Unlike those two proud ones. And one or two others who also chose to stay out, but who soon developed unstanchable running sores, and died. It was the daughter's doing, she was the stronger one; but it was the mother who really remembered. They're buried? You're sure? You saw them laid in the grave? Maria dug the grave, dear Maria."

"I laid them in myself. I laid them side by side. And I covered them deep in earth. She told me to."

"Ah. Did she? That is her gift to me, though I suppose the people think otherwise. She knew I couldn't take them down myself. The burning alone was my duty, for which of course I am generally blamed. Well, no help for that. It is the way in late times; when wills clash, how can they be reconciled? The king being dead. As good as dead. They think him dead. You say her sleeping is peaceful? Altogether peaceful?

"Yes." Her long black eyelashes were fringing her cheeks and her loose black hair was overflowing the pillow. "Peaceful and deep."

"Ah. I'm very glad. It has been quite a peaceful time while you have been in each other's arms. People have seemed a little less wan, have had even a little spring in their walk as they have gone out to the fields. Very little, but yet... I even believe that the line about Black Melk's castle is a little...well that indeed only a very little...indeed I won't say it, it is too much to hope that... But, still, it may be happening all of itself, there may even be no further need of my…of the raven's…. Just his being perhaps has somehow…and your return of course… They saw them buried, did they, they all saw them buried?" His head was turning one way and then another and he was fingering the cord at his throat again and twisting it, he was so uneasy that she was beginning to move a little in her sleep her eyelids were beginning to quiver.

"They were all around the grave, as close around as they could be. I left them all around it."

"Ah, did you? That's good then, good. Then I can be quiet, I can rest. The red line will surely fade quite away in time and Black Melk withdraw back into the hills. Now that she is well. He won't any longer insist on his rights as the eldest…he will yield to her. And the hills will be just as they were before the old king saw him returning to claim his…" He stared steadily out the window.

"We were three, you know. Don't know. But they, of course, all know. I was the youngest, he was the eldest, and the old king stood between… Yes, he will go now, I know he will go…" What was wrong, Maria's whole body was quivering and her eyelashes were fluttering. "The plain will bear again now, I know it will. And the people will bear again, and you and Maria…and now that your blood has burned clear the channels in the outer garden, and the king is back by the fountain…I am at peace…nearly at peace…" He was walking back and forth in the room and looking around it every way. She was turning in the bed and turning back, her hair was tangled round her throat, he spread his arms out to her and around her drawing her close to him his lips brushed against hers her heart was beating and beating…

"The line is sharper. Harsher," Fenwick said abruptly. He was standing still and looking across the plain at the far hills. "Something is happening." Black clouds were

299

rising up from the hills into the clear sky over them, and their shadow on the plain was like a swift-flowing purple stain, with veins in it like darting jagged fire; and around the edges of Black Melk's castle the red line was pulsing against the black clouds like living flame. Fenwick was trembling. Maria's warm body in his arms was quieter, it was turning gently, and stretching. Fenwick crossed quickly to the window and pulled hard on the bell-rope beside it, and the bell overhead began clanging noisily.

"He's not giving up," he said, reaching into the drawer of his desk with one hand and beckoning him to him with the other; it seemed he wanted him beside him at the window. Already the black cloud was covering nearly half the sky; and the swiftly approaching purple shadow below it seemed to be teeming with shapes, horses they looked like, and men riding them, both enclosed in a fine red line. Maria's lips were brushing warmly against his throat. Fenwick was holding his little round mirror.

"He is semding in his private bodyguard," he said. "He has never been so open in his aims before, always he has tried to cloak them in natural events, drought and disease and storms. And spies. It's a measure of his present desperation that he has dropped his mask. Hold the other side of this mirror, I'll need your strength to steady my aim." It was so small that their fingertips touched behind it. Outside, the whole plain seemed to be quivering a little.

"Hold it steady," Fenwick said in sharp whisper. "And we must both concentrate our attention. Otherwise we haven't a chance. Now, tip it upwards to catch the sun. There. Now very slowly tilt it downwards, carrying the sun with us; that's right, follow me; make sure we don't lose the sunlight. Now aim it into the shadow, at the first of the horsemen, just hold it steady and I'll guide... There!" At the very front edge of the fastapproaching shadow one of the horsemen and his horse exploded in a flash of red light, leaving only a puff of pale smoke. Just as the horseman beside him was glancing fearfully at what had happened, he exploded as well. And then a third.

"We must hold the leading edge back," Fenwick said. His breathing was fast and shallow. Maria's warm arms were folding about William's body, sliding over his arms her hands were gliding down his back. "It's that which is bringing the cloud forward; if the cloud once covers the sun we will no longer be able to hold them off, but will be at their mercy. It is only by great good fortune that I saw in time what he was aiming at. But what I don't see is how, if she is sleeping peacefully as you say..." Another horseman was struck by the sun's reflection in the mirror, and exploded. But still the purple shadow was sweeping forward under the black cloud. Fenwick glanced up in great unease at the sky, and struck three horsemen in succession with beams of light. "How can he be attacking so strongly while she is sleeping peacefully? Perhaps, after you left..."

"She is asleep. Deep asleep," he said, feeling her body against his, her belly against his belly, their child...

"Look!" Fenwick cried out. "At the horizon. How his castle is rising above the hills, all red and distended..." How warm and easy her breathing was, and her body; it was hard to keep his mind with Fenwick's. but it was true that the castle shape on the far hills seemed to be pulsing with harsher red light. "He is putting all his strength into the battle. He knows it is now or never. Hold onto the mirror tightly." He held onto his side of it as well as he could, while Fenwick turned it this way and that, striking horseman after horseman with sharp beams of light; but still the dark shadow was flowing forward over the plain. And the foremost horsemen were now striking with their swords at the few men who had gone out from the town with the cows, or to cut and gather the thin grain. They were striking at cows as well, they were plunging their swords into men and cows indiscriminately, whichever came to hand. The cows were hardly bleeding, but blood was pouring out of the men in rivers, and they were sinking to the earth just where they were stricken. Two wounded cows were leaning against each other, they were sinking to their knees while the man who had been herding them was still pushing and kicking them to drive them back towards the town gates. A horseman rode up behind him and struck off his head, which rolled and bounced away over the dry ground. The man's blood-gushing body was turning white. The horseman exploded in red light.

"How *can* she sleep...? Fenwick muttered fiercely. "They are *her* people. I am only the caretaker." It was ever harder to hold onto the mirror the way he was turning it this way and that. Everywhere on the nearer plain now there were puffs of pale grey smoke from exploded horsemen, but still they were coming on there were still very many of them, and still the purple shadow and the deep black cloud were slowly advancing on the town and the sun, and Black Melk's castle was uprearing higher and higher and was throbbing and swollen and blood-red. He gazed at it while his hand holding the little mirror was pulled by Fenwick every which way, and wondered how it was so different from what he saw from the burning plain on the other side, where it was green and soft against the burning sun, and seemed full of glistening fountains...

"Hold to the mirror, hold tight," Fenwick hissed. "He's trying to hide them in the smoke of their own exploding. He's making it spread and glisten. Look!" It was true, there seemed to be a mist low over the plain everywhere now, and it was queerly bright with fine glistening light. And it seemed to be moving, to be swaying back and forth as if with wind or breathing; and it was blurring the horsemen with their upraised swords, just as Fenwick was aiming the light-beam at them the misty smoke drifted in front of them and the beam sprayed outwards like a fountain of light against the smoke, and seemed to stay there like fine drops of water, glistening and gathering and slowly trickling down the smoke to the ground. Every moment there seemed to be more and more water, the horses' hooves were splashing in it as they galloped; a fleeing man slipped and fell in it and a horseman speared him to the ground with his sword, and then hoisted him up on the sword and watched him wriggle he wasn't a man at all he was a bright gleaming fish and the face of the horseman was as pleased as a child's the lights dancing from the fish's body were dancing in his eyes; another man pulling a thin cow by a rope was struggling fearfully past him to escape him, but the horseman wasn't moving he was only gazing fascinated at the fish.

"Hold the mirror steady and we've got him," Fenwick said, and the horseman was suddenly lit up in a great flash and the fish melted from his sword and his sword melted and his arm and his whole body flowed away in sparkling drops over his melting horse, and the man pulled his cow through their fading bodies as if they weren't there. To right and left there were other horsemen melting, and bright fish trickling in rainbows down their upright swords, melting their bodies with their own melting, and around them the mist was clearing and there were open patches of ground green with all the water flowing; and flowers were springing up and opening pale petals, even bushes were blossoming and leafing, and young thin trees as straight as around the old man's glade, rows and rows of them were appearing through the mist and blossoming, and the horses alone now without their riders were making their slow and quiet way among them, all russet horses, grazing on the fresh grass and drinking from the rivulets and streams, and wading across the broad shallow river glinting with sunlight. The old man himself was sitting on the grassy bank, and his long beard was trailing in the rippling water as he bent over and gazed into it, and his face gazing up out of the water was rippled but his eyes were as clear as jewels, as emeralds, they were so brilliant he could hardly bear to keep looking at them, in the centre of them the very centre there was the shape of someone he was moving like water he seemed to be beckoning him... "Your son," the old man was saying, his lips were rippling with the water. "Go to him, he is waiting. Come to him, he is waiting."

Maria was stirring, her body was stretching and stretching through the cool sheets and her eyes were glowing through her eyelids, and her arms were reaching out for him they were wrapping slowly round him her lips were half-parted and brushing against his...

Fenwick was holding his wrist and screeching at him, it seemed he had let the mirror loose from his hand. He took hold of it and felt his hand again being dragged after Fenwick's hand. The plain was heavy now with smoky mist, so dense he could hardly make out even the nearest horsemen. The light-beams from the mirror were striking against the mist and bursting it into bright particles, opening holes in it to the bare ground and horsemen approaching over it; but almost immediately more mist flowed into the holes, blurring and hiding them. The mist was growing brighter and brighter with all the light they were beaming into it, it was full of sparkling lights, and darts like fine lightning. Some of the darts were breaking out of the mist, and flying towards them; they were striking against the walls of the town and were shooting into the room through the windows they were striking his body and Fenwick's body. They seemed to be causing Fenwick great pain, he was trying to catch them with the mirrorand send them back into the mist, but there were too many, far too many the whole room was alive with them. On his own body they were melting like fine waterdrops against his skin; his grey robe was glistening with water and his pentangle was gleaming through his robe brightly it seemed to be catching every dart of light. He could see her eyes in the mist, the old woman's golden eyes, they were shining out through the mist and her old lips were smiling and her long red hair was flowing and rippling around her in the mist. "Come to him," she said. "He is waiting for you. Please come."

"What am I to do?" It was Fenwick's voice, where was he? "How can I strike what I can't see?" He had sunk to his knees on the window seat and was holding the little mirror against the sill in both hands; it seemed he had somehow let go of his half of it again, both his own hands were hanging down at his sides. Beyond the narrow band of sunlight outside the window the pale grey mist rose like a wall from the earth to the sky. "In a moment now the mist will blot out the sun, and it will be the end. He has won." Maria was stretching and stretching in the bed, her beautiful brown arms were outstretching...

"What's that?" Fenwick said sharply, looking down. Something was moving at the edge of the mist, moving out of the mist into the sunlight. A cow. And behind it another cow. And behind them both a man on foot, herding them. Fenwick looked down aghast.

"It's not possible," he said. "That man was dead. I saw him killed, and bleed white. Black Melk is using the mist as cover to make changlings, he is using dead bodies to make spies. I must stop him." He pulled himself to his feet and leant out of the window and trained his little mirror on the man. The sharp sun's rays struck him full in the face, but nothing happened, he didn't explode; he only lifted his hand to his eyes to shelter them from the glare, and continued driving his cows towards the gate. Fenwick then turned the mirror on the cows, but they too only continued their slow way under the goading of the man. And now there were other men and cows emerging from the mist and making their way unhurriedly towards the gate. Fenwick trained the mirror on one after another in a growing frenzy, but none of them exploded.

"I don't understand," he said in a despairing voice. "How can he do it? What has he made them of that the sunlight won't burst their masks?" One after another the men reached the gate and the gatemen let them pass. "He's bribed the gatemen, the only men I trusted; look at them, they're hardly examining them, they're just gazing blankly at the mist." He reached up and seized the bell-rope, and made the bell clang wildly to alert them, but they didn't even seem to hear it; and they were letting the men come into the town as if they weren't even seeing them, they were gazing unmoving at the mist what were they seeing in the mist? Maria's warm body was sliding against his, her breasts were warm against his chest her breath was warm against his throat…

The mist was slowly thinning, slowly parting, and within it something was growing, was rising up from the black ground. The ground itself was rising and bodies lying on it were turning over and slowly rolling down it, and were finding their feet as they rolled, and were standing up and starting to walk towards the town gates like the others.

"I don't believe it," Fenwick said, staring in horror. "It's not possible."

The ground was rising higher and higher, the whole black plain seemed to be swelling upwards and the mist now was flowing down it in pale streams, and wherever it flowed fine shoots of green grass were appearing through the surface of the earth, they were growing and spreading, and flowers were appearing among them again. He could feel Fenwick's body quivering beside him, and he rested his hand on his old bony shoulder to calm him if he could. The middle of the plain was so high now its crest was even with the window and it was gushing with streams they were bright in the sunlight, pouring down over rocks and shattering in glittering drops against rocks and flowing together again, they were all flowing into a silver river which was flowing around the great hill, spiralling down-wards through fields and stone walls.

"He can't build his castle here," Fenwick said in a whisper, his whole body trembling like a leaf. "Not in the middle of the plain, not…"

There was a light at the bottom of the hill, small and sharp and bright. It seemed to be floating on the river, it seemed to be gliding up it, against its flowing, around the hill through terraced fields and thousands of bright flow-ers and young spring-green trees; it disappeared behind the hill and appeared again, still gliding up the silver river, and where it passed the flowers and grasses were pale to blankness, and the banks of the rivers to ashy whiteness. It was burning its trail higher and higher up the hill, it was gone around behind it again, there was only the white track of it slowly fading as colour flowed out of the river back into the banks and the grass and flowers. The light burst like the sun from behind the hill and floated higher and higher up the hill, and the white track of its pass-ing was spreading wider, whole fields now were burning, the trees in the fields were bursting into flames they were burnt first black and then white they were drifting in soft ash down to the burnt earth, even the stones of the walls and loose rocks were being burnt, the brilliant dead white was overspreading the whole crown of the hill and the river was glittering brighter and brighter under the light, it was overflowing its banks and flowing up into the bright air it was turning to vapour and small thin rainbows were arching out of it, curling round and round the ever rising light, the river was now all vapour, it was blurring the light and swelling it bigger and bigger it was filling the whole crest of the hill it was melting into the hill and the hill was melting into the light and the rainbows were dancing in their millions in millions of incandescent waterdrops...

It was nearly dark. The red upper edge of the sun was just disappearing below the horizon. His arms were wrapped tightly around Fenwick's bony body and both of them were still. Below them, what looked like all the people of the town were standing outside the walls, gazing out at the black empty plain. Fenwick stirred and struggled against his encircling arms. He let them fall to his sides; and looked out at the bare plain and the clear sky, which seemed more beautiful than he could understand.

"For the moment it's quiet," Fenwick said, pushing him back to give himself room. Maria was stirring, her legs and arms were sliding between the silky sheets and her eyes were opening onto the darkening room. He wanted to go to her. Fenwick leaned out of the window and waved his arms at all the people below.

"Go inside. Go inside," he shouted. "The sun has set." He reached up to the bell-rope and pulled it sharply and the bell clanged. "They no longer have any minds of their own," he muttered, as they began to shuffle their way towards the gates and through them, all glancing back again and again at the still and quiet plain. Fenwick watched them closely. Maria was sitting up in the bed. She was listening, and her body was slowly breathing the big room...

The gates slammed shut. Fenwick stood back from the window. Three floors below them the raven was knocking.

"But now, right in the town" Fenwick said, looking down at the little mirror cupped in his hand like a still pool of water, "We have all these new spies." Maria was sitting on the edge of the bed with her feet on the smooth wooden floor. What was she listening for? He wanted to be with her. The twilight was swiftly deepening over the plain.

"She is listening to the raven," Fenwick murmured. "She will be going to it very soon. You must stay away from her for now." He laid the mirror on the desk and looked out across the plain. The red line around Black Melk's castle was sharp against the dark. The sound of the raven's knocking was louder.

"You see how strong he feels?" Fenwick said. "He thinks that he has nearly overcome us. Well, we'll see. I have been waiting years for this night." Maria was standing naked in the middle of the room, turning slowly round and round. Her hair was rippling over her shoulders and her breasts. Why couldn't he go to her? Fenwick had taken him by the hand and was drawing him across the room towards the door.

"I'll show you," he said, unbolting the door and pulling it open. Maria was turning round and round him and around within him, he was turning with her turning... Fenwick was drawing him by the hand to the railing at the edge of the landing. The knocking of the raven was shivering the floor against his feet.

"Look down," Fenwick said. He looked down and saw her coming out of the dark hallway onto the dark landing below them, her white dress glowing like a night flower; the scent of her rose to his nostrils and flowed into his body. He started towards the stairs to go down to her; but Fenwick was holding to his hand.

"She is going to the raven," he whispered. "Wait." Her palely glowing shape passed down the stairway floor by

309

floor, her hand gliding down the railing; and the raven began its harsh croaking. There was a rattling of the raven's gate, and the sound of it creaking open and closing again. Her feet were silent in the dust of the long dark hallway. Fenwick let go of his hand.

"She goes every evening now," he murmured. "I had to allow it, the raven's knocking and croaking was exceeding all limits, I feared he might break through the very walls of the ballroom. As night falls it begins, whether it is fed or not, and nothing will quiet it except her presence; except these last days when you... I don't know why that should... Listen." She was near the old ballroom now, he could feel her feet against the floor, and her hand touching the separating wall; and the noise of the raven was dying, it was still. The deep dusk on the landing was lightened just near him by the bright glowing of the pentangle under his robe. It was silvering Fenwick's face like moonlight and was sparkling in his dark watching eyes. He was raising his hand toward it.

"Is it warm?" he asked. "Or cold? Or neither? I mean the light it gives."

"Cool. Like fresh water."

"Ah. Cool. I don't quite..." His voice trailed away and his half-raised hand fell back to his side. Maria was resting her hands flat against the wall between her and the raven.

"Come," Fenwick said, crossing the landing back into his room. "We must wait in here until the time." When they were both in the room, Fenwick closed and bolted the door.

"We mustn't sleep," he said. "Lest he attempt to attack us again before we can attack him." He walked across the room to the window facing across the plain to Black Melk's castle; and as he looked, the flaming edge around it seemed to grow brighter.

310

"He knows we're here, and waiting," he said. "And he never has attacked while Maria was awake; not wishing her to see his evil, so that her only report of it is through me, and the evident damage. I think that has been his motive, but I am not any longer sure, many things have become unsure; even Maria herself is not, is perhaps not... else why should the raven be...no, that can't of course be, I don't know why I allow myself to have such... Look, his castle is rising higher, surely it is rising higher."

It seemed unchanged; he peered at it across the room and past Fenwick's thin silhouette and across the plain: there was only a ver faint jagged edging of red between the solid black of the earth and the clear black of the sky. The stars were sharp and brilliant in the sky, and their light on the earth was soft; and blurred and very slowly gliding past the window; he could feel the time flowing past him like water, and he felt strangely blithe and light. He could feel Maria walking back and forth through his body, trailing her fingers separating her from the raven, and he could feel its great bulk slumped up against the other side of the wall. Fenwick was standing beside him again and was gazing at the glowing pentangle. The stars were wheeling slowly through the sky and over the floor.

"Is it light from the well?" Fenwick asked, in a strangely soft voice, soft and young. His hands were both upraised and his palms were gleaming with the light of the pentangle.

"The old woman's well?" he asked. Fenwick nodded. "I don't know. I think so."

"We saw it," Fenwick murmured. "Maria and I. It streamed up through the globe and over the ceiling of the room and out of the windows and down to the ground, like water itself. Yes, that's right; and it sprayed right over the two poor corpses below, making them glisten with rainbows. Maria stared and stared at them; and I saw light in her eyes for the first time since..." She was resting her body full against the wall between her and the great raven, she was sliding her belly back and forth against the wall. Fenwick was holding his hands up in front of his face as if the glow of the pentangle was too bright for his eyes. He was backing away.

"You have aged me," he murmured, backing and backing. "You have taken my strength." He was stumbling back through the tracks of the wheeling stars, back towards the window. "I helped where I could, but my strength wasn't enough. That's why I fell over and you laid me in the water and laid stones on my body. I was tired and overborne. The light was too much. I am old." He sank down onto the window seat.

"That was you...?" The starlight was glistening on his nodding grey hair and bony shoulders. The plain beyond him was a flood of starlight to the very horizon. There was no trace of the far hills or of Black Melk's castle. "You saved me. I was burning..." Fenwick was waving his words away with both hands.

"It was only a matter of weaving a bower around you," he said. "It wasn't much. But my strength wasn't much. And now it is much less. I hope it will be sufficient. But you see how high Black Melk's castle has risen above the plain; it will take all our strength and skill..."

He couldn't see the castle at all through the plain awash in starlight; the only sign of it was a faint melting rosiness flowing between the earth's far edge and the sky. Maria's lips were softly kissing the wall between her and the raven.

Fenwick was standing beside him again, touching his arm. All the stars in the heavens were in other places, the night had gone on. Fenwick was carrying things, he was giving them to him to carry. He took them. they were soft, they seemed to be wool. And there were what felt and smelled like thick leather thongs.

"It is time to go," Fenwick said.

"Go where?" The plain was still swimming with starlight, and the room. He didn't want to go anywhere.

"To Black Melk's castle. We must go now, this night between moons, while the old king is still sitting by the fountain. He won't be able to stay there long, his strength is little and depends on ours. It must be now. Come."

"But how?" There was no sign at all of the castle, there was only silver starlight. Fenwick was pulling him by the arm with his sharp fingers. He let himself be pulled out of the room and onto the landing. He could feel Maria's body lying quiet in the dark hallway below. He heard the lock click into place.

"The raven will carry us there," Fenwick said, pulling him by the arm to the stairs and down them. "That's what he is for. Now that at last he is full-grown."

They went down flight after flight of stairs to the first floor, where he waited in the gentle darkness which spread away from his glowing pentangle, while Fenwick opened the gate and drew him through it and along the dusty hallway. He could feel Maria nearer and nearer. A cat slithered past his legs, and another. Fenwick was holding more and more tightly to his arm.

"She has let them in," he muttered. "I told her to be careful, but she... Not that it matters now." She was only a little way ahead of them now, he could feel her body by the wall he could feel her turning and turning in his arms her lips brushing against his ear, his lips... Fenwick's fingers against his arm were so sharp they seemed to be tearing his flesh.

"The cloaks. The cloaks," Fenwick said in a little shrill voice. "We must put them on now. Stop here. We must put them on so we seem part of the raven, so Black Melk

313

will not discern us." He was pulling at the soft wool in his arms. In the distance, through the caressing dark, he could see the pale bloom of Maria resting against the wall, unmoving. But he could feel her moving, her whole body was moving against his... Fenwick pulled so sharply at the woollen bundle that it fell to the floor.

"Put one on me and the other on yourself."

By the pale light of the pentangle he lifted up one of the cloaks and found the right way of it and settled it around Fenwick's shoulders. Then he settled the other around his own. It was thick and soft.

"When we are on the raven you must cover the pentangle with it," Fenwick said. His voice was like a thin wire. "Of all things, Black Melk must not see that; and uncovered it will be as bright as a falling star. Now take up the thongs and bind me to you, to your back."

He knelt to the floor and felt through the thick dust for the thongs and gathered them up, and tied Fenwick's body to his own, so that he was resting against his back with his head just behind and beside his own. Fenwick was trembling.

"Is that all right?" he asked him.

"Yes. Yes. Now we must hurry. There is very little time. The sun is already rising upwards again towards our horizon."

Standing as atraight as he could under his burden, he began walking again along the dark hallway towards the pale glowing which was Maria. Fenwick with one hand was searching through his bundle of keys, holding them in front of the pentangle for light. He found one and held it out for him to take. Maria was in the light of the pentangle now, she was turned towards him and was smiling at him, her eyes were shining in the pale light,

"Give her the key," Fenwick said, trembling worse than before. His hand touched her hand and the bundle of

314

keys passed to her. He bent and kissed her shoulder as she stooped to unlock the sliding door. Soft thongs with loose knots in them were hanging loosely about her neck.

"Stand back, away from the door," Fenwick hissed shrilly, "The wind now is like a hurricane." He stood to the side of the door as Maria unlocked it and slid it open. There was no wind. She handed the bundle of keys back to Fenwick's clutching hand, and stooped through the low doorway into the room. There was a sound of breathing, of a great animal breathing, and a creaking of the floor that he could feel in his own feet; and he could feel the raven lift itself away from the wall beside him and waddle slowly across the room after Maria, and its head just brushing the ceiling.

"Don't move," Fenwick whispered. "Wait." The raven was standing still beside Maria, it seemed quiet and gentle; he could feel its head hanging down and its beak, as big as her body, resting like a breeze on the crown of her head.

"I don't know why there's no wind for her," Fenwick murmured. "It began to die when she saw the women…" She was coming back over the floor thick with the raven's dung, she was reaching a hand through the low doorway, around the doorway, she was holding out the end of a leather thong.

"Take it," Fenwick said. He took it from her, his hand just grazing hers as she drew it back; but she wasn't gone, she was still close to him…

"Now," Fenwick said sharply. We must try to reach the raven. Stoop down and go through the doorway, try to go through it. And don't, whatever you do, lose hold of the thong, or we'll be flung back and broken on the walls."

He stooped down to the low doorway, with Fenwick trembling violently against his back and all his sharp fingers digging into his shoulders; and the instant he was in

315

front of the doorway the wind howled out of it in a gale so fierce he could hardly stand. He held with all his strength to the taut knotted thong, and pulled himself forward step by step through the doorway and into the room, into the teeth of the shrieking wind. He struggled forward knot by knot along the thong, digging his toes into the thick dung on the floor, towards the immense wind-blurred shape of the raven. And just over him, just beside him, the wind was even stronger than where he was struggling, it was whistling like a hurricane past his head, and hitting so hard against Fenwick's head he could feel his whole body being dragged from his back, he couldn't feel him against his back any longer, all he could feel were the thongs holding him cutting like knives into the flesh of his chest and belly. Ahead of him, like a beacon, the great eye of the raven was gazing at him out of the middle of the wind, wavering from red to yellow as he staggered towards it inch by inch, from knot to knot, while all around him and around the raven he could feel Maria slowly turning and turning, her long black hair fanning gently out into the darkness, her mouth smiling and her eyes full of a golden black light.

His hand touched a feather of the raven; so black it was the light from his pentangle melted into it and vanished. He laid his hand full on the raven's feathers, and felt Fenwick's fingers on his shoulders again, and the wind die suddenly away. And Maria was beside him, her body was close to his, she was nearly touching him. Fenwick on his back felt broken; but he moved a little and he was whispering something, it was faint and far...

"Climb. Climb," he was saying. "Don't let go of the thong. Pull us up on its back. Pull!" He began pulling himself and Fenwick hand over hand up the flank of the raven, towards its great neck, she had fixed the thong round its neck. She was moving slowly round the raven's great body she was stroking its black feathers her hands were lost in the blackness of its feathers, her arms, half her body was lost in the blackness of its feathers.

"How can she? How *can* she?" Fenwick was wailing into his ear. "She is the king's daughter, she is the heir to the kingdom, she will be the queen..." She was turning round and round against the raven, half in the room half lost in its feathers, her unblinking eyes were pools of black gold.

His leg slid over the crest of the raven's great neck and down the other side, and slowly and cautiously he let himself sink down, until he was sitting deep in among the black black feathers into which all the light of his pentangle was pouring, and held onto the thong and waited. Maria was standing in front of the raven now, and her hands were cupped together and outstretched towards its beak; she was moving slowly backwards towards the high windows and it was lurching clumsily after her. He held fast to the thong round its huge neck and felt Fenwick's clawlike hands holding fast to him. Maria was pulling open the grilled gate in front of the middle window, the window itself was creaking open, she was pulling back both its dusty great frames, the smell of the open night was flowing into the room and the light of the stars was resting on her face and bare arms. She was gliding away from the window into the middle of the room she was turning slowly round and round with both her arms wrapped round her belly, how it seemed to have swollen was it with his child, his...

"Cover your pentangle," Fenwick hissed. He wrapped his cloak close around himself. The raven let out a deafening screech, and hopped onto the low windowsill.

"Don't let go of the thong," Fenwick screamed through the raven's screeching, his mouth right against his ear. "Whatever happens, don't let go." They were facing out into the black starlit night, perched over the empty town square. Behind them Maria was turning round and round under the great cobwebbed chandelier, her eyes as black as the room and night, sprinkled with sparkling stars.

They were afloat over the square. The raven was slowly flapping its great wings, their tips seemed almost to be brushing against the houses around the square, and they were rising up and up into the cold air of the silent dying night.

"Hold on, hold on," Fenwick whispered in his ear. The raven was flying high over the plain towards the far hills, straight towards the jagged red outlining of Black Melk's castle. It seemed very very far. The wind was cold and all around them was blackness, so black that even the raven's great wings were invisible, all the far starlight was being swallowed by its immense black body. He hunched down deep in its feathers for shelter, peering into the wind through half-closed eyes to see when they were nearer the hills and the castle. But they didn't seem to come any nearer.

"They will be nearer suddenly," Fenwick whispered. "We must be ready. Ready to leap off. Wait until I tell you. Not before we arrive, not even a moment before, or we'll be flung high into the air and fall to the ground miles away. And not a moment after we arrive, or we'll be broken against the castle walls. But for a second, only a second, the wind will drop, if we've timed it correctly. That will be the second to leap free."

The wind was stronger, and colder. He crouched deeper down into the raven's feathers, but still it tore at his hair and cloak, and was like ice against his hands clutching the thong. It felt full of sharp needles, icy needles which lodged a moment in his flesh before melting.

"It's Black Melk's armoury," Fenwick murmured, his body quivering close against his back. "He has seen us despite our disguise. Hold tight to the thong. He can't repel the raven. The raven is his own." The icy needles were striking them now from every side, his hands and his face and all his body were covered with them, they were digging deep into his flesh and the pain of them was driving further and further into his body, it was piercing through his blood and his muscles to his very bones...

"Now," Fenwick shouted. "Jump!"

He jumped, he didn't know how or where, into the air; and landed on something hard, on his feet. there was a sudden harsh sound, like the cracking of a whip.

"Look," Fenwick whispered. "Look down." Below them a stone wall fell away sheer, and into it the great tailfeather of the raven was disappearing; and the thong by which he had held to it was slithering down the wall into the gloom far below.

He was standing on the parapet of a castle which rose high above him in tower after black tower. There was nobody near them, nobody to be seen anywhere defending it, nor any sound of anyone, nor any sound of anything. The air was still, and overhead the stars were being paled away by the lightening sky. And at the far horizon in the direction they had come from he could see the first melting signs of the spreading dawn. The pain of the needles in his body had disappeared to nothing.

"Untie me," Fenwick said. "Quickly. We must be ready for him." He lowered himself and Fenwick down from the parapet onto a broad flagstoned terrace, and untied the thongs binding them together; and then held him a moment until he could stand on his own. The whole while Fenwick was glancing about in alarm. But he himself felt strangely peaceful.

"Shall we go and look inside?" he asked. At the far end of the terrace there were heavy double doors. He began walking slowly towards them; and Fenwick walked beside him, nearly touching him, unsteady on his feet and shivering. The air was cool and as fresh as clear water. The sky overhead was slowly becoming white.

"Don't be fooled," Fenwick said, plucking at his cloak. "He knows we're here. He's luring us deeper... Watch out!" he suddenly hissed, and half-sheltered behind him as one of the double doors just in front of them half-opened. Around it a figure drifted, a young woman, pale pink she seemed, or pale yellow, another was drifting past behind her, they seemed together to be pale green. He could see the doors and the stone walls through them, and through others drifting out the doors after them. They were drifting palely across the terrace, flowing to every part of it, and they seemed to be filling with the light beginning to flow more strongly from the horizon, they were drifting over the parapet into the twilight.

"Don't let them lure you," Fenwick whispered from behind him. "Close your eyes against them." He watched them drift away into the air as more and more of them filtered out through the doorway, they were already veiling in colour the brightening sky.

They were beckoning him in through the doorway; they were palely smiling and their flowing hands were calling him. He passed in through the doorway, in among them, with Fenwick clutching onto his cloak from behind, and found himself at the top of a broad shallow flight of steps, and began slowly to walk down them; they were as black as the raven, and cool and smooth against his feet, and the reflections in them of all the passing smiling women were like flowing colours in a deep black pool. Their sheer dresses were drifting against him now as they glided past him up the stairway to either side, and the pale scent of them was fresh and sweet. They were stroking at his cloak with their passing hands, and their pale lips and eyes were smiling and smiling. He felt his cloak slide from his shoulder and slide down his body, and Fenwick behind him seemed to be stumbling over it, but he was still clinging to him somehow. The stairway was now curving very gently round to the left, and the smiling women were closer on each side he could feel their softness brushing against him as he made his way through them, their dresses were deeper in colour and the black polished stone of the walls beyond them was barely visible through their gliding bodies, which just in passing him were brightened by the glowing of his pentangle against them, all their bodies were breathing sweet perfume.

"Don't lose it, don't lose it," Fenwick was whispering fearfully from behind him. It seemed he meant the pentangle. The women were all stretching out their passing hands towards it, they were stroking and caressing it through his robe, it was so bright through their hands it was as if their hands were melting. their bodies were closer still against him now, he was pressing against their sliding softness with every step he took down the ever narrower stairway their bodies were so solid now he couldn't see the walls through them any longer, and the perfume of them was sweeter and stronger they were all looking at him with eyes full of love and the light of his pentangle was pouring over their passing bodies they were stroking his body all over with every part of their own he was so in the midst of them and the rainbow colours of them were so burying him he couldn't even see the stairway he seemed to be turning round and round and their bodies were close against him and the scent of them was flooding through him he could feel himself pushing still deeper into their ever-yielding soft bodies the colours of them now were as deep and rich as jewels glowing with the light of his pentangle...

They were gone. The dark was open all around him, warm and dense with perfume. Where had they gone?

Fenwick was clinging with both arms to his arm, sheltering and shuddering against his body. The floor under his feet was as smooth as glass. It seemed that he was in a great hall.

"We've come too far," Fenwick whispered. "He's trapped us. We're not armed for when he shows his true face."

There seemed nothing to be frightened of, the dark seemed gentle. And far ahead in the way he was facing it seemed less dark, and something seemed to be moving, some faint glimmering light. He began to walk towards it. After a while he brushed against what felt like a young tree, and then another and another, they seemed to be growing close around him. But they weren't trees, they had long pointed fleshy leaves growing from their stems, and just above his head they were flowering, great blurred trumpet flowers, all white. They were lilies, great lilies, their perfume was the perfume of the flowing women it was flowing over him now and flowing through him. Fenwick was choking and holding to him ever more tightly; he wrapped an arm about his old body and held him close against his side. All around him and farawy into the dark the lilies were flowering like thousands of soft perfumed stars, and their reflections were misty lights in the polished floor over which he was walking.

The reflections seemed to be flowing under the floor, flowing towards their feet and past them, as if the floor was built over water; everywhere he looked the reflections were drifting, they were floating under the lilies and rippling and melting into each other. And his own reflection and Fenwick's reflection were rippling in the midst of them, breaking away from their feet and reforming and breaking away.

"Don't look, don't look," Fenwick said, his voice was only a little wisp of sound. Ahead of them the light was clearer, it was a tall thin light rising high into the gloomy hall; it seemed to be beckoning him nearer.

"No!" Fenwick cried. His feet were dragging after him now over the polished black floor, he seemed to have no have no more strength in his body. The tall thin light was wavering in the midst of the thousands of blurred lilies.

"It's him, I see him!" Fenwick cried out in terror. "He has caught us in his trap." He looked higher and higher up the tall narrow light to see the face in it that Fenwick seemed to see. But there wasn't any face, there was only a gathering of pale light in a column, a moving quivering column.

It was a column of water. It was pouring down out of the high darkness to the gleaming black floor; and through the floor and gushing under the floor, carrying all the lily-reflections with it, past his feet. It was a waterfall.

"No!" Fenwick said, his voice barely a whisper. "It's a disguise. I know him. It's a disguise." He was sliding down his body to the floor, all his strength was gone, he was sagging limply against the front of his legs his old cheek was lying on the black floor lilies were flowing past his old head.

High in the gloomy air, far above the soft lily lights, a blackness blacker than the air was slowly swelling within the waterfall. It was growing and growing and it was growing even blacker it was drawing up into it all the pale lily light in the hall it was swelling into the whole upper body of the waterfall, all the lilies and their reflections were lost in it now, even the light of his pentangle was lost he couldn't see Fenwick or the floor at his feet or even himself.

At the centre of the blackness at the very height of the waterfall there was a needle point of light. As he stared at it it grew brighter, and brighter, and the black was blacker and blacker and blacker...

"Black... Melk..." Fenwick's voice barely breathed. "For...give me. I...."

The black was bleeding from the water. Into the floor, under the floor. He could see the blur of Fenwick at his feet, and the reflections of the lilies washing again under the floor, and the lilies in the air around him. And the point of light in the waterfall was the whole of the waterfall and was floating down through the waterfall, and down, his pentangle was catching its light it was trembling against his chest and his whole robe was glowing he could hardly look at the light it was opening and opening out of the waterfall it was right in front of him...

It was a boy. He was smiling at him out of the waterfall he was stretching out his arms to him his eyes were as blue as the sky, and in his left ear was a gold earring.

His own arms were outstretched and he was walking towards the waterfall, his feet had scattered Fenwick's bones as he moved, they were slithering and breaking on the polished floor, and bursting into bright motes of dust around his footsteps. His grey robe was melted away and his pentangle was scattering silver light into the gold which was flooding from the boy. His fingertips touched the falling water and he was touching the boy's hands his radiant face was against his own his body was against his own. His pentangle was melting and the boy's earring was melting...

Right over his head she was floating, as she promised she would be, her great wings were as wide as the sky. And her eyes were everywhere in the water springing up around him. And she was dancing in the rainbows which were arching up out of the water, everywhere he looked she was dancing, and everywhere she danced lilies and roses were springing out of the rainbows, as far as he looked lilies and roses were springing, wherever the sun was shining on the unmoving surface of the golden lake.

ISBN 141206452-X